The
Wedding
Vow

Also by Dandy Smith

The Wedding Vow

DANDY SMITH

embla books

First published in Great Britain in 2025 by

embla
books

Bonnier Books UK Limited
HYLO, 5th Floor, 103-105 Bunhill Row, London, EC1Y 8LZ
Owned by Bonnier Books
Sveavägen 56, Stockholm, Sweden

A CIP catalogue record for this book is available from the British Library.

1

ISBN: 9781471416477

This book is typeset using Atomik ePublisher.

Printed and bound in Great Britain by Clays Ltd, Elcograf S.p.A.

Embla Books is an imprint of Bonnier Books UK.
www.bonnierbooks.co.uk

For Lucy Perkins
My soul sister. Geek love. xXx

Prologue

The Wife

My husband isn't answering his phone. While not entirely out of character, it still makes anxiety flutter in my chest. On the train, I scroll back through our messages; Linden hasn't responded since I left for Oakleaf Yoga Retreat yesterday morning. He's supposed to collect me from the station when I arrive but, as the connecting train from Oxford to Bath was delayed by fifty minutes, I'll be getting in much later than planned. Linden has no idea though, and all my calls are going unanswered. I'd be agitated if I had to wait around for him for an unknown stretch, but my husband has a more laissez-faire approach to life. I try not to worry; he'd usually pop into the coffee shop across the road and settle himself down with a newspaper. I don't know anyone else under forty who still buys the paper, but before his death, Linden's uncle was a reporter for one of the big internationals, and the smell of ink reminds Linden of his childhood. Still, I try his number one more time. Again, he doesn't answer.

'Verity, is everything OK?' asks Flora. She's sitting across from me, surrounded by pamphlets for Oakleaf Yoga Retreat and all the notes she wrote during our visit. Being so young, I expected she'd work from her phone, but, like Linden, she's an old soul, preferring pens and paper.

'All good,' I tell her with a too-bright smile. I fire off one last message to Linden before sliding my phone onto the little table between us.

The carriage isn't as busy as expected, but then, it's a Sunday in first class. In the seat adjacent to us is a man with polished leather shoes and a heavy, expensive watch, engrossed in his Kindle. A little further up is a rosy-cheeked, mousy-haired woman minding two immaculately behaved children, both dressed head to toe in Boden's latest autumn collection. When she sees me looking, she smiles, and I smile back before picking up my phone to check for a reply from my husband. 'Nothing,' I say out loud. 'Brilliant.'

'Sorry?' says Flora.

I give her a distracted smile. 'Just . . . Linden.'

'Oh.' She looks away and I put my phone down again, feeling restless. 'So,' she says, 'are we going ahead with the Oakleaf collaboration?'

I force the whirling anxiety to the back of my mind and concentrate on the task at hand. 'I think so, yes. They're a good fit. Their technology ban is on trend for the burnt-out millennial.' When I arrived at the retreat yesterday morning, I'm ashamed to say I felt naked without my mobile and, heart racing, kept patting myself down for it. Heidi, our in-house graphic designer, eagerly handed over her devices. She's been talking about this retreat for weeks. Though, as a mother of three, it's a rare break from her hectic home life. 'Let's feature them on the website in November. See if we can get a Christmas discount for our subscribers.'

We're only half an hour from Bath now. Unusually, Linden hasn't called to find out where I am and how long I've been delayed. I should've taken Heidi up on her offer of a lift since we're all headed back to Somerset but as I live in Bath and she lives in Frome, she'd have had to drive twenty minutes out of her way. That, and her car is always littered with children's toys and stray socks, and once, there was a bottle of curdled breast milk forgotten under the passenger's seat in the height of summer.

'Thanks again for inviting me to join you this morning,' says Flora.

I pull a face. 'Sorry I couldn't get you in for the entire weekend. I needed Heidi with me to take the photographs.'

'Oh, no worries. I had plans last night anyway.' Before I can enquire, she adds, 'My skin feels incredible after that Oakleaf mud bath.'

'Still happy to write up a review of their treatments?'

She nods. 'Absolutely.'

'Do you think you can get the first draft to me by Friday?'

Another enthusiastic nod.

Flora has been my assistant for the last year but her ambition lies in content creation. It's a shame; I don't know what I'd do without her as an assistant but if I want to keep her at Verity Rose at all, I need to let her branch out. Still, my head aches with the prospect of finding a replacement – all those awkward interviews and sweaty, overly eager candidates.

Flora goes back to scribbling in her notebook. Her teeth bite into her full lower lip as she writes. She's attractive, with her long red hair and pretty green eyes. She's self-assured, but inexperienced. Idealistic, but talented. And twenty-three. So young. Though I am only seven years her senior, I feel old around her. Out of step. She is the sort of young that can drink cheap tequila and even cheaper wine, crawl home at four in the morning and wake up a few hours later, fresh-faced and hangover-free. So young that finding The One isn't important. So young that there is enough time to fall in love again and again and make mistakes because, at twenty-three, no decision will ever leave you stuck, *truly* stuck, on a path you no longer want to walk.

I think about the girl I was at twenty-three, so different from the woman I am now.

Flora is bright. Brighter than I was at her age. She's Oxbridge-educated but, unfortunately, that isn't what will open doors for her in life. It's her shapely legs and smooth, dewy skin, because whether we like it or not, sex still sells. Of course, being a young, attractive woman in the workplace isn't always easy. It can breed jealousy among the older women who eye your bare legs in a heatwave and still make comments like, 'Just looking at you makes me feel cold.' Not because they are concerned, but because they are jealous, threatened by someone they feel is more desirable. And the men are worse. The ones who patronise. Who lean in a little too close. Who leer at your bare legs, not with jealousy, but with something darker and stickier. Then blame you for their unwanted attention because you had the audacity to wear a skirt in summer. Flora doesn't realise how lucky she is to work for a website run *by* women, *for* women.

When I started my lifestyle blog from my bedroom six years ago, I never imagined it would grow into a household name. What was once interior design tips and smoothie recipes read by only a handful of people and solely managed by me, is now a global well-being and lifestyle website, dealing in topics from home decor to sex and relationships, from culture to health and beauty. I still do the bulk of the writing, but we've worked with renowned guest writers and partnered with huge brands. Verity Rose expanded so quickly that two years ago, I had to put together a small team: a marketing manager, a graphic designer, an assistant.

I look out at the darkening, rain-laden clouds. It's mid-September. The summer heat has waned quickly and there's a chill in the air. Without Linden to collect me, I'll be stuck waiting for a taxi without a coat. I pull my phone towards me. As anticipated, no call.

'Sure you're all right?' presses Flora.

I stare at my seven unanswered messages and finally, I shake my head. 'Linden isn't responding. It's just . . . unusual.'

She wrinkles her nose. 'Oh. Well, maybe he fell asleep?'

'Perhaps,' I say, even though at 6 p.m. it's unlikely.

'Could someone check on him? If he's taking a nap, the doorbell might be enough to wake him.'

I nod, thinking of Mimi. We live on a private road, set back from the main thoroughfare, separated by a low stone wall and a row of tall evergreen trees. There are only two houses on Rook Lane. Windermere, which is ours, and Ullswater, which is Mimi's. As a freelance book translator, she works from home. If it were a weekday, I'd be confident she'd be there, but Mimi fills her weekends with an eclectic mix of hobbies, from pottery classes to archery. She says it's because she has a broad spectrum of interests, but the death of her mother three years ago and the breakdown of a long-term relationship a few months before that has left her with a void.

I'm surprised when she answers on the fifth ring. 'I'm just coming back from this fantastic cooking class,' she enthuses, as though we are mid-conversation. 'When you come over for supper tomorrow, you're going to dine on the most incredible gnocchi you've ever eaten. It's so good, you'll think you're in northern Italy.'

Despite my churning unease, I smile. 'You *are* Italian. Didn't you already know how to make gnocchi?'

'Half Italian, and yes, but the teacher didn't know that and now I am the star of the class,' she sing-songs.

'Naturally,' I say. 'Look, Mimi, can you do me a favour and please pop round to check on Linden?'

She's driving. I hear the rhythmic clicking of her indicator. 'Why?'

'He isn't picking up his phone and he's supposed to collect me from the station. I'm delayed.'

Silence. 'You mean . . . you aren't home?'

'No. I've been at Oakleaf Yoga Retreat since Saturday morning. Why?'

'Oh. I thought . . .' She trails off.

My pulse kicks. 'Thought what?'

'Nothing. I just . . . I didn't realise Linden was home alone.'

'Well, at thirty-seven, I tend to trust him not to run with scissors or open the door to strangers late at night,' I deadpan.

'There's that Verity Lockwood charm,' she teases. 'Maybe he left his phone behind when he drove out to get you? He's probably waiting at Café au Lait with a newspaper.'

'Left his phone at home . . . of course,' I say, unconvinced. He's a perpetual scroller and wouldn't last five minutes without his phone in his hand. 'I didn't even think of that.'

More silence.

'You're worrying, aren't you?' she asks.

'No,' I lie.

'You are, aren't you?' she presses.

'I mean, Linden's fit. He takes care of himself. It's not as though he'd have suffered a heart attack or stroke. But a fall down the stairs or slipping in the shower . . .' I wince.

She sighs. 'I'll be home in ten and then I'll head over.'

Relief sweeps through me. 'You sure?'

'I've got a key. It will only take a couple of minutes.'

'Thank you.'

'But Verity? Text him so he knows I'm coming round. I don't want him jumping down my throat the second he sees me.'

When I ring off, I send Linden another message, warning him to expect Mimi. He doesn't like that she has a key. Just as he doesn't like how much time Mimi and I spend together. For the most part, my husband is effusive; just occasionally though, he is sullen, borderline sulky. Quality time is important to him, important to any successful relationship, but lately, between running Verity Rose, keeping on top of the house, exercising and juggling a busy social life, it's a tight schedule, and Linden feels he doesn't get a large enough portion of it. He wasn't overjoyed about me going away to Oakleaf for the weekend, but it's a big brand and I needed to check it out for myself before recommending it to our audience. It's not that I don't trust my team's opinion, it's just . . . Verity Rose is my baby. My only baby. And, as expected, handing it over to others is challenging. Like I've told Linden, one day, in the next few years, I can step back a little more.

By the time we disembark, I still haven't heard from Linden or from Mimi.

Distracted, I wheel my suitcase through the crowd, catching people's heels as I weave in and out. Flora jogs to keep up. I can't slow. Can't shake the crawling sense of disquiet. Just as I thought, Linden isn't milling in the foyer and he isn't standing outside on the street either.

People scuttle along the pavement in a steady stream. I stand on my tiptoes, scanning the crowd for his golden head, his tall, lean frame. He isn't here. Still, I decide to duck into Café au Lait. Too impatient to wait for the green light, I stride into the flow of slow-moving traffic. A cyclist slams on his brakes and yells at me. I don't so much as glance his way. Flora staggers after me. She's talking, but I can't hear her over the rush of blood in my ears as I stand in the café and see that Linden isn't at a table with a newspaper.

'Shall we share a taxi?' asks Flora. 'It will be quicker than the bus.'

As we approach the house, I feel sick with dread. Flora is wittering on about Oakleaf, probably to distract me, and I fight down the urge to snap at her. Mimi should've been in touch by now.

'Left,' I instruct the driver. 'Just here.'

It's a tight turn, missed by most. He swings onto our road. Our house is a double-fronted Georgian affair in Bath's signature cream stone. Far too big for just the two of us, but Linden was really taken with it. It looms into view. Its large bay windows like two wide, petrified eyes. The black front door like an open, screaming mouth. We pull up and I pay the driver. I'm just climbing out of the taxi when the front door of my house is flung wide. Mimi hurtles onto the driveway, shrieking. A continuous, high-pitched, blood-curdling cry of fear. I stumble towards her. Mimi crashes into me, her dark curls coming loose from her bun.

'What is it? What's happened?'

Her huge hazel eyes find mine. They are glazed over in horror. She is trembling. Violently trembling. 'Police!' she manages. Then louder, 'Police!'

I am vaguely aware of people behind me. A man's voice at my back. 'I'll call them, love. What's happened?'

Mimi starts sobbing. Thick, clotted cries of terror.

I grab her arm. 'Mimi, what is it?'

But she bends over double and retches. Then she is on her knees, vomiting onto the pavement. I look towards the house.

Linden.

I dart around her.

'Verity, no!' shouts Flora.

Ignoring her, I race along the path, up the stone steps and tumble into the house through the open front door. I skid to a halt in the foyer. I stop and listen. Silence. The kind that settles over mouldering bones in a graveyard. To my left is his study. To my right is the lounge. Ahead of me is the entrance to the kitchen. Only one of the doors is open. I pivot slowly towards the lounge. I feel my pulse in my fingertips as I step inside.

Something squelches underfoot. I look down. My black leather boot is in a puddle of dark, sticky blood. With a hot rush of horror, my gaze lands on Linden. He's in a heap on the wooden floor in front of the fireplace. One arm is down by his side, the other stretched out in front of him, as though reaching for the door. I stare at that hand. It takes me a moment to realise there is a hole in his palm. Raw and

7

bloodied. Something has been stabbed through it. Blood is spattered up the walls and matts his golden hair, pooling beneath him. His face is turned to one side. His head littered with ugly gashes. His nose broken, bent at an unusual angle, and swollen like a pig's snout.

The truth sinks in slowly, like a blade into my chest: he's dead.

My husband has been murdered.

Chapter One

The Wife

'Verity, are you sure you're ready to do this?' asks Addison.

We are standing outside the master bedroom I once shared with my husband. I haven't slept even one night in our bed since his murder a year ago. When the police tape was finally ripped down and I could return, I moved into the bedroom at the back of the house. Of course I thought about selling our home and starting afresh, but Linden had adored Windermere and living here makes me feel closer to him. These last twelve months have been difficult but I'm stronger now and I have a plan. It's time to move forward.

'We don't have to do this today,' she reassures me.

'We do,' I tell her. 'I'm ready.'

I push open the door to our bedroom and step across the threshold, breathing in the stale air. Other than the thick layer of dust, it's exactly how we left it. The wooden floor, the large cream rug, the panelled, olive-green walls.

In the centre of the room, directly in front of me, is our king-size bed. Untouched since Linden's death. I step towards it and run my hand along the oak frame. We spent more than a thousand nights in this bed together. I remember when it was delivered. The second the drivers left, Linden lifted me easily and spun me. I wrapped my legs around his waist and laughed into his neck before he flung me onto the mattress. Later, under the sheets, his naked body on top of mine, he whispered, 'I love you, Mrs Lockwood. I knew it

9

the moment I set eyes on you.' He showered my face with kisses. 'The very moment.'

'Where shall we start?' asks Addison, stepping into the room behind me.

'The windows,' I answer distractedly, my mind still in bed with my husband. 'We should air the room out.'

She moves past me and throws them open, letting in the chilly October breeze.

I turn towards the wall opposite the bed. The fireplace is flanked by two double doors painted in Farrow & Ball 'Slipper Satin' that lead to the his-and-hers walk-in wardrobes.

'I think we should start small,' I say. 'With the chest of drawers.'

She nods, then unrolls the bin liners.

'Thanks for doing this with me,' I tell her.

'You don't ever need to thank me.'

I smile and she gives my hand an affectionate squeeze. She may only be my cousin, but she's always felt more like a sister. We're both only children, born to our twin mothers which, genetically speaking, makes us as close as half-siblings. We look so much alike that we're often mistaken for one another with our espresso-dark hair, square chin and full mouth. Though we both have our mothers' deep-set eyes, mine are olive, like our mothers', Addison's are chestnut, presumably like her father's. When we were children, our mothers kept our hair long, tumbling in a glossy waterfall down our backs. Now though, mine is shorter, hovering between chin and collarbone. Addison has kept hers long. Sometimes, I feel a stitch of regret for having chopped it off. But Linden had been so fond of my long dark hair that whenever I saw myself in the mirror, I felt the ghost of his fingers running through it.

We have only sorted through one drawer when we hear the rumble of an engine outside. With a sigh, Addison pushes to her feet. 'I told the charity they couldn't collect until tomorrow.' She goes to the window. 'Oh. It isn't the charity. It's a moving van. Are your neighbours leaving?'

I glance over my shoulder in surprise. 'I don't know. I don't have much to do with them.' A deliberate choice. After how things turned out with Mimi, I avoided getting close to the woman next door. It's almost unbelievable how much can change in a year. I join Addison by the window. The willowy blonde is holding a cardboard box as she talks to the two movers in navy polo shirts.

'I still can't believe Mimi upped and left like that,' says Addison. 'And she loved that house. Though God only knows how she afforded it.'

'It was her mother's. No mortgage. Mimi renovated it herself.'

'I didn't know it was her mum's.' There's a snap of envy in her voice. My aunt never owned her own home. She spent her life moving around the country, embroiled in one wild love affair after another, a disgruntled Addison in tow. When my aunt ran away for good, she left Addison with nothing. 'Where was she living before?'

'Rented a place near the canal, I think?'

'But she moved to Rook Lane *before* her mother died?'

I nod. 'She put the house in Mimi's name when she went into the hospice.'

'And Mimi sold it?'

I shake my head. 'Rents it out.'

We watch as the movers duck inside.

The woman stands on the driveway and is joined by her husband. She's visibly upset. He pulls her to him and they stare forlornly up at the house they've been renting for eleven months. In the brief conversation I had with them, they said they planned to stay for the next few years and even hoped to buy the property from Mimi if she was willing to sell. So why are they moving out now? What's changed?

'And where's Mimi these days?' asks Addison.

'A friend of a friend mentioned Leeds?' I stop myself from adding that the reason I'm unsure is because she blocked me on all her social media accounts and even changed her phone number. The rejection is so raw, so brutal, it's like a hot iron being pressed into my skin. A wound I don't want examined. Yet, Addison continues.

'Do you ever hear from her?'

'Not since the funeral.'

Though Mimi attended, she stood at the back, as far away from me as possible. She didn't talk to me. Didn't look my way. She stared resolutely at the coffin but, unlike every other mourner in the

11

room, there wasn't sadness in her expression. There was flintiness. It hardened her usually soft features. I was determined to talk to her at the wake and ask why she hadn't replied to a single one of my messages or returned any of my calls or even answered the door when I knocked, but she left the second the service ended. Mimi was my best friend, and I was grieving my murdered husband, yet she was as lost to me as he was.

'I'm sorry,' says Addison, though I'm not sure she is. When she and Mimi first met, they got on really well, bonding over their similar family situations: no mother, and an aloof, or, in Addison's case, anonymous father. They even had lunches together, just the two of them, which, I'm ashamed to admit, made me feel a twinge of jealousy. Then, a month or so before Linden's death, the lunches stopped and they avoided each other entirely. On the rare occasions they were in the same room, the tension was palpable. Of course, I asked what had happened, but they denied anything had. After that, I often felt like the child of divorced parents, caught between them, not knowing enough about the situation to choose a side. 'Remind me, when did she leave?'

'The moment the police gave her the OK. Around two months after his death.' Addison's lips thin in disapproval, and despite how bruised I am by Mimi's abandonment, I rush to her defence. 'Well, she did discover his body. It was . . . horrific. So violent and . . .' I can't catch my breath as Linden's bloodied head and wide, unseeing eyes flash into my mind. I wish I'd never asked her to look in on him. 'Maybe she couldn't bear living next door anymore. Too many terrible memories.'

'But why cut you off?'

I shrug against the blade of betrayal, though I have my theories. Perhaps, since I was the one who guilted her into checking on Linden, she blames me for what she saw.

'Do innocent people flee town only a couple of months after their neighbour is murdered?' presses Addison.

'The police obviously thought so.'

'The police have been utterly useless,' she remarks and, catching the hiss of anger in her voice, I'm irritated. As though she's stolen it from me. As Linden's wife, that anger is mine. But Addison has a habit of asserting herself into places she isn't always needed. After one too many glasses of wine, Mimi once referred to Addison as bindweed in a bed of roses. And even though a small, shameful part of me agreed, I rebuffed Mimi's assertions, insisting my cousin's ardent approach is often mistaken for intrusiveness.

'Did they even search Mimi's home for the fire poker?' she asks.

Linden's injuries, along with the missing fire poker from our hearth, were all the police needed to conclude it was the weapon used to beat him to death. It had been part of a brass set I'd picked up at a vintage market the autumn before. I wince, thinking about it striking his skull. I hear the crack of bone. Feel the blood spatter across my face. Nausea rolls through me. No one else dares reference the brutal way in which my husband was killed. But Addison is known for her direct manner. I suppose, as a stay-at-home wife, her day-to-day life doesn't require her to be tactful. Not like it does for someone who works within or, like me, manages a team. Though Addison and I look alike, we're very different people, raised by two very different women. Addison's done some admin and photography work for Verity Rose in the past but she prefers running a household. If it were me, I'd be bored to tears, decorating and cleaning and organising the Ocado deliveries. Addison says she's her own boss but I'm not convinced the weekly allowance she takes from Harry could be classed as a wage.

'If they suspected Mimi, of course they would have searched her home,' I assure her. I picture that fire poker often, crusted with his dried blood, stuffed in a basement along with the secret that it's responsible for a man's death. 'I know Mimi. She isn't capable of what you're suggesting.'

She turns to me. Those dark eyes hard like conkers. 'Under the right circumstances, we can all commit murder, Verity.'

My heart thuds in my lips. I open my mouth to speak when an almighty bang makes me jump. The movers have dropped a bedframe. The ivory wood now sports an ugly split along one side. It takes just a second for something perfect to be broken.

'Right,' says Addison, turning away from the melodrama unfolding below. 'Let's finish clearing out these drawers.'

Before long, we turn our attention towards his walk-in wardrobe. I pull open the Shaker doors, anticipation hot in my blood, and breathe in his smell. It's so familiar to me, the warm, spicy scent of him. And beneath it something sweet and dark – chocolate. It brings with it a million memories. For a moment, all I can do is stand and let the grief crest over me. I fight to keep breathing. To keep my head above the murky waters of sorrow. I step inside and run my fingers over his shirts. I stop when I reach my favourite. It's the colour of crushed blueberries and did nice things for his eyes. I bought it for him. A gift. I laid it out on our bed and told him to put it on for the date I'd planned. Just as he'd done for me a hundred times when we were first together. As Verity Rose gained traction and I was the one earning very good money, it was a thrill to be able to treat him. To take him to a fancy restaurant. To pay the bill. I can still taste the wine and the blackberry crumble on his lips as we kissed in the taxi on the way home. Can still feel the buttons of his shirt beneath my fingers as I undid them.

'Charity or keep?' prompts Addison at my back.

'Keep.'

An hour later, the wardrobe is half-empty and, despite the autumn chill, we are both hot and sweaty.

'You still wear your rings,' observes Addison.

I glance down and realise I've been spinning my engagement ring on my finger. An old habit. It's a large oval sapphire encircled by a halo of diamonds and set on a gold band. A Lockwood family heirloom. Much like the locket around my neck – it is gold and round, engraved with a cursive L. Even though Addison didn't ask a question, I feel obliged to answer. 'I don't think I'll ever stop being his wife. Even now, it would feel like a betrayal to remove my rings,' I say. 'Imagine if it were Harry.'

'Of course.' She swallows, her cheeks colouring. 'I didn't mean . . . and did you ever get his ring back?'

I shake my head. The newspapers got hold of a lot of gory details regarding Linden's murder, including the fire poker. What the public don't know is that the murder weapon isn't the only thing his killer took. They stole his watch and wedding band, too. The police think Linden's death was the last in a spate of robberies happening across Bath, that whoever attacked him didn't expect him to fight back and when he did, they accidentally killed him. They argued that as Windermere is old, with creaking pipes and shutters that slam closed in the wind, it's possible his assailant mistook the noise for another occupant in the house and ran, only having the time to grab the watch and ring. The bifold doors were found wide open so the police think his attacker fled out the back and across the fields.

I'm still spinning my engagement ring when it comes loose and slips from my finger, clattering to the floor. I drop to my knees to retrieve it. It's skittered into the furthest corner of the walk-in wardrobe, behind some shoe boxes. On all fours, I shove them aside. Above me, Addison is swishing suit jackets along the rail to allow me more room. I feel around for it, putting most of my weight on my left hand. Then I shriek as the floorboard beneath my palm flips up. When I rear back, it crashes down, but doesn't slot back into place.

'Jesus,' hisses Addison. 'That scared the life out of me. That's a hazard. Should we call someone to look at it? Harry's handy. I can ask him to stop by after work.'

Harry works in finance. I've never seen him with a hammer or a drill, and struggle to imagine him hanging a picture frame, let alone fixing the hardwood floor. I pick up my engagement ring and slide it onto my finger.

'I can phone Harry now,' offers Addison.

But I'm no longer listening. My entire body is a live wire of tension as I catch a glimpse of something shiny in the space beneath the loose floorboard.

'What're you doing?' she asks, watching me slide the board free.

'There's something in there.'

She crouches beside me, so close her shoulder is pressed against mine.

I move the upended oak board aside and prop it against the wall. Then I reach inside the hole. My fingers brush something smooth and hard but the gap is too small for me to retrieve whatever's down there. I wiggle the floorboards on either side. The one to the left is loose too. I remove it easily and pass it to Addison.

'Verity, should we . . .'

But I don't hear her. I am reaching inside and pulling things out: a silver laptop, a phone and a thick wedge of papers. Hidden beneath the floor of my deceased husband's wardrobe. Blood pounds in my ears. The phone is basic. A Nokia. A burner phone. I press the button on the side to turn it on but, disappointingly, it doesn't blink to life. And neither does the laptop. Then I take the wedge of papers. They're thick lilac sheets of A4. Dozens of them folded in half. I take the first one in the pile and open it up, catching a faint whiff of another woman's sweet perfume.

'What are they?' asks Addison, peering over my shoulder. She gasps. She reads what I am reading.

'Letters,' I answer. '*Love* letters.' This truth goes up my spine, down my shoulders and through my fingertips. Chilling my blood. Sinking into my bones. Crystallising in my marrow. I feel myself chip and splinter and break, tiny pieces of me shattering on the wooden floorboards and skittering into the secret hole. The truth burrows out of my mouth. A wriggling, anaemic maggot falling from my lips. 'Linden was having an affair.'

Chapter Two

The Other Woman

She wakes up to Linden putting on his clothes. It is early morning; the summer sun streams through the hotel window. The sight of his naked back ignites a deep, humid sex memory within her, last night coming back in delicious pieces that melt on her tongue like dark chocolate. His hips between her thighs as he moved over her. The sore sweetness of his teeth sinking into her shoulder. The sex is the best she's ever had. With him, she doesn't have to pretend, to fake an orgasm just to massage his ego. 'Tell me how you want it,' he said. No one has ever asked her that before. He taught her how to be truthful and unashamed and greedy. To ask for more, for rougher, harder. It's refreshing. It's addictive. After, she scrawled her name across his chest with her fingertip. Over and over, branding him, wishing they could live forever in the heady happiness of that July evening.

'You're leaving?' she asks.

He slips into his shirt. 'I need to get back home.'

She is silent, wearing disappointment like a gag.

He looks over his shoulder and when he sees her sullen expression, his handsome face creases in sympathy. 'I don't want to leave you.'

She knows she is pouting. It's a childish gesture; one she is usually careful to avoid because she wants him to think of her as educated and worldly. Even so, she is pouting. He climbs back onto the bed, his shirt only half buttoned. He slowly pulls the bedsheet away from her naked body and she lets him. Then he kisses his way up her throat.

She unwillingly melts against him. Candlewax to his lit wick. He circles her wrists with his large, soft hands and yanks them above her head. Pinning her to the mattress. Desire glitters in her veins and then his mouth claims hers. Hungrily, desperately. When he pulls back, she stares up into his eyes, the colour of caramel, and knows she'll never stop wanting Linden Lockwood.

He runs his thumb over her bottom lip. 'I'm only ever truly home when I'm with you.'

From anyone else, it would be a cringeworthy line, one she'd recite to her friends to make them laugh, but from him, from Linden Lockwood, it is everything. A diamond she will take out and marvel at again and again, before slipping it carefully back into the folds of her memory.

'Stay,' he tells her. 'Order breakfast. No need to rush off. It's all paid for.'

'Don't you ever worry she'll see your bank statements?'

He tenses as he bends to pull on his shoes. 'She knows I'm at a hotel for work.'

'But not that you're with me?'

He is quiet as he zips up his bag. 'Obviously not.'

She feels a stab of jealousy when she thinks about him and his wife, together in the home they share, doing things normal couples do: cooking dinner, bickering over laundry, having sex in a familiar bed, in a familiar house that smells of their combined scents. Sure, it was a thrill in the beginning, sneaking around, the danger of being caught spiking their lust with an urgency she'd never felt with anyone else, but it has become more than that in the three months they've been together. So much more. Whenever he leaves and goes back to his wife, he takes a piece of her with him and she worries that if he never returned, it would be lost.

She looks around the hotel room. It is expensive with its velvet sofa, plush carpet and large walk-in shower. One of the nicer ones they'd stayed in, but it isn't a home. It isn't theirs.

'I wish we had a place that's all our own,' she tells him, flopping back down onto the duck feather pillows. 'Anonymous hotel rooms are sleazy.'

But that's what she signed up for, isn't it? After all, she's not his wife. She's the *other woman*. The nightmare that lurks in the corner of every seemingly happy marriage. The temptation that spouses convince themselves their partners will never give into. She is the forbidden apple in the Garden of Eden. Or, if she's being unkind to herself, she's a married man's dirty, disposable secret. The snake in the grass.

'It's only sleazy if we smoke afterwards,' he teases.

She smiles and wants to say something clichéd about him being her only addiction, but then he picks up his overnight bag.

She kisses him at the door and knows that when he gets to the end of the corridor, he'll slip his ring from his trouser pocket and slide it back onto his finger. Is she forgotten then? Remembered as vaguely as a dream upon waking?

She takes a shower, washing him from her skin, and orders breakfast. While she waits for it to arrive, she scrolls through her phone. When the affair began and she and Linden disappeared to hotel rooms or sneaked into his house on the rare occasions they were brave enough, her phone bustled with messages from friends, asking about her weekend, wondering where she was, what she was doing, who she was with. She lied and lied and lied again. Being with Linden has meant being at his beck and call, cancelling plans with friends or leaving an evening early to be with him in the short windows of time he's able to escape his wife. Friendships are like plants, they require time and attention, pruning and watering often. Since being with Linden, she knows she's been neglectful of them, leaving them to wilt. She misses her friends, but how can she stay close to them without being able to talk about the most important thing in her life, and she knows she can't tell anyone about Linden. Even if she wanted to, what would she say? No; what she needs are cacti, the kinds of friendships that survive without much attention. Even so, Linden takes up so much space, winding through every waking moment like an exotic vine.

By the time breakfast arrives, she's no longer hungry. She spends the morning lounging around in the hotel. It's much nicer than her little studio. When she eventually leaves, it is raining. The summer sun has been swallowed by a thick blanket of clouds, the early July afternoon sticky and grey. As she crosses the car park, she feels eyes on her. Her skin prickles. She stops. Slowly, she looks around. Except for the parked cars, the place is empty.

If she'd known that months from now it would end in blood and tears, maybe she'd have searched a little harder.

Chapter Three

The Wife

His betrayal is a hot spear lodged in my chest. I claw at it. Falling to my knees in the walk-in wardrobe. 'No.' My voice is a thin whistle of grief. 'No, he'd never . . .'

Addison sinks down beside me. 'Verity, I'm so sorry.'

The full weight of Linden's treachery crushes me so hard I can barely breathe. I feel my ribs cracking. Bones breaking. Heart tearing. I thought he loved me the way I loved him: unwaveringly. I had no idea he was unhappy. That he would stray. Why would he have an affair? The need to know pushes back the grief. I'm still clutching the first lilac love letter, balling it up. I sit back on my haunches and with frantic, fearful fingers I press it into the cool wood and smooth it out with the flat of my palm so I can read it again.

'Maybe you shouldn't,' says Addison tentatively. 'You're in shock.'

'I need to know,' I bite out. I reread it until I feel sick. 'Who is she? There's nothing in this letter to tell me who she is.' I reach for another but Addison snatches them up.

'You're in a state. Let's get out of this wardrobe. I'll make us some tea, then we can sit down and go through each one together, OK?'

I glance at the hole the loose floorboards have left. To think, a year ago I was lying in our bed, only feet from his darkest secret, and I had no idea.

The kitchen is bright and airy, with floor-to-ceiling bifold doors and a skylight over the island. Addison makes us fresh mint tea, plucking the herb from the terracotta pots on the windowsill. I love this kitchen. Together, Linden and I chose the stone-coloured Shaker cupboard doors and gold hardware, the ceramic butler sink, the thick oak countertops and the off-white wall tiles. All the while I thought we were building a home together, a life, and behind closed doors he was busy tearing it apart.

Addison serves the tea. She takes a seat opposite. 'Are you sure you want to read through all these letters? Will it make you feel better or worse?' I can tell she's choosing her words carefully, worried I am a fragile glass vase. One chink and I will shatter, but I know if our positions were reversed, she'd comb through each sentence looking for answers.

'I need to know, Addison. Linden was having an affair. We were married for *four years* and he was with someone else.' I shake my head. 'I don't understand. Why cheat? Why didn't he just leave me and start over?' My chest heaves as sobs break from my ribs and expel themselves in frantic gasps. Addison takes my hand and squeezes it. 'I can't ask him . . . he's dead, but if I can find the other woman, I can talk to her and find out why.'

'What makes you think she'll talk to you? Or that you can trust anything she says?'

Our eyes lock. 'Because she owes me that.'

She bites her lip against the pleas for me to let it go because she knows, with or without her, I am reading these letters. And after all we've been through together, she won't let me do it alone.

Addison was only seventeen when her mother abandoned her for good. My parents took her in and Addison and I became closer than ever. When I passed my driving test, I drove me and Addison to the beach two hours away. The rain lashed against the windows, so loud our voices were lost to it. The beach was dark and empty and it was raining so hard, we shivered in our summer dresses. I was exalted, high on my new-found freedom. Far from home and the watchful eyes of my parents. So I stripped.

'Get naked,' I told her. 'We're skinny-dipping.'

'Look at the sea,' she yelled over the waves crashing against the rocks. 'We'll drown.'

'I'd never let you drown.' I slid my fingers beneath the hem of her dress and pulled it up and over her head. Then, hand in hand, we raced down to the raging water.

We've always been there for one another, which is how I know she'll agree to stay and help me uncover the identity of this other woman. She sighs. 'Fine, but I think it's a terrible idea.'

As I don't have a charger for the phone or the laptop, we can't search either, but we do read through the letters, hunting for clues. After an hour though, we haven't discovered a single piece of helpful information. Addison was right; reading about my husband fucking someone else, the intimate, almost obsessive feelings the author had for Linden, makes nausea and fury wash through me.

'I just don't understand why he would be unfaithful,' I say in a small voice.

'I wish I had an answer. Linden and I weren't close but when we were all together, it was obvious to me how much he loved you.'

Hot tears prick my eyes. 'I wasn't enough.' I toss the letter I'm holding onto the counter. 'Obviously.'

We fall silent, staring at the evidence of my husband's infidelity. For a moment, I am so jealous of Addison and her intact marriage that I can't bear to look at her. The grief and shock are subsiding, leaving only a burning rage. I gave up so much for Linden, *gave* him so much. This house, a life spectacular enough to rival even his brother's perfect existence, I gave Linden everything he asked for, didn't I? So why wasn't it enough? Why wasn't *I* enough? Self-pity sludges in, dousing the flames of my fury.

'I need to take this to the police,' I say.

Addison frowns. 'Why?'

I look at her in confusion. 'Because the woman who was having an affair with my husband could also be his killer.'

She opens her mouth, perplexed, and then says, 'That seems like a leap.'

'Does it? His wedding ring was missing. Maybe she took it out of spite.'

Addison blanches. 'But so was his watch. It was a robbery, wasn't it? The police said whoever attacked him only managed to get the watch and ring before being spooked and taking off.'

'They did, but—'

'And didn't the break-ins stop after Linden was found?'

'Yes, but that could be because there was an increased police presence as a result of his murder, not because they took it too far and accidentally killed him. The police are certain his death wasn't planned since the murder weapon was an item already found in the house and not something his attacker brought with them. Now we know about the affair, it all makes sense,' I tell Addison. '*She* killed him. She took the watch to make it look like a robbery.'

'And the ring?'

'She stole my husband. Maybe taking his wedding band was some kind of trophy.'

She nods but doesn't look convinced. 'Did the police ever ask if he was unfaithful?'

'Yes, but I told them I'd never suspected a thing. That we were happy. I told them the truth. Or . . . what I believed was the truth.' I close my eyes against the image of Linden touching another woman, and I feel sick all over again.

Addison is silent, her teeth digging into her bottom lip.

'What is it?' I ask.

She lifts her dark eyes to mine. Hesitantly, she says, 'The thing is, Verity, if you go to the police now and tell them Linden was having an affair, they might turn their attention to you.'

Dread crawls up my spine. 'What do you mean?'

'Just that they always look at the spouse, don't they? And they might assume you knew about the affair before we discovered the letters.'

'But I didn't.'

'I know, but if they think you did, even for a moment, they could . . . they might assume . . .'

'What?'

Her cheeks are reddening. She doesn't want to say what she is about to say. I remain silent. Daring her. 'That you killed Linden.'

I feel myself turning to stone. 'You can't be serious.'

She pulls her mug towards her, refusing to meet my eye.

'I didn't murder my husband, Addison.'

'I know that. Of course I do. I just worry that this could put you in the hot seat.'

I push myself to my feet. 'Let it. I have nothing to hide. I was at a rural yoga retreat seventy miles away. I was seen by thirty people. I didn't even have my car. I got the train home, for Christ's sake. I . . .'

'I know,' she says, standing. 'You're right. I'm sorry. I just . . . worry. You're the only family I have left.' She shakes her head, tears glistening in her dark eyes. 'Thank God you weren't in this house when Linden was attacked. It could've been you.'

'Sometimes I feel guilty I wasn't here. If I'd been here, I might've stopped the assault. *Saved* him.'

She pulls me into a hug. I breathe in the Jo Malone Blackberry and Bay perfume I got her for Christmas. I buy her a bottle every year because Harry refuses to spend so much on fragrance. Unlike Linden, Harry is mindful of money. 'You can't think that way, Verity. His death wasn't your fault.' She pulls back to stare into my eyes. 'You really believe the woman he was sleeping with is the same person who beat him to death?'

'Yes. Maybe she's in a relationship too and Linden threatened to tell her partner, or maybe she threatened to tell me and things got out of hand.' I shrug. 'Whatever happened, I'm not going to let her get away with it.'

It's late by the time Addison leaves and I agree to wait to take the things we found to the police. Addison is still worried they'll turn their attention to me and insists I call my lawyer first and take a couple of days to process the affair. I don't have the energy to argue with her so I agree.

I have a shower and slip into my favourite baggy T-shirt and harem pants. When we moved into this grand house, nearly four years ago now, I only wore Gilda & Pearl silk pyjama sets and lacy nightgowns. I never wanted to become one of those stale couples who got too comfortable, spending their evenings in loungewear sat in front of Netflix. Endless grey nights filled with average conversation, average TV and average sex. It's laughable now, that I thought silk and lace would save us. Still, what about how we lived our lives? We travelled – Norway and Bali, Italy and the Maldives – somewhere different every year. My career meant we were invited to exclusive events – gallery openings, book launches, festivals. And I never stopped giving him blow jobs or became one of those women who insisted he washed his cock in the sink first. Though Mimi once said, 'It's called a blow job for a reason. I expect my workspace to be clean, thank you very much.' While I poured time and effort into our marriage, he was with another woman.

My cheeks colour as I remember how smug I felt whenever we met up with our other married friends, feeling as though what I had with Linden was so special. On the way home, we'd say things to one another like, 'Did you notice how he rolls his eyes every time she speaks?' and 'Did you hear how she snapped at him after dessert?' I'm ashamed of myself. It's only now, in the echoing silence of my bedroom, that it dawns on me those other couples were likely talking the same way about me and Linden, spotting all the signs I missed that we weren't as happy as I believed us to be.

I sit up in bed, unable to sleep. When I close my eyes, I see Linden with her. Maybe Addison is right and the police will take a closer look at me if I hand over what we found. But I don't care. They won't find anything to suggest I killed my husband. But maybe they will find the other woman, expose her, because that is what she deserves. I hope when people find out what kind of person she is, it ruins her life the way she has ruined mine. It's a spiteful thought. We're told not to ever bring other women down. To remain a supportive part of the sisterhood. But I can't exactly punish Linden now he's dead. She's the only one left. And I can't wait a second longer.

Decision made, I go downstairs, snatch up the laptop, the phone and the lilac love letters, and drive them to the police station.

Chapter Four

The Other Woman

Linden takes her to a vintage clothes shop after hours. A man in a suit lets them inside. At the back is a large mahogany wardrobe which Linden opens with a flourish and says, 'Step inside, Lucy.'

Growing up, *The Lion, the Witch and the Wardrobe* was her favourite book but she preferred Susan, who was brave and took charge. She is giddy as she moves coats and dresses aside before stepping into a bar. A speakeasy. Inside it is dimly lit. The exposed-brick walls are decorated with dozens of vintage paintings in vintage frames. All the wooden tables are mismatched, and each is home to a crystal decanter, cut tumblers and a tealight in a saucer.

She's still buoyant as she and Linden are seated at a little round table in the corner.

'Sorry if that was a little gimmicky,' whispers Linden.

'Whimsical,' she corrects. 'And I loved it.'

She browses the drink selection, settling on her favourite: a raspberry mojito. But then he takes the paper menu from her and replaces it with the posh kind, bound in leather. 'This is better,' he assures her.

She runs her eyes down the list. 'It's all wine. I don't like wine.'

'That's because you only drink the cheap stuff.'

He orders them a bottle of a fancy Italian red she can't pronounce. She realises then that admitting you don't like wine is like admitting you don't like ballet. It tells people you're uncultured, maybe even uneducated. That's not how she wants him to see her. It's not who she wants to be. So she drinks the red, and in the toilet, she googles the bottle so when she returns she can talk about the oaky aftertaste as though she's a seasoned connoisseur. His mouth quirks. He knows.

He goes to the bar and orders them more drinks, leaving his phone on the table, screen up. A message from his wife flashes across it. They never speak her name when they're together and she never thinks it either, referring to her simply as 'his wife' or 'the wife'. It makes it easier to fuck another woman's husband if his wife is reduced to an inconsequential title. And even though she *knows* his wife, when she conjures up her image, she is a cartoon character. A 1950s cookie cutter with a bouffant, swing skirt and a tray of freshly baked cakes. So different from the high-powered entrepreneur she really is. So different from her, his mistress.

She's never asked Linden why he strayed from his beautiful, ambitious, witty wife. Why he has chosen her to stray with. Without his answer, she can pretend it's because she is special. *More* beautiful, *more* ambitious, wittier. It is a lie. But one she finds comfort in. She wonders if Linden has ever questioned why *she* was drawn to *him*. Wonders whether men ever dip their toe into the pool of self-doubt that women seem to be submerged in most days. Wonders now how long it will be before Linden tires of her. Just as the lovers who came before did. She supposes it is only a matter of time. She tries to shake off the sickening grief that slowly creeps over her at the thought of being without Linden. Reminds herself that in five years from now, with Linden in the rear-view mirror of her life, she will look back on this time with bemusement, shocked that she dared have an affair with a married man. If she thinks of their relationship as though it is already over, it will not hurt quite so much when it comes to an end.

Linden returns with two white wines. She can already taste the acidity hitting the back of her throat. She smiles up at him. He grins – all dimples and straight white teeth. His smile falters when his eyes find his phone and spots his wife's name on the screen. He reads her message, a frown furrowing his brow.

'Everything OK?' she asks.

He pauses before answering, 'Yeah, sure. Let's get a hotel tonight.'

He says it with the same nonchalance her friends would say, 'Let's get a takeaway.'

'Aren't you worried she'll wonder where you are?'

'No.'

'Because she trusts you?'

'Because she's going to London for a meeting.' He sips his wine and then nods to her glass. 'You need to drink that. We've got more on the way.'

Later, in the toilet, the room spins away from her. Her face is hot. She grips the sink to keep herself upright. Alcohol clings to the back of her throat and coats her mouth. She has become best friends with a willowy, dark-haired woman – Marissa – whom she met outside the cubicle. Public toilets are a petri dish, a breeding ground for fast female friendships. Some of these bonds are like midnight snacks, consumed quickly and forgotten easily. Others become comfort food, a staple dish you return to again and again. She knows her new best friend will only be a snack because as *the other woman* her life is too complex for something meaningful, the kind of friendship that requires you to give away your secrets like one-penny sweets. Besides, being on Linden's timetable doesn't allow her the flexibility to pour energy into other people.

The two of them sing along to 'You Can't Hurry Love' by The Supremes. When the song is over, Marissa says, 'I should probably get back to my husband, he'll wonder where I am.'

'You're married?'

She nods, reapplying her scarlet lipstick in the mirror. 'Two years. Our wedding didn't go to plan, but the marriage has been smooth sailing.'

It's on the tip of her loose, drunk tongue to tell Marissa it's only smooth sailing until another woman, a siren such as herself, bewitches said husband to shipwreck their boat on the rocks of an affair.

Marissa talks about her lawyer husband, her exciting career as a designer, their house in the heart of Bath. Marissa giggles. 'Sorry, all I've done is go on about myself. I don't even know your name.'

'Juliet,' she lies, feeling envy for Marissa's life hardening in her throat.

'Are you married, Juliet?'

'No.' She feels a second lie snaking up her throat. 'But I think he might propose.'

Marissa's eyes widen. 'How do you know?'

'I found a ring in his bedside table.'

She squeals. 'That's *so* exciting. Congratulations.' Marissa pulls her into a hug as though they've known each other all their lives. 'How did you meet?'

'Fate,' she answers. 'I found his wallet on the street and walked it to the address on his driving licence. When he opened the door and smiled, I just . . . I knew. We've been together ever since.'

'That's so romantic.'

And so much better than the truth.

It is how her mother met her father. Maybe since her love story with Linden doesn't have a pretty beginning, it will have a better ending than her parents' story did.

She returns to Linden. There's another large glass of wine. She drinks it quickly. Marissa stops by their table on her way out. 'Have a lovely night, Juliet.'

Her face reddens. 'You too.'

When she's gone, Linden raises an eyebrow. 'Juliet?'

'I didn't want to give her my real name . . . just in case.'

His grin is lazy. 'Does this make me Romeo?'

She doesn't answer. Her mind snagging on how Romeo and Juliet's story is tragic. How they both die in the end.

Linden captures her silence with his mouth, kissing her hard.

Two glasses of wine later, and she is stumbling into a taxi with him. Unlike hers, his movements are certain and coordinated. The entire world swims beneath the current of alcohol in her blood. Her head flops back against the taxi seat. Her body is heavy. Linden's hand sweeps up her thigh and beneath her dress. He pushes his fingers into her. Dimly, she wonders if the driver is watching them.

The hotel foyer is a blur. She's vaguely aware of someone offering her a glass of water and then Linden's voice, 'Don't worry, I'll make sure my wife drinks plenty.'

Wife. My wife. She supposes people are less likely to question his intentions if she is his wife, as opposed to a one-night stand or, heaven forbid, a mistress. He guides her to their room, one hand pressing the small of her back. She staggers as though her heels have been replaced with clogs. Soon though, they are gone and she is naked beneath him.

Linden rises early and leaves before breakfast. She's so hungover, she's sure if she eats even one bite of anything right now, she will vomit. So she showers and dresses quickly.

In the foyer, the receptionist calls to her. 'Miss, excuse me, miss?' She turns.

The receptionist has come around the desk and is holding a folded piece of paper. 'A message was left for you this morning.'

As she takes it, she is only vaguely aware of the receptionist's fretful expression. Still, she smiles and says goodbye. She gets a giddy rush, like a schoolgirl being passed a note in the classroom. Linden has never left her a note before. It's only when she steps out into the summer sun that she reads it and discovers it isn't from Linden at all.

I know what you're doing. It makes me sick.

Chapter Five

The Wife

On Monday morning, I go to work as usual but I am exhausted after a night stretched thin answering questions in the police station about what I found, how I found it, when. As Addison predicted, I was asked if I'd known about the affair prior to Linden's murder. I told them I didn't. I'm not sure they believed me. Still, they thanked me for everything I'd handed over, promising to keep me informed.

The temptation to work from home or not at all is almost overwhelming, but as much as I don't want to be around people, the distraction will be good for me. So I head into our little office, right above Crumb Coat Bakery in Bathampton. It is all exposed brick and parquet flooring, wood panelling and plants, brass hardware and oak desks. A lot of the products we advertise to our Verity Rose readership is photographed in-house, so it made sense to invest in its aesthetic. It's small yet there's enough space for the four of us. Colette, Heidi and Flora each have a desk in the open-plan area, while my office is at the back.

I arrive just after nine, carrying a box of pastries from Crumb Coat. Flora and Heidi greet me warmly and each take a croissant. My marketing manager, Colette, on the other hand, stands back with an imperious expression and makes a show of checking the slim gold watch that hangs from her bony wrist. As though she's *my* boss and *I'm* a tardy employee. After Linden's death, I took almost three months away from Verity Rose and, as Colette is the most experienced of my team, it made sense to put her in charge. The trouble now is that she's convinced she can run my business better than I can. Still, I choose to kill her with kindness. 'Rhubarb Danish, Colette?'

She wrinkles her nose. In the three years we've worked together, I've never seen her eat processed sugar or carbs. Maybe that's why she's so miserable. 'No, thank you,' she says curtly. Her attitude as sharp and severe as her appearance. She's wearing another trouser suit, this one in plum. I imagine a meticulously organised wardrobe housing a rainbow of trouser suits set exactly one centimetre apart. 'Have you finalised that piece on the ten most effective meditation and breathing apps to reduce anxiety? I need Heidi to whip up some graphics for collaborator approval.'

It's a listicle. I can do them in my sleep. 'Yes, Colette, it's done. It'll be with Heidi as soon as I get to my desk.'

'I see.' A terse little silence follows. She does this a lot, uses silence like a noose in the hope you'll hang yourself. I stare impassively back until she clicks her tongue in annoyance and adds, 'It would be great if we have something to share with our collaborators this morning.'

I press my lips together to stop myself from snapping that I've been a little preoccupied sorting through my murdered husband's things and uncovering his affair, and instead say evenly, 'As I said, it'll be with Heidi as soon as possible.' Then I add, in saccharine tones, 'Sure you don't want this Danish?'

She smiles tightly. 'As I said, no thank you.'

I shrug, plucking it from the box, and even though I don't like rhubarb, I stuff it into my mouth.

Colette turns and stalks away. As the founder of Verity Rose, I *should* spend less time writing and more time focusing on the bigger-picture stuff. The boring stuff. Colette is always telling me so. But Verity Rose was built on *my* voice. *My* point of view. So I hold on to as many of the articles as I can, commissioning the surplus or anything that doesn't grab me to our pool of freelancers.

I feel Colette's brown eyes burning into the side of my skull because I haven't immediately scuttled to my office. Instead, I take the time to ask Heidi and Flora about their weekends. From beneath her newly cut-back-in fringe, Heidi gives me a knowing smile. Though she's far too nice to say so, I think she finds Colette's pointed edge just a tad too sharp. 'Well, the children had swimming on Saturday morning, and then it was a mad rush to get Jamie to a birthday party in Bristol,' says Heidi. Her northern accent has softened after years spent living in Somerset. 'And Cleo's just started gymnastics, so we had to dash back across to Frome for that. Then it was the usual bath time, bedtime routine, but the baby is teething so I got almost *no* sleep. I'm exhausted, and she's been far more difficult than the first two and—' She stops, catching herself, and then rearranges her frown into a soft, maternal smile. 'But it's worth it, isn't it? Being a mother is one of the best jobs in the world.'

I'm nodding and wondering why parents feel the need to smooth over a vaguely negative comment about their children with a good one. Like Polyfilla over a crack.

'Anyway,' she continues. 'There was *another* birthday party on Sunday. Then Jamie had rugby training and I spent the rest of the day catching up on chores. It was a hectic one, to be honest.'

I nod and smile, thinking this would've been a much shorter story if she'd led with 'I spent my weekend being an under-appreciated housemaid and an unpaid taxi service to three children who have busier social lives than I do.' Instead I asked, 'And what did your husband do this weekend?'

She shifts uncomfortably in her seat and starts tearing the croissant into pieces without making eye contact. 'Oh, well, Darren had some DIY projects, so he was working away in the garage, and then on Sunday he had a really important game of golf.'

Really important game of golf? That's an oxymoron if I ever heard one.

'He works so hard,' she says loyally.

'So do you.'

She looks up at me, a smile stretching across her round face, and I wonder whether Darren ever thanks his wife for raising their children alongside working and juggling a household so he can have a weekend entirely to himself.

Across the room, Colette starts passive-aggressively sighing. Ignoring her, I turn to Flora. 'And you, any wild weekend escapades?'

She doesn't look up. 'Nothing that will make the front page.'

Heidi's bright blue eyes glitter in a way that is unique only to women who have a piece of office gossip. 'Flora was whisked away on a romantic weekend break by her new boyfriend.'

Flora's cheeks flush a deep scarlet.

I smile even as I feel a pang of sadness at being the last in the office to know. As much as I try to be one of my team, I'm their boss so there's a gap I can't bridge. Still, I'm happy for Flora. Last year, barely a month after Linden's death, I bumped into her at Novel Wines – Linden's favourite. I almost didn't recognise her. She was pale with dark circles under her eyes, her red hair greasy and limp. I looked much the same, caught in a whorl of grief and clutching a bottle of red. I worried that whatever Flora was going through was my fault, convinced that being with me the day Linden was discovered had shaken her. I wanted to talk but she practically ran from me. Months later, when I returned to work, Heidi told me Flora had been struggling with a terrible break-up. I hadn't even known she'd had a boyfriend. None of us did. Even as I grieved Linden, I ached for Flora, remembering the burn of every heartbreak I endured before finding my husband.

'Will we get to meet this one?' Heidi asks Flora hopefully. 'You could bring him to the winter party.'

She stiffens. 'Maybe.'

'How do you know him?' she presses, not picking up on the social cue to drop it.

'University,' says Flora, reaching for her headphones.

'Have you been together long?'

'Sorry, Heidi, can we chat later? I really need to get this done before lunch.'

Heidi nods, though I can see she's disappointed. Flora slips her earbuds in and starts typing. Unperturbed, Heidi turns her smile on me. 'And you? Good weekend?'

I think about my dead husband's secrets, squirrelled away beneath the floorboards, and my stomach twists. 'Yes,' I lie.

'What did you do?'

I swallow, more lies sticking in my throat. I'm too exhausted to keep spinning tales so I choose honesty instead. Or at least, a slice of honesty because, quite frankly, the truth is like the chocolate cake Bruce Bogtrotter stole from Miss Trunchbull – too much of it will make you sick. So I offer Heidi just one easy-to-digest serving.

'Actually ... I ... took some time to sort through Linden's things.'

There's a heavy, sombre silence.

'That mustn't have been easy,' she sympathises.

My smile is wry. 'More difficult than you'd think.'

Though Flora's gaze is fixed on her screen, I notice she's removed an earbud to tune back into the conversation.

'I'm sorry,' says Heidi, pressing her lips together in a show of compassion.

'It's fine. It needed doing. I've put it off for a year now.'

'When we went through my grandmother's things we found all sorts,' says Heidi. 'Antiques, every birthday and Christmas card she'd ever received, diaries. The diaries were really interesting, actually. Turns out my grandmother had a wilder side in her youth.'

I nod. 'It's startling, the things you find out about a person after they're gone.'

At this, Flora's gaze whips up to mine. Our eyes lock. In hers, I see something I can't quite place. My heart races. She looks away quickly and starts tapping at her keyboard as though this conversation is happening far above her head, but there's a line of tension running across her shoulders and she refuses to meet my eye again.

36

Chapter Six

The Wife

In my office, I wonder about Flora's reaction. I wanted to question her but it wasn't appropriate in front of Heidi and Colette. Was her fear a figment of my imagination? Did I read her wrong entirely? It's possible. After all, I'm shattered and stressed and my world has been cast into disarray. Still, I know Flora isn't the other woman. She wasn't having an affair with my husband. For a start, she only met Linden a handful of times.

My office has a window that overlooks the rest of our workspace. Flora's desk is the closest. She's in profile, head down, earphones in, scribbling in a notepad. She hasn't so much as glanced my way since that odd interaction an hour ago. Is that guilt or nonchalance? I study her now. Her full mouth and doe eyes. Her long red hair and dewy skin. Wouldn't it be a shameful cliché of my husband to have had an affair with a younger woman? Flora has proven herself to be reliable and smart, even a little reserved. Picturing her engaging in an affair with a married man is almost laughable. She isn't sly or daring, thrill-seeking or deceptive.

Refusing to dwell on Linden and those lilac love letters anymore, I throw myself into my work, ticking things off my to-do list at speed. Linden used to mock me for my lists. I have at least three on the go at any given time. I'm organised. A meticulous planner. I'd be lost without them. Today, I'm supposed to be meeting with my accountant, Amy, but I reschedule for next week because number-centric conversations always require more of my attention and, even though I've promised not to think about Linden, my mind keeps dragging me back into the murky depths of his deceit. I can't stop picturing him with another woman. His exploring hands. His tongue between her thighs. His body moving over hers in a rhythm all their own. Different from ours.

Then I'm caught in a memory. Our first night at Windermere. Our bedframe wasn't due to arrive for another month so we were tangled together on our king-size mattress. We were naked, drinking champagne and eating the pizza we ordered from the little Italian in town. He told me I was beautiful. That he was so lucky. The *luckiest*.

'But will you still love me when I'm no longer young and attractive?' I teased.

He nipped at my bottom lip. 'Yes.'

'When I'm old enough to tuck my boobs into my socks?'

He laughed. 'Even then.'

'When my face resembles a walnut?'

He brushed my hair back, stroking it across the silk pillow. 'I'll love you even when you have nothing left but your aching soul.' And I ate up his words, like ice cream off a spoon, getting fat and happy on his promises. 'It's always been you,' he said. 'It will *always* be you.'

But it wasn't, was it? My reign was short and I was easily dethroned.

For the rest of the afternoon, I pendulum-swing between missing Linden and hating him. I start dissecting our relationship as though it's a cadaver on a steel table, desperate to uncover its cause of death. I know he had an issue with how much I worked. How much I earned. When we bought the house, my money made up the vast majority of the deposit. Linden was an English Literature professor and a published novelist. His first book, a literary fiction title, did remarkably well and was translated into nine languages, but his second was subpar. Over the years, his royalty cheques dried up, though he was never honest about this with his family. The Lockwoods are a pack of high achievers and even higher earners. The family company, Lockies Shortbread, has been a household name since the 1930s, passed from father to eldest son since its inception. Linden should have been at the helm but his younger brother was their father's choice, breaking four generations of tradition. Linden always said he was glad Felix took it off his hands so he could focus on his writing, but I knew there was more to it. He and his brother are fiercely competitive. It's a toxic environment I tried to avoid. We only saw his family for big holidays and extra-special occasions. Though Felix's wife Céline was the favourite daughter-in-law, she was always frosty towards me. It didn't escape my notice that, at gatherings, she went out of her way to talk to Linden.

At our housewarming party, I overheard Linden boasting to Felix about his literary success. 'The book sales are phenomenal. I'm in demand, travelling all over the country to guest-lecture. It's a shame that Lockies Shortbread anchors you to dreary old England, brother.' It didn't really bother me that he wanted people to think our home was paid for by his income. I know some men's egos can be a slippery glass ball and so I've always handled it with care. But, other than that, we were happy. So happy. We rarely argued, only ever bickering about him forgetting to take the bins out, or that I am forever leaving the back door unlocked. In fact, we had very few rows in all the years we were together. The fact is, we never stopped wanting each other. So many of my friends have complained about their lacklustre sex lives and though I'd nod sympathetically, I could never relate. The day before I left for Oakleaf Yoga Retreat, we had sex on the stairs, too hungry for each other to make it all the way to the bedroom. We talked. Laughed. Shared stories and secrets, swapping them like playing cards each night over supper. OK, so, as Verity Rose snowballed, I didn't make it home for supper every single night, but he was away sometimes too. Though, looking back, was he really guest-lecturing, or was he with her?

Just then, Amy calls. I answer, grateful for the distraction.

'Verity, I just got your email to reschedule our meeting. Next Tuesday good for you?'

'Absolutely. Great. Sorry to mess you around.'

'Oh, no bother.' She is somewhere loud. I imagine her striding through Bath, her pale blonde ponytail swinging behind her, a takeaway cup of coffee in one hand and her phone in the other. 'Actually, I have some news.'

Baby, I think. Even though I'm not sure whether she is married, I am convinced she's going to tell me that she is expecting her first child. I'm at the age now where pregnancy announcements are as common as summer colds. I feel a brief dart of selfish panic. Amy is the best accountant I've ever had. Linden introduced us. He'd been a client of hers long before I met him. Right now, I could really do without the stress of having to find another accountant. Even if she only takes a few months of maternity leave, she won't come back full-time. She'll say she will because that's what they all say but everything changes the second the baby comes. She'll be flooded with maternal hormones and then her friends from NCT won't go back, so she'll feel guilty and neglectful if she does. These are all things Linden and I discussed when we debated whether or not to have children.

'I'm leaving Waterhouse Accounting.'

'Oh . . . wow. That *is* big news,' I say, waiting for the inevitable 'because I'm pregnant' cheer. Even though she can't see me, I plaster on a smile, hoping it will make my obligatory 'congratulations!' sound more genuine. When she doesn't reply, I add, 'You've been there years.'

'On to pastures new.'

I frown. 'What do you mean?'

'I'm opening my own accountancy company!'

'Oh, that's fantastic,' I say, my enthusiasm almost rivalling my relief. 'Congratulations, Amy!'

'Thank you. It's all rather exciting. Rather busy too. Of course I'd love for you to come with me on this new venture.'

'Definitely.' I had no idea she was thinking of branching out on her own. But then, as much as I'd like us to be, we aren't exactly friends. A couple of times we've arranged to go for a drink or for dinner but Amy has always cancelled last minute. I think she's intent on keeping things professional, but maybe that will change now she's working for herself. Ever since Mimi cut me off, there's a chasm in my life that I haven't been able to fill. 'You can tell me all about it next week. Shall we make it a lunch meeting? On me. We can celebrate your new company.'

'Perfect.'

When we ring off, the silence in my office engulfs me. The same echoing silence that lives in my house now Linden is gone. It is absolute. Like darkness. Like a blindfold over my eyes. A gag in my mouth. I miss him so much. I hate him, too. What would I do if he appeared in my office right now? Would I fling myself into his arms, breathe in the familiar, comforting scent of him, melt into his strong, certain embrace? Or would I beat him to death with a fire poker? I hear Addison telling me that, under the right circumstances, we can all commit murder.

I decide to go home. Flora has already left for lunch so I tell Colette and Heidi I have a headache. Colette's pinched, angular face tightens in disapproval but I ignore her in favour of Heidi, whose freckled visage creases in sympathy.

I don't really want to return to an empty house, but what choice do I have? I think about heading to Addison's but I know she'll be put out that I didn't wait to go with her to take the letters, laptop and phone to the police. As I don't have the energy to defend myself, I decide to indulge in a bottle of wine in the hope it'll help me sleep. It's not healthy and not something I'd ever recommend to my Verity Rose readers, of course. Would any of them – my readers, the brands I work with – take me seriously if they knew what a thorny, tangled mess my life really is? I doubt it. I think about all those articles I wrote advising others on how to maintain a healthy relationship and I feel like a fraud.

I'm pulling up to my house when I see a familiar petite, curvy frame crossing the driveway next door. She's dressed in denim dungarees over a mustard sweater. Her curly dark hair is piled high on her head, secured with a silky, burnt-orange scarf. I watch as she carries a cardboard box from her Nissan to the open front door of her house. There are a few more boxes on her porch.

She's back.

Mimi is back.

Without thinking, I am getting out of my car and crossing my driveway towards her. 'Mimi!'

She spins on her heel, eyes wide as they meet mine. Her olive complexion pales at the sight of me.

41

I jog up the two steps to join her on the porch. There used to be a bistro table set out here where, during the warmer months, we'd share a pitcher of mojitos and our deepest secrets.

'You're back,' I say. 'I didn't know you were coming back.' But then, I didn't know she was leaving until I knocked on her door and a woman I'd never met answered. The pain of that memory, of being abandoned, shoots through me afresh.

Mimi is silent. Staring at me warily, as though I'm a wild animal she isn't sure will lash out and bite. I should be angry with Mimi for how she left but instead I am only relieved that she's returned. I've missed her so much. 'Why now?' I ask. 'It's been a year.'

She lifts her chin in a familiar gesture of defiance. 'Because it's my home and I refuse to be chased out of it.' Before I can question who she's referring to, she says, 'You shouldn't be here, Verity.'

Her usually warm hazel eyes are cold and unforgiving. I don't understand what I've done wrong. Why she left. Why she's ignored me for twelve months. 'I live next door . . . where else did you expect me to be?'

She glances towards my house. 'I thought you might have sold it, to be honest. I can't believe you still live there after what happened in your lounge.'

And I see something in her face I've never seen before: judgement. How dare she look down on me for continuing to live in the house *I* paid for. A house filled with some of my happiest memories. And memories are all I have left. 'Because it's my home and I refuse to be chased out of it,' I retort.

She grips the box so tightly her knuckles are turning white. 'Just stay away from me.'

Then she spins back towards the house and crosses the threshold, dropping the box onto the console table in the hallway. I hover, wrestling with this foreign hostility. Baffled by it. 'I don't know what I did wrong . . .'

Mimi whirls towards me again. 'Stay. Away.'

'But—'

'*Please*, just leave me alone,' she says, somewhere between a plea and a command.

I am an unwelcome stray begging for scraps, being shooed away, but still, I don't leave. I can't. 'I've missed you, Mimi.'

And, just for a second, she softens and I think that finally, she'll talk to me. She'll explain what it is I've done. Then she closes her eyes as though she is fighting off a headache. When she opens them again, a kaleidoscope of emotions plays across her features: fury, devastation, *fear*. 'I mean it, Verity. Don't ever talk to me again.'

And then she slams the door in my face.

Chapter Seven

The Other Woman

It has been nearly two weeks since she received that strange note at the hotel. For a few days, she worried someone knew her secret. She turned her paranoia onto everyone, shining it in their faces like torchlight. She'd become suspicious of her colleagues, the friends she walked away from, his wife. Yet no other notes have been sent. Besides, the first didn't cite her or Linden by name. It didn't even reference an affair.

I know what you're doing. It makes me sick.

Vague and impersonal. She had to let it go; perhaps it wasn't meant for her at all.

She hasn't seen Linden in ten days. Today, he comes back from his holiday with his wife. She tries not to be concerned that a week in Lake Bled will remedy their marriage, the getaway acting as a warm cloth over a festering wound, and she, an infection to be drawn out. Still, this concern isn't as easily tossed aside as that note. She cannot stop fretting over what she will do with her time if Linden puts an end to their relationship upon his return. If he decides to leave her, who will fill the hours in her days and in her head?

She dreams that it is her exploring Lake Bled with Linden, eating cream cakes and hiring a boat to row across to the island. But then she wakes up, a sadness in her chest, as dark as spilled ink, spreading through her, staining her insides black with mourning.

She's barely heard from him this past week. He has sent her a few messages, fired off at odd hours of the night, presumably when his wife is asleep. She misses him. Thinks about him constantly. She *fantasises* about him all the time. Sometimes, they are sugary sweet indulgences: picnics in the park where they feed each other chocolate-covered strawberries, and he kisses her chastely on the mouth. Sometimes, usually at night while alone in her bed, she yearns for something richer, spicier. She thinks of sweat and heat, of breathless excitement and his naked body slamming into hers. Sugary sweet or rich and spicy, he is what she craves.

As she walks home, she misses the air-conditioned office. The summer heat is almost unbearable, laying its flat, unwelcome palm against her chest. Though it is only early evening, people spill onto the pavement outside bars, clumsy and sunburnt and drunk, sloshing apple cider poured over pint glasses of ice. She grows hotter still. Wanting Linden has become a fever that bubbles beneath her skin.

Across the street to her right, she spies a group of three women laughing loud and shrill and leaning into each other. She knows these women. They were her friends. She shed them months ago, peeling them off like sweat-damp clothes because juggling her affair with Linden and her friendships with them had become too complicated. She hadn't given those women, ones she had loved deeply, much thought recently. Like a mug of tea forgotten and left to go cold. Linden had moved like expanding foam through her mind, her life, filling in the gaps her friends had left. But now, seeing them together, their bond just as strong without her, unearths a deep, dank well of loneliness. She has come to a stop on the pavement and is staring at them with a longing so strong, it briefly eclipses thoughts of Linden. Anna, her best friend from university, looks up and their gazes lock. For a moment, she believes Anna will call out to her. Ask her to join them. She doesn't. Anna turns her face away. All those cancelled plans and white lies and ignored calls have eroded their friendship to dust.

She takes out her phone and there, standing on the pavement, she deletes Anna's number. Then she walks determinedly away, their laughter following her down the street. She lifts her chin and sends Linden a message: Thinking only of you.

She is sweaty and exhausted by the time she reaches her road. It is only as she pushes open the front gate to her studio apartment – an annexe that adjoins a larger property – that she sees her belongings strewn across the tiny patch of brown grass that makes up the front garden. She stumbles up the path, heart racing, trying to understand. She picks up a bin bag. It is filled with her clothes. The front door swings open and a man with dark hair and dark skin whom she recognises only vaguely, steps outside to dump another box of her things onto the grass.

When he notices her, he holds up his hands as though to ward off the anger he knows blisters on her tongue. 'I need you out. I did call. Couldn't get hold of you.'

Then she places him – her landlord. She only met him once, the day he handed over the keys. He'd been clean-shaven then and smiling. 'I haven't had any missed calls.'

He shrugs.

Her wild, panicked gaze ranges over her haphazardly packed belongings. 'What's happening?'

'I need my place back.'

'But it's *my* place. I've paid you on time every single month. I—'

'Girlfriend kicked me out,' he says, as though this explains everything.

'You can't just toss my things onto the street and—'

'We don't have a contract.'

She'd been living in the studio for eight months. It was small but affordable and, most importantly, available immediately. She'd been so desperate to get away from her mother that she'd moved in without signing anything but the landlord had promised her the studio for at least a year. She'd made it her own in the short time she'd been there. Decorating it with throws and pillows and candles she'd bought from charity shops and markets.

'But I don't have anywhere else to go.' The truth of it sets like concrete in her stomach. 'Please—'

He either doesn't hear her or, more likely, doesn't care. He turns back into the house. She rushes after him, shoving her arm into the door but he slams it anyway. She shrieks and staggers back, clutching the throbbing limb to her chest. The door slams shut. She hears the lock sliding into place on the other side. Tears, born from frustration and pain, fill her eyes. Cradling her arm, she sinks onto the grass, among everything she's ever owned. It isn't a lot. But she has nowhere to put any of it. If she wasn't still smarting from Anna's rejection and Linden's silence, maybe she'd have the energy to throw herself at the door, to rage at her landlord. *Ex*-landlord. Not that she thinks that would get her anywhere.

She has a degree. A job. Yet, she is homeless. She truly doesn't have anywhere to go. Nor does she have enough money in her account to stay in a hotel until she can sort out another place to rent. She doesn't have friends. At least, not anymore. None she can turn to after months of radio silence. The only family she is close to, that would help her, is living abroad. Of course Penelope, her mother, isn't far, but returning to her childhood home where her mother's grief sits like a thick, greasy film over everything, isn't an option. Her mother had warned her that if she left, she'd fail. That renting alone was expensive. A waste of money. But that was her mother's fear talking. Penelope was afraid to be lonely. With her husband gone and her daughter too, she'd rattle around in that too-big house.

If she slinks back to her mother now, tail between her legs, she'll never hear the end of it. Perhaps it's selfish but she finds her mother's bouts of depression suffocating. She can't face one more day in the bleak, grey landscape of her mother's mourning. No. She won't go back.

Determination runs through her like a steel spine. And though she isn't one to believe men are the white knights of fairy tales, she isn't stubborn or naive enough to think this is a situation in which she can rescue herself. So she turns to the only person she trusts. That still cares about her. And hopes his proclamations of love are not just sugar-spun lies. She calls Linden.

Chapter Eight

The Wife

The following Friday, Addison and I meet for dinner at Hall & Woodhouse in Bath. In the summer, we like to sit on the roof terrace and enjoy the view of the city with its cream stone architecture and cobbled streets. Now though, early October, the evenings are cooler so we choose a table in the restaurant beside the impressive sweeping staircase.

Addison flicks her long dark hair over her shoulder and I feel a stab of regret at having ever cut mine.

'I love your boots,' she says. They're knee-high, in buttery-soft black suede with a square toe. 'Where are they from?'

And because they were expensive, I hesitate. 'Russell & Bromley,' I answer reluctantly, then I tack on a lie. 'In the sale.'

Her smile is stiff. 'Well, they're gorgeous.'

Though Addison has never directly admonished me for my spending habits, she's made comments. When I got my first brand deal five years ago, I treated myself to a Gucci belt, the black leather one with the brass double-G buckle. I still remember Addison's round, disbelieving eyes when I admitted how much it cost. 'Goodness, Verity. Is it a magic belt? Does it grant wishes?' But there'd been an edge to her voice that belied her teasing. Still, it was so much more to me than just a belt. It was a symbol of my success. I started the blog in my bedroom a few months after the clothing brand I worked for went under. Linden doubted my blog would ever make a penny but it made thousands, and, over the years, has gone on to make much more. Back then, as everything was starting to take off, when I wore that belt I felt validated.

'How've you been?' she asks.

'Keeping busy,' I say honestly. I've been waking early, running as the sun rises, and then heading into the office. I used to love working from home but now I wander through my house and imagine all the places my husband had sex with his mistress. 'You?'

'I've been to three baby showers this week.'

'*Three*? Is that a new record?'

She nods. 'We're at that age, aren't we? Just one lemming after another, leaping off a cliff.'

She says it with derision but I know she wishes she was leaping off that cliff, too. She's always wanted to be a mother. Since we were children, she's kept a list of potential baby names scribbled in diaries and then, later, saved on her phone. Addison's mother was flighty and negligent, eager to drop Addison off like a bag of unwanted clothes whenever she could with my mum, our nan, whoever would take her. Addison's father wasn't around. My aunt told our nan he'd died but my mother was adamant she only claimed he was dead to hide the truth: she didn't know who Addison's father was. I think Addison's fraught childhood has driven her desire to start a family of her own. To be the mother she wished she'd had. She was only a few months into her marriage when she told me she and Harry were trying for a baby. After that, every time she refused a glass of wine or complained of feeling nauseous, I wondered if she was pregnant. It's been eight years, and the room reserved for a nursery is still empty.

'Beth had her baby last week,' she tells me with forced cheer.

I frown. 'Beth?'

'My sister-in-law.'

'Sorry, of course.' Addison and Beth have always been in an odd little competition to win their mothers-in-law's favour. Addison longed to be close to Harry's family, and she was . . . until Harry's brother met Beth. Now, less than two years into her marriage, Beth has birthed the Abbotts' first grandchild. Though Addison's trying to hide it, I can tell she's upset. 'So you're an auntie?' I ask, trying to lift the mood.

Tight-lipped, she nods. 'Yep.'

But not a mother. Eyes downcast, she slowly stirs her mojito with a straw.

'A baby girl – Paige. Seven pounds and three ounces. Beth did this whole post on her socials yesterday.'

'With a photo of her cupping her newborn's foot?'

Her smile is wry. 'That's the one.'

'It's so weird to me that parents announce their baby's weight online. Surely you only need that information if you're planning to post the baby via Royal Mail.'

'I'll tell that to Beth.'

'Write it in her card along with, "congratulations to you, condolences to your vagina".'

'Not a bad idea.' She tries to smile. 'Beth's talking about moving from Bath to the countryside.'

I wince. This is Addison's dream: a baby and a dog and a rural cottage.

We order our food and when the waiter leaves, Addison leans in. 'Really, though, Verity, how're you doing?'

She wants to know how I'm coping after we unearthed my dead husband's affair, but I'm not ready to talk about it. Instead, I tell her about the strange conversation I had with Mimi. I'm just recounting how she slammed the door in my face when our food arrives. 'I have no idea what I've done wrong.'

Addison's eyes are wide. 'I can't believe she treated you like that. What the hell has got into her?'

I shrug. 'No idea. I mean, I've never had so much as a cross word with Mimi before.' I bite my lip, not sure how to ask the question I desperately want answered. I decide to be direct. 'Why did you and Mimi fall out?'

Addison picks up her knife and fork and starts cutting into her salmon. 'I told you, we didn't fall out, we just drifted apart.' I'm not sure I believe her. I'm about to press for more information when she says, 'Have you considered Mimi might be the other woman?'

I set my cutlery down. 'What? No.'

'Why not?'

I'm so stunned by the suggestion, for a moment I can't find my voice. 'Mimi and Linden didn't even get on.'

'Could that have been an act? The two of them moved in the same circles. Mimi translates books for Harrier's and they're the house that published Linden's novels, aren't they?'

My heart quickens. She's right. I'd never thought of that. Still, I know she's wrong about Mimi and Linden.

'Isn't it possible they knew each other *before* you bought that house?' she continues. 'That he wanted to move there because it was convenient?'

I swallow thickly. 'Convenient?'

'To have his mistress live next door . . .'

I want to tell her to stop being so absurd but I can't deny her theory carries some weight. After all, it was Linden who was desperate to move into Windermere. He fell in love with that house, but I can't imagine him falling in love with Mimi. He barely tolerated her. 'Mimi is a good person. My best friend. She'd never do that to me.'

'But she did stop talking to you after your husband died . . .' Addison holds my gaze and spears a piece of asparagus on her plate.

'Yes, but that doesn't mean she was sleeping with him. Anyway,' I say, 'if Mimi *is* the other woman, the police will confirm it sooner rather than later.'

She stills, fork halfway to mouth. 'What do you mean?'

I brace myself, knowing Addison won't like that I went to the police without her. She likes to be involved, to feel important, and I remind myself to be patient with her because her need to feel valued harks back to how her mother made it known that Addison was only ever a burden. 'I handed it all over to them – the laptop, the phone, the lilac love letters.'

She blanches. 'But . . .'

51

'Don't worry, they're never going to come to the conclusion *I* killed my husband. They know it isn't possible.'

She lowers her fork. 'You really think his mistress killed him?'

'*Yes*,' I say. 'And even if she didn't, I'm sure the police will find something on Linden's devices that will tell us who the other woman is. At least that way I can confront her myself. And if it *is* Mimi, I owe you dinner.'

'I don't want to win a prize. I don't even want to be right about Mimi. I just don't want you to get hurt any more than you already have been. Are you sure you want to know who she is, Verity? What good will that do you now?'

I arch a brow. 'Wouldn't *you* want to confront the woman who had an affair with *your* husband?'

'Maybe . . .' She tucks her long hair behind her ear. 'I don't know.'

'She could be married too. Doesn't her husband deserve to know who his wife really is?'

She sits back in her chair and reaches for her mojito. 'You're right. I'd probably want to meet her.' She sips her drink. 'Who do you think it is?'

'I'm not sure. Linden sometimes travelled for work, guest-lecturing at various universities across the country. It could be a random, enamoured student. Someone a decade younger than me, I suppose. He did tell me a few of them had a crush on him.'

'Maybe.' She picks up her cutlery. 'Either way, I'm here if you need me.'

I smile. 'Thanks, Addison.'

'This salmon is delicious,' she says, cutting a piece off and offering it to me. 'Want to try it?'

I recoil. 'Are you trying to kill me?'

She frowns. 'What?'

'I'm allergic. Even the stench of it makes me feel sick.'

She lowers her fork. 'Oh, God, yes, sorry. I'm always forgetting. I could've sworn when we were kids and your parents took us to Devon we ate fish and chips on the beach.'

I shake my head. 'Not me. I'm allergic.'

Her face flushes. 'Sorry. Yes. Of course. I'm just tired. I've barely slept this week.' She dabs at her mouth with a napkin before smoothing it out across the table and neatly folding it. 'There was something else I wanted to talk about,' she says quietly.

'OK?'

She takes a breath. 'I was wondering if I could pick up some more freelance work for Verity Rose.'

I try to hide my surprise. Addison hasn't worked for me since Linden's death. In fact, she hasn't worked at all, choosing instead to focus on her home renovations. Since meeting Harry, she hasn't needed a full-time job. He's a few years older and, by the time they got together, he already had a mortgage and a highly-paid job in a bank. After only a few months together, Addison moved in with him and her interest in her budding career as a photographer waned. While I scrambled to find a graduate position that paid a living wage, she dipped in and out of various roles, cushioned by her partner's income. Addison works hard to be the antithesis of her nomadic, promiscuous mother, which is why she was so eager to put down roots and marry. 'Sure. Admin work or photography?'

'Both,' she says. 'Anything. I don't mind.'

I nod. 'I'll have Flora set something up.'

She relaxes a little. 'Thanks.'

I reach for my drink. 'Why now?' Though Addison and Harry aren't as financially comfortable as Linden and I have become over the years, Harry makes a good living. As far as I know, they don't have any serious financial worries. Though Addison encourages Harry to strive for any and all promotions, even if it means they spend less time together as a result.

'The house renovations are done. It's decorated to within an inch of its life. I'm bored, I suppose.'

Maybe she hoped that, by now, she'd have a baby to fill her time. I want to ask her whether they're still trying but I don't want to pry and upset her. Addison is like a cat, coming to you on her terms, making you feel chosen when she allows you close, only to turn and lash out the second you make a misstep. So I swallow my questions and decide she'll open up when she's ready.

After dinner, Addison suggests a gin bar around the corner. It's dark and moody with black hardware and low ceilings. It's busy and loud. After ten minutes of lingering by the bar, we grab a table by the door. Addison orders gimlets. I'm only halfway through my drink when someone stumbles into our table. Addison's glass topples and then smashes. She leaps to her feet but her drink has sloshed across her silk skirt.

'Oh my God, I'm so sorry,' a woman slurs.

My head whips up. I know that voice. Flora clumsily pushes her hair away from her sweaty, flushed face before toppling into the door frame. I get to my feet and grab her elbow as she wobbles atop her heels.

Addison's scowl quickly slides off her face as she recognises Flora. I don't blame her for taking a moment to place her. At the office, Flora is almost always dressed in neutrals: long sleeves and high necks, hair scooped up in a high ponytail. Tonight though, in her tight red dress, hair tumbling down her back and lips painted scarlet, she could be mistaken for a model at an after-party.

She's either too drunk to recognise me or too preoccupied because she shrugs out of my grip without so much as looking at me before stumbling towards the exit. A man in dark green trousers and a crisp white shirt rolled to his elbows is close behind her. He's at least fifteen years her senior and looks so much like Linden with his golden hair and square jaw, that my breath catches. He whips out his wallet and slaps two twenty-pound notes onto the table. 'Sorry about your drinks,' he says and then he follows Flora out into the night.

I stand and turn towards the window behind our table. Outside, the man has caught up with Flora. He pulls her to him, arm snaking around her waist. She beams up at him and touches a hand to his cheek in an easy, familiar gesture that tells me this is not a one-night stand. Then they are kissing. Devouring each other right there on the street in front of the bar. That is when I see it: the silver wedding band on his left hand, glinting beneath the streetlight.

Chapter Nine

The Other Woman

She is still sitting on the lawn surrounded by her belongings when Linden pulls up outside the house. She gets to her feet and lifts her chin, refusing to cry. But the helplessness of her situation washes over her until she is drowning in it. What does she expect him to do? Move her into his house alongside his wife? The thought is so absurd, she almost laughs. His gaze roams over the bin bags, the suitcases, the moth-eaten cardboard boxes that contain her entire life.

'He can't do this to you,' he says.

'He already has.'

Linden shakes his head and marches towards the front door. She lays a hand on his arm. 'There's no point. I didn't sign a lease. I've got no legal claim to that house.'

Beneath her fingers, his muscles are tense. He wants to save her and she loves him for it. Really though, she didn't expect him to rescue her. She just didn't want to be alone, and he is the only person left for her to call. Linden pulls her into him. He's broad and solid and safe. To her mortification, a sob wells in her chest and breaks from her lips in a wet gasp. He holds her tighter. 'Don't worry,' he soothes. 'It's going to be fine.'

She pulls away from him, scrubbing a weary hand over her face. 'I have nowhere to go, Linden.'

'I'm going to take care of you.' He is so confident that she finds herself believing him. She dares to hope. Linden picks up a box and carries it to his car. He places it inside, not caring that the lawn clippings stuck to the underside of the cardboard fall onto his expensive leather seats. 'Get your things. I'm taking you home.'

They drive with the air conditioning turned up and the radio down low. She rests her forehead against the glass. The summer sunset casts a golden glow over the cream stone buildings. She opens the window a crack and on the air is the smokiness of a barbecue. It is a glorious evening and she marvels at how the world still turns even as her life crumbles to dust around her. If it weren't for Linden, she'd crumble with it.

She hasn't the energy to ask where he's taking her. For a moment, she lets herself pretend Linden is divorced and is whisking her away to his home. She imagines herself in their shared kitchen, stirring a risotto on one of those grand Agas, while he pours them a glass of white wine from the fridge.

Now, he takes her hand in his. It is warm and reassuring. She glances at him and manages a smile. Then she closes her eyes and leans back against the headrest. She indulges in another game of pretend. In this fantasy, they are driving to the countryside for a minibreak. Their toddler is strapped into a car seat and their golden retriever snoozes in the boot. She imagines a ball chucked across a field. Their chunky toddler splashing through muddy puddles. And Linden kissing her, whispering against her mouth that they should try for a second baby. These are all things she doesn't know for sure she wants, but they are so much better than what she currently has . . . which isn't a lot. A carful of her possessions and a man who belongs to somebody else.

Soon, they are pulling onto a driveway. She blinks up at a neat cream brick house with a tiled porch awning, a dark green front door and sash windows. The front garden is well kept, with a manicured lawn and an apple tree. Linden gets out of the car and then comes around to the passenger side and opens the door. She gets out and watches as he strides across the lawn, taking a key from his trouser pocket. She knows for a fact this is not the house he shares with his wife. Confused, she stumbles after him.

A wooden plaque on the wall reads PADDLEDOWN. He opens the front door and motions for her to step inside. She crosses the threshold into a small hallway. It has solid-wood floors and a little console table with a large stone lamp. To her left is a staircase, straight ahead and to her right are closed doors. Linden moves past her to the one on her right and pushes it open. Then, eyes glittering, he says, 'Coming?'

He disappears into the room and, with a frisson of excitement, she follows. The kitchen is cosy, with grey cupboard doors and warm wooden countertops. Through an archway is a dining room with an oak table and a small two-sweater sofa positioned beside bifold doors.

'Next room over is the lounge,' he tells her. 'Upstairs, there are two bedrooms. A family bathroom.' She wanders over to the glass doors and looks out across the back garden. He takes her hand and leads her outside. 'This is the best bit,' he whispers to her. The garden is long and thin and leads down to the canal. The sun is setting in a lazy spill of pink and orange and gold. The colours ink the water, too. It's a moment of beauty in an ugly, tumultuous day.

Linden winds an arm around her waist and pulls her to his side. She's exhausted but her mind is fizzing with questions. 'Whose house is this?'

'Mine.'

'Yours?'

'Mine,' he says again.

'And you're going to let me stay here?'

'Yes.'

'For how long?'

He shrugs. 'As long as you need.'

She stiffens because this is too good to be true. In all the months they've been together, he has never brought her here. *Why* has he never brought her here? 'Is your wife likely to show up?'

'She doesn't know about Paddledown.'

'How?'

'I bought it before I met her.'

He'd talked about an investment he'd made with the money he inherited after his grandfather's passing; he must have meant

Paddledown. She grew up eating Lockies Shortbread, Linden's family business. Although his younger brother runs it, Linden told her he was happy to let Felix have it; he never wanted to be the managing director of a confectioners, so he struck out on his own. She admires him for that, to be brave enough to walk away from tradition to forge his own path.

'But *why* doesn't your wife know about it?'

'Because I've never told her.' She is quiet, leaving a silence for him to fill. He considers her and she can tell he's weighing up how honest he can be. 'It's no secret that she's the breadwinner. Most of what we have is hers, but this' – he throws an arm out in the direction of the house – 'this is all mine.'

She knows Linden has his secrets. After all, she's one of them. And while a number of men will have a secret mistress, how many will have a secret house? Has Linden ever brought other women here? He swore she is his first and only affair but is that the truth? 'Do you rent this place out? I mean, what do you want with somewhere all your own?' She shrugs as though his answer is of no interest but she watches him carefully, scanning his face for lies.

'I come here to write. To think. To exist in a space that's just mine. Or, *was* just mine.' She raises an eyebrow and he turns to her, hooking his thumb beneath her chin and tilting her mouth up to his. 'Didn't you want somewhere that was just ours?'

She kisses him. He tastes of strong coffee and mint toothpaste. She feels like a neglected animal that's been rescued and rehoused. Dimly, beneath the warmth of his mouth on hers, she is aware how much she depends on him, for affection, for sex, for conversation, for feeling connected to the world. And now, for shelter, too. She knows it is not a good thing to be this reliant on another person. The way her mother was with her father. The loss of him had made the vivid ink of her mother fade until it was like viewing her through tracing paper.

When Linden pulls away, she says, 'This is an incredible gesture, but I don't know if I can afford it . . .' The studio was expensive, but just about within her budget. A two-bedroom house that backs on to the canal most certainly isn't.

He laughs. 'You think I'm going to charge you to live here?'

'Well, yes, of course.'

He shakes his head dotingly as though she is a child caught too easily in a game of hide-and-seek. 'Never.'

She hesitates, remembering how, when they first started dating, he'd insist on picking up the bill but she refused to let him. She was aware there was an imbalance of power between them, factors she couldn't control, like their age, their education, their careers, their wealth, but she could, at the very least, pay for herself. Though she knew from the tightness of his smile as she pulled out her debit card that it bothered him. 'I want to give you rent money.'

'Well, I don't want to take it.'

Before she can argue, he takes the nape of her neck and pulls him towards her, hard. He kisses her again, rough and demanding. Then there is no time for talking. Soon, they are in the lounge. Really, she is too exhausted for sex, and is shaken by the events of the day, but he has just given her a house. So she lets him bend her over the arm of a cream linen sofa, and thinks of a high-end sex worker, the kind that isn't meant to be loved or kissed on the mouth.

Though he says he wants to, Linden can't stay the night. She knows this is because his wife is expecting him home. When he's gone, she looks around the kitchen which is now filled with boxes and bin bags and suitcases, but she can't bring herself to unpack so she goes upstairs and has a shower. Then, naked, she crawls into the soft, unfamiliar bed.

She does not notice the figure on the driveway, staring up at the house.

Chapter Ten

The Wife

It's been four days since I saw Flora with her married lover. On Monday she worked from home and today I'm meeting my accountant, Amy. I'm glad for it because as curious as I am about Flora, it would be unprofessional to ask an employee about her sex life, and I know as soon as I see her, questions will inch their way up my throat.

Amy and I share a table at the Rye Bakery in Frome. It's one of my favourite spots in the little Somerset market town. The converted church has retained some of its original features: the ornate ceilings, the leaded-glass windows, the pews, and a magnificent organ, set against a mural of a midnight sky.

'This place is gorgeous,' says Amy.

She's a couple of years younger than me and the type of beautiful that people notice. She's tall and athletic with waist-length pale blonde hair and piercing blue eyes. Her skin is flawless, as though she has been carved from marble. Today, she's wearing a black mock-neck jumper, a dark grey woollen coat in an expensive cut and tan trousers tucked into glossy dark brown riding boots. She reminds me of those clean-faced models in country life magazines. She's one of those women you know was popular as a girl. The kind with a swishy ponytail who knew how to do a perfect cartwheel and orchestrated the dance routines in the playground.

We spend an hour going through my tax information and I try

not to glaze over. I nod like I am knowledgeable and sign whatever she puts in front of me. Usually, this is when she exits stage left as quickly as possible, but today she agrees to stay and I order us tea and a fat slice of chocolate cake. She accepts the tea but eyes the cake warily. 'I'm not sure I should indulge. I'm actually training for the Bath half-marathon.'

'Will all the sugar and butter slow you down?' I tease.

As I take in her toned thighs, I feel my own rising like dough. And suddenly, I'm not sure I want the cake either. But then she sighs and says, 'Fine, but if it does slow me down, it's all your fault.'

I grin. 'Bill me.'

She picks up the second fork and helps herself to a mouthful of chocolate ganache. Eyes closed, she groans in pleasure. 'God, that is so good.'

'Heavenly,' I agree. 'You know, every year I promise myself I'm going to run the half-marathon and every year . . . I don't.'

'You should. It's hard work, but it's so rewarding. The trick for me was finding a cause I really believed in.'

'What's your cause?'

'Men's Minds Matter.'

I rack my brains. Verity Rose sponsors a new charity every quarter but I've never heard of that one. 'What is it?'

'A men's suicide intervention and prevention charity.'

'Oh . . .' I shift in my seat, trying to find the right words. 'Is that because . . .'

She nods.

I don't feel comfortable asking who in her life took theirs, so instead I say, 'I'm so sorry.'

'It was a long time ago now.' We lapse into silence and I wonder whether I *should* ask questions. The truth is, though, until now, our relationship has been strictly professional. And while I don't want her to think I'm not interested, I don't want to seem as though I'm prying, either. Before I can tie myself in knots, she brightens and says, 'I think if you find a cause you care about, running will be easier. Something for Linden, maybe?'

It is on the tip of my tongue to quip that there is no specific charity for deceitful, adulterous, murdered husbands. 'Maybe,' I concede.

Another silence settles around us. The secret that Linden was having an affair squirms beneath my skin like a parasite, eating me up from the inside, and I am desperate to purge myself of it. To talk to someone. To gather as many opinions about my relationship as possible in the hopes that they form a puzzle I can slot together for a full, unbiased picture of my marriage. Even though I was blind to Linden's extramarital activities, I'm sure there are those in my life who suspected. Is Amy one of them? Is that why she never wanted to get too close to me? It occurs to me I don't know a lot about Amy and Linden's relationship, so I ask. 'Did you ever tell me how you and Linden met?'

She sips her tea. 'He was a client.'

'But how did you meet?'

She pulls her long blonde ponytail over her shoulder and runs her fingers through it. 'Probably through a friend. Or another client. Honestly, Vee, I can't remember.'

I feel a jolt of shock. *Vee.* Linden is the only person who has ever called me Vee and even then it was an accident. I hated it. 'But—'

Amy's eyes widen as though suddenly struck by an idea. 'Shall we split another slice of cake?'

I look down at the one that is still only half finished. 'Sure.'

Then she is up and moving towards the counter. She'd been reluctant to share *one* slice of cake and now she's suggesting a second . . . I feel she just wanted to get away from me. Her vagueness about Linden and her reluctance to engage needles me.

Amy returns a few minutes later. And when she opens her mouth, I know she is about to change the subject, but I am not done talking about my husband, so I say, 'I think Linden told me you met at a work party.'

'Did he? Your memory is much better than mine.' She laughs. But it's a half-strangled thing, and her annoyance is clear. Not wanting to be pressed by me anymore, she steers the discussion in another direction. 'I can't believe it's been more than a year since . . .' She trails off. Having sprinted headlong into this conversation, she's now reluctant to go any closer to the cliff edge of it.

'Since he was murdered?' I offer, forcing her to look down the steep drop.

She closes her eyes and shakes her head. 'Sorry . . . I didn't mean to . . .'

'It's fine,' I say, instantly feeling guilty for making her uncomfortable. I am about to slice into the cake Amy has brought back from the counter when I realise it is red velvet: Linden's favourite.

'You OK?' she asks, noting my hesitation.

I nod and force the cake into my mouth. Did she know it was Linden's favourite? I press my lips together to stop myself from asking because no matter how I phrase it I'll sound deluded and paranoid. 'So, congratulations on starting your own company. It's a huge achievement.'

'Thank you. It's a huge risk, too.'

'So why now?'

'I work better alone. The tedium of spending eighty per cent of my week with people I probably wouldn't want to share a drink with outside of the office finally got to me. Frankly, most people either bore or irritate me.' I'm too slow to hide my shock at her candour. She isn't repentant and makes no effort to blunt the sharp dagger of her words. 'My mother used to say I'm like dark chocolate.'

I frown. 'Bitter?'

She laughs, properly this time, throwing her head back so I can see all her perfect white teeth. When she sobers, she says, 'No, but it's good to know what you think of me.'

My cheeks redden. 'No, I don't—'

She holds up a hand to stop what we both know will be a babbled apology. 'She said I was like dark chocolate because I'm overpowering and best in small doses.'

'Oh . . . are you and your mother close?' I ask, knowing most people would be upset if their mother thought that of them.

'No. Not since my father died.' She shrugs as though she doesn't care but the tightness in her shoulders betrays her. Maybe it is her father who took his own life. 'He'd be proud; I've come a long way in the last few years. I used to live in a tiny studio and now I have a beautiful home and my own business.'

'There's lots to celebrate,' I say. 'Do you have someone special to celebrate with?'

She relaxes a little and seizes upon this new topic. 'No one special. I went on a date with a guy last week who I immediately thought was odd.'

'Why?'

She hesitates just a moment, as though weighing up whether we know each other well enough for her to talk to me about her personal life. 'He set his jacket down on the seat of a table behind us.'

'OK . . .'

'Like it's normal to take off his coat and put it on the back of a *random* chair at a *random* table where another couple are sitting. When he went to retrieve his jacket, he was furious to find it gone. He shouted at the staff and accused them of stealing it, but it had actually been handed in to lost property as soon as the couple realised the jacket didn't belong to either of them.'

'Who puts their belongings on someone else's table? Why did he do that?'

'Male arrogance. As though he feels entitled to any and *all* space around him.'

I nod solemnly. 'Manspreading but with clothes.'

She grins. 'Exactly. And he spent the entire night slagging off his "crazy" ex because she had the audacity to move out of their house and change her number without telling him.'

I wince. 'What did he do to make her run away from him like that?'

'God only knows.'

'Was his jacket red and in the shape of a flag?'

She smiles then stabs at the cake. 'Honestly, don't date. It's brutal.'

Cold realisation drips down my spine because if I ever want love in my life again, I'll have to join the dating pool. Though, from what friends have said, it's less like a pool and more like a swamp. It's been a year since I last felt the warm embrace of a relationship. Of having someone to come home to at the end of every day and fall asleep with each night. I dread creating an online dating profile and entering the world of unsolicited dick pics and ghosting and awkward small talk. 'It can't be that bad, can it?'

'It is. Men can be pigs.' Linden's corpse flashes into my mind, his nose so badly broken, it resembles a pig's snout. 'Sorry, I don't mean to frighten you. Maybe I'm just too picky. I've got to stop comparing everyone I date to—' She cuts herself off so abruptly, I look up from my tea. Amy's rosebud lips are parted, as though she wishes she could gather the words up and shove them back into her mouth.

'To . . . ?' I prompt.

She arranges her face into a neutral half-smile but doesn't elaborate.

'There's always one that got away, isn't there?' I say, groping for more information, for a connection. I like Amy, and want her to like me, too. 'What was so special about him?'

She looks up at me from beneath her lashes. 'Who said it was a "him"?'

I flush. 'Sorry, I didn't mean to assume—'

Smiling, she shakes her head. 'Don't worry, I'm teasing. I mean, I've been with men and women but you weren't to know. And you're right, there's always one that gets away.'

'So what happened?'

'Me. I poured far too much time into other projects. And by the time I realised, it was too late. It was over.'

I feel an ache of recognition. I dedicated so much of myself to work and, in Linden's opinion, not enough of myself to him. Still, there were years where I was sure while he was my entire world, I was only ever a small piece of his. I had my career and my friends, but spinning at the centre of it all was him. Finding out he was having an affair made me realise that although he was always on my mind, I was often pushed from his in place of *her*. 'I'm sorry.'

She shrugs one slender shoulder. 'Heartbreak isn't the worst thing that can happen to a person though, is it?'

'No, but I suppose it's a type of temporary madness.'

'A madness that drives people to do unforgivable things.' Our eyes lock and a peculiar atmosphere grows between us, the air like a suspended breath, held in anticipation. Then she smiles and it's dispelled. 'Anyway, I want something long-lasting. Steady. I want marriage, a dog, children. Then I can just be done. Settled.'

And before I can stop myself, I'm saying, 'It's so strange to me, this narrative that, for women, marriage is the end of our story. The full stop at the end of a sentence. We're fed this idea when we're just girls. The princess is married off to the prince and then the credits roll.' I want to tell her that sometimes, princes are warlocks in gentlemen's clothing, but I don't want to sound like a bitter widow, so instead I say, 'Marrying Linden wasn't the end of my story, it was just the bit in the middle. It was after we married that my career took off, that I found an incredible group of friends, that I started to travel and see the world. What I'm trying to say is, plan beyond marriage and children because that life isn't a meal that satisfies you forever. You need more sustenance than that.'

She's nodding, listening intently, and I feel like a wise old crone in a fairy tale, handing out pearls of wisdom to beautiful maidens. 'You and Linden never had children?'

And it is like she has just spilled her hot tea in my lap. 'No. We didn't,' I say, sure I can *feel* my ovaries withering. 'If he were here to tell people *why* we don't have children, he'd say it's because I was too preoccupied with my career to be a mother.'

She bites her full bottom lip. 'And is that true?'

'Is that what he told you?' In the silence, she matches the intensity of my stare with one of her own. She isn't as surprised by my question as I thought she would be. Rather, the corner of her mouth turns up in an almost-smile, and I feel as though we are playing a game. My heart flutters in my chest as I wait for her to answer, to reveal her hand, but we're interrupted by a woman with sleek red hair and a narrow waist.

'Amy, hi,' she says excitedly, hovering beside our table. 'What're you doing in Frome?'

Amy looks up and pales. 'Oh. Hi. I'm . . . working.' She glances towards me. 'This is a business meeting.'

The redhead winces. 'Gosh, sorry, I didn't realise.'

I open my mouth to introduce myself but Amy's wide eyes find mine and she pushes so suddenly to her feet, my mouth snaps shut again. The redhead frowns, as confused by Amy's skittishness as I am. 'Do you mind if I have a quick chat with my friend?' she asks me.

'Not at all,' I say politely, even though I think it's a little rude. Why can't they talk here? And why is Amy so hassled? 'Go ahead.'

Amy's smile is forced. She steers the bewildered-looking redhead across the room and for the next couple of minutes, I watch them. I can't hear their conversation over the noise of the café, but the redhead keeps glancing my way, her expression somewhere between shock and disgust. Then she leaves without meeting my eye.

When Amy returns, I ask after her friend. 'Everything OK?'

'Fine,' she says, reaching for her tea. Though she's trying to appear calm, I can see she's rattled.

'It's just, you whipped your friend away so quickly, I didn't even catch her name,' I say because Amy obviously didn't want to introduce us. But why? I'm not brave enough to be direct and ask, so instead, I hope she'll volunteer some information. Of course, she doesn't. She just smiles blandly and shortly after, she excuses herself. As I drive home, I wonder who the redhead was and whether I'm right in thinking Amy knew Linden more intimately than she's letting on.

Chapter Eleven

The Other Woman

She has been living at Paddledown for two weeks. It's a longer commute to work and means she needs to get the bus to and from, but she doesn't mind because the house is beautiful, situated in a quiet neighbourhood. It isn't as grand as the home Linden shares with his wife, but she can imagine herself living here with him, along with the golden retriever and chunky toddler from her game of pretend.

She and Linden cook together, salmon and summer vegetables. They sit and eat it at the dining table with a bottle of red wine. 'Did you manage to get the rest of your things from your landlord?'

She spears a piece of salmon. 'Some of it.'

'Only some?'

She sighs. 'He threw away most of my furniture. Well, he said he did but I think he probably sold it.'

Linden sets down his fork. 'Like what?'

'Side tables. My dressing table. My gorgeous olive-green armchair.'

His eyes narrow. 'He's a scheming fuck. At least this place is fully furnished.' She nods, trying not to think about her armchair, but Linden senses the dark cloud that has settled over her. 'What's wrong?'

'It's just . . .' She shrugs. 'That armchair meant a lot to me.'

'Go on . . .'

'It's the first piece of furniture I ever bought. Me and my dad went to this fancy interiors shop and I fell in love with it. It was pricey but I'd just got my first pay cheque. I knew my mother wouldn't

68

approve – she was all about saving for my own house, not throwing money away on expensive armchairs.' She rolls her eyes, thinking of all the times she'd had to explain to her mother that the housing market was a different kind of beast and that, with house prices ten times the average wage, not buying coffees out wasn't going to make her any more likely to drum up fifty thousand for a deposit. 'But Dad gave me his twinkly smile and told me if that armchair would bring me joy, it was worth every penny.'

'You never talk about your parents.'

Another shrug. 'There isn't much to say.'

'Are you close to them?'

'I used to be, but my mother changed after . . .' She trails off, feeling as though she is veering too close to an open flame, but Linden presses her. 'After?'

She's restless and doesn't want to talk about her family but she worries closing the conversation down will upset him. 'My dad. He's . . . gone.' She remembers how the loss of her father had consumed her mother. Her grief a stomach in which she was slowly digested.

Linden takes her hand. 'I'm sorry to hear that.'

'It was his choice.'

'Suicide?' He is shocked. 'Jesus, that's terrible.'

She draws breath, wanting to open up to Linden, but then she hears the angry snap of her mother's voice. 'Your father's gone. He's *dead*. Don't think about ghosts because they certainly don't think about you.'

Linden squeezes her hand. 'Are you OK?'

'I'm fine, but I'd rather not talk about my dad.' She gives him a weak smile. 'Let's talk about *your* family instead.'

He snorts. 'I'd rather have a stroke.'

'That bad?'

'Worse.'

He's made reference to how his younger brother Felix is the reigning king in the court of their parents' favour, and though Linden claims he is unbothered by this, she knows he is lying. 'God, this salmon is great.'

She laughs at the joy on his face as he puts another forkful into his mouth. 'You're devouring that like it's your last meal.'

'Well, it *is* the last time I'll eat seafood for a while.'

She raises a querying eyebrow.

'You know she has a fish allergy.'

She. The wife. 'Ah, yes. Of course.'

'It's inconvenient but, you know, handy if I ever need to kill her off.' She expects him to laugh but his expression is all earnest sobriety. Her insides somersault and she is frozen, fork halfway to mouth. Linden grins. 'Sorry, that was in poor taste.' He's still smiling as he tops up her wine. The tension slowly dissolves and she eats the pink fish.

She feels foolish for taking him seriously, if only for a second. 'And where is *Mrs Lockwood* tonight?'

'Work trip. She's not back until Monday evening.'

She reaches for her glass and, not for the first time, wonders *why* he is here, with her, rather than with his wife. She's half a bottle of wine deep and brave enough to ask.

At first he's surprised by her question and then he is thoughtful. 'Because you're beautiful and intelligent. You care deeply. And . . .'

He trails off. She gets the feeling it's not because he has run out of things to say but because whatever is on the tip of his tongue might be a poisonous dart. 'Go on.'

His expression is intent as he weighs up whether to continue. She keeps her face neutral and leans back in her chair, waiting. He nods. 'You make me feel needed.'

She rolls the word around on her tongue, not sure whether it is bitter or sweet. 'Needed?'

He leans back in his chair too. 'Needed.'

'And what makes you think I *need* you, Linden?'

His smile is private, his eyes penetrating, as though he knows something she doesn't. 'When you were at a low point, when you lost your house and needed someone, you called me.'

She bites the inside of her cheek. He's right. Without Paddledown, she'd be forced into a crowded, overpriced house share that would limit her privacy and strangle her relationship with her married boyfriend. But is this how she wants to be perceived? As a woman who *needs* a man just to get by?

'It isn't weak to need someone,' he tells her, as though reading her thoughts. 'There's strength in that. The night you called me was good for us. It made me trust you.'

'Trust me . . .' She feels a pinch of hurt. 'Didn't you trust me before?'

'Yes, of course, but doesn't everyone want to feel needed?'

She disagrees. Her mother needed her. Needed her so much in the weeks and months after they lost her father, Penelope's grip became so tight it was painful, but she can't voice her opinion without delving further into her complex relationship with her parents so instead, she asks, 'Does your wife need you?'

His laughter is hollow. 'No. Not anymore. She did. When we were first together, I was the one with the career. She was a little directionless. Didn't take much interest in her professional life, and I stepped in and filled her personal one. We were together more often than we were apart. It was passion and good conversation and something . . . more.' He's smiling, lost to the memory of their romance. 'Until it all changed. Her company, her *brand*, took off and we saw each other less and less until one day, I wondered if she'd even notice if she woke up and I wasn't there.' He sighs. 'Honestly, I don't think I've been needed by anyone in a long time. Not by my wife. Certainly not by my parents or my perfect brother.'

She can feel his pain. The short, sharp slap of rejection. She is in love with his vulnerability. With the idea of pleasing him. 'But isn't it better to be loved by someone because they *choose* you than it is to be loved by someone because they *need* you?'

He raises an eyebrow. 'Do you?'

'Do I what?'

'Love me?'

And though she thinks she might, she isn't ready to admit to it because the last person she loved left her. She understands that love is giving someone the power to ruin you and blindly hoping they'll choose not to. She isn't ready to give Linden that sovereignty. So, instead of answering his question, she gets up and goes to him. She kisses him deeply, with an urgency she feels in her bones.

In the morning, Linden leaves. It is only when he is gone that she finds the handwritten note that has been pushed through the letterbox.

He's married.

Chapter Twelve

The Wife

On Wednesday morning, I'm back in the office and I can't stop thinking about the conversation I had with Amy yesterday. I am sure she is hiding something. For whatever reasons, she didn't want to introduce me to the redhead but, the more I think about it and about how Amy is a private person, it's likely she isn't keen on mixing business with pleasure. Although, I still wonder whether Amy was more to Linden than just an accountant. Maybe I'm being paranoid, but I no longer feel I can trust anyone. If Linden, the person I loved most, betrayed me, then anyone can. And Amy doesn't owe me loyalty; we aren't friends and she isn't my family. I imagine the two of them having sex. Her long, slender legs wrapped around his waist, his fingers in her shiny blonde hair, the excited pant of his breath as he slams into her. Jealousy whiplashes through me at the thought of my husband with another woman, accompanied by a rage so potent it tastes like battery acid on my tongue.

Forcing Amy from my mind, I turn my attention to my mounting inbox and for a few hours, I lose myself in mind-numbing admin. By lunchtime though, Addison is in my office to iron out the details of her return to Verity Rose. Her long dark hair spills in a sleek stream down her back and I feel a dart of envy. Self-consciously, I touch the ends of my short, blunt cut, wishing I could tug it down past my shoulders. She hands me a chai latte and a pastry she bought from the coffee shop down the street. I was so distracted this morning, stomach churning with anxiety, that I didn't have breakfast. I thank her but still can't bring myself to touch the croissant. 'Where is everyone?' she asks.

'The Wild Café. I treat the team to lunch there on Wednesdays but Heidi's gone to pick up a new camera. She'll be back soon.'

'A free lunch every Wednesday – I think I'll enjoy working here again.'

I try to smile but it feels strained. 'Three days a week? Is that OK?'

Addison doesn't answer. She has noticed the hand which trembles around the takeaway coffee cup. 'Are you OK?'

'Fine,' I say too quickly. I don't want to think about Amy and my gnawing suspicions so I launch back into the topic of work. 'It might be easier if you worked from the office for the first few weeks, and then—'

'Verity, what's going on?' She cuts me off and leans forward, determined to shine a spotlight on the issue I want to keep in the dark. 'Is it Flora?'

I frown. 'Flora?'

'Yes, Flora. Did you speak to her about the married man we saw her with?'

I have fallen so far down the rabbit hole of Amy and Linden that it takes me a moment to haul myself out. 'Oh. No. I haven't.'

She stares at me as though I've lost my mind. 'Why not? I thought you were going to speak to her.'

'I can't. She's an employee, it's none of my business who she spends her time with outside of work.'

'Except you just found out your husband was having an affair, and now you know one of your employees has a penchant for dating married men . . .'

'Just because she's been with one married man it doesn't mean she's been with them all.'

'But he looks *so* much like Linden.'

My stomach drops. She's right. He does. But that could still be a coincidence. Flora is so reserved, so sensible and coltish.

The girl in the red dress kissing a married man outside the bar feels like a stranger. So much so, I wonder if Flora has a wild, temptress twin.

'Maybe married men are her type,' says Addison.

'Her type?' I echo. 'Why do you think *any* woman would want to get involved with someone else's husband?'

She stares at me, apparently surprised I'd ask. I remain silent, waiting for her to answer. 'I don't know,' she says eventually.

'Addison, you always have an opinion. Don't pretend you have nothing to say.'

Her eyes find mine. She considers me. And even as my heart races in anticipation, I am careful to keep my expression neutral because I want to hear her take. She sits back in the chair. 'I think there are a few reasons women are drawn to married men. It's thrilling, exciting, maybe even a little dangerous. Perhaps her life is mundane and having sex with someone else's husband is a splash of colour.' I imagine a woman with a double life: on Monday morning she is hoovering carpets and folding laundry, by Monday evening she is meeting her married lover in a hotel room and indulging in loud, sweaty orgasms. 'Maybe she just wants to feel powerful.'

'Powerful?' I can't keep the incredulity from my voice.

She arches a brow. 'You don't think there's power in luring a man from another woman? In being a more tempting option than the wife he chose?'

More tempting. She means *more attractive, more exciting, superior.* I feel my blood scalding in my veins. Beneath the desk, my hands curl into fists.

Oblivious, she continues, 'There's power in being wanted so much by another person, they're willing to risk it all just to spend a night with you.'

The air seems to grow hotter and hotter. Too hot to breathe. I boil over. 'Well, a man so easily swayed isn't worth keeping because if he strays once, trust me, he'll stray again. Whoever the other woman is, she isn't as special as she thinks.' I'm breathing hard, fury bubbling beneath my skin. This is my fault. If I wasn't prepared for the answer,

I should never have asked for Addison's view. She watches me warily, as though I am a rabid dog, foaming at the mouth. 'Maybe this other woman has daddy issues.'

Addison pulls a face. 'Daddy issues?'

'You know, attachment challenges that come from a dysfunctional relationship with a father figure.'

'I know what daddy issues are, Verity.' She pulls her shoulders back. 'Don't you think that's a little clichéd?'

'Aren't a lot of clichés based on evidence?' I counter. 'Maybe she has a subconscious desire to mend a broken relationship with her emotionally unavailable or absent father, so she ends up bedding emotionally unavailable men hoping she can fix them in a way she could never fix the man who should have raised her.'

Addison shrugs but doesn't respond. She looks shocked and even a little wounded, as though my words are pins being pushed into her flesh.

'Sorry,' I say. 'I know your father wasn't around, but it doesn't mean I think you'd sleep with someone else's husband.'

She tucks a lock of dark hair behind her ear. 'Well, no, but everyone deals with situations differently, don't they?'

I nod. 'I don't know anything about Flora's family,' I concede. 'She's very private.'

'There are a lot of reasons Flora might be drawn to married men.'

I take a deep, calming breath. 'I just can't bear the thought of Linden with Flora, or Amy, or—'

'Amy?'

I close my eyes, frustrated with myself for being so careless.

'Who's Amy?'

I sigh because I know she will only push and push until I relent. 'My accountant.'

'OK . . . but what has she got to do with Linden?'

'Linden actually introduced me to Amy. They knew each other before.'

Her eyes narrow. 'How?'

'He told me he was a client of hers, but then that could've been a lie. He was obviously a very accomplished liar, wasn't he? He hid an entire relationship from me for God only knows how long.'

'And you think Amy could be the other woman?'

'Maybe,' I say honestly.

Her dark brows knit together. 'I don't understand.'

I tell her everything. About Amy's vagueness around how she and Linden met; her reluctance to talk about him; how she's always kept me at arm's length. I even tell her about the red velvet cake and how she seemed to already know why Linden and I hadn't had children. I consider telling her about Amy's reluctance to introduce me to the redhead, but I'm not sure it's relevant so I keep quiet.

Even so, Addison is shocked and appalled. 'Have I ever met this woman?'

I shake my head. 'Don't think so. She's stunning. Tall, athletic, blonde. You'd remember her.'

'*Blonde*?' She snorts. 'I can't imagine Linden with a blonde.'

'She's objectively attractive.'

'Like Flora?'

My stomach knots. 'Like Flora.' We fall silent. It's a cliché that men will leave you for a younger woman. Though I am barely a handful of years older than Amy, there's almost a decade between me and Flora. At the time of Linden's death, I was only thirty. Linden once joked that I was the oldest woman he'd ever been with, despite being seven years my senior himself.

What if I'd started to become invisible to Linden? I was warned by women in their forties that it happens, but by my thirtieth birthday, I started noticing groups of teens and twenty-somethings looking through me as I walked along the street towards them. Or, as I stood at a busy bar, waving my debit card, the staff served the younger women around me first. Addison assured me I was just being paranoid, and that we were thirty, not dead. I let myself believe her, content in the knowledge my husband couldn't keep his hands off me. But what if all the while he was longing for the twenty-something version of me? Or his twenty-something accountant? Maybe even his wife's twenty-something assistant?

In this moment, I feel a burning indignation that while greying women fade into obscurity, greying men are dubbed silver foxes; in this moment, I feel small and insecure that my husband didn't want me as much as I wanted him.

Addison leans forward, perching on the edge of her chair. 'I'm sorry, Verity. I know how much you're hurting.'

But she doesn't, does she? Her husband is faithful and alive, her marriage and her sanity still intact. I spit out my jealousy like bitter fruit pips and force myself to breathe through it. The truth is, I am alone. My situation – a murdered, deceitful husband – isn't a common one. I can't expect anyone to fully understand. I remind myself that one day I'll find happiness. That the pain and loneliness I feel now is only temporary.

Just then, there's a knock on my door and Heidi appears. Her round, freckled face is earnest. I'm about to ask her when she returned from the camera shop when I notice the office phone in her hand. 'It's the police,' she says. 'They want to talk to you. Apparently they couldn't get through on your mobile?'

I'd set it on silent so I could get some work done. I come around my desk and take the phone from her. My heart canters in my chest – do the police know who the other woman is? 'Thanks, Heidi.'

Addison gets to her feet. 'Do you want us to . . .'

'Stay.' Even though Addison doesn't agree with me taking what we found to the police, I need her here with me. Heidi and Addison exchange a look. I go from hot to cold and back again as I press the phone to my ear. Heidi turns to leave but I grab her hand as though I am drowning and she is a life raft. I cling to her, not worrying whether it's inappropriate and unprofessional. Right now, I need Heidi. She is compassion and comfort. Warmth and home-made bread.

Detective Inspector Jones tells me they discovered letters on the laptop in the recycle bin. Ones Linden had written to his lover, but there were no details as to her identity. He says they've combed through the lilac love letters to no avail. I am so heavy with disappointment I sink into my chair. He reveals that the burner phone has only ever been used to call one other number which belongs to a second untraceable burner phone. The text messages they found are perfunctory: Call me and Are you alone? and Meet me at our usual place. It's maddening. I was hoping there would be *something* on that phone to help the police. But then he says, 'We did find something of interest.'

I sit up straighter.

Addison sucks in a breath.

'Yes,' he goes on. 'We found a message in the drafts folder on the phone.'

'OK . . .'

'It appears Linden intended to break off the affair.'

Addison's mouth hangs agape and Heidi squeezes my hand.

'It appears the message was composed the night your husband died,' he continues.

I swallow. 'But he never sent it?'

'No. It's likely he ended the relationship when he met with her.'

'And so she flew into a rage and killed him?'

He clears his throat. 'That's our working theory.'

Addison looks like she might be sick.

'We need you to come to the station to provide us with a list of all the women who were known to Linden.'

'Like his friends? Colleagues?'

'Yes. And yours.'

'*Mine?*'

Opposite me, Addison pales and mouths, 'Why?'

'I'm sorry, Mrs Lockwood,' he says, 'but given the content of some of the text messages, his mistress was aware of your work, your schedule. It's likely she's someone known to both of you.'

When I ring off, there is a shared, stunned silence. My hand slips from Heidi's and I stare at the black screen of my phone. 'I am so sorry, Verity,' says Heidi. 'I had no idea Linden was—'

Beyond my closed office door there is a dull thud that makes us jump. We freeze. Then I hear the unmistakable sound of retreating footsteps. I push to my feet and hurry around my desk. Heidi and Addison follow closely behind. I swing open the door and step into the open-plan room. But no one else is there. I'm about to turn back into my office when I see the upturned plant pot on the rug right outside my door. The long, slender neck of the monstera, snapped.

Chapter Thirteen

The Other Woman

On the bus journey home from work, she stares at the crumpled handwritten note for the thousandth time since she received it only three days ago. She doesn't recognise the writing. She thinks of the message left for her at the hotel reception all those weeks ago.

I know what you're doing. It makes me sick.

She'd naively, *keenly*, dismissed it. But this . . . this note was posted through the door of her lover's house. She's told no one, not even her own mother, that she's moved out of her studio. Still, someone knows about her change of address and, worse, about the affair, that much is clear from this new note: *He's married*. Short but effective. She feels a twirling, merry-go-round dizziness and closes her eyes against another wave of panic. She does not know how to tell Linden about the notes. She is terrified that once she does, he will end their relationship. Write it off as easily as a wrecked car, knowing she can be replaced by a newer, more exciting model in the future. If he leaves her, what does she have left? She'd sacrificed her social life to be with him. As her tongue blackened with lies, she felt the only way to protect her relationship with Linden was to cut out the people who might unearth her deceit. She even took a step back from her mother, worried she would discover their secret. The truth is, without Linden, she has nothing. Without Linden, she *is* nothing. Though she is ashamed to admit it, he is the most thrilling thing about her.

She opens her eyes and looks down at the paper scrunched in her fist. Her list of suspects is short. Of course, at the top is Linden's wife. Surely it can't be her though. She'd have confronted Linden by now.

Linden has been virtually uncontactable since the morning she found the note. Until this afternoon, her calls and messages had gone unanswered but, voice thick with excitement, Linden phoned and told her he'd meet her at Paddledown after work.

The bus trundles along, winding down residential streets. She swings from desperation to speak to Linden to fear of facing him. But she *needs* to know if it's possible his wife is aware of their affair. At the same time, he mustn't find out about the notes. She takes a deep, steadying breath and, as she finally steps off the bus at her stop, she slips the note carefully into her bag.

Less than five minutes later, she pushes open the door to Paddledown. Linden is in the hallway, waiting for her. He bubbles with excitement like a bottle of champagne ready to be popped. If she weren't so afraid, his joy might be catching.

'I've got something to show you,' he says with a grin. He takes her hand and tugs her towards the lounge but she digs her heels into the floor. She must speak to him. Now.

'Linden, wait,' she says, voice quivering.

He turns to face her, his smile slipping. 'What is it?'

'Look, I need to ask you . . .' She gazes up at him, wondering whether her question will make him skittish enough to bolt. For a moment, she considers not asking at all. Whoever is sending her these notes isn't brave enough to confront her directly. She could just ignore them. Pretend she never received them. But what if the anonymous author sends notes to Linden instead?

He pulls her close to him. 'What's happened?'

She wants to run from this conversation but she knows that isn't an option. 'Does she know about our affair?'

His brow wrinkles. 'Who?'

'Your wife.'

'No.' He's adamant. 'Why?'

She glances down and notices his rust-coloured socks. She bought them for his birthday. It was the first gift she ever gave to him. It had to be generic, of course, so as not to arouse suspicion from his wife; something that could be easily concealed or passed off as a gift from a colleague. But they were luxury socks. The most expensive pair she'd ever bought, selected from Jollys. She'd chosen the rust-coloured pair because in the sunlight his caramel eyes are flecked with amber. In this moment, she realises how desperate she is to be the person who buys him socks. It's such a ridiculous thought, she almost laughs. 'I'm worried someone knows about us.'

His face creases and, as she feared, he drops her hand. 'Why?'

'Maybe I'm being paranoid. I just . . . we've been together for four months now. That's a long time without getting caught.'

'We're careful.'

'I know but . . .'

He reaches for her. 'If Vee knew, don't you think she'd have confronted me?'

'I suppose.'

'Don't you think she'd have confronted *you*? She isn't exactly the shy, retiring type.'

'That's true.'

'And weren't you with her all day today? Did she say anything?'

'No,' she answers honestly.

He shrugs. 'There you go. You're worrying about nothing.'

Some of the tension seeps out of her. 'But if she did find out, what do you think she'd do?'

'Forgive me,' he says easily, almost smugly.

'Really?' She doesn't bother to keep the cynicism from her voice.

'Marriage is important to her.'

She wrinkles her nose. 'If it's important to her, wouldn't she be furious you broke your wedding vows?'

He shakes his head as though she is one of his particularly slow students. 'She doesn't believe in divorce. She'd have us in couples counselling or some remote yoga retreat in Bali before she contacted a divorce lawyer.'

She feels a thud of disappointment. She's never wanted their affair to be discovered but, in her quiet fantasies, if his wife ever did find out, the marriage would end so they could stop sneaking around. She's so enamoured with this idea, she pushes Linden for more details. 'You said your wife doesn't need you. If that's true, why would she hold on to someone she doesn't need?'

'Because she loves me. She's *in* love with me.'

It's on the tip of her tongue to ask him if *he* would ever divorce *her*. If he would leave his wife to be with his lover. And if not, why not? Why cheat on his wife with someone *less*? Someone who isn't worth the trouble? She supposes this is what she uses to assuage her conscience, the idea that she is, in some ways, more suited to Linden than his wife because why else would he risk it all? But, hearing him talk about his marriage now, she wonders if she's much more to him than a cheap ride at an amusement park. Something to pass the time. A blink of excitement in a landscape of mundanity.

He shrugs. 'Marriage is for life.'

'Until death do us part?'

'That's right.'

She's always thought of marriage as tedious. As a trap. As endless trivial bickering and terrible sex. But then she met Linden. Still, she will not be *that* other woman. The unoriginal one who asks her lover to leave his spouse. If he is to end his marriage, it has to be because *he* wants to.

Since receiving the note and convincing herself Linden's wife is the author, she's been unable to sleep. Now she knows his wife didn't write it, the adrenaline rushes from her body and she is suddenly exhausted. She wants to be alone. She wants to go upstairs and take a bath and watch TV until she can no longer keep her eyes open, but it doesn't feel right to ask Linden to leave the house he owns.

He reaches for her and she lets him tug her to his side. 'I came here to give you a gift, not to talk about the woes of marriage.'

She smiles weakly at him, her mood lifting a little. 'I've asked you a dozen times not to buy me gifts.'

'No,' he says, an edge to his voice. 'You *demand* I never buy you gifts.'

It's true. She believes if she lets him ply her with presents, it cheapens what they have and makes the difference between her and the caricature Other Woman who resides rent-free in her mind, the scarlet lady who's only in it for the great sex and the hard cash, less and less. The hypocrisy is not lost on her that while she refuses underwear and jewellery, she has accepted a house. Still, a home is a necessity, and she plans to be at Paddledown only for as long as it takes to find a new place.

'You're going to *love* this,' he tells her, taking her hand again. 'You can't be mad at me for getting you a gift if you love it.'

'And if I hate it?'

He grins. 'If you *really* hate it, you can beat me to death with it.'

She rolls her eyes good-humouredly. 'Deal.'

He stands in front of the lounge door and, with a flourish, opens it. She steps inside. In the middle of the room is a plush olive-green armchair. *Her* armchair. The one she chose with her father. It's so incongruous, she blinks, sure she's imagining it.

'What do you think?' Linden whispers in her ear.

She forces herself to look away from it and drags her gaze up to his. 'You did this?'

He nods.

'And it's mine?' she asks, walking over to it. She strokes the soft velvet. 'My exact one?'

'When you told me how important it was, I knew I had to get it back.'

'But how?'

'I paid a visit to your old landlord. Don't look so worried, I didn't punch him, though I was tempted after how he treated you. I asked him for the buyer's details and—'

'And he just gave them to you?'

'I may have given him some cash.'

'You bribed him?'

'You really wanted that armchair.'

She feels a swell of affection. This is the kindest thing anyone has ever done for her. It's romantic and sweet without being cheesy or too flash. 'Linden, you didn't have to do this.'

'The buyer drove a hard bargain but I got what I wanted in the end.' He grins in a way that tells her he is used to getting what he wants.

She dares not ask how much he paid for it but she can imagine it was much more than it's worth. 'Thank you,' she says, knowing he can hear the fullness in her throat, the raw and undiluted adoration that she usually masks with flirtation or sex.

She imagines him driving all over town for her and then wrestling her armchair into his BMW. The notes are forgotten. The complicated nature of their relationship and the reality that he will never leave his wife for her is forgotten, too. She doesn't care about any of it. She cares only that she has it with a man who listens, *really* listens, and who goes out of his way to ensure her happiness.

She kisses him then, winding her fingers through his silky golden hair. He groans appreciatively into her mouth. They undress. Soon, they are naked and she is straddling him on her olive-green armchair. This time, the sex isn't all sweat and heat and frantic, groping hands. Their rhythm, which is usually feverish, mellows into something slower, softer, more meaningful.

After, still naked and now entangled in one another on the living room floor in front of the fireplace, she knows she is in love with him. Deeply and irrevocably in love with Linden Lockwood. She opens her mouth to tell him but then he is on top of her. The solid weight of him is reassuring. He is looking at her with so much intensity, her breath catches in her throat. He smooths her hair away from her face and before she can speak he says, 'I know. I love you too.'

Chapter Fourteen

The Wife

I clean up the fallen plant pot, scooping up soil and cutting away any damaged leaves.

'Who was eavesdropping?' asks Addison.

'It could've just fallen over by itself,' offers Heidi. 'There's no one out here now.'

I nod though I don't agree. Someone was listening to our conversation. Colette maybe, or Flora. But why?

'Verity, are you OK?' asks Heidi with such sincerity, I feel myself crumble, tears pricking behind my eyes. I blink and blink and blink, willing them away. Grief is like a wound. Over time, it scabs over. It heals. It turns into a scar. One you occasionally catch sight of and remember the pain you felt the day it happened. Over time, losing Linden has become a puckered, shiny scar. Lifting those loose floorboards and reading those lilac love letters has slashed open that wound. Now, I am bleeding all over my office. All over Heidi and Addison. But it's inappropriate. Unprofessional. I crossed a line when I clutched Heidi's hand. I cannot be the boss who clings to her employee and cries on her, too. But then she adds in a soothing, motherly tone, 'I'm in shock. I can't believe Linden was having an affair, and with someone you know, too. I always thought you were the perfect couple. It's OK to not be OK.'

And I come undone. Without another word passing between us, I start to sob. Heidi wraps her arms around me and holds me as though I am one of her children with a scraped knee in the park. She smells of lilies and detergent, strong coffee and shampoo. 'It's going to be all right,' she soothes. 'It will all be fine.'

She tells me to go home. That she will explain to Colette and Flora that I have a migraine. Addison declares I'm not fit to drive and so she takes me in her car. We don't speak much. I press my forehead against the cool glass and wonder how many times my husband betrayed me. Then I am ambushed by a thought so tart it makes my mouth water: once Addison drops me off, she will return to her husband. Her generous, kind-hearted, loyal husband, and she will breathe a sigh of relief that her life is nothing like mine. That her family is unbroken. That tonight she will sleep beside a warm body and not a ghost.

'Do you think it was a good idea to involve Heidi like that?' asks Addison, a crack of annoyance in her tone.

I'm so surprised by her question, it takes me a moment to process it. 'I didn't intend to.'

'You grabbed her hand.'

My cheeks flush at the memory of desperately reaching for Heidi. 'I didn't think.'

'But you need to think, Verity,' she says with the authority of a parent dealing with a difficult child. 'You write a weekly advice column on how to sustain a healthy relationship. Your entire brand is built on you being aspirational. On people wanting what you have. If Heidi lets slip to your readers that your marriage wasn't as perfect as you made it out to be then this could ruin everything.'

After finding out about the affair, these are concerns I've secretly had but kept buried. Now my cousin is exhuming them. Bringing the corpse of my fears to the surface and forcing me to acknowledge them. Of course I don't want people to think I'm a fraud but, at the time I wrote about my marriage, I believed it to be authentic and enduring. A rare, golden pearl of marital bliss. It's Linden who has made me a fraud, revealing our relationship to be a common piece of plastic costume jewellery.

'I just worry about you,' she says as we reach the traffic lights. 'You've lost your husband and I don't want you to lose your business too.'

'I didn't *lose* my husband, Addison. I didn't misplace him. He isn't a set of fucking car keys. He was murdered. He was murdered because he was sleeping with someone else. Quite frankly, my *brand* has been the last thing on my mind.'

Silence.

I stare out of the passenger's side window. We pull away from the traffic lights and pass Victoria Park. Even though it is November, parents push their children on swings and wait for them at the bottom of the slides. A couple stroll hand in hand. The woman rests her head on her husband's shoulder and he whispers something into her hair. She laughs. Even though I *hate* Linden, I love him, too. Missing him is a physical ache.

Soon, Addison is parking on the driveway outside my house. I move to get out but she reaches for me. 'I'm sorry. I'm not handling this very well . . . I just . . . I don't know how to help you. You're like a sister to me, Verity. We grew up together. We've always been there for one another. I want to *always* be here for you,' she says, voice thick with emotion. 'I'm just sorry this is happening.'

I meet her gaze, my smile weak. 'You didn't kill him, did you?'

She presses her lips together. 'No, I didn't.' She lifts her chin. 'But if I'd found out what Linden was doing behind your back, I might've done.'

In the house, Addison tells me to go upstairs and have a shower while she makes lunch. I'm so anxious, the fluttery feeling in my gut won't allow me to eat the sandwiches but I drink the mint tea and swallow the pills she hands me. 'Something for your headache. You always get them after you cry,' she explains.

The first time Addison ever saw me sob like this, with impotent rage and desolation, we'd been fifteen. My aunt had left Addison with us for the summer. I'd saved my birthday and Christmas money and bought Glastonbury Festival tickets for us both even though I knew my parents would never let us go. My aunt met her first love, the man she ran off with who introduced her to a nomadic lifestyle at Glastonbury. I think my mother recognised in me that same wild, free spirit, and she did all she could to crush it beneath her sensible loafers. When my parents found the tickets, they tore them up. I was devastated. And though Addison seemingly shared in my disappointment, I knew she was secretly relieved. She'd spent her entire life traipsing from town to town on her mother's whim, being dragged around parties and festivals and warehouse raves. Addison was grateful for the warm, perfectly made bed and hot chocolate my mother offered. Where I found my parents' rules tedious, Addison found them comforting. Sometimes I wonder whether it was Addison who told them about the tickets, keen to keep my head out of the clouds and my feet on the ground, always wanting the best for me even when I couldn't see what was best for myself.

So I take the tablets and she leaves half an hour later. Body heavy with exhaustion, I climb into bed. Soon, I fall into a deep, dreamless sleep.

When I wake, my head feels as though it is packed with lead. I'm disorientated and have no idea what time it is. It's still dark outside. The curtains are open just a crack. I reach for my phone but it isn't on the bedside table where I usually let it charge. I pull open the drawer and riffle through it until I find my smartwatch. It's just after six in the morning. I've been asleep for fourteen hours. *How* have I been asleep for fourteen hours? Then I remember all the nights this week I have lain awake, unable to shut off my racing thoughts, and I'm not surprised I basically slipped into a coma.

I set the watch down and, as I do, I hear creaking beyond my closed bedroom door. Unease scuttles across my skin. I hold my breath and listen, convinced I'm not alone. Is someone in the house? Panic whirls in my stomach. I climb out of bed and slowly move towards the door but, as my fingers close around the handle, I picture Linden on the other side just as he was in the wake of his death. His cracked skull, thick ribbons of loose flesh torn from his scalp, peeling like a banana skin to reveal bone. His broken nose, red and swollen like a pig's snout. I squeeze my eyes shut but I can still see him. My heart races so fast, I feel light-headed.

Then I take a deep breath and tell myself I'm being ridiculous. I am alone in this house. There is no one stalking the landing and no corpse waiting for me beyond the door. I open it. I wait. I'm greeted only by silence.

'Get a grip,' I say into the dark.

It feels good to break the silence. Satisfying, like cracking the thin layer of ice that forms over puddles in winter. I'm wide awake now, too wired to sleep, so I decide to go downstairs and make myself a tea. As I descend the stairs, I feel the drop in temperature. It's like stepping into a fridge. Or a morgue. The hallway is cast in darkness. I don't bother fumbling for the light switch, instead I move quickly towards the kitchen at the back of the house. It's only as I cross the threshold that I understand why it's so cold: the bifold doors are wide open, yawning into the dark. I didn't leave them unlocked yesterday . . . Someone has been inside my house. Fear winds itself across my chest. I turn on the lights. Leaves have blown into the kitchen and skitter across the floor.

I feel as though I'm being watched and imagine someone lurking on the patio. I jog across the icy tiles. I've almost made it to the doors when I slip. Then I am falling. I hit the ground hard enough to knock the air from my lungs. Pain radiates across my ribs and I gasp into the tiles. I breathe through my mouth, through the agony. Slowly, I push myself onto my elbows but my ribs shriek in protest and I squeeze my eyes shut against the pain. If they aren't broken, they're certainly bruised.

Then I open my eyes again.

And I see it. Nightmarish and haunting.

I scream.

I scream so loudly my ears ring.

Chapter Fifteen

The Other Woman

She and Linden are spending the day together. They're shopping for paint and homewares because everything inside Paddledown is white and, in her opinion, has the creative flair of an unseasoned bowl of porridge. If you ignore the fact that they must drive an hour away to avoid being seen by his wife or anyone they know, it's all very normal. The kind of things her parents did together. They get snacks for the car journey, chocolate and salty bags of crisps, ice-cold fizzy drinks and hot takeaway coffees from Starbucks. The August heat is thick and relentless. She's nervous about dropping chocolate on the leather seats, but Linden insists it's fine. He pops the protective lid off his coffee cup. His wife wouldn't approve. In all likelihood, it was her who bought this car.

It's difficult *not* to make observations about her lover's marriage. She's sure Linden isn't comfortable that his wife's career is more successful than his, and so he punishes her by spilling coffee on the cream leather seats and fucking his mistress in the car his profession failed to pay for. This side of him, the bitter, churlish side, is one she glimpses only occasionally, but it is at odds with the ebullient, charismatic man she has fallen in love with. The one who gave her a house and rescued her olive-green armchair. She decides that it is his wife who brings out the worst in him and *she* who brings out the best and that, at least for the moment, eases the guilt that she is enjoying a day out with another woman's husband.

* * *

It's the biggest DIY shop she's ever been in. Coming here was Linden's idea. He wants her to make Paddledown her home. As an adult, she has always rented from landlords who insist on magnolia walls and beige floors, so she's excited to put her stamp on a place even if it isn't truly hers. Linden was thrilled she agreed and gifted her a jubilant smile. Sometimes, with him, she feels like a wounded animal being nursed back to health, and he, her rescuer. She supposes, when they met, that she was wounded. Her heart recently broken, crushed beneath the boot of a man she should never have given it to, the last of her close family moving abroad, her father gone, her mother left in ruins and *she* bearing the weight of it all. When Linden showed interest in her, it felt like a burst of colour in a world that had slid into greyscale. She couldn't believe someone as attractive and confident and educated as Linden Lockwood would want anything to do with her.

She glances over at him now. He's at the information desk, talking to an employee and gesturing enthusiastically. He has his back to her, so she can't see Linden's face, but she can see that the young man serving him is smiling. It's a genuine smile. That's the thing about Linden; he's got this easy, magnetic personality. People like him. They're drawn to him. Just as she is.

She's browsing the tester pots of paint when Linden returns. 'Picked one?'

She shakes her head. 'Too much choice.'

'Why do they give paint colours such utterly ridiculous names?'

'What's ridiculous about Pine Green?'

He raises an eyebrow. 'What's sensible about Elephant's Breath?' He plucks one of the little pots from the shelf. 'And this one, Pennies From Heaven . . . *Pennies* . . . From Heaven?' His eyes are comically wide. 'Pennies? Is there a financial crisis happening up there too?'

She smiles.

He picks up another, turning it over in his hand to read the label aloud: 'Pretty Ugly.'

'Now you're just making things up.'

'Nope.' He tosses it to her.

'It is indeed called Pretty Ugly,' she concedes, but grimaces at the putrid-green colour.

'At least it's self-aware.' He picks up another. 'What about this one? Humorous Green.' He pulls a face. 'Christ, there's nothing funny about the price.'

Grinning, she takes it from him and puts it back on the shelf. 'Well, *you're* not the one paying for it.'

He rolls his eyes in an exaggerated show of disapproval. 'You're not a very good mistress, you know.'

'I'm not?'

'Aren't you supposed to want me for my sexual prowess and money?' he teases. 'You won't even let me buy you a tin of paint.'

'I let you give me a house.'

'Ah, yes, how very generous of me.' He pulls her to him and kisses her softly on the lips. She breathes in the warm, spicy scent of him. Black pepper and ginger. Then he returns his attention to the tester pots, scanning the labels, but her mouth still tingles. 'Christ,' he says, picking up one more.

'What is it?'

'Dead Salmon,' he says flatly. 'Sounds . . . delicious.'

'You're meant to paint the walls with it, not eat it.'

'Paint the walls with a deceased fish?' he asks, bemused. 'The world's gone doolally.'

Her favourite colour is lilac but it's the shade used to decorate her childhood bedroom so she selects something different, something grown-up.

'Go on then,' he says nodding at the pot in her hand. 'What's it called?'

She bites her lip. 'Anal Beads.'

He grins. 'No prizes for guessing what colour *that* one is.'

Laughing, she holds up the tester pot. 'I chose Sage Green.'

'A classic.'

They walk hand in hand down the aisles and she manages to forget that his heart doesn't belong only to her. The shop isn't very busy. A woman's clarion laughter rings out. Linden's head snaps up at the sound. He stiffens. 'What is it?' she asks. He's frowning, eyes fixed in the direction of the laughter. She squeezes his hand to get his attention. 'What?'

'I thought . . .'

Then a tall, slim woman with long, glossy hair rounds the corner, talking into her phone.

Linden's hand slips from hers and he quickly crosses to the other side of the aisle, as far from her as he can get. Her heart starts racing; he knows the woman. She and Linden have never before bumped into people they know. Following his cue, she pretends to browse light fixtures but she is too afraid to move for fear of drawing attention to herself.

'Linden?' calls the woman.

He turns to her, managing to sound surprised. 'Good to see you!' They hug. 'What're you doing in Cirencester?'

'I had a meeting nearby and decided to swing in here to pick up some paint.'

'Don't tell me my cousin is thinking about painting that lounge again?'

'No. No, Vee doesn't actually know I'm here.'

'Oh?'

He leans in conspiratorially. 'I decided to redo my study.'

'But you've only just finished it!'

'Hence the secret mission. I figured I'd make this a surgical strike: get in, get the paint, slap it on the walls before she can stop me.'

She smiles warmly. '*Great* idea. I don't know what I'm looking forward to more: seeing what you do with the space or her reaction after she spent a silly amount of money on that interior designer.'

'Well, if she kicks me out, can I stay with you?'

She laughs. 'Always.'

They say goodbye. Once the woman rounds the next corner and is out of sight, Linden breathes a sigh of relief. And so does she, but she's still too afraid to approach him in case the woman returns. Linden gets out his phone and taps away at the screen. She receives a message: Pay for the paint and walk down the road. I'll pick you up.

Ten minutes later, she slides into his BMW, the tins of paint clanging together in the plastic bag. Before she can speak, he says, 'That was too close.'

Tension runs through him and she wants to reach over and rub his leg reassuringly but she knows it won't help. 'You did well. I don't think she even noticed me.'

He keeps his eyes on the road. 'Maybe.'

An awkward, agitated silence seeps into the car. She rushes to fill it. 'They're cousins?'

He nods.

'Makes sense. They look a lot alike. They're both really beautiful.'

They stop at the traffic lights. He takes her hand. '*You're* really beautiful.' They smile at one another. 'Let's get back.'

Linden doesn't stay as planned. Instead, he helps load the bags into Paddledown and distractedly kisses her goodbye. Then he is gone. She stands for a moment after his car has pulled away and stares out at the empty street. The sky is turning grey with clouds. The afternoon she had imagined for them – wine in the garden down by the canal – is washed away. She sighs and closes the door. That is when she finds another note. With trepidation pulsing through her, she picks it up off the door mat and reads it: *His wife deserves to know the truth.*

Chapter Sixteen

The Wife

Ignoring the pain in my ribs, I scramble to my feet. On the patio, in full view of the bifold doors, is a severed pig's head. Embedded in its skull is a knife. As I get closer, I see the note the blade has speared in place. The pig's skin is grey and pink and wrinkled. Its eyes milky and blank. Dried blood crusts the thick, severed neck. Then I notice its mouth has been crudely sewn shut with thin brown twine. Even though it is dead, I hear its panicked squeals as it's slaughtered. See the knife sawing through skin and flesh and bone. I breathe in the stench of rotting meat and then I am running to the sink, slip-sliding across the tiles, and retching into it. I stare into the brass plughole and feel my insides churn. I taste fear, empty and hot, at the back of my throat. I can still hear that squealing pig.

Running from the room, I swallow against the pain in my ribs, and skid into the hall. This time, I turn on the light and search until I find my bag. Inside is my phone. I call Addison. I ring and ring and ring again. I'm just about to phone Harry when Addison calls me back. Her voice is groggy with sleep. 'Verity, are you OK?'

'No,' I gasp. 'No, I'm not OK at all.'

I hear the swish of fabric and imagine her sitting up in bed. 'What's wrong?'

'Can you come to the house?'

Within forty minutes, Addison is standing by my side as we stare, horrified and repulsed, at the severed head. Her hand covers her mouth and her eyes are two enormous pools of darkness. 'The smell . . .'

I can taste the decaying flesh as though it is congealing on my tongue.

'And what's that?' she asks, lowering her hand. 'Is that a note?'

'I haven't touched it.' Revulsion maggot-crawls across my skin. 'I can't.'

She bites her full lower lip. 'Do you want me to . . . ?'

I nod. She reaches forward, tears the folded cream paper free and opens it. She frowns down at whatever it says and even though I don't want to get close to the pig, I take a step forward and hold out my hand to receive the note. Brow still furrowed, she gives it to me.

Keep your pig mouth shut.

I look back at the head, at the mouth that has been haphazardly sewn closed. Why a pig? What does the note even mean? And then it clicks into place . . . 'This is because I went to the police.'

She raises one dark eyebrow. 'What?'

'I went *squealing* to the police. To the pigs. Whoever left this at my door is warning me not to get them involved.'

Slowly, she glances back at the severed head. 'Are you sure that—'

'Did you do this?' I demand.

She spins towards me. '*What*?'

'Did you?'

Her mouth drops open, aghast. 'Are you insane? Of course I didn't.' She is seething, indignation coming off her like steam. 'What the hell, Verity? Why would you even *think* that?'

My entire body quivers, fear and adrenaline flooding my veins. 'You never wanted me to talk to the police.'

'Because I was worried they'd suspect you. I've got nothing to hide.' Her eyes narrow. 'Do you think *I'm* the other woman?'

I feel my pulse in my lips as I search her gaze. I take several deep breaths to compose myself and then I say, 'No. No, I don't.'

'But you do think I left a severed head on your patio alongside some cryptic note?'

'No.' I screw up the note in my hand and dig my nails into my palm so hard it hurts. 'I'm sorry. I'm terrified, Addison. Linden's killer is still out there, and now this.'

She softens. 'You need to call the police.'

'But—'

She digs her phone out of her jogging bottoms. They're far too big for her. I picture her staggering out of bed, frantic to reach me, grabbing a pair of Harry's bottoms and sliding into them so as not to waste time. I called her and she rushed right over to be with me. Whenever Linden went away, I'd potter around the house in one of his T-shirts, comforted by the warm, spicy scent of his cologne lingering on his clothes.

I look down at the phone but I don't take it and I don't call the police. The reality is, Linden has been dead over a year and they haven't a clue who's responsible. Even with all I gave to them, they weren't able to unearth a single useful detail about the other woman. If I want to know who left a grotesque pig's head for me to find, I have to do it myself. 'I don't trust the police to help,' I admit.

She nods slowly. 'I suppose they haven't done you much good so far, but this is terrifying, Verity. It's ghastly. I think you should call them.'

'It's awful,' I agree, 'but my doors were wide open. Whoever did this didn't want to hurt me. If they did, it'd be *my* head that blade is driven through. This was a warning.' My heart hammers at the thought of someone creeping into my bedroom with a knife. 'And what happens if the author of that note finds out I went to the police again straight after they demanded I don't?'

She frowns. 'True . . .' Her eyes dart from me to the pig. 'Do you really think whoever left that head would hurt you?'

'There's a killer on the loose, Addison.'

The silence that follows is eerie and too still. Outside, the sun is rising in an inky swell of amber and cerise. If it weren't for the decomposing pig's head just a few feet away, it would be a beautiful sight.

'OK,' says Addison after a moment. 'We should call round the local butchers and abattoirs. There can't be that many places a person can just pick up a pig's head, right?'

'That's smart,' I say, nodding. 'But you should really go back to Harry. He'll wonder where you are.'

'He knows. I told him before I left.' She pulls me into a hug. I rest my chin on her shoulder and breathe in her rhubarb and rose shampoo. 'I'm not going anywhere. It's me and you. Always.'

Before we bag up the head, I take a photo of it on my phone in case I ever need to show it to the police. It takes three black bin bags to trap the rancid stench of rotting flesh. I've retched so many times, my throat aches. After, we drink chamomile tea and wait for the local butchers and abattoirs to open.

It doesn't take long before we find the right shop. The man on the other end of the phone has a thick Somerset accent, creamy like churned butter. 'Ah, yes, that's right. We sold that head yesterday.'

'To who?'

'I thought it was a woman who rang to ask if we had anything but it was a man who turned up.'

'A *man*?'

'That's right.'

But it doesn't make any sense. 'What did he look like?'

'My wife would've thought him a looker, I'm sure. Tall, blond.'

My stomach drops. 'Did he leave a name?'

'Let me have a look for you.' I hear the rustle of papers and then the phone switching hands. 'Ah yes, here it is. Lockwood,' he tells me. 'Linden Lockwood.'

Chapter Seventeen

The Other Woman

What if the person sending the notes isn't connected to *her*, but to Linden's wife? Is it possible the cousin has been following them? Going as far as to stalk them to the DIY shop? Maybe the cousin is the author of all these notes? But then, why not confront Linden or his wife? Why plague *her*? She wonders whether she should tell Linden, but then she recalls how stressed he was after almost being seen together and knows he is a teetering tower of cards: one wrong move and he'll topple. No. She refuses to burden him with this. The problem is, she's invested now. She cares if their affair is discovered because it will mean the end of their relationship. Yes, he says he loves her, but while his wife doesn't need him, *he* needs his wife. She owns everything they have. All of it. Even if Linden resents that he isn't the moneymaker in their relationship, his wife's career allows him to work part-time and to focus on his beloved novels, all while enjoying an expensive, honeyed lifestyle. Truth is, between their affair and his lecturing career, he isn't getting much writing done. She thinks about how, if they could be a proper couple, out in the open, Linden would be content and fulfilled. They both would. Though they'll never get a happily-ever-after if the author of these notes follows through with their threat. How can she stop them when she doesn't know who they are?

Her head is throbbing. She sets down the paintbrush and stands back to survey her work. The sage green is pretty and makes her olive armchair pop. She likes her outfit, the dungarees and the silk scarf she's used to secure her hair. Before Linden, she'd have snapped a photo and sent it to Anna. It's Saturday, and while she is alone with nothing but paint fumes for company, Anna is probably enjoying brunch with friends. No bother; Linden is coming to visit tomorrow. They will spend an entire day in bed. A lazy Sunday. She pretends this is because he wants her naked and not because he is afraid to ever step foot outside of Paddledown with her again.

Her phone rings.

It is her mother.

She has ignored Penelope's calls for weeks, ever since she moved. She sighs, knowing she can't do it forever. As soon as she answers, her mother says, 'So you're alive then?'

She rolls her eyes. 'Obviously.'

'Well, how would I know? You don't call. Don't text. Don't return a single one of my voicemails.'

'I'm sorry.'

'You don't sound sorry. Where are you?'

She bites her lip.

'Well?' pushes Penelope.

'Home.'

'Liar. I've just been to your studio and a rather rude man informed me you no longer live there. Is that true?'

She sucks in a breath. 'I'm sorry.'

Her mother's disappointment hurtles down the line. 'You're my daughter. You're my daughter, and you moved house without bothering to tell me? Do you know how that makes me feel?'

There's a snap of guilt, like an elastic band pinged against her skin. 'Mum . . .'

'Really, your father's gone and now you are too.'

'I'm not gone. I've just . . . moved, and I was busy with the move. I haven't had a second to breathe.'

'Send me the address. I want to see you.'

Her heart races. What would Linden say if she invited her mother to Paddledown? He hasn't told her she can't have people in the house. He's encouraged her to treat it as her own but still, there is something very *wrong* about hosting your mother in your married lover's secret second home. 'Actually, I've been painting, so—'

'If you don't send me your address so I can see you aren't living in some crack den, I'm going to call the police and report you missing myself.'

Disbelief floods her. 'Mum—'

'The choice is yours.'

But there isn't a choice at all. Not really. 'Fine,' she relents. 'I'll text you the address.'

Her mother wanders around the house with an appraising eye. 'You've certainly landed on your feet,' she says, running a hand over the wooden worktops. 'This is lovely.'

'Thank you.'

'Promotion at work?'

'No. Why?'

'I'm just trying to figure out how you've gone from a studio with a view of wheelie bins to a two-bedroom house with a view of the canal.'

She clears her throat and busies herself making tea. 'The landlord doesn't have a mortgage on the property and he isn't in the business of extorting from people.'

'Well, that's very generous of him.'

She shrugs but doesn't meet her mother's eye. 'The house was actually in a bit of a state when I moved in,' she lies. 'So I agreed to pay for paint and any other small DIY jobs.'

'That's savvy.'

They take their tea to the small oak dining table. It's just starting to rain. She doesn't mind. Usually, she would curl up on the little sofa that overlooks the garden and read a book. She enjoys the sound of rain against the windows. Instead, she is tense, sipping too-hot tea and burning her tongue in a bid to move her mother along as soon as possible. Linden isn't due until tomorrow, but she is still worried that her mother will poke around and find a man's stray sock or an old bill with his name on it.

'It's been quite a while since we caught up,' comments Penelope.

'Has it?' she asks, even though she knows it has.

'Yes.'

'Then . . . let's catch up. What's new?'

Penelope blows on her tea. 'Well, I've started running again and last month I returned to work.'

Involuntarily, her eyebrows shoot up. 'Full-time?'

'Don't look so surprised. I'm not an invalid.'

But when she'd been living with Penelope, just over a year ago, her mother hadn't been capable of much at all. She'd been a wreck, consumed by the loss of her husband. Penelope didn't turn to drink or try to harm herself, nothing quite so dramatic, but she did retreat, withdrawing from friends and hobbies and work, all the while holding on too tightly to her daughter, crushing her within desperate, clenched fists. 'Well, that's fantastic. I'm glad.'

'And you?'

She sips her tea. 'I moved, and . . .' She casts around for something else, knowing a crumb of gossip won't be enough to satiate her mother. Yet she cannot tell her about Linden. Penelope would never in a million years forgive her daughter for becoming The Other Woman. 'And that's it, really.'

'We haven't seen one another in more than two months and that's all you have to say?'

She bites the inside of her cheek because she and her mother have never been the sort to gossip or swap stories. Though she wanted a relationship with her mother that was vibrant and fun, it always felt formal and taxing.

'I was thinking we could go away for a few days,' says Penelope.

She chokes, shocked by the suggestion. 'When?' she asks, wiping her mouth with the back of her hand. Though her friends often enjoyed brunch dates and cocktails, minibreaks and trips to the spa with their mothers, when she had suggested the same to Penelope, she'd been met with a derisive, 'I'm your mother, not your best friend.'

'Tomorrow.'

Her eyes widen. '*Tomorrow*?'

'Leave on Sunday, back by Tuesday evening.'

But tomorrow Linden is spending the night. Then he will be gone for a week, travelling with his wife. She needs to see him before he

The Wedding Vow

goes. Wanting him burns like a fever for which he is the only remedy. She is never more alive than when his hands are on her. She can't go away with her mother because she can't go without seeing Linden. 'Mum, I really can't get the time off work at such short notice.'

Penelope's face falls. And while she feels guilty for rejecting her mother's attempt to reconnect, she knows Penelope's happiness will vanish like sugar in hot water the moment something reminds her of her husband, and then the two of them will revert to their former roles of manic depressive and bumbling carer. When Penelope fell into that well of sadness, she, the dutiful daughter, moved back in with her mother, but nothing she did was right. The tea she made was too hot. The film she'd chosen too boring. The food she cooked too bland. The conversation too superficial. Penelope chipped away at her daughter's worth every day because she didn't like herself and didn't want anyone else to like themselves either. One day, her mother took it further than a few well-aimed digs and erupted, spewing hate, saying the *unthinkable*. And it is because of that hate-filled remark that she fled her mother's house a year after having moved in to help her.

'I see,' says Penelope, even though it is plain she doesn't. The silence that follows is taut. 'Look,' continues her mother after a moment, 'I know that after your father, I fell apart. And I was far too protective of you.'

She tries not to snort at this. Penelope has always been overly protective, but in her depression, she became controlling, deciding who her daughter talked to, when, where she went, who she went with. Penelope was a python constricting her. Now, her daughter bites down on her lip to stop herself from yelling all this at her mother, and swallows that old, acid anger like cheap white wine.

'But I want to be part of your life again,' Penelope continues. 'Daughters need their mothers and . . .' She swallows thickly. 'And mothers need their daughters.' Then she reaches across the table and lays a hand over hers. 'I just want us to be closer.'

Penelope's sincerity thaws her but then she thinks of Linden, and the idea of not seeing him for over a week sends panic rolling through her. They don't get to spend a lot of time together so when

105

the opportunity arises, she must grab hold of it. Before she can come up with another excuse, she hears a key in the lock. She jumps to her feet, heart in her mouth, and races to the front door. Linden steps inside, smile wide. She feels Penelope appear over her shoulder. Linden's smile falters and then vanishes completely. The three of them stand stock-still in the small hallway which seems to shrink around them. She swallows again and again and then says, 'Mum, this is my landlord.'

Linden's gaze darts between the two women and then he plasters on his most charming smile. 'Nice to meet you,' he says, nodding towards her mother.

Penelope steps around her daughter to clasp Linden's outstretched hand. 'And you.'

Linden's eyes come to rest on her again. 'Thank you for coming over on a Saturday,' she tells Linden. 'I just wanted to make sure you were OK with the paint colour I chose for the kitchen.'

Linden nods and says, 'No problem. I was passing by.' His eyes slide over Penelope. 'I can see you've got company, so why don't I come back next week, or you can just email me a photograph of the swatches. I'm sure whatever you've chosen is fine.'

Her heart is pounding so hard, she feels dizzy. She can tell from the tense line of his shoulders and the tightness of his mouth that he is livid. 'I was thinking Elephant's Breath,' she says, hoping an inside joke will lighten the mood. It doesn't.

'As I said, whatever you've chosen will be acceptable, I'm sure.'

She swallows. 'Well, I'm sorry you drove all the way out here.'

His expression is stony. 'No problem.' He turns to her mother. 'Lovely to meet you.'

And then he is gone, shutting the door behind him.

Penelope returns to the kitchen but she does not follow. Can't. She stares at the closed door and forces herself not to chase after him. She listens to his car pull away from the house and her stomach drops. He is furious. She pushes her fingers back through her hair and claps her mouth shut to stop herself from screaming. She needs to fix this. How can she fix this?

'Why are you still dithering in the hallway?' calls her mother.

Anger displacing her desperation, she turns on her heel and stalks into the kitchen. 'Mum, I'm really not feeling well. I've been breathing in paint fumes all day. I'm tired. Can we please do this another time?'

'*This?*' she hisses. 'As though I'm a work meeting you can just move around. I'm your mother. Not some colleague. Not a stranger.'

But they aren't close, especially not since that last big row.

'I can't believe you don't want to spend time with me,' laments Penelope. 'I won't be around forever, you know. Your father's dead and one day I will be, too.'

'Mum—'

Penelope holds up a hand. 'No. Don't worry. I'm leaving.' Then her mother's gaze locks with hers. 'Maybe I do feel like a stranger to you, but you feel like a stranger to me, too. At least I'm trying.'

And with that, her mother storms out of the house, slamming the front door.

Chapter Eighteen

The Wife

Linden is dead. There is no way he left the pig's head at my door. Someone is playing a very sick game. Is it his mistress, trying to ward me off? It's one thing to be a homewrecker, it's another to be psychotic about it. Or is it someone else?

'Who else knows you went to the police?' asks Addison.

'Heidi.'

She raises a brow. 'But why would Heidi do this?'

I shake my head. I've always felt at ease around Heidi. She's one of those rare uncomplicated people. She's never malicious or short-tempered, and she's always taking care of others before taking care of herself. I can't imagine for one moment that Heidi is behind this.

'How well do you know Heidi?' she asks.

'What do you mean?'

'She talks about a family, but have you ever met them? Met her husband?'

I bristle. 'You aren't suggesting Heidi is the other woman, are you?'

Addison tucks her hair behind her ear. 'I don't know. I just think you need to be careful who you trust. What about whoever was eavesdropping yesterday? You don't really think that brass planter fell over all by itself?'

'No. I don't.' Someone had lurked outside my office door, maybe the same someone I felt skulking in the hallway this morning, just before I found the pig. And even though I don't want to consider it, what about Flora? Flora who has a wilder, darker side. Who drinks too much and kisses married men on cobbled streets. He was tall and blond, just like Linden. Could *she* have been the woman who enquired on the phone about the head? And could *he* have been the man who collected it? But *why*? To what end? What does Flora not want me to find out?

I decide not to go into the office. Addison offers to stay with me but I tell her to go home and get some sleep. There are purple shadows beneath her eyes and she's pale. As much as I don't want to be alone, I don't want to be around people either. I don't have the energy to wear a mask of normality, not today.

I set myself up in the lounge and sit in the little window seat with a Noah Pine book. Not that I can concentrate. Still, I force myself to keep reading until the words on the page blur. Then I slap the book shut. The silence closes in around me. I feel as though I am being watched. Or maybe I'm not. Maybe I am living with the ghost of my husband. Murdered in front of the fireplace, feet from where I am sitting. I set the book on the arm of the window seat cushion and walk until I am standing over the spot where he died. I still haven't replaced the brass fire poker used to beat him to death. I kneel down, pressing my shins into the cool floorboards, and I rest the palm of my hand against the place where his head had lain. The patch of wood is lighter. I had to bleach the floorboards to remove the blood. Sometimes, when I walk into this room, I can still taste the metallic tang of it on my tongue. I can see him, can see the fire poker cracking against his skull, can hear him screaming for help. And I *hate* the other woman for it. Hate that she ruined my marriage. Ruined my life. Stole from me everything I ever wanted. The man I loved. The life we built. *She* is the reason my husband is dead. And now I have to live my life without Linden. Alone. Always alone.

I miss Mimi. I miss her dark sense of humour and her laugh. The kind of contagious, gravelly laugh you can pick out in a crowd. I miss sitting in her kitchen, drinking her famous raspberry mojitos, and then complaining about our hangovers the next day. I miss that I am never more myself than when I am with her.

The difference between Mimi and Addison is that I always felt, as family, Addison was obligated to love me, but there was something fragile, yet special, in that Mimi *chose* to love me. Linden never understood how I could be so close to two very different women. Where Addison is perfectly made beds and strong coffee and effort, Mimi is curiosity and art and enthusiasm. But I loved them both.

I'm trying not to cry. I never thought this would be my life: a widow at thirty-one, rattling around in a too-big house, too paranoid to trust anyone in my life. I have a career I love, a company I started all by myself – but what's the point in any of it if I feel this alone? I reach for my phone and I do something I almost never do: I call my father.

He moved to Belgium years ago. He's remarried now to a baker called Agathe. They live together in a little cottage along the coast. My mother loathed him for divorcing her but, to his credit, he didn't have an affair. He did things the 'right' way. My father is honourable and kind, patient and well-meaning. The type of man I should have married. He didn't intend to hurt us when he left. His departure was like surgically losing an infected limb; you're prepped, numbed, the cut clean and sterile, the wound primed to heal, yet you still mourn its absence and long to be whole again.

I don't see my father very often. Not as much as I'd like. Maybe, once this is all done, I will take a few weeks away from Verity Rose and visit him and Agathe. I picture myself sitting with him and his wife on their garden patio, sharing good wine and good conversation, no longer feeling the cold embrace of loneliness, but the warmth of sun on my face.

'Verity, are you all right?' he asks and I immediately feel guilty for not calling more.

'Yes,' I lie. 'I just, it's been too long, hasn't it?'

We talk for a while. I go back to the window seat and let the familiar timbre of his voice chase away the horrors of this morning. For half an hour, I let myself forget about Linden and his affair, his murder and the severed head. But then I see Mimi. Her little orange Nissan passes my window and I hear it crunching over the gravel drive outside her house.

'I'm so sorry, Dad. I need to go,' I tell him hurriedly. 'I'll call again soon.'

I ring off and then I am sliding off the window seat and hurrying to the front door. I don't stop to grab a coat or put on shoes. I know she has warned me away from her house, but like an abandoned pet, I find myself returning, longing to be wanted once more. The ground is cold, the beige gravel sharp. I step onto her porch. Mimi is dressed in a fuchsia pink coat over blue jeans and cream Dr. Martens. Her mass of curly hair is tied up with an emerald-green silk scarf. It's noon and I am still wearing the navy button-up pyjamas I went to bed in, my hair unbrushed. She eyes me warily.

'Mimi, can we please talk?'

She turns away and unlocks her front door.

'Mimi?'

She whips towards me. 'I told you to stay away from me. Jesus, Verity, what about that is so difficult for you to understand?'

My cheeks burn as though I've been slapped. But I can't cower, can't run away, tail between my legs, because I need her help. So, still smarting from her rejection, I ask, 'Did you see anyone come to the house this morning? Or last night?'

'Why?'

I remember the pig's head, bloodied and wrinkled. My stomach turns over. 'Something was left on my back patio.'

She shrugs. 'No idea.' Then she's turning into the house.

'Is this because I asked you to check on Linden that morning?' I blurt out. 'Is that why you won't talk to me?'

She stiffens and then slowly twists towards me. 'What?'

'I wish I could take it back. I wish I'd never asked you to look in on him.'

Chewing on the inside of her cheek, she considers me. I can't work out what's she's thinking. It's strange, not being able to read her. Before, we were so connected, we could finish each other's sentences. 'I don't want to have to relocate again.'

'Who said you had to?' I move towards her but she takes a step back as though I'm a venomous snake. 'Why won't you just tell me what it is I've done? Can you please—'

'Just keep your deranged cousin away from me,' she warns as she steps inside and places herself in the gap, as though she's worried I might try barging my way into her house.

'Addison?'

'I don't want anything to do with either of you.'

I frown. 'When did you see Addison?'

'Why don't you ask her?'

'Because I'm asking you.'

She tips her head back and says to the sky, 'I knew I shouldn't have come back.'

'So why did you?' This time, I don't bother to contain my anger or the hurt I feel that she abandoned me when I needed her most.

'This is my home. I didn't want to keep running.'

And finally, a pearl of truth spills from her mouth. I pick it up and examine it in the autumn light. 'Running? Running from what?'

She presses her lips together and I can't decide whether she looks guilty or scared. What does she know? My heart starts to race.

I lower my voice, make it sweet like honey. 'Mimi, you can tell me anything. If you're in danger or—'

Her laughter is devoid of its usual warmth. It is strangled and hollow. '*Danger?* Is that a threat, Verity?'

I blanch. 'Of course not.'

She shakes her head at the ground, a wry smile creasing her lips. 'I want to believe you, but you know as well as I do, everyone's a liar.' Then she looks up and our gazes meet. Hers seems to burn straight through me.

Behind her, I catch movement. A figure passing the archway that leads into the kitchen. Tall and lean. A man. Mimi glances over her shoulder and then quickly back at me. And for the second time since her return to Rook Lane, she slams the front door shut in my face.

Chapter Nineteen

The Other Woman

The next morning, having barely slept, she sits up in the double bed and reaches for her phone. She feels awful for hurting her mother. She should have bitten her tongue, but she was so frantic about upsetting Linden that she snapped. She sends her mother an apology message that she knows will go unanswered. Then she calls Linden again. And again. And again. Eventually, he picks up. 'I can't talk.' His voice is cold and hard like the pebbles at the bottom of the canal.

'Can't or won't?'

Silence.

She is sick with fear. Not because she is afraid of him, but because she is afraid of losing him. She searches for something to say that will make it all better. 'Linden, I didn't know you were coming over.'

'So this is my fault?'

'I didn't say that.' She swallows and tugs at the emerald-green scarf tied to the bedpost and remembers how, just last week, Linden had used it to secure her hands behind her back. She twists the silk fabric around her finger until it hurts. 'I don't know why you're so upset. Nothing even happened.'

'No one but *you* is supposed to know I own that house, yet you branded me your landlord in front of your mother. I *trusted* you.'

She closes her eyes against her own stupidity but she's adamant she didn't have a better option at the time. 'What was I supposed to say when you let yourself in without warning? Would you have preferred I was honest? That I told my mum you're Linden Lockwood, my married lover? Would that have been better?'

'Don't be obtuse.'

She sighs. 'I said what I thought was best in the moment. Mum believes you're my landlord. She doesn't even know your name and even if she did, who would she tell? Who would care?'

'*I* care,' he says, voice like the crack of a whip. 'No one can find out about us.'

'Don't you think I know that? There's a lot at stake for me too.'

His laughter is mirthless. 'Is there?'

'Yes! My job, my reputation.'

'Your job is hardly a skyrocketing career, is it?' Humiliation flushes her cheeks. It is on the tip of her tongue to snap 'And your career as a one-hit wonder and part-time lecturer is?' but she doesn't because she isn't willing to hurt him the way he has just hurt her. Instead, she says, 'I've given up a lot to make this relationship work.'

He scoffs. 'Do tell.'

She squeezes the phone against his mocking tone. 'For a start, my friends.'

'I never asked you to give up your friends.'

'If I wanted you, did I have a choice? I couldn't be honest with them about who I was spending so much time with. I couldn't sit with them at brunch and lie and lie and—'

'I am *not* taking responsibility for your loneliness.'

Her mouth snaps shut, stunned by his unearthing of her. She never said she was lonely. But she realises she is . . . desperately so. If she's honest, she's been feeling lonely for a long while now. Linden is right, though – he never asked her to sacrifice her social life. Or the chance to go on a minibreak to reconnect with her mother. These were her own choices and she made them freely. 'I don't want to fight.'

'Neither do I, but here we are.' She can hear the rustle of fabric as his phone changes hands. She wonders where he is. Where his wife is. God, she misses him. She longs to be with him so fiercely, there is an ache in her chest. A burn that she knows will only be soothed once she's with him again. Being touched by him again. She opens her mouth to ask him to come over but he says, 'If you'd warned me you had company, I'd never have come by the house.'

'I know.' Her voice is small and remorseful. She drops the silk scarf and gets out of the bed. She moves across to the window. She does not spot the person walking away from Paddledown. The person that just moments ago was watching her. Instead, she is caught in a tailspin of panic at the thought of losing Linden. 'But, be fair, if I'd had any idea you were planning to visit, of course I'd have warned you. I'd never go out of my way to cause trouble.'

There's another longer, stonier silence. He sighs again. 'This is all becoming very complicated.'

She swallows. 'It's always been complicated.' In the following quiet, her heart races in her ears. 'Linden . . .'

'I leave for York tomorrow. We can't talk while I'm away with my wife. I'll be in touch once I'm back.'

'Linden, please—'

But he has already hung up.

Chapter Twenty

The Wife

I drive to Addison's house the following morning. On the way, I replay the conversation I had with Mimi the day before, and two key phrases lie beneath my skin like splinters.

I didn't want to keep running.

Everyone's a liar.

Who is Mimi running from? When did Addison talk to her? And why did she keep it from me? Addison won't approve of me stopping by without calling ahead first. She likes to be prepared, to plump the cushions and whip the hoover round, to light a candle and add sliced lemons to the jug of water she keeps in the fridge. If she has time, she will top up her perfume and redo her lipstick before opening the door. The perfect home kept by the perfect wife. I pull up onto their drive. Though she refers to their house as semi-detached, it's an end-of-terrace. It's not large or grand or, at least, not as large or as grand as she'd wanted, but it's beautifully done.

It's just before 9 a.m. when I ring the doorbell.

Addison is surprised to see me, and just as I thought, not happy I've popped by without warning. 'Did I know you were coming over?' she asks in the same tone you'd say 'What the hell are you doing here?'

'No,' I answer just as briskly. 'Can I come in?'

Brow furrowing, she steps aside. Judging by her running outfit, a black Sweaty Betty set I bought her for her birthday, she was on her way out. I follow her into the kitchen. 'Can I get you a drink?'

I shake my head, suddenly nervous. I know this isn't going to be an easy conversation.

'Everything OK?' she asks.

Nothing has been OK since I found out my husband was having an affair, but the world continues to turn and I continue to search for answers. Answers I think my cousin has. 'I spoke to Mimi yesterday.'

I watch carefully for her reaction. Surprise flickers across her face but she composes herself quickly. 'Didn't she ask you to stay away from her, Verity? Aren't you at all worried she'll tell the police you're harassing her?'

'Harassing? I'm not harassing her,' I say, affronted. It's on the tip of my tongue to tell Addison I still miss my best friend. To explain that, in a moment of weakness, of floundering in the gloomy depths of loneliness, I reached out for her, longing for her to throw me a rope, only to be washed away by the force of her rejection. But I can't confess this to Addison because I know she will think I am weak for wanting a person who deserted me at my lowest ebb. Just as Addison's mother abandoned her, leaving her behind in favour of another adventure, another man, ditching her on a whim. In Addison's mind, if she can move on from her own mother deserting her, why can't I move on from Mimi? 'Mimi told me to keep you away from her.' I wait for Addison to react but her face is carefully blank. 'Don't you think that's odd?'

She flicks up her chin. 'Actually, what I think is odd is that she ran away right after her best friend's husband was murdered next door.'

I refuse to be baited into another heated discussion as to why Mimi left Rook Lane. 'You went to see her, didn't you? When? Why?'

She glowers. 'If you and Mimi are so close again, why don't you ask her?'

I always suspected Addison was threatened by my friendship with Mimi. Addison is like a sister to me. More so than our mothers were to each other. We grew up together. We depended on one another. We shared everything. I'd never loved anyone with the same ferocity

with which I loved Addison. That is, until I met Mimi. I hoped
by introducing the two of them, and encouraging a friendship, it
would negate any jealousy on Addison's part. Apparently, though,
it was a doomed endeavour because now she wears her jealousy
like an emerald choker. 'I did ask Mimi, but she told me to ask
you. Jesus, Addison, I am so tired of these games. Of both of you
keeping secrets.'

She scowls. 'What's the point in me telling you anything, Verity?
You never listen to me.'

'Yes, I do.'

'No you don't. Especially not when it comes to Mimi.'

I pull a face. 'What do you mean?'

'I tried to tell you after we found those letters.'

'Tell me what?'

She closes her eyes and pinches the bridge of her nose as though
staving off a headache.

I know the polite thing to do would be to leave. To apologise
for coming over unannounced. For interrogating her. But between
my best friend cutting me out of her life without explanation and
a severed pig's head being left at my back door, I am desperate
and lost and Addison knows something I don't. 'Tell me what,
Addison?'

And when she looks at me again, she is afraid. Truly afraid. 'I
think Mimi murdered Linden.'

It takes me a moment to speak. 'Why?'

And slowly, in the face of my obvious doubt, her fear dissolves,
replaced by something steelier, 'You refuse to see the bad in her, don't
you? From the moment you met her, you were smitten, enamoured
with your shiny new penny.'

'Addison . . .'

'Our relationship was never the same after she waltzed into your
life. I was tossed aside like a toy you'd outgrown. Just like you, Mimi
lived in a big, beautiful house and she had money and you could do
exciting things together. Trips away, spa days, dinner at exclusive
restaurants. You knew I could never keep up and you didn't care.'

I see the hurt I've unwittingly caused her. I always offered to pay for Addison to come to all those places but she wouldn't allow it, which is why I spoil her for birthdays and Christmases. She's so upset, I don't bother pointing this out. Instead, I apologise. 'I'm sorry, Addison. I never wanted you to feel like that.'

'Well, I did. There are things that happened to me that you have no idea about.'

'What things?'

Her eyes fill with tears and I am certain she's referring to the lack of a child. A miscarriage, maybe. I always suspected but didn't ask her for fear of adding to her pain. 'Things I never bothered you with because you were too busy having the perfect life. The perfect career, the perfect husband, the perfect house, the perfect best friend.'

I recoil at the sharp slap of her words. 'Perfect life? My husband had an affair, Addison. He was murdered. Linden is dead.'

'And I think Mimi killed him!'

'Why? Why would you think that?'

'I DON'T KNOW!' She throws up her hands.

We tumble into a thorny silence.

She leans against the kitchen counter and chews her thumbnail. 'Or, maybe I do know. I'm not sure . . .' Her eyes are fixed on mine and I can see she's trying to decide something. Weighing up whether she can say what it is she's thinking. It's so rare for Addison to hesitate before speaking that I know whatever is on her mind is going to be painful to hear. 'Verity, are you certain he wasn't sleeping with *multiple* women behind your back?'

My mouth falls open and for a moment, I am too shocked to speak. When I do, my words burble up like acidic hiccups. '*Multiple?* Because betraying me once wasn't enough? I was so terrible a wife, he had to fuck more than one other woman to rid me from his thoughts?'

'That's obviously not what I'm saying.' She shakes her head. 'I just meant that since you told me about Amy, and the draft message found on the burner phone ending an affair, I've wondered whether Linden had more than one mistress. Maybe *that's* why he was killed.'

'You think one of his mistresses found out about the other and lost it?'

119

She nods. 'I know the police say it was a robbery gone wrong but nothing about that attack was controlled. It was feral. How many times did they say he was struck?'

I swallow. 'Nine.'

She closes her eyes as though trying to banish the image but I am seized by it. I am back in the living room staring at the gashes littering his skull, horrified by his swollen pig nose and the strips of torn flesh. I blink and blink until I am back in Addison's kitchen. 'Is that why you went to see Mimi?' I ask. 'To accuse her of murdering Linden?'

'Not exactly.' She folds her arms across her chest. 'I wanted to understand why she left so quickly after his death. I wanted to know how close she and Linden really were before his murder because Mimi isn't perfect, Verity. She's a liar. She's been lying to you.'

She levels at me a stare so hard my breath catches in my throat.

But I am done with vagaries and crumbs of truth. 'Please, Addison, just tell me what you know.'

She considers me, weighing up her options. And I hold myself very still because I'm afraid if I don't, I will lunge at her and shake her until she tells me everything she knows. My patience is on the verge of snapping when finally, she sighs and turns away from me. She crosses the kitchen to the sideboard behind the dining table where she opens a drawer and takes out a photograph. Impatient, I cross the kitchen to meet her.

'I told Mimi to tell you,' she says quietly. 'I found out a month or so before Linden died.'

Around the same time Mimi and Addison stopped being friends.

She holds out the photograph to me. I almost don't want to take it because I sense my world is about to slide from beneath my feet. But I do take it. I take it because hiding from the truth doesn't erase it and ignorance isn't always bliss.

It is a photograph of Mimi and Linden. Mimi is wearing a silver sequin minidress, her curly dark hair loose around her shoulders, framing her pretty face. Linden is dressed in grey trousers and a white shirt, the cuffs rolled to his elbows. He's holding a glass of wine. His other hand rests on the violin curve of her waist. His arm is wrapped around her, pulling her into his side. She fits perfectly against him, as though they were made to slot together. They're both grinning, gazing into one another's eyes. And behind them, in rainbow glitter, is a New Year's Eve banner dated two years *before* Mimi and Linden supposedly met on the doorstep of Windermere . . .

Chapter Twenty-One

The Other Woman

It's been a week since she last saw Linden. This morning though, he called and asked her to meet him at a pub in the village of Mells. He's booked them a table under the name Capulet, which has become an inside joke since she told the woman she met at the secret bar that her name was Juliet. Now, she's seated in the corner, wearing a slinky wine-coloured dress with a sweetheart neckline and side slit.

A waiter comes to take her drinks order. As she scans the menu one last time, she feels his eyes on her legs. She wants to order her favourite cocktail, a raspberry mojito, but she chooses a wine she knows Linden likes. This week, she has struggled to eat or sleep, so she promises herself that tonight, she will only have one drink.

As she waits for her wine, she surveys the pub; it's quaint with its low beams, wood-panelled walls and candlelight. There are rooms upstairs too, and she hopes this is the reason Linden chose The Talbot Inn. She imagines them now, drunk and wanting, him fumbling with the zip of her dress, her biting his bottom lip, both of them too desperate for one another to make it to the bed.

Around her, happy couples sit together, clinking glasses and laughing loudly. She sinks into her chair, loneliness spreading through her like black mould. Just for something to do, she takes out her phone. There are no unread messages to reply to, no friends enquiring about her weekend plans. She scrolls through her list of contacts, skimming names of people that, over the months, have become strangers.

A shadow looms over her. She looks up. It isn't Linden. To her shock, it is Peter. The last time she saw him was the day she moved out of his Bristol apartment almost two years ago. He'd been standing in the doorway, hard and cold like granite, and stared impassively on as she begged him not to break her heart.

'What're you doing here?' she asks.

'Nice to see you too.' He grins at her. 'My friend is the manager.' He inclines his beer bottle. 'Free drinks.'

She nods. 'I see.'

They appraise one another. His dark hair is shorter now, the floppy fringe she'd once loved is swept back off his face. The stubble is new. It makes him look older. More refined. Though he's still wearing black skinny jeans and band T-shirts.

'You look great,' he tells her.

'Thank you,' she says, though she knows the concealer beneath her eyes has done little to hide the dark circles. So as not to be churlish, she adds, 'You too.'

He grins. He has a wide mouth and straight teeth and a gold lip ring. It is a smile that is almost as familiar to her as her own. Though they were an item for less than a year, they've known each other since primary school. As a girl, she was sure she would marry Peter Holland, and as a teenager, she would mimic the lovesick heroines of TV and film, scribbling *Mrs Holland* in the back of every exercise book. It's only in recent years she has decided that if she marries, she won't give up her surname. It is the very last string that tethers her to her father.

'Can I sit?' he asks.

She'd rather he didn't. Linden will be here soon. 'I'm actually waiting for someone.'

'I promise I'll scarper as soon as your . . .' He clears his throat, searching for the right word.

'Date?' she offers.

'Yes,' he says, and scratches the back of his neck with his thumb. 'I'll make myself scarce as soon as your date arrives.'

She thinks about the black swill of loneliness within her and wonders if some company would be cleansing. 'OK.'

He slides into the seat opposite her. 'So, how've you been?'

She considers his question. This week, she has felt like an abandoned dog pining after its master, but she can't admit that to Peter. In fact, she can't talk to anyone about how she's been, not without exposing Linden, and that would detonate a bomb in both their lives. *This* is why she is so lonely. *This* is why she relies on Linden for so much. *This* is why she must lie. Or, at the very least, feed Peter only partial truths. 'Great,' she says. 'I've been great. I love my job, I've taken up running, I've just moved into a gorgeous little house.' She sips her wine. 'You?' She doesn't really want to compare notes because she is very aware that if every break-up has a loser, it is her.

After Peter ended their relationship, she returned to her mother's house. By this time, her father was gone and her mother was steeped in grief. Alone at night, in her childhood bedroom, the door shut tight against her mother's mourning, she found herself scrolling through Peter's social media. Her friends told her not to, that she was just torturing herself, but it had become a compulsion. She'd stare at photographs of Peter in his shiny new relationship, in the shiny new house he bought with his shiny new girlfriend, and felt her mouth sour. Meanwhile, what did she have? A ruined family and a handful of friends who were moving on with their lives even as hers stagnated.

In her darkest hours, she would cyberstalk Peter's new girlfriend, and obsess over every detail of his lover and their life together. It was in these moments that she would think about how much easier it would be to move on if, instead of breaking up with her, Peter had died. The truth is that grief is a less complicated, purer and more socially acceptable emotion than jealousy. With him dead, she wouldn't fixate on all the ways in which his girlfriend must be better: smarter, funnier, prettier. She wouldn't lie awake and replay each time she criticised him or nagged him or showed blatant disinterest in his work stories. With him dead, she could relax into the role of hapless victim instead of finding ways in which she was the villain of their love story. These were ugly, irrational thoughts, but at the height of her heartbreak, they were ones she couldn't shake.

'Yeah, I've been . . . good,' he tells her, but then he falls quiet, staring down into his bottle. She's about to ask if he's OK when he says, 'That's a lie.' He shakes his head. 'I've had a shit few months, actually.'

'Oh.' She feels suddenly awkward, as though she's walked in on him naked. She has no idea what's happening in his life anymore. Since meeting Linden, she has barely thought of Peter Holland. Or of anything else. 'I'm sorry. Is it . . . What's happened?'

'I had to sell my house in Clifton and now I'm living back with my parents, but the commute from their house to my job in Bristol was too long so I had to quit. I'm working for my dad now.'

'I didn't think you were interested in stonemasonry.'

'I'm not. It's a dying art, despite what my dad says.' He shrugs and swigs his beer. 'But needs must.'

Peter comes from four generations of stonemasons. The Hollands' workshop in Wells has been there for nearly a century. Rejecting stonemasonry deeply disappointed his father but she'd supported Peter, encouraging him to pursue graphic design like he'd always wanted. 'But why?' she asks. 'Why did you have to move?'

He drains his beer. 'Tammy and I broke up.'

'I'm sorry,' she says and is surprised that it is honest. She *is* sorry. Peter isn't a bad person, he just stopped loving her.

'Thanks.' He puts his empty bottle on the table. 'I'm sorry, too.'

'For what?'

'The way things ended between us. The way *I* ended things.'

She thinks about how sudden it was. One day, they were talking about buying a house and the next, he admitted he wasn't in love with her anymore. Hadn't been for weeks.

'You never asked why,' he says.

'Knowing wouldn't have changed anything,' she offers. Really, though, she'd been too afraid to hear the answer. She didn't want to know what it was about her that made her so unlovable, especially if it wasn't something she could fix.

'It wasn't your fault,' he tells her, as though reading her mind.

'You don't need to—'

'I do. We were friends before we were more.' His mouth quirks up in a grin. 'And I've missed you.'

But has she missed him? She digs out the memories she'd pushed to the bottom of herself and then flips through them like a forgotten photo album: evenings spent on his large corner sofa, with snacks and whatever TV series everyone was talking about that week; walking hand in hand through the city and stopping at the Society Café for coffee; tucking into a Sunday roast at his parents' countryside cottage; the pine and cedarwood scent of his cologne; the way she fit perfectly into the groove between his neck and shoulder; the sweaty, breathless heat of the two of them beneath the sheets of his double bed. She feels a pang of longing but can't decide if it's for him or for the easiness of an uncomplicated, drama-free relationship.

'You were so excited to buy a house, get married, start a family, but I wasn't ready for any of that,' Peter says. 'And I was too much of a coward to tell you, so I ran from you instead. I thought I'd enjoy being selfish for a while. Go where I wanted, when I wanted, without having to think about someone else.'

She searches for dishonesty in his words but he sounds sincere. 'You know it's possible to do all those things in a relationship.'

'No. Not with you. I could never be selfish with you.' Their eyes meet and her pulse quickens. 'After we broke up, I felt hollow. I thought a new relationship would fix it but it didn't. Tammy and I weren't a good fit.'

'Why?'

He leans forward, so close she breathes in the familiar pine and cedarwood scent of him. 'Because she was so different.'

'From what?'

'You.'

Her cheeks flush. In the weeks following their break-up, she'd longed for this. She'd daydreamed a thousand ways in which Peter Holland would apologise, take back what he'd said, piece together the heart he'd shattered. She looks down at their knees, pressed against one another, then up into his eyes. She could kiss Peter. She could make her first argument with Linden her last. With Peter's mouth on hers, she could slip back into her old life and into a relationship that could spin, wild and free, out in the open, but it's too late for that because she is irrevocably in love with Linden. 'I'm with someone else.'

He holds her gaze and in it she sees his burgeoning disappointment. 'And you aren't the cheating type.'

She searches his face for some sign that he is toying with her. That he *knows*. But she is met with only honest innocence.

'I think you might be the most morally grounded person I know,' he says.

She reaches for her wine. 'I doubt that.'

'Even when we were children you had this burning sense of right and wrong.'

She raises a querying brow.

'We were nine, maybe ten years old, when that house martin flew into your French doors.'

'OK...'

'And you spent a whole weekend taking care of it.'

She remembers digging through her mother's wardrobe with Peter, looking for a shoe box to house the injured bird. The two of them decorated it with seashells and Pokémon stickers. 'You were supposed to go on a trip with your dad to Newquay. You'd talked about it for months.'

She adored their annual father-daughter minibreaks. They'd spend a weekend paddleboarding and hiking the coastal paths, eating salty fish and chips out of newspaper cones and playing in the arcades. She feels a deep, lacerating grief at the memories. She takes a glug of wine and then another and another. Peter continues, 'You were so excited for that trip but you gave it up to nurse Martin.'

She smiles; she'd forgotten Peter had come up with the *least* imaginative name possible for their injured bird. 'You mean Martina. She was a girl.'

He grins. 'Fine. Martina. You gave up that time with your dad to take care of a stunned bird. Not many kids would do that.'

Her father must've been disappointed she'd pulled out of their trip but he hid it well, never once making her feel guilty. He is so very different from her mother.

'And the way you took care of your mum after what happened ...'

He's looking at her as though she is a rare jewel. 'I know it wasn't easy. She took it all out on you.'

'Her entire life fell apart,' she says, defending her mother even as she remembers the snark and criticisms flung her way after they lost him.

He nods. 'But you were there for her.'

'You don't abandon your family,' she says, parroting her mother.

He nods. 'Like I said, you're the most morally grounded person I know.'

She swallows thickly. What would he think of her if he knew she was sleeping with a married man? Is *in love* with a married man? Is living in that married man's secret house? That her entire world has been reduced to him and their affair? There is nothing morally grounded about her life now. She's acutely aware that the loss of her father changed her mother. Until now, she hadn't considered how much it had changed her, too. She'd been an easy, conscientious teenager, never getting into trouble. She'd gone to university, got a job, settled into a stable relationship, ticked all the boxes you are told to tick to find happiness, and still her father made his choice.

Just then, her phone vibrates with a message from Linden. As she reads it, disappointment sinks like a stone in her gut.

'Everything OK?' asks Peter.

She drags her gaze from her screen. 'He's cancelled.'

'Ah. Poor form.'

The night she imagined, one of reconciliation and great sex, dissolves. She can't bear the thought of another night spent all alone at Paddledown, so when Peter asks if she wants another drink, she agrees. 'Raspberry mojito, right?'

'You remembered.' She takes a moment to digest how she feels about Peter. She reaches for the rawness of their break-up, but where she expected a weeping wound, or even a scar, she is pleasantly surprised to find only smooth, unmarred skin. And, as he orders her a cocktail, she feels a familiar, uncomplicated affection for him that has been exhumed from the topsoil of post break-up anger and grief and frustration.

They sit and talk and drink, the promise she made to herself to just have the one glass of wine forgotten. They reminisce, the sunlight of their past warming her skin. Soon, the pub walls sway and the floor slip-slides from beneath her heels. As Peter helps her into a taxi, she can taste the tequila shots they did earlier. With her head in that perfect nook between neck and shoulder, she breathes in pine and cedarwood, and she falls asleep.

She is woken by Peter's hand on her arm, gently shaking her. 'Home sweet home,' he says.

She stumbles out of the taxi and is surprised to see Paddledown, sure she didn't give the taxi driver her address. Peter pays. She fumbles in her bag for her house key but has trouble getting it into the lock. Peter's body is warm and solid against her back. She hears the taxi pulling away and wonders why he is still here. She turns to him, intending to ask him to go. As she does, he swoops, his mouth claiming hers. She tastes tequila and beer. She whips her head to the side and Peter rears back. 'Sorry, I thought . . .'

She brings her fingers to her lips and shakes her head. Then she turns away from him and slips into the house. He follows. 'I'm so sorry. Can we just—'

'You need to leave.'

'But—'

The door to their right opens. Linden fills it.

'What're you doing here?' she breathes.

He looks past her, his gaze zeroing in on Peter. 'She asked you to leave.'

There is a long, terrible silence.

She steps towards Peter, wanting to quietly tell him to go, but Linden grabs her wrist. It doesn't hurt but surprises her enough that she yelps.

'Stop,' barks Peter, reaching to help her. Linden lets her go and steps around her, shoving Peter into the door frame. The sound of him hitting the wood makes her wince. Peter rights himself, hands balling into fists.

'Don't,' she pleads with him. When they were teenagers, he took a lead pipe to the car of a neighbour who'd hit his dog, killing the greyhound, and driven off without stopping. Peter was so furious, she worried that if the neighbour caught them, tried to stop him, Peter might beat him to death. But Peter's father found them and wrestled the lead pipe from his son. Seeing the same murderous look on his face now, she is glad Peter doesn't have a weapon. 'Just go home.'

As Peter's eyes find hers, his rage dissipates and is replaced with something much worse: hurt. He is hurt that she is sending him away. That she didn't kiss him back. But she can't think about that now. Not with Linden standing so close.

Peter leaves without a word and as she watches him go, she wonders how he knew her address. And whether it's the first time he's ever been to Paddledown.

Chapter Twenty-Two

The Wife

Our first day at Windermere was hectic. The movers arrived late and they had another client to get to so Linden and I were running back and forth unloading boxes from the lorry. Later, sweaty and exhausted, I stood in our new living room, surrounded by a mound of chaos. The movers were gone and Linden was nowhere to be seen. I called for him. My voice echoed around the house I knew was too big for just the two of us. When he didn't answer, I went searching for him. Then I heard the low, unmistakable burr of my husband's voice. We'd been married for almost eighteen months and I was only just getting used to calling him 'husband'. It'd felt akin to putting on my mother's stilettos as a child and tottering around in them. I didn't feel grown up enough to be someone's wife. Being married was for older people. *Real* people. Ones who fully understood mortgages and tax forms and how to clean the dishwasher filter.

Linden was outside talking to a pretty woman with olive skin and a mane of dark curls. She was wearing a pair of bright yellow Dr. Martens that, on her, looked cool, and on me, would look clumsy. Linden noticed me first. He spun in my direction and I remember thinking he looked like a boy caught with his hand in the cookie jar but then his eyes crinkled at their corners.

'And this is my beautiful wife,' he'd said, holding his hand out to me. I took it and let him lead me down the steps to join them. 'Verity, meet our new neighbour . . .' He trailed off, gaze sliding apologetically to the woman. 'Sorry, I didn't catch your name.'

There was a beat of silence before she turned to me with a smile. 'Mimi,' she offered.

Linden nodded. 'Good to meet you, Mimi.'

Why did they pretend not to know one another? I replay that moment over and over. How close had they been standing together when I discovered them? Was his hand on her waist? Was she gazing up into his eyes just as she was in that photograph? And what had they been talking about? I imagine them whispering to one another in low, flirtatious voices right before I opened the front door and then later, naked and lounging together, laughing about how easily I was deceived and congratulating themselves on a plan well executed.

Addison babbles to me about how she saw the photograph at Mimi's when she'd gone over for lunch. That it was on the coffee table with a bunch of other old pictures Mimi had been sorting through. She tells me that, when confronted, Mimi became defensive, refusing to explain how she knew Linden and why they'd been dishonest about it. That she'd warned Addison to keep quiet and insisted nothing untoward was going on. How Addison had been dubious but, like me, couldn't imagine Mimi and Linden together. I'm struggling to organise my thoughts, to contain the mounting rage that my best friend and my husband betrayed me. And that my cousin kept it from me.

Mimi and Linden weren't even friendly. Occasionally, I'd catch her looking at him as though he were a rat scurrying along her kitchen counter. But maybe she knew I was watching her and it was all an Oscar-worthy act. Once, after too many raspberry mojitos in her lounge, I'd said, 'You don't like my husband, do you?'

She'd stiffened and stared into her drink. I felt the change in atmosphere as clearly as if it was the clang of a gong. It had slipped from giddy elation to something strained and uncomfortable. But then Mimi smiled, dispelling the tension so quickly I wondered if I'd imagined it, and said, 'Well, I certainly don't like him as much as you do, but that's probably for the best, isn't it?'

'I wanted to talk to Linden about it,' Addison is saying. 'I was going to insist he come clean with you but I was never alone with him and then . . . well . . . then he died.'

My breath is coming too fast. I grip the kitchen counter. I cannot believe . . . cannot *believe* Mimi lied to me. Fury bubbles beneath my skin like acid. I turn on Addison and spit, 'Why didn't you tell me *yourself*?'

She blanches. 'I didn't have all the facts.'

'You had a fucking photograph.'

'That I *stole* from your adored best friend. Truly, Verity, I thought you'd shoot the messenger.'

I bite my lip to stop myself from saying something she'll regret hearing. Pushing my fingers back through my hair, even amid my confusion and grief and fury, I find myself hating how short it is. 'You've known for over a year . . .'

'Yes, but it wasn't really my place, was it? Mimi took off. I thought if the police questioned her as thoroughly as you said they did that they'd have found out the two of them had known one another for a long time. I was sure if anything nefarious had happened between them that the police would know and feed it back to you. It's only after we found those lilac lover letters stowed beneath the floorboards that I wondered whether Mimi and Linden were more than just neighbours. When I suggested as much, you shot me down.'

She's right. I dismissed her. Dismissed all of it. If she'd shown me the photograph, I'd have confronted Mimi myself, before she fled Rook Lane. 'Why are you only telling me this now?'

'The pig's head,' she said. 'I suspected Mimi was behind it. That she was trying to scare you into disengaging with the police so they didn't uncover her secret. So, after you fell asleep, I went next door. I thought if I confronted her, told her I suspected *she* had been having an affair with Linden, she wouldn't be bold enough to attempt any more stunts.' She sighs deeply. 'I was just trying to protect you.'

I am quiet, trying to work out how much of Addison's story I believe. She is convinced Mimi killed Linden. Discovering now that Mimi has been lying to me for *years*, she feels like a stranger and I wonder if you can ever truly know someone. 'Everyone's a liar,' I say, feeling the truth of Mimi's words thrumming through my bones.

'I didn't lie,' insists Addison. 'I omitted.'

'SAME THING!'

She stumbles back, shocked by my outburst. I'm so angry, so *wrecked*, I am shaking.

'I thought you'd want to know,' she says after a moment.

She is like a cat dropping a dead bird at my feet. She thinks she has given me a gift when, in reality, she has given me a horrific mess to clean up. If I don't leave right now, I will explode and leave black smears of myself, of our friendship, all over the off-white walls of her home. So I go. I turn and I leave. She's still calling after me as I get into my car and drive away.

I cannot believe I handed out my trust as readily as one-penny sweets. I drive around Bath for a while. I am too livid to go home. I know if I do, I will hammer on Mimi's door until she answers. The way she looked at Linden in that photograph . . . it's so familiar, so intimate. I try to imagine them fucking. Try to picture my best friend riding my husband. His fingers in the mane of dark curls, pulling her head back to expose her throat. I feel queasy. I reject the image of them together. Even with the photograph, I can't believe they were ever romantically involved.

And I can't believe Mimi would hurt me like that. We were close. Like family. After a night spent watching another true-crime documentary on Netflix, Mimi joked, 'If I ever need to bury a body, I'm calling you.'

I grinned. 'I'll provide the shovel and the alibi.'

Addison is right; things between me and her changed after I met Mimi. My inner circle expanded while hers did not. For a moment, I wonder if Addison somehow faked the photograph – after all, she has a degree in photography. But no . . . I don't think she'd do that, not when a simple conversation with Mimi would unveil her lie. Which means Mimi and Linden knew each other long before they claimed they did. But why hide it?

Mimi and I shared an intense bond. One Addison had, on occasion, referred to as 'suffocating', but I didn't find anything suffocating about how Mimi and I loved each other. My friendship with her made me feel safe because I knew, no matter what time of day or night, we'd always be there for one another. That, at the end of every stressful work situation or disagreement with Linden, there was Mimi, waiting with a pitcher of raspberry mojitos and a sympathetic ear. I never felt suffocated; rather, I felt I could breathe more easily knowing she'd always be by my side. Mimi was bounce and art and spontaneity. She was up for anything. She was always on the move, always turning her hand to a new hobby, and dragging me along with her, insisting I shouldn't spend all my time on Verity Rose and Linden. We once got kicked out of a pottery class after sneaking in a flask of gin and re-enacting that scene from *Ghost*. I can still hear Mimi's off-key rendition of 'Unchained Melody'. We'd got a taxi home and stood before Linden like two giggling schoolgirls caught by a disappointed parent. Linden had escorted Mimi next door which, at the time, I'd thought was sweet of him. Now though, I wonder if he lingered on her doorstep. Kissed her. But I just . . . I can't imagine them together. I really believed, *really* believed, Mimi disliked my husband and I was *sure* he disliked her too. They never had a row or a cross word but they often dug at one another. Just a few months before his death, Mimi and I were having supper together. Linden was supposed to be out with friends but they'd cancelled and so he moped around the house like a child on a rainy day. He scoffed at Mimi's supermarket-bought rosé and insisted he'd never drink anything from a screw-cap bottle, then proceeded to insult her job translating books for Harrier's. 'I could never spend all day reading *genre fiction*. If I were you, my brain would leak out of my ears. No, I need something a lot more challenging, the kind of writing where the words on the page really matter.'

'Like your books, you mean?' she'd quipped. 'And how is that third novel coming along, Linden? Are there any words on the page yet, or . . .'

He'd pressed his lips tightly together before turning on his heel and stalking away. She'd watched him go, trying to hide her smile behind her wine glass.

But was that all an act? A game of pretend? Were they treating each other with snark just to stop me from sniffing out their affair? Any why her? Why my best friend? Jesus, how many women was my husband fucking behind my back?

I drive around for another forty-five minutes because I'm afraid of what I'll do if I see Mimi. Instead of calming down though, I wind myself into a frenzy imagining the two of them keeping secrets, whispering in corners, *lying* to me, but remind myself that I've won because though Linden was once a man who could fill a room all by himself, now he can fill only an urn. I'm glad he's dead because dead men can't hurt or deceive or betray. These are dark, sour thoughts I know I will be ashamed of later once the rage has burnt off. At this moment, though, I stoke it because I'd rather burn with fury than weep with devastation.

Finally, I pull into Rook Lane. I bang on Mimi's door until my knuckles redden. She either isn't in or is smart enough not to answer, but I want her to be aware I know her secret so I take the photograph and post it through her letterbox.

Chapter Twenty-Three

The Other Woman

When Peter is gone, she whirls towards Linden, an explanation already on her lips. She expects to be met with anger. Instead, he comes close enough that she can breathe him in. Black pepper and ginger. Shampoo and wine. He reaches out and brushes her hair back from her face. He says one word: 'Upstairs.'

She is drunk, and keeps missing the steps. He leads her to the bathroom where he takes his time undressing her. She stands before him, naked, while he is fully clothed. His gaze travels over her body and she's pleased when his breath comes faster: he wants her. She may not have a ring on her finger, but she still wields power because she is desirable. Linden kisses her, grabbing the back of her neck and pulling her to him. He runs the shower and soon he is naked too and they are beneath its hot spray. It's not long before he's inside her, rougher with her than usual. He bites down on her shoulder hard enough to bruise, branding her, marking her as his.

She doesn't remember getting into bed but when she wakes, she is alone. For one terrifying minute, she is sure Linden is gone forever, but then she hears the fridge closing and the sound of pans being taken from the cupboard as he makes breakfast. Relieved, she flops back onto her pillow, her head pounding. But by the time the smell of cooked bacon wafts up the stairs, she has showered and slipped into a pretty sundress. She applies a thick layer of moisturiser to her face because alcohol always makes her skin dry. Then she dabs light-reflecting concealer under her eyes. She uses a tinted lip balm, mascara, a stroke of blusher. She is determined to be better than the girl she was last night. The one who shared too many raspberry mojitos with her ex-boyfriend. She thinks of the ominous notes that she has hidden in her underwear drawer and wonders whether Peter is the author. She still can't remember telling him where she lived. So how did he know? She decides she will confront him. But first, she and Linden are going to reconcile. She will not lose him. When they met, she'd been determined to keep her heart out of it. Their tryst was meant to be all about the thrill, the great sex, the fleeting impermanence of it all. But now, almost five months deep, she realises she'd been naive because even though she recovered from her last heartbreak, she is certain she wouldn't survive losing Linden.

He is serving up fat bacon rolls as she enters the kitchen. He doesn't smile. In silence, she goes to the fridge and pours two glasses of orange juice. Linden carries the breakfast to the little oak table. They sit but she is too anxious to eat. She feels like a wayward child in the headmaster's office.

'Who is he?' asks Linden.

She tries to sound light and easy when she answers. 'Peter.' He raises one, querying brow and waits for her to elaborate. She shifts uncomfortably on the wooden seat. 'My ex.'

'Ah.'

The silence that settles around them is thick with disappointment.

'I bumped into him at The Talbot. I didn't invite him to Paddledown . . . it wasn't like that.'

'Like what?' He is daring her to say it, to bring sex into it, but she refuses to be goaded.

'He was just making sure I got home safely.'

'I'm not convinced the only thing he had on his mind was your safety.'

She blushes. 'I told him to leave.'

'And I made him go.'

She can feel his anger rising like steam and, for just a moment, she wishes she was back at The Talbot with Peter. Easy, uncomplicated Peter. 'It was just a couple of drinks.'

'Did you want it to be more?'

'No. Of course not. Of the two of us, *I'm* not sleeping with anyone else, am I?'

He dumps his roll onto his plate. 'Meaning?'

She's making this worse, but she can't back out of this conversation now. 'Let's not pretend you're trapped in a sexless marriage, Linden.'

He scowls. 'So last night was what? A taste of my own medicine?'

'No.' She sighs. She doesn't want to argue. She loves Linden even if loving him isn't easy. 'I didn't choose The Talbot, *you* did.' Her tone is gentler now. 'I had no idea Peter would be there and no clue you'd be waiting for me here.'

'Do you wish I wasn't?'

'No.'

'Did you want to fuck him?'

'No.'

'You should,' he says. His earlier antagonism lies forgotten alongside his breakfast. He looks defeated. The summer sun streams through the French doors and she notices how tired he looks. 'He's closer to your age. He's probably single. He can take you for dinner without looking over his shoulder. You can go out in the daylight instead of skulking around in the dark.'

She remembers Linden sinking his teeth into her shoulder last night and thinks of vampires. But if Linden is Dracula, she can't claim to be Dracula's Bride. Just the mistress. Just the secret he keeps hidden in the house by the canal.

Linden stands then walks around to her side of the table and offers her his hand. She takes it and he tugs her to her feet. Then he winds his arms around her waist and pulls her to him. 'I'm sorry I was upset about your mother being here. I was being irrational.'

She softens. 'No, you weren't. It's your house.'

He squeezes her. '*Our* house,' he corrects. 'It would be so much easier if you lived closer. You know, I've considered selling Paddledown and putting in an offer for the house next door to mine.'

'Why?'

'For you.'

She frowns. 'What do you mean . . . ?'

He leans in conspiratorially. 'Wouldn't this' – he gestures between the two of them – 'be so much easier if you were only a stone's throw away?'

She studies his face. Sees that he is serious. 'I don't think I could cope watching you and your wife playing house every day. And she isn't stupid. She'd sniff us out in a heartbeat.'

There is more to Linden's suggestion than ease. He wants her close to ward off other men. Men like Peter. Even though she knows it shouldn't, Linden's spark of jealousy pleases her. It means he really cares.

'We'll put on a play. Pretend to hate each other.' He kisses his way up her throat. It feels so good, she presses herself against him.

'Warring neighbours on the streets, lovers between the sheets?'

He grins into her neck. 'Exactly.' His teeth graze her throat and then his mouth finds hers. She wants him. Wants him naked and inside her again but then he sighs and pulls away.

'What is it?'

He looks pained. 'I just can't bear the thought of someone finding out about us and this, us, coming to an end.'

She stiffens. She always suspected he would cut her out of his life if anyone uncovered their affair, but thinking it and hearing him say it are two very different things. A sickening dread swirls within her and she knows she can *never* tell Linden about the notes. If she wants the two of them to stay together, she must find the author before they start sending letters to Linden. Or, worse, before they go to Linden's wife, just as they'd threatened. If not, she'll lose him.

Chapter Twenty-Four

The Wife

Mimi doesn't seek me out to explain or apologise like I hoped she would when I posted the photograph through her door. In fact, I'm not sure she's even staying at her house. The lights are off and her car hasn't appeared outside. I've knocked a couple of times but she never answers.

Addison sends flowers and chocolates and my favourite perfume. She calls a dozen times a day for a week. She apologises over and over again. I don't go into the office. I work from home, from coffee shops, and I ignore my cousin's pleas for forgiveness. Maybe I am being too harsh but I am so angry at Linden, at Mimi, at her, at the dishonesty of it all.

It's all become so complicated. I find myself missing my life before Linden's murder. Missing how close I was to Addison. Though she'd been there for me since my husband's death and Mimi leaving, I've had my guard up. Built walls tall enough to keep out everyone I once loved. But now, in the face of yet more lies, I long for the relationship I had with Addison before my world was shattered. Neither of us had a sister but in each other, it felt like we did.

During the long stints in which my aunt dumped Addison at our grandmother's house, I'd spend as much time with her as possible. It was always the same; in the first few days after being deserted by her mother, Addison had the look of a dog abandoned at a shelter. She was nervous and pining, fearful and too thin. Even at the height of summer, Nanna Violet would bundle us into her small kitchen to bake. 'It's good for the soul,' she'd say in her creamy Somerset accent. Addison would brighten and Nanna Violet would serve her an extra slice of cake, frowning at her protruding collarbones and the sharpness of her jaw. Even after our grandmother died, Addison and I would bake together when one of us was feeling low or stressed. We'd blast nineties hits while we whisked flour and eggs and ate too much of whatever chocolate was intended for the recipe. A year into her marriage with Harry, she showed up on my doorstep with a bag of raw ingredients and red-rimmed eyes. Wordlessly, I let her inside. It was only after we'd shut the oven door that she sank to the floor in front of it and said, 'I got my period again.'

We've always been there for each other. It's rare to know a person long enough that they love you as a girl and as a woman. We have so much history and yet all of it less complicated than our present.

Almost nine days after our fight, as I pull onto my driveway, Addison is waiting for me on the stone steps. She looks tired, her dark hair is limp and there are shadows beneath her eyes. She stands to greet me, clutching a bulging tote bag. 'I'm sorry.'

Then I see that in the bag is flour and eggs, butter and caster sugar. 'It's good for the soul,' she says.

And for the first time in days, a small smile curls my lips.

'I'm sorry,' she repeats, tears in her dark eyes.

I'm exhausted. Too exhausted to hold on to another grudge. I need Addison. From the moment we stepped into that wardrobe and found Linden's secrets squirrelled away beneath the floorboards, we've been on a path together, searching for breadcrumbs, making our way to the gingerbread house of revelations. I can't do it alone.

So I tell her I forgive her and she promises never to lie to me again.

Chapter Twenty-Five

The Wife

We hold the Verity Rose Winter Party every year. Though last November, in the wake of Linden's death, it was cancelled. One of the harshest lessons I learned after the loss of my husband is that even when your world comes to a grinding halt, for everyone else, it just keeps turning. When the deepest sympathy cards stop arriving and the bouquets of flowers around you start to wilt, so too does people's interest in your pain. Even while you can't move on, as gripped by grief as you are, they can. Your living nightmare becomes their passing thought.

Despite my adulterous, murdered husband, the severed pig's head and my lying friend, Addison insists the party must go on, reminding me I have a brand to protect and a life to rebuild. As I slip into a silver beaded cocktail dress, I transform from Verity Lockwood, Linden's window, to Verity Rose, CEO and hostess.

Though our office is beautiful, it isn't big enough to hold two hundred guests, so we hired Lullington Manor, a stately home on the outskirts of Bath. It's all high ceilings, dark wood and grand, sweeping staircases. Servers glide through the crowds with trays of canapés and glasses of champagne. There's a live band in the ballroom and a bar set up in the library. Outside on the lawn is a firepit and a hot chocolate wagon. It's the perfect networking event, packed with influencers, bloggers, journalists, brand reps, PR agents and our freelancers.

During the last winter party we held, I'd stood off to the side to give myself a moment to drink it all in. I felt bewildered and grateful that so many people had taken time out of their lives to celebrate another year of Verity Rose. It's strange to think this is the first one I've hosted without Linden. I want to pretend he was unwaveringly supportive of this party, but that wouldn't be truthful. The year before his murder, he'd been surly and irritable. His usual glass of red was dismissed in favour of whisky, which he only drank when he was in a sour mood. He'd stood on the fringes, staring down into the amber liquid as though he wanted to drown himself in it.

'What's wrong?' I'd asked, voice low and cajoling. 'Not feeling well?'

'This entire event is ridiculous,' he'd said, and I felt as though he'd thrown his drink over me. 'Don't you think it's all a bit much?'

Words jammed in my throat. I was *proud* of this event. The brand I'd built. The life it allowed us to lead. But Linden never wanted a wife with a career. With a passion outside of our marriage. Outside of him. From the day we met, it was apparent to us both that he was smarter, more sophisticated, more successful. And that's the way he preferred it. But things had changed. It surprised me that someone so handsome, so educated, born into so much wealth, could be so insecure. So *incapable* of sharing the limelight. I told myself he didn't mean what he said. That he loved me. That I'd spent less time with him and he was hurt. So I made myself smaller. Shortened my speech. Left my party early. At home, I used sex to soothe him. Let him take charge. Let him have me however he wanted. After, he apologised for his behaviour. Told me I was Verity Lockwood, Queen of Hearts, and he an unworthy king. But my reign was short. I didn't know it then, but I'd been usurped from my throne.

'Penny for them?' says Addison, arriving at my side with two glasses of pale champagne.

I take one from her. 'Sorry?'

'Your thoughts . . .'

'Oh. Right. Yes, sorry. I was just thinking about Linden.'

She nods. 'He did love a party.'

When it was about him, I think. The more I've learned about my husband since his death, the more I've noticed the chinks and scratches in our 'perfect' marriage. 'You look incredible,' I tell Addison. She's wearing a floor-length navy gown with a high neck and a low back.

She swishes the skirt of her dress and bobs a curtsey. 'Why thank you.'

'And where's Harry?'

'He's talking to the travel blogger Luke Northman about the Jordan desert. I think he fancies himself as an explorer.'

'The two of you did live abroad for a couple of years.'

'Yes. In America. Where there are bathrooms and restaurants, not endless sand and searing heat.'

Then, to my shock, we are joined by Colette. The ivory suit is tailored to perfection, striking against her dark skin. 'You're here?'

Too late, I realise how rude that sounded. I open my mouth to apologise but she beats me to it. 'I do still work with you, don't I?' she says with a little mirthless laugh.

Technically, she works *for* me but I don't correct her, knowing it will only anger her further. 'Of course. I just meant . . . you haven't come to the winter party before.'

'Well, I'm usually busy. No one ever consults me about the date for the party but, on this occasion, I didn't have any other plans.'

Addison glances between the two of us with a morbid glee unique to those able to watch a drama unfold without being at the centre of it.

'OK, well, excellent. As always, Colette, it's a pleasure. Do help yourself to the canapés,' I say, knowing she won't. I'm pretty sure she only feeds off air and the tears of virgins. As long as they're organic.

The smile she turns on me is one of contempt. Then, without another word, she slithers back into the crowd.

'She really doesn't like you, does she?' asks Addison, staring after her.

'Not at all.'

'Why?'

I sip my champagne. 'Never asked.'

'I'd fire her if she spoke to me like that. Why haven't you fired her?'

I shrug. 'She's great at her job,' I say, thinking of how well she steered the company in my absence. Without her, it would have all fallen apart.

'But don't you want to know *why* she doesn't like you?'

'If it was that important, don't you think she'd have told me herself?'

We move through the ballroom and I spot Flora by the bar. Her long red hair tumbles down her back. Her ivory dress is silk with a boat neckline and fluttery angel sleeves. A vision of innocence. So different from the short scarlet number she was wearing the night I saw her kissing someone else's husband.

Despite telling her she could bring someone, she's come alone. Did I really expect her to show up with her married lover? He looked *so* much like Linden. I wonder again about the woman who ordered the pig's head from the butcher's and the man who picked it up and gave them my husband's name. It certainly fits, doesn't it? But why would they be involved?

The night winds on. I give the crowd my dimples and my charm and my glowing, golden gratitude that they came. Heidi arrives late because her youngest wouldn't settle. I don't ask why her husband isn't capable of putting his own child to bed and instead I summon a passing waitress for a glass of wine. Heidi takes it gratefully and downs it in three gulps. 'It really was such a faff trying to get all the children to sleep,' she's telling me. 'I even whipped out *The Lion, the Witch and the Wardrobe*.'

'That was my favourite book when I was little,' remarks Colette as she joins our group. I try *not* to look at her for fear her withering glare might melt the skin from my bones.

'I did say you could bring the kids,' I tell Heidi.

'Yes, but last time Jamie spent the evening sliding across the dance floor and Cleo put her entire face in the chocolate fountain. Honestly, I love being a mum but you should all make the most of your child-free time.'

I glance over at Addison who has stiffened, her fingers tightening around the stem of her glass. Heidi, unaware of her blunder, ploughs on. 'My three adore you, Verity. You're so good with children, you'd make an excellent mother.'

In a bid to erase Addison's frown, I quip, 'I'd make an excellent crack dealer too, but I'm not going to do that anytime soon either.'

There's a stunned silence.

To my relief, Addison laughs. And the corner of Colette's mouth lifts in a rare, genuine smile.

The party spins around me. People grow louder, clumsier, drunker. Addison has gone to find us more drinks. My feet are aching in my heels and I'm already looking forward to taking off my makeup and climbing into bed. Then I see Amy. She is standing by herself, sipping a blood-red cocktail, gaze roaming slowly over the guests. She's content to be alone. Most people would be reaching for the social crutch of their mobile. Not her. She exudes confidence. It pours out of her, and I find myself wishing it was something you could bottle and spritz like perfume. Her dress is the same icy blue as her eyes. Her pale blonde hair is pulled up in a high, sleek ponytail. The swishy kind that would've made her popular at school. She'd have been the athletic type, the girl everyone wanted on their team for sports day. I imagine she had a charmed childhood. That is until I remember someone close to her killed themselves.

She looks up. Our eyes lock. It would be rude not to go over and talk to her. She's so self-assured and unshakeable, I become clunky and awkward in her presence. Reminding myself I am the head of a global brand and this is my party, I make my way over. 'Thank you for coming,' I say. 'Are you alone?'

'Guilty,' she says.

'You could've brought someone with you. A date, a friend. The redhead?' I say. I'm fishing for information but, as anticipated, Amy doesn't take the bait.

'Redhead?'

'The woman who came by our table at the Rye Bakery,' I say, not convinced she's forgotten.

'Oh. Yes.' She sips her drink. 'To be honest, I'm quite comfortable coming to parties alone. More time to people-watch. Meet interesting people. Mingle, that sort of thing.'

Doubt creeps in; maybe I'm being paranoid about Amy not wanting to introduce me to her friend. 'It's the first Verity Rose ball you've attended, isn't it?'

She holds up her glass. 'Yes, and with the open bar it won't be my last.'

I smile. 'It's safe to assume you won't be going for a late-night run after this?'

'Can you imagine? I'd be running sideways after a few more drinks.'

'You like to run?' asks Addison, emerging from the crowd. She hands me a glass of champagne.

Amy's gaze slides over her. 'I do.'

'Amy, this is my cousin Addison,' I offer.

Amy nods. 'Nice to meet you.'

Addison sips her wine but doesn't reply, openly appraising Amy with a critical, penetrating eye. If she's looking for flaws, she won't find any. From her pale blonde hair to her Louboutin heels, Amy is perfect.

A thin layer of frost has formed. In an attempt to thaw it, I say, 'Amy's running the Bath half-marathon in March. She's raising money for Men's Minds Matter. It's a suicide prevention charity.'

Addison raises one dark brow. 'Someone you know killed themselves?'

The colour drains from my face; her question isn't just blunt, it's *invasive*.

Amy isn't rattled, though. She sips her blood-red cocktail and says, 'My father.'

'That's terrible,' says Addison without feeling. 'How did he do it?'

I open my mouth to admonish her but close it again when Amy says, 'Threw himself into the River Avon. My mother insists he jumped but I think he fell.'

Addison's nose wrinkles. 'If you don't think he took his own life, why are you raising money for suicide prevention?'

'Because it's important to my mother.'

Addison nods. 'Right.'

Amy watches her with bemusement. My cousin has extracted more information from Amy in three minutes than I have in three years. As embarrassed by her directness as I am, I can't help being impressed by it, too.

'Verity told me you and Linden go quite far back,' says Addison.

All at once, Amy's bemused smile slips and is replaced by a hard, thin line. 'That's right.'

'And how is it you two knew each other?'

I know I should intervene, change the subject, but I don't because I want to hear what Amy has to say. With me, she was evasive but maybe she'll respond better to Addison's more cut-throat approach.

'Like I told Verity, I don't really remember.'

'That's vague.'

Amy's eyes narrow. 'And how about you, Addison? Were you and Linden close?'

She shrugs. 'Not particularly, but then I didn't know him as long as you did.'

'I hardly think the length of a relationship determines its intensity, do you?'

They are glaring at one another. The atmosphere is tangible; you could reach out and pluck it like a violin string.

Addison sips her drink, eyes fixed on Amy over the rim of her glass. 'Did you and Linden ever date?'

'*Addison!*' I scold.

Amy brings herself to her full height. She's a few inches taller than Addison. 'No,' she says in cool, measured tones. 'We didn't date. Why would you think we did?'

She shrugs. 'I just wondered if that's why you were being so evasive.'

'Evasive?' There's an edge to Amy's voice now, sharp like cut glass. 'You look a lot like Verity. If Linden had a type . . .'

Something dark and resolute passes over Addison's face. She opens her mouth to snap back at Amy but I've had enough. 'Don't,' I warn. The two of them turn their attention to me, as though suddenly remembering I'm still here. I don't know whether it's the alcohol or the intensity of their exchange that is making my head spin.

'Verity, are you OK?' Addison's voice is gentle and ripe with concern.

'I'm fine.'

Amy steps closer to me. 'You don't look fine.'

And to my horror, my vision swims. I don't know where the tears have come from. I want to blame the alcohol but I've only had a couple of glasses. Being here tonight, for the first time without Linden, has made me feel acutely alone. I was blind in my marriage to Linden even though I went in with my eyes wide open. I thought I knew every inch of the man I loved. Even the dark, dangerous parts most would run from. But he obviously couldn't be trusted. Addison's instincts are right. I can *feel* it in my bones, just as I did that day at the Rye Bakery: Amy has slept with my husband. How many others were there? How many times did the love of my life plunge a knife into my back, and why is it only now that I feel the blade cutting through flesh? One moment I want to shake the truth from Amy and, in the next, I want to run from her so I never have to hear it.

'Verity, do you need to sit down?' asks Amy.

I blink up into her impossibly beautiful face. 'I found some letters,' I hear myself say. And I watch carefully for her reaction. 'Love letters.'

'Verity, don't,' warns Addison. I know when I ask her later *why* she didn't want me to tell Amy about Linden's affair, she'll say it's because she's worried about my brand and what will happen to it if people realise I didn't have the perfect relationship I wrote about and advised others on finding.

In this moment though, I don't care. I *need* to know what Amy will say in the face of Linden's betrayal. 'From another woman.'

In my peripheral vision, I see my cousin shake her head.

'Oh,' says Amy. Disappointingly, her expression is as unreadable as ever. 'Right. That's . . . I'm sorry. I—'

But she's cut off by a flustered-looking Flora. 'Verity, you're needed. There's been an issue in the cloakroom. The guy who was managing it has gone home unwell but he locked the door and no one can find a key, so any guests who are leaving can't get to their coats.'

I seize the distraction with both hands. 'There's a box of spare keys in the study at the back of the house. I'll come and sort it out.'

Flora looks visibly relieved. 'Great. Thanks.' She turns to Amy and Addison. 'Sorry for interrupting.'

Amy is watching Flora with measured interest. 'I don't think we've been introduced.'

She smiles. 'Flora,' she offers. 'Verity's assistant.'

'Flora,' says Amy, turning the younger woman's name over in her mouth like a boiled sweet. Amy's smile is small and private. I wonder what the joke is, but I'm not brave enough to ask.

'Verity, are you feeling all right?' asks Flora, green eyes searching my face. 'You're really pale.'

'Think I've had one too many drinks,' I lie.

After finding the spare key, Flora agrees to a stint managing the cloakroom, and I return to the party. The music is too loud and the large house too hot. I am desperate for this night to be over, for the crowd to thin and dwindle to a trickle of guests so I can make my escape, but the throng seems to swell, a steady rush of people surging around me. Addison and Amy are nowhere to be seen.

I'm in the foyer, turning towards the library to look for Addison when a waitress makes a beeline for me. 'Mrs Lockwood?' she asks.

It's been such a long time since anyone addressed me as Mrs Lockwood. Am I still a Mrs if my husband is dead? And do I want to keep his name? Honestly, I wasn't keen on taking it in the first place but Linden insisted. 'Really, Verity, you're being very difficult. Your name isn't even yours anyway. It's your father's.'

Of course it was *my* name. Even if it had been my father's first, it was mine at birth and I wasn't sure if I wanted to give it up, but Linden pointed out that his family name was a household name and that I'd alienate my soon-to-be in-laws if I didn't honour that.

'I have a note for you,' says the waitress, and hands me a folded piece of cream paper. 'A guest asked me to pass it on.'

I open it.

If you want answers, join me for a drink in the wine cellar at 11 p.m. L x

Dread slithers into the pit of my stomach. 'Who gave this to you?'

'A man.'

'What man? What did he look like?'

She shrugs. 'Tall, blond, attractive.'

My heart is racing so fast, I feel faint. 'Thank you,' I say and pocket the note. The waitress moves off. The grandfather clock in the foyer tells me I have only a minute to get to the cellar. I automatically reach for my phone but it is in my handbag somewhere in this sprawling house. Even if I had it, who would I call? Addison, Heidi? I'm sure the author of that note intended for me to come alone. I cast around for someone I know but I am looking at a wall of only vaguely familiar faces. I could grab a random guest, but how would I explain why I'm dragging them into a cellar? If this were a horror film, I'd be screaming at the idiot woman who is seriously considering going into the basement of an old manor all by herself, but this is real life and there are people everywhere. All over this house. How much danger can I really be in? If someone wanted to hurt me, they wouldn't do it at a party teeming with guests. I know Linden isn't waiting for me. He's dead. But whoever's been tormenting me might be in that cellar, and they're right, I do want answers. More than that, I *need* them. I want to know for sure who left the pig's head outside my back door. I want to know *why* they don't want me talking to the police. I want to know exactly who they are. Maybe this is a game of humiliation and I'll go to that cellar only to be left standing alone in the dark. There's one way to find out.

Decision made, I hurry towards the cellar at the back of the house.

Chapter Twenty-Six

The Other Woman

Two days after reconciling with Linden, another note appears through her door. This one is typed and folded. *He can't be trusted.*

As she reads it, anger ripples to the surface. Why is this person interfering? Why do they even care? She is sure Peter is behind this. After all, he knew about Paddledown even though she'd never told him. Perhaps they hadn't simply bumped into one another at The Talbot. Maybe he followed her there, too. Strange, he never struck her as the stalking type. If Peter is responsible for the notes, and she's pretty certain he is, she is furious with him. He was the one who ended their relationship, and two years later he's decided to meddle in her life because he's holding on to some virtuous version of her that she burnt after he broke her heart. She worries she deleted Peter's phone number along with Anna's and anyone else she hadn't spoken to in months, but she's relieved to see she hasn't. She must put an end to these wretched notes before he takes it any further. She sends him a message, asking to meet. He replies almost immediately.

Two hours later, she waits for him outside Bath Abbey. It's too hot. Her long hair clings to her face in sweat-damp clumps. She stares out across the square and watches people passing by. Businessmen shiny with sweat, on their way to meetings; tourists posing for photographs outside The Pump Room; vendors selling ice creams and overpriced bottles of water; groups of women laden with glossy shopping bags; carefree couples walking together, fingers entwined. She feels a stab of pain that she and Linden can't do that. For as long as he is married, they can't stroll together through the city in broad daylight.

She spots Peter crossing the square towards her. Even in this heat, he is wearing faded black skinny jeans and a band T-shirt. Despite how angry she is with him, when he smiles at her, she feels herself relax a little. 'I was surprised you wanted to see me after last time.'

She remembers his mouth on hers. How it felt both unexpected and inevitable. But then she blinks the memory away and decides to get straight to the point. 'How did you know where I lived?'

He looks taken aback. 'What?'

'You gave the taxi driver my address,' she says, not knowing if this is accurate but feeling sure she didn't give it to him herself. 'How did you know where I lived? I didn't tell you.'

'Your mum told me.'

'My mum?' she asks, not bothering to hide her disbelief. Though her mother was always fond of Peter, if not his lip piercing or his scuffed Vans, she can't imagine the two of them gossiping together.

'I bumped into her at a supermarket a few days before The Talbot and she told me you'd moved into a house by the canal. Paddledown.'

Her eyes narrow. 'Why would she tell you that?'

'Because I asked after you . . .' She doesn't know whether he's being honest but she's sure he isn't stupid enough to tell a lie she could simply uncover in one conversation with her mother. 'She said the two of you fell out. That you haven't been to see her since?'

'When did you and my mother become best friends?' she snaps, feeling guilty that her ex seems chattier with her mother than she is.

'We're worried about you,' he says. '*I'm* worried about you.'

'Why?'

'Because I care.'

And then he catches her wrist, his thumb stroking over her pulse, just as he did when he met her off the train on their first date. She had been late, her train delayed and delayed again. By the time they reached the fancy Italian restaurant he'd booked, it was closed. She worried he'd be annoyed but there was an easiness about Peter, a buoyancy. Unperturbed, he'd taken her hand and they'd walked through the city. It was late. The only place open was a run-down-looking fish and chip shop. 'They'll probably be the best fish and chips we've ever had,' he enthused. They weren't. The fish was mostly batter and the chips were hard enough to crack teeth but she'd never felt as connected to someone as she did to Peter. He asked her questions and was genuinely interested in her answers. And at the end of the night, he kissed the salt from her mouth. Staring up into his eyes now, she believes he cares about her in a time in her life when many people don't. So why play games? Why post letters through her door? She snatches her wrist away from him and he winces as though she has slapped him. 'Have you been sending me notes?'

He frowns. 'Notes . . . ?'

'Yes. Notes. Threatening, ominous notes.'

His eyebrows shoot up. 'You really think I'd do that?'

She shrugs.

'You know me,' he insists. 'I know you.'

But he doesn't, does he? Not anymore. When he left her, it made her feel disposable. She spent months sifting through herself, panning for impurities, looking for whatever it was that made her so easy to abandon. Even if Peter has suddenly decided she's now deserving of his affection, she's turned herself into someone who isn't. 'Just stop sending me notes, stop following me, stop talking to my mother.'

A crowd of tourists with bulging rucksacks and bulky cameras surges towards them. She's said what she needs to say, so she starts walking away. Peter calls her name and jogs after her, dodging between people in the crowd. He catches up easily and swings into her path. 'Can you please just listen to me. I haven't sent you any notes. I'd never . . .' She searches his face for deceit but finds only genuine confusion. 'What do the notes say?'

She wants to tell him. Wants to talk to *someone* about her life. About Linden. The affair. About sex and power and what it means. About the notes. But she can't. Telling Peter would be like setting alight her relationship with Linden and watching it burn to ash. 'Doesn't matter.'

'I'm worried for you.'

'I'm fine.'

She makes to move past him but he blocks her path again. 'Who was that man in your house?'

'None of your business.'

'He isn't right for you.'

'You don't know him.'

'I know you and I know you aren't happy.'

She freezes. It feels as though he has just ripped the shower curtain down to expose her naked, wet body. She swallows. 'Don't be ridiculous.'

He moves closer and she lets him. 'You deserve to be happy.'

She shakes her head.

'There are other people who miss you,' he tells her. 'Your mum, your friends. Anna said—'

'You spoke to Anna? But Anna doesn't even like you,' she says. Maybe that was unkind and not entirely accurate. Anna did like Peter but she was jealous of how much time he took up. 'Did you bump into her too? Just like you *happened* to bump into my mother at the supermarket and then me at The Talbot?'

His cheeks turn pink. 'I'm not some crazed stalker.'

'If the shoe fits . . .'

His eyes search her face again. 'What has he done to you?'

The question pierces her skin. She feels it enter her bloodstream, slicing as it moves within her.

'Anna said you cut her off. Lucy said she hasn't heard from you in months. Mel told me you bailed on her birthday. You've disappeared from your entire social circle.'

She turns on her heel and strides away from him, past The Abbey, walking towards Performer's Square where a man plays Vivaldi on a violin. Peter bounds after her again. A Labrador that won't be left behind. 'Stop following me.'

'Will you please just—'

'Stop stalking me. Stop harassing me. Stop sending me notes.'

'I'M NOT SENDING YOU NOTES!' Pigeons take flight. The man with the violin falters. Dozens of pairs of eyes turn their way. Peter's cheeks are bright pink. He lowers his voice. 'Is this erratic behaviour because of your dad, or—'

'No.' She feels as though an icy hand has reached inside her chest and taken hold of her lungs. 'Leave him out of it.'

'Then it's that guy, the one who was at Paddledown. Are you together?'

'Stop.'

'It's his house, isn't it? Is that how you can afford to live there by yourself?'

'It's none of your business.'

'I *care* about you, even if you don't care about yourself. You're so thin, and you look sad and tired.'

'Thanks.'

'Is he stopping you from seeing your friends? Your mum?'

'No. Linden wouldn't—'

'Linden?'

And too late she realises her mistake. She wants to take the word and cram it back into her mouth. 'I've been busy.' She thinks of the seconds and hours and days she pours into Linden. 'Busy with work,' she lies. 'That's why I haven't had time to hang out in coffee shops or go for drinks or . . . Anna has a trust fund. I mean, it's OK for her. She can just dip into Daddy's money whenever she wants to go to an expensive restaurant or club.'

But Peter doesn't take the bait. He refuses to be derailed. He zeroes in on Linden. 'He's older.'

'No, he isn't . . . not by much,' she says, defensive now because if a younger woman with a complex relationship with her father deigns to date an older man, the 'daddy issues' alarm bells start to chime. Ones she can see are ringing loudly in Peter's head.

'Does he make a habit of housing his girlfriends?'

'No.'

'You don't really think you're the only one he's let live in that house?'

He has found a purple bruise and presses his thumb into it.

'I know men like him,' he tells her. 'The BMW, the Rolex, the expensive suit. You're just another shiny object he wants to keep all to himself.'

'You have no idea *what* you're talking about.'

'He isn't good for you. Relying on someone this much isn't good for you.'

'He gave me somewhere to live when I needed it.'

'You mean he waited until you were vulnerable before swooping in and scooping you up. He took advantage. You're like the house martin we rescued. The one that was stunned and injured, only he hasn't given you a home, a safe place to heal, he's given you a gilded cage. Men like him don't set women like you free.'

She is breathing hard, his words hitting her like bullets. 'You don't get to do this,' she says. 'You don't get to drop back into my life after two years and tell me how to live it. You don't know me. I'm not innocent, Peter. Have you ever wondered whether *I'm* the one taking advantage of *him*?'

He shakes his head. 'You're a good person.'

'No, I'm not.'

'You're selfless.'

'You're wrong.'

'Penelope asked something of you that no mother should but you did it anyway. For her. Because you're selfless. Because—'

'Linden's married!' she yelps like a dog that's been kicked. Then she claps a hand over her mouth. But it's too late. Peter pales. She feels sick, regretting it immediately. But why? Hasn't she got exactly what she wanted? She took a sledgehammer to the fictional version of her that he holds dear and smashed it to pieces.

Chapter Twenty-Seven

The Wife

The first year we hosted this event at Lullington Manor, we stored some wine in the cellar so I have a vague memory of where it's located at the back of the house. Along the way, I pass a waiter and, thinking quickly, ask him to tell Addison I'm meeting Linden down there and to join us there as soon as she gets the message. Obviously, he has no idea who Addison is so I describe her dress and explain she looks like me but with long hair. He nods, though he's clearly baffled.

With time running out, I move past him and through the dimly lit warren of corridors. I come across a console table tucked away in an alcove. I open the drawers, searching for something to use as a weapon. Just in case. I find loose sheets of paper, a broken brooch and a silver letter opener. I pick it up. It's blunt but better than nothing. The more I think about it, the surer I become that no one will be there to meet me. I believe the pig's head and this note were sent by the same person. Someone who sends threats from a distance, who prefers to remain anonymous. So why would they arrange a face-to-face meeting? It's more than likely that this is a way for them to exercise power over me. To clap their hands and see if I will dance. Still, I don't want to turn back now. I want to go to the cellar to prove whoever is tormenting me is as cowardly as I think they are.

As I venture deeper into the belly of the house, the noise of the party gets further and further away. Then I am standing outside the heavy barn-style door that leads into the wine cellar, painfully aware of how quiet it is. How far removed I am from the safety of the crowds. Surely if I can't hear the guests, the guests can't hear me, either.

I stand statue-still, fingers on the latch, ready to lift it and let myself inside. I'd been so sure that if I came here, no one would be brazen enough or stupid enough to attack me when there are people crawling all over this house, but the cellar is not as close to the party as I anticipated. My earlier bravado drains from me; I snatch my fingers from the latch and back away from the door. I can't believe how reckless, how *stupid* I've been. I'm turning to leave when I hear it. A man's voice calling my name. A man with Linden's public-school drawl. Goose bumps bloom across my skin and my heart stutters in my chest. The voice rises from the depths of the wine cellar. I am torn between terror and curiosity. And even though it killed the cat, I take a step closer and press my ear against the wood.

I wait.

I listen.

Silence.

Feeling an idiot, I am about to pull away when I hear it again. 'Verity.'

It's as though my entire body has been submerged in iced water. The shock of it renders me still. Unable to draw breath. It is definitely a man's voice. Before I can stop myself, I am flipping up the latch and wrenching open the door. I hurry down the stone steps but almost tumble in my heels. I stop and wrestle them off my feet, dropping them on the stairs. Then I sprint until I hit the bottom. The cellar is cold and damp and dark, lit only by a single anaemic light that does little to illuminate the vast space. It's laid out like a library with rows of shelves steeped in shadow. Plenty of hiding places.

'Who are you?' I call out into the dark.

No one answers.

But I feel eyes on me.

The only thing worse than being alone in the cellar of an old manor is sensing that you aren't. I clutch the letter opener in one hand and remind myself that I am not defenceless and that Addison will likely be here any minute. I move slowly and quietly away from the steps, eyes running down each aisle. I hear him breathing. Somewhere in this cellar, he waits.

'Why're you doing this?' I say into the dark.

There's movement to my left, the rustle of fabric, and I spin towards the noise. I can't see anything, though; the corners are thick with shadow. Getting any closer would mean moving away from the stone steps and my only exit. Fear curls like smoke through my blood. I hold my breath and listen. I'm met with an eerie, absolute silence but I can *feel* him watching. And I decide the best thing is to go upstairs and lock the door behind me, trapping him down here until Addison arrives.

I back up, fingers tightly clasped around the letter opener, and keep my gaze trained on that shadowed corner. I imagine him leaping from it, running at me, tackling me to the cold stone floor. Still walking backwards, I crash into something warm and hard. A scream unfurls in my throat but a hand clamps over my mouth and an arm locks around my middle, pinning me in place. I struggle but he's bigger than me, taller, stronger. So much stronger. The letter opener slips from my fingers and clatters to the ground. He kicks it away and it spins into the gloom. I pitch forward, hoping to unbalance him but his grip around me only tightens until I think my ribs might break. I am a wild, thrashing thing in his arms. Then he swings me round, up and off my feet. I scream into his hand. He hurls me to the ground. My head cracks against the stone floor and I am sucked into the dark.

Chapter Twenty-Eight

The Other Woman

She cannot believe she was impulsive enough, foolish enough, to tell Peter that Linden is married. Months of careful secrecy. One conversation to undo it all. She can still see Peter's face, looking at her in disgust. In disappointment. Like he had finally travelled to the end of the rainbow and realised there was no pot of gold. Just a chest of dirty pennies.

She steps off the bus onto the Lakeside Campus. It's August, so most of the university students have gone home for the summer, but she knows that somewhere Linden is here. The need to see him floods her bloodstream, making her feverish. He can't ever know how she has just betrayed them. Can't ever know about the anonymous notes. She is sure that as soon as she is in Linden's arms, the panic will subside.

She walks the main path through the sprawling campus. To her right is the student accommodation, to her left is a postcard-perfect view of the blue skies and cloud-white sheep grazing green fields. Bath Springs University is steeped in history with its twelfth-century castle tower, grand Georgian manor and lake. Linden is lucky to work somewhere this beautiful. She thinks about her desk with its browning calathea plant and view of a magnolia wall.

Linden isn't in his office. She knocks and knocks but he doesn't answer. She calls him but it rings through to voicemail. She is gripped by the irrational fear that he knows she told Peter about their affair, that he knows she's been receiving anonymous notes, and he has decided to snip her from his life as easily as a split end. But of course he doesn't know. He can't. Still, he isn't at the refectory and the library is closed for refurbishments. Urgency pounds within her. She feels like an untethered kite in a storm. She strides past the amphitheatre and veers off the path in the direction of the lake. Her heart is beating too fast in her chest. She can't breathe. Can't think. She stands on the hill that rolls down towards the lake.

Water has always made her feel calmer. When she was a child, her father took her to Mayfly Ponds. She remembers the first time she saw the tub of slimy, writhing worms. He taught her how to bait a hook. She'd hated the pop and crunch of the metal sliding into the wriggling worm. When they finally caught a fish, she cried at the sight of its bloodied mouth and wide, unblinking eyes. Her father threw it back into the water. Then he kissed her cheek and told her she was his 'gentle soul'. They spent the rest of that afternoon drinking hot chocolate from flasks and watching the sun set, enjoying the gold spill of dwindling light on the lake's still surface. She wants to feel that serenity now. Longs for it. Longs for her father.

Reeds gather in the brackish shallows of the campus lake. It's fringed by a grass slope and bowing willow trees that graze the water. Among them is a weathered stone temple with three open arches and a bench made of the same cream brick. It's collecting just enough moss to look pretty. Linden took her there once after dark, during the Easter break. He had a basket of tealight candles, strong cheese, fruity wine. It rained. The two of them huddled together inside the temple. She can still feel the icy water dripping down her back, and the warmth of his mouth on hers.

She is caught in the memory of his fingers moving her underwear to one side when Linden strides into view and she is thrust into the present. His blond hair gleams in the sunlight as he steps into the temple and is framed in the middle archway. She is about to call his name when he is joined by a girl. Not a *girl*, exactly; a young woman. A young, attractive woman wearing tiny denim shorts and a fitted white T-shirt. Her long, shiny hair streams down her back. They are much too far away for their conversation to be overheard and the girl is in profile, too distant to clearly make out her features. But her body language speaks volumes – she seems to be pleading with Linden. She reaches out to grab the sleeve of his shirt but he steps calmly out of reach. She covers her face with her hands. Linden is talking, his mouth moving quickly, but she only shakes her head, as though she can't bear to hear it. Then Linden says something that makes the girl's head jerk up. She lunges at him, her hand shooting out to slap his face, but Linden is faster, seizing her wrist and holding it captive. Their eyes lock. Their faces are so close, all the girl would have to do is tilt her mouth up to his and they could kiss. But instead she tries to pull herself free. Linden holds on to her for a moment longer before finally releasing her. The girl turns on her heel and jogs away from him, down the stone steps. Linden thrusts his hands into his pockets and watches her go.

Chapter Twenty-Nine

The Wife

As I surface from the depths of unconsciousness, I am in pain. Everything aches. There are hands on me. Turning me onto my back. I whimper, terror tightening my muscles.

'Verity, can you hear me? Can you open your eyes?' And at the sound of Addison's voice, relief spreads through me like butter on hot toast.

'Do we need to call an ambulance?' Another voice – northern – and shot through with panic.

'Heidi, do you have any signal down here?' asks Addison.

I force my eyes open but am momentarily blinded by the sickly, anaemic light overhead. My mouth is dry and my head throbs. I struggle to sit up. Pain shoots through my ribs and radiates across the front of my skull. Addison is kneeling beside me, dark eyes laden with worry. I'm still in the cellar but at least I'm not alone.

'That's a nasty cut,' says Heidi, examining my forehead. 'I think we should call an ambulance.'

I touch it, wincing as it stings, and my fingers come away sticky with blood. 'Don't,' I manage. 'Please.'

Addison and Heidi exchange a look.

'Did you fall?' asks Heidi in a tone I imagine she uses to soothe her children.

'I . . .' My heart leaps around like a rabbit caught in a trap as I am accosted by the memory of a man's hand covering my mouth, stifling my scream, and the frightening ease with which he tossed me aside.

165

Dandy Smith

Addison's gaze finds mine. 'I was with Heidi when I got your message.'

'I really think we need to call an ambulance,' says Heidi again, pulling her phone from her clutch bag.

'No,' I yelp. 'No, don't. I had too much to drink and I fell ... I feel like an idiot as it is.' Addison presses her lips together. She knows I am lying. 'An ambulance will worry the guests, and it'll be the only thing people remember about this party.' This, at least, is the truth.

Heidi's round face creases in disapproval. 'You've had a nasty knock to the head. I think—'

'I'll take care of her.' Addison's tone leaves no room for discussion. She holds out her hand and hauls me to my feet. I'm a little unsteady. The room spins around me and I have to fight the urge to sit back down.

I look to Addison. 'Can we get out of here?'

After assuring Heidi I'll see a doctor tomorrow, I make her promise not to tell anyone I took a tumble down the cellar stairs and then I send her back into the party. The second floor of Lullington Manor is out of bounds to guests, so Addison and I head up there for some privacy. The landing is vast and grand; the walls are adorned with oil paintings in heavy frames and the floor is decorated with a thick Persian rug. We cross it to the French doors that open on to a balcony. Below is the front garden, elaborate with its topiary hedges and statues, fountains and twinkling fairy lights strung between carved wooden poles. The November wind whips around me and I shiver, though I haven't been able to get warm since I entered the cellar. Addison ducks back inside and emerges moments later with a damp cloth. I take it from her and press it to the gash on my forehead, baring my teeth against the sting.

'What happened?' asks Addison. Her cheeks are flushed and her long dark hair streams like inky ribbons in the wind. 'The waiter said you were going into the cellar to meet *Linden*?'

I tell her about the note the waitress handed to me and the description of the man who gave it to her.

'Well, it wasn't Linden ...' she says.

'Of course not, but I think it could be the man we saw with Flora.'

'But Flora came alone.'

'I know.' I lean against the iron railing and rub at the dense fog building between my eyes.

'Why would your assistant's married lover lure you to a cellar to attack you? That doesn't seem likely.'

'But the corpse of my murdered husband does?'

'No,' she concedes. 'Obviously not. But then why . . .'

'I don't know. I think the pig's head and the cellar, using Linden's name, it's all to scare me or . . . distract me, maybe?'

'Distract you? Distract you from what?'

'Finding out the truth. Linden clearly had a lot of secrets.'

We lapse into silence. I can feel Addison turning it all over in her mind. 'What about Amy?'

I take a deep breath, remembering how my cousin had interrogated her. 'You were one evasive answer away from waterboarding her.'

She straightens, defensive. 'Hardly. I only asked if she'd ever dated Linden. It's not like I demanded to know her bra size.'

'You don't like her.'

'No, and I don't trust her either,' she says icily. 'Do you?'

'No,' I admit. 'I don't.'

'Then why tell her about the affair?'

'I wanted to gauge her reaction.'

'And?'

I swallow around the jealousy and hurt, the betrayal and white-hot fury. 'I think she slept with him, though I'm not sure when. Maybe it was before Linden and I were married.'

Addison nods but doesn't comment. Her silent doubt coats my hope like thick black soot. The gravel driveway is bathed in a warm glow as guests leave the party with raised spirits and loud voices.

'Can I please say something without you getting angry?' asks Addison after a moment.

If someone requests you *not* get angry at what they're about to say, it usually means they're about to say something to make you angry, but refusing to hear her out would be immature and I'll spend the rest of the night wondering. 'Go ahead,' I say and brace myself.

'Your success is built on people believing you have the perfect life: the perfect house, the perfect career, the perfect relationship. Is it really a good idea to tell anyone he was sleeping with someone else? Don't look at me like that, Verity, I'm trying to protect your brand. I'm trying to help. And before you tell me Linden's murder proved your life isn't perfect, I disagree. Your readers saw it for what it was: a tragedy out of your control. But when it comes to straying husbands, people are less forgiving. Whether they admit it or not, they always wonder what it is the woman did to make him stray. Whether we like it or not, women are held responsible for men's bad behaviour.'

I want to tell her she's wrong but there's truth in what she's saying. I nod sagely into the dark. Then I see a willowy blonde woman stepping out into the night. She is wrapped up in a gorgeous white fur coat: Amy. We watch in silence as she taps away at her phone. A car winds down the gravel driveway. She looks up, sees it and makes her way over. She pockets her phone. Then stills. She pulls out a piece of paper.

Lilac paper.

My world tilts off its axis.

She turns it over in her hands before scrunching it into a ball and thrusting it back into her pocket.

Chapter Thirty

The Wife

It's been three days since the Verity Rose Winter Party. I am plagued by nightmares of men emerging from shadows. In my dreams, he picks up a fire poker and beats me to death with it. I wake with a start, sweat-drenched and nauseous. I've barely slept. Every time I climb into bed, questions buzz around my mind like a thousand restless bees, stinging me awake.

I have called and emailed Amy a stalkerish number of times. She's ignoring me. Yesterday I finally got through to her new office where a bored-sounding receptionist informed me that for the next few days Amy's in Germany. I'm not sure I believe her but I know how to find out. First, I drive to her office in Frome and even though it's a Tuesday afternoon, it's closed. I suppose, though, if Amy really *is* away, it would make sense for her sole employee to work from home.

I curb the urge to scream. I want to talk to her about the lilac paper, the same paper used to pen love letters to my husband. In Addison's mind, this has cemented Amy as the other woman, but *why* would she bring a single sheet of lilac paper to a party? Still, I trust the instinct that tells me Amy and Linden were once together. To what extent and when, I'm not sure, but I'm determined to find out.

Bradford-on-Avon is a little market town bustling with character: winding cobbled streets, buildings and bridges in creamy Cotswold stone. Through its heart runs the river. It's a crisp day, the sun is golden and bright in the vast blue sky. Christmas is in the air. I stop and look at the lights in the shop windows. Last year, I spent the holiday in Belgium with my father and Agathe. We pottered around winter markets with steaming cups of gluhwein and ate bûche de Noël. I long to go back this year, but with everything that is happening here, leaving would feel like running. I have to see this through. Lately, my life has felt like one giant puzzle that I am hunched over, scrabbling for pieces with frantic, fumbling fingers. Impossible to complete unless I unearth the nature of Amy's relationship with Linden.

I keep walking, discovering pockets of pretty houses I've never seen before. Eventually, I reach the three-storey building I've been looking for. Amy lives on the top floor. I still have her address from all the years we sent Christmas and birthday cards. Hoping she hasn't moved in the last few months, I ring the buzzer for her apartment. No one answers and though I suspected as much, I feel a pang of disappointment. I loiter outside. A man in a Barbour jacket walking a boisterous springer spaniel is striding in my direction. He eyes me warily, as though I am dressed in a stripy black and white T-shirt, wearing an eye mask and carrying a bag labelled 'swag'. I give him what I hope is a disarming smile as he passes, and he nods brusquely in my direction. Then I take my phone from my coat pocket and pretend to scroll through it so as not to draw attention to myself while I consider what to do next. Maybe Amy really is abroad, but I'm not leaving without answers. I go back to the panel of buttons and press each one. The first two apartments I try don't pick up but, much to my relief, the third one does.

'I'm trying to get up to Amy Carter's apartment,' I say vaguely into the speaker.

'Oh, yes, are you the house-sitter?' A woman's smooth Somerset accent comes through the tinny speaker.

'Yes,' I lie. I hold my breath, praying she won't ask my name. She doesn't.

'Oh, good, you're early. Come right up.'

Heart racing in triumph, I am buzzed inside the building.

As I reach the third floor, I am greeted by an older woman with grey hair and wide hips. 'Amy has left a list of instructions on the kitchen countertop. I'd usually take care of the place myself but I'm visiting my brother in Dorset,' she explains. 'My train leaves in an hour.'

I nod but decide the less I say, the better. She produces a brass key on a monogrammed leather fob and offers it to me. I hesitate, just a moment, feeling a pang of guilt because no matter how I try to justify it, I am taking advantage of this elderly lady's trusting nature, fooling her into thinking I'm someone I'm not. But what's the alternative? Go home and keep obsessing? Live the rest of my life without ever knowing the truth? This may be my only opportunity. As my hand closes over hers, I imagine a Venus flytrap clamping shut around a small, oblivious insect.

I let myself inside Amy's apartment. It's light and spacious with hardwood floors and quartz countertops. The lounge and kitchen are done in moody slate greys and dark navys, but her bedroom is softer, with creams and touches of dusky pink. I walk around the apartment a few times, not sure where to start or what it is, exactly, I'm looking for.

In the kitchen, I open drawers and cupboard doors but I'm met with all the things you expect to find: utensils and cutlery, cleaning products and pans. I pick up the pestle and mortar on the side. At the bottom of the bowl is a sprinkle of green herb dust. Of course Amy is the type of together woman that owns and actually *uses* a pestle and mortar. I bet she grinds her own kale for her super-green smoothie every morning before she goes on a run. I wouldn't be surprised to learn that her sweat smells like a Jo Malone perfume.

In the lounge, I riffle through the sideboard but find nothing more interesting than old birthday cards and half a dozen Diptyque candles. Her books are arranged by colour, flowing seamlessly from light to dark. Linden would have hated that. I'd wanted to arrange our bookshelves in the same way but he'd said, 'Books are to be read and studied and devoured. They aren't ornamental, Verity. They aren't for show.' I find yoga manuals and healthy cookbooks, travel guides and the occasional thriller.

I look around the apartment of this perfect woman and feel painfully inadequate. I've been writing about my life for years. Putting out into the public eye a carefully curated version of myself. Since finding out about Linden's affair, whenever I look back at those articles, I feel like a fraud. As though it is a lie. A life I wanted, or rather, wanted people to think I had, instead of the life I was actually living. But Amy *is* the woman I was pretending to be. From the matching pots and pans in the kitchen to the shampoo and conditioner she has decanted into amber bottles in the bathroom, everything in Amy's apartment, everything in Amy's life, is meticulous and perfect. On the windowsill is a photograph of her with the redhead from the Rye Bakery. They are standing, arms wrapped around one another, in front of the Eiffel Tower. They must be very close if they're on holiday together. The only other framed photo is of Amy with her mother; they're cheek to cheek, smiling brightly into the camera. I feel a sharp pang remembering the last time I saw my mother before she died.

I go back to the bedroom and open up the wardrobe. I see the white fur coat she wore on the night of the party and search the pockets. The lilac paper is gone. Then I get down on my hands and knees to test the base of the wardrobe. It's solid. I crawl over to the bed and pull out the wicker storage baskets beneath it. In the first, I find spare linen; in the second, I find a large wooden box. I take it out and set it on the cream rug beside me. I stare at it. And I know that I am about to uncover something I'd probably rather not, but ignorance isn't always bliss. In fact, in my experience, it is maddening. So I open the lid.

Inside are photographs. Dozens and dozens of photographs. They are of Linden, mostly taken unawares: him browsing a shop window, sunglasses resting on his head; sitting on a park bench in winter, nursing a takeaway cup of coffee; having dinner in a restaurant we'd visited together a hundred times. I flip through the images, faster and faster, my thoughts whirling. She's been watching him for years. I go from hot to cold and back again. Did Linden know? Did he have any idea his accountant was also his stalker? Maybe they didn't sleep together. Maybe Amy only wishes they did. While I'm appalled, I'm also secretly relieved Amy wasn't another of Linden's mistresses. No wonder she hasn't been able to settle into another long-term relationship; she's too preoccupied fantasising over mine.

Even though I know she is out of the country, my skin still prickles with panic at the thought of her returning to find me knee-deep in her darkest secret. Is it possible *she's* behind the severed pig's head? Was she trying to ward me off, distract me from finding out she's an obsessive stalker? Even though I know the head was collected from a butcher, I imagine Amy slaughtering the squealing pig herself. Hacking at it, cutting through flesh and muscle, tendon and bone. I retch, remembering its putrid stench.

Addison would advise me to get out. To call the police and tell them Linden was being followed for years before his murder. But how would I explain that I moonlighted as a house-sitter to gain access to Amy's property? Surely any evidence I gathered would be inadmissible in court? The police usually require a warrant to enter someone's home, not a lie and a bit of luck. Even though I didn't smash a window or kick down a door to gain entry, I'm pretty sure this is classed as a break-in. Still, I take out my phone and snap some photographs of what I've found, worried if I take any of it, Amy might notice.

I'm scooping them all up and putting them back in the box when I see the corner of a book I recognise. Pushing the remaining photographs and polaroids aside, I uncover a copy of Linden's first novel. I lift it from the box and turn it over in my hands. Unlike the paperbacks on her shelf, the pages of this book are yellowing and dog-eared. It's well loved. Or, much to Linden's gratification, it has been visibly *read and studied and devoured*. I flip to the first page and a volt of electricity zips through me when I see a hand-scrawled note from my husband:

I would know your soul anywhere. The shape and taste and touch of it. I will love you always. In this lifetime and the next. In death and everything that comes after. L x

Chapter Thirty-One

The Other Woman

She believed Linden when he said she was the only woman he'd had outside of his marriage. He'd made her feel chosen. Special. Desired. There had been power in knowing that she, and she alone, was enough to lure another man from his marital bed. That she was wanted enough for him to risk everything just to have her. His one and only mistress. But he and the girl were too intimate with one another, too volatile, to be anything other than lovers. He has lied to her. He has tricked her. Her heart beats so fast against her ribs that she is sure they will splinter and break. She hates him. Hates his blond hair and his amber eyes. Hates that he is charismatic and gorgeous and fun. Hates even more that he is exploitative and selfish. Hates that he is terrible at housework but brilliant at sex. Hates most of all that he has her whole heart and has chosen to squash it beneath his expensive leather shoes. She hates him so much she imagines hitting him with a rock and drowning him in the lake.

He does not see her standing up on the hill, watching him. He doesn't chase after the girl. Instead, he turns and walks leisurely in the opposite direction, following the path up the slope which will eventually lead him to the kissing gate on her right. She storms across the hillside to meet him. His eyes widen when he sees her. 'What're you doing here?'

Her chest is heaving. Fury curls her hands into fists. 'Who was that?'

He frowns. 'Who was who?'

She swallows around the lump of anger in her throat. 'The girl. The girl you were just with. Who is she?'

Surprise flickers across his face but it quickly hardens into accusation. 'Were you spying on me?'

'Who is she, Linden?'

He lifts his chin. 'Who do you think she is?'

'Are you sleeping with her?'

His eyes narrow. 'No.'

'Who is she then?'

He shakes his head and walks past her. She stands, staring down the dusty, well-trodden path beyond the kissing gate. She cannot believe he has dismissed her as though she is one of his students. She spins on her heel and follows him. She wants to hit him. Wants to keep hitting him until he doesn't get back up. She isn't her father's 'gentle soul' anymore. She is a woman spurned and tricked and used. 'WHO IS SHE?' she screams at his retreating back. Birds scatter.

Linden whips around and stalks towards her. 'Do *not* do this here,' he says with such menace, she knows she should probably be scared.

'Then where?'

He snatches her wrist and starts towing her across campus, his long legs moving quickly. She stumbles to keep up. They stop outside the library which is closed over the summer for renovations. He pulls a key card from his pocket and uses it to unlock the doors. Inside, it is cool and dimly lit. Anger comes off him in waves. 'What do you think you're playing at?' he snaps. 'Turning up to my place of work and screaming like a banshee, for fuck's sake.'

She stares up into his face, searching for the adoration, the affection, the desire that normally greets her. But there is only fury. Her own rage seems to have drained from her. She feels shaky and weak and, to her horror, a sob swells in her chest. She chokes it back. 'Just tell me who she is.'

He considers her a moment before answering. 'A disgruntled student.'

'You expect me to believe that?'

'She didn't get the grade on her dissertation that she wanted.'

She can taste his deception. Linden is lying to her. Or at least, he is not giving her the whole truth. 'She tried to slap you.'

Surprise flickers across his face. He hadn't realised how much of their exchange she'd witnessed. 'She isn't stable.'

'OK. What's that got to do with you?'

He stares at her, weighing up how much to tell her. She resists the urge to pepper him with questions, hoping he will fill the silence. 'She's infatuated with me.'

Just for a second, his mouth quirks upward, smug. Of course Linden is pleased to be the subject of a young woman's obsession, but was it one-way? She doubts that. 'Has anything happened between you?'

'No,' he affirms. 'She's a student.'

She searches his face for signs that he is lying but his expression is carefully blank. 'Go on,' she says.

His lips thin. He wants her to drop it but she *needs* him to convince her he's telling the truth. 'She comes from a difficult family situation. I could see she was struggling with the course so I offered to help. That's how her infatuation began. When I realised how out of hand it had become, I told her to transfer to another class.'

'And?'

'She refused.'

'Why didn't *you* ask for her to be transferred?'

'Because then I'd have to explain to my head of department why.'

'But why not confide in him? If you really have nothing to hide ...'

'I didn't want to ruin the girl's reputation. She's a promising young woman. I don't want to be responsible for depriving her of future opportunities. It's rare for a woman to come out of these situations smelling of roses.'

She doubts him. Wants to extract the truth from him like a rotten tooth. 'Or were you worried you'd get in trouble for encouraging her?'

'I didn't do anything wrong,' he snaps. 'She was following me to my car at night, turning up outside my house, writing me letters, slipping notes into my bag.'

Her skin prickles. 'Notes?'

'Yes. Notes.'

Is this girl the one who's been tormenting her? If she's been following Linden then she will know about Paddledown. About the two of them. It occurs to her that the girl would more likely attack Linden's lover than Linden himself, perhaps in the hope of driving a wedge between them and clearing the path for herself.

'I'm being honest,' he insists, reaching out and clasping her shoulders. 'There is nothing between me and Millie.'

'Millie?'

'She's just a silly girl with a silly crush.'

'Does your wife know?'

'Not all of it. Just that one of my students has a thing for me.'

'Does she care?'

'You mean, is she threatened?' He frowns. 'No. She trusts me.'

Silly her, she thinks, and wonders if she is silly too because she believes him. Believes Millie is enamoured with him. Has stalked him. Has stalked her. 'Why didn't you tell me?'

'Because Millie doesn't matter to me. I haven't seen her since term ended in June. I didn't expect her to turn up here today. That's the first time she's ever physically lashed out.'

'Do you think you should call the police?'

He shakes his head. 'I've got her under control. She isn't a deranged bunny boiler.'

'Are you sure?' she asks. She is on the verge of telling him about the notes. Maybe if she does, he can talk to Millie and make her stop.

'I'm sure. I don't want to complicate things. If I involve the police and they do some digging . . .'

'They could find me.'

'And that can't happen,' he tells her. Then he grabs her wrist and pulls her to him, moving his free hand up her arm and closing it around her throat. He kisses her. She isn't sure she wants to be kissed so soon after a fight, but the taste of him is intoxicating. Just as she starts to kiss him back, he pulls away, reminding her that he is in control. Always in control. 'I've missed you. When I'm not with you, I'm thinking about you. I can't lose you.' The hand around her throat tightens and she feels not like a lover, but like a possession. 'I won't.'

She thinks about Peter's warning, insisting she is an injured bird trapped in a gilded cage of Linden's making. But what if she doesn't want to be set free? What if she is exactly where she wants to be? Exactly where she deserves to be? Maybe she will only ever be Linden Lockwood's mistress but, as long as she is the only one, perhaps she can accept that.

She reaches up and kisses him with such force, he stumbles back into some shelves. There's the thud of paperbacks hitting the floor. He groans into her mouth, his hands tangling in her long hair. She feels him harden against her. Then, mouth still on hers, he lifts her skirt up and pulls her knickers down her thighs. He turns her. Bends her over. She grips the bookshelves. As he pushes into her, she hears Peter's warning again: *Men like him don't set women like you free.*

Chapter Thirty-Two

The Wife

The note isn't dated. It's possible he wrote it before he and I were ever together. Amy would've been young. Linden is at least a decade her senior. Even if he wasn't aware of Amy following him, he lied to me about the nature of their relationship. It clearly wasn't just professional or platonic. I can't help myself; I tear the pages free and slap the book shut. Then I shove it haphazardly into the wooden box and throw it into the wicker one. Once I've kicked it beneath her bed, I storm into the lounge. I feel like a natural disaster. I want to whirl through her apartment and destroy it all. There's a violence in me so dark, so powerful, that it frightens me. I want to smash and tear, beat and break everything in my path. I have to hold myself perfectly still until the urge subsides. I leave, slamming the door shut behind me. I drop the key onto the mat then jog down the carpeted stairs and out into the sun.

I should go back to work. I have several pieces to write and a handful of contracts to sign before everyone starts winding down for Christmas, but I can't bring myself to go into the office and act as though I haven't just uncovered *another* of my husband's dirty secrets. He knew Mimi years before he claimed to have met her and though it's possible there was nothing romantic between them, why hide it from me? He was clearly involved with Amy at some point in the past and lied about that, too. What else was Linden doing

179

behind my back? And when did the fantasy of me stop living up to the reality? Linden lived for the thrill of beginnings. That much was obvious in how he would dream up new ideas for novels. He'd become infatuated then grow bored and discard them before ever putting pen to paper. Was it the same for him and women? Maybe, once the intoxicating, temporary madness of lust burnt away and he was left only with the mundanity of everyday life, he sought out heat in others. It's crushing to know my love, deep and unfathomable as it was, left my husband cold.

While I'm driving back to Rook Lane, Addison calls me. I don't pick up. I didn't tell her about my planned excursion to Amy's today. I think if I had, she'd have insisted on coming. She took an instant dislike to Amy. Having initially dismissed my suspicion that she and Linden were once lovers, claiming she couldn't imagine Linden with a blonde, I wonder how Addison will feel when I tell her about the photographs and the signed book. Still, I can't face dealing with her outrage on top of my own.

When I arrive home, I notice a car in Mimi's driveway. Not her orange Nissan. This is black and sleek. I get out and move towards it. Has she taken off again, moved elsewhere and decided to rent out her property? Does this car belong to my new neighbour? I'm still eyeing it when I hear her front door open. A man with a mop of dark hair, carrying a leather holdall, walks down the steps towards me. He's wearing skintight black jeans and an aubergine velvet blazer. As he nears me, I note the black nail polish and lip ring. 'Big fan of cars?' he muses.

I smile. 'As long as it gets me from A to B without breaking down, I'm happy.'

'You're pretty easy to please, then.'

'I like to think so.'

He grins, his lip ring glinting in the sunlight. He feels familiar, the type of guy I would have dated in my youth: sulky-faced and alternative. The kind you could share eyeliner with and trust to take you to all the best record shops in Camden. He's what Addison would describe as an Elder Emo. His gaze briefly flits to the healing cut on my forehead. The memory of being in that cellar makes my breath hitch in my throat. Worried he might ask how I got it, I say, 'Is Mimi around?'

'Sorry, no.' He nods towards the holdall in the boot. 'I was just swinging by to collect a few things for her.'

I frown. Is she so desperate to avoid me that she's fled her own home and won't even return to collect her belongings? Or am I being paranoid? Self-involved, even? Maybe this has nothing to do with me and everything to do with this tall, dark stranger. I remember the last time I spoke to Mimi, I'd seen the figure of a man behind her in the kitchen and wonder if this is him. 'I didn't know Mimi had a brother,' I say, knowing she doesn't, but hoping it'll nudge him into telling me the nature of their relationship.

'God, no, I'm not her brother,' he says so vehemently I suppress a smile. 'I'm actually her . . .' His cheeks colour. 'An old friend.'

And the way he says 'friend' as though it is a square peg being shoved into a round hole tells me it isn't quite the right fit. A new boyfriend? Or an ex? She's always careful who she gives her heart to.

'Love isn't a fairy tale,' she'd told me once. 'And even if it was, I wouldn't want it. I mean, look at Cinderella. She settled for a man who forced her to try on a heel because he couldn't recognise her without a full face of makeup.'

'Sorry,' he says. 'I didn't catch your name?'

'Verity.'

His expression darkens. 'Linden's wife?'

I'm so taken aback at the mention of Linden, for a moment I can't find my voice. 'Widow,' I correct.

And he smirks.

I open my mouth to demand *why* he's smirking when he turns away and slams the boot shut. The noise is bullet-loud and makes me jump. Then he stalks around the side of the car and I follow. Riled by his blatant rancour, I say, 'Most people offer their condolences.'

He yanks open the driver's side door. 'Only if they're sorry for your loss.'

I put my hand out to stop him from sliding inside. 'I'm sorry, did you know my husband?'

He lowers his head so our eyes can meet. 'Did you?'

Though his tone is silky, his question cuts deeply. The look he's giving me is so unsettling, my hand drops to my side. I'm still trying to figure out what he meant and how to answer when he ducks into his car and pulls away.

Chapter Thirty-Three

The Other Woman

She spends the next few days keeping an eye out for Millie. Not that she would recognise her in a crowd. The girl had been too far away to make out her features. Still, she is wary of any young, slender woman who veers too close in a crowd.

She feels guilty for accusing Peter of stalking her and terrified he will tell someone about her affair. She makes a smoothie, already knowing her churning anxiety won't let her finish it, and takes it into the garden. She sits at the little bistro set on the wooden jetty that extends into the canal, turning her phone over in her hands. She decides to call him. He picks up just before it rings through to voicemail.

'Yes?' His tone is cold and hard like pebbles in winter.

'Peter . . . I'm sorry for everything I said. I know it wasn't you sending the notes.' Silence rushes down the line. She pulls the phone away from her ear to make sure the call is still connected. When she realises it is, she says, 'I know you must be disgusted with me and I'm sorry for that, but please don't tell anyone.'

He scoffs.

'Peter, *please*.'

'Are you worried he'll kick you out of that house if people find out his dirty little secret?'

Dirty little secret. Is that what he's reduced her to now? Isn't that what she's reduced herself to as well? 'I don't care about the house,' she says honestly. 'I care about him, Peter. I love him.'

He's quiet again. Hurt or angry, she isn't sure. 'And you think a man like that is capable of loving anyone but himself? He's married. He made a vow to another woman and he's broken it.'

'You're right, but what Linden and I have is special, it's—'

'It's no different to what he and his wife had at the beginning of *their* relationship.' This is a slap, stunning her into a nauseating silence. 'I know this is hard for you to hear but he can never love you the way you love him.'

She clutches the phone so hard, her hand starts to hurt. 'You're wrong.'

'And you're deluded.'

She swallows around the thickening lump in her throat and stares out across the water, longing for the calm it used to bring her on boating trips with her father, but still she is swept beneath an undercurrent of guilt and shame and unease.

He exhales, long and hard into her ear. 'He's turned you into someone you aren't.'

She wants to tell Peter there is no point in him making excuses for her, trying to polish out the dents and scratches left by so many disappointments, because she is damaged goods. At least Linden accepts her exactly how she is and doesn't make her feel as though she isn't as shiny as she could be. 'Peter, I just need you to promise you won't tell anyone. You broke my heart and turned my life upside down. Don't you at least owe me this?' It's a cheap shot but she isn't afraid to take it.

'Who would I tell? Who would even care? You've cut everyone you ever loved out of your life.'

She crunches on his words, on the truth of them, as though they are gravel, but she doesn't speak.

'I won't tell anyone,' he concedes after a moment.

She's relieved but she doesn't feel the rush of triumph she thought she might. 'Thank you.'

'But listen to me,' he says in a low, dangerous voice that frightens her. 'If he ever hurts you, *really* hurts you, I'll kill him myself.'

Chapter Thirty-Four

The Wife

The day after sneaking into Amy's house, and my run-in with the man with the lip ring, I email the office and tell them I'm not well and not to expect me. Colette's reply is just as brusque, demanding to know whether I'll be gracing them with my presence tomorrow as I still have a pile of papers waiting for me. I don't bother responding. I can't even bring myself to care. In the last five days, I have been lured into a cellar and attacked, I've discovered my accountant is a stalker who was once involved with my husband and I had a chilling encounter with a dark-haired, smirking stranger next door. And I still don't know who is behind the pig's head and luring me to the cellar or whether they're even related . . . though my gut *insists* they are.

Addison calls and calls again. I don't answer. I fire off a message telling her I have a migraine and I'll be in touch tomorrow. I want to process everything that's happened before dissecting it with her. She's so forceful in her opinions and theories that I don't want her to steamroller over mine.

I shower and pick out some underwear, automatically reaching for something comfy that I can slum around the house in, but stop when I notice the unworn, dark green lingerie I'd bought for a romantic break with Linden. He died before we went. I lift the scant, expensive lace from the drawer. I remember choosing them, dragging Addison into the boutique and gushing excitedly about a few days alone with my husband. She'd hovered awkwardly, glancing around at all the underwear she couldn't afford. I felt so guilty, I offered to treat her, but she refused, saying Harry would think she'd become a wealthy man's mistress.

I wonder how many women Linden bought underwear for while we were together.

I yank off the tag and slip into the balconette and thong. In the changing rooms, they'd fitted like a glove. The bra just grazed my nipples, pushing my modest breasts up until they sat beneath my chin, The thong was so sheer, it was almost invisible. I'd felt all the things you want to feel when you're standing in new underwear: powerful, sexy, desirable. Now though, the cups of the bra flap and the thong keeps slipping down my hipbone.

From the moment I met Linden, I fell easily under his spell. I let his confident, experienced hands mould me. Then he was murdered and now I'm having to learn who I am without him. Not wanting to face the woman I've become in the wake of his death, I've avoided my reflection, but I can't do that indefinitely so I step in front of the floor-length mirror now. And I gasp. The woman staring back at me is shapeless. Not curvy like Mimi, or toned like Addison; not slender like Flora, or athletic like Amy. Just skin and bone.

In my early twenties, I'd longed to be thin in a way I think a lot of women secretly do. I'd wanted elegant, protruding collarbones and a thigh gap. But what I'm met with now is a parody of what I'd wanted. I remind myself of those frail Italian greyhounds with huge eyes and visible ribs, that shiver even in summer. I've lost more weight than I thought this last year. Most of it since walking into that wardrobe with Addison. It wasn't intentional. But the stress of dealing with Linden's affair and then being ambushed by threats and a dismembered head has left me with a sickening anxiety that turns everything I eat into a handful of lint.

The gash above my eye is healing nicely, crusted to a dark rust. My hair is limp and unwashed and, between chin and shoulder, still feels too short. I want to grow it but then I think of how much Linden loved it and I get the urge to hack more of it off. What was it Amy implied? That if Linden had a type, Addison, who looks so much like me, would be his pick.

I take the underwear off, toss it back in the drawer and change into a soft, cream loungewear set. Even though the house is already clean, I decide to spend my afternoon polishing and mopping and hoovering just so I have something to do with my hands. I take out my phone to write a to-do list, already looking forward to the dopamine hit I'll get from ticking off each task. But when I open up the notes on my phone, I catch sight of one I'd written the week after Linden's death.

Linden, being loved by you was like feeling the sun on my skin for the very first time. Some days, the pain of losing you pours out of me like a wave that builds and builds until it crests over my head and I am drowning. I cannot breathe or think. I ache to feel the peace I once did during those long, warm nights spent in the golden harbour of your embrace.

I stare at what I'd written and wince at the lovesick, wallowing woman I was in those early days. Then I delete it and type a new one.

How could you? How could you? How could you? You did this to me. You ruined me. Wrecked me. Turned me inside out. I hate you. I hate you. I hate—

I toss my phone across the room and scream into a pillow until my throat is raw.

Chapter Thirty-Five

The Other Woman

She doesn't know where Linden is taking her. He says it's a surprise. Told her to pack an overnight bag.

It is late September now and the leaves are starting to turn on the trees. The car window is open just a crack. She breathes in the smokiness of a bonfire. She thinks of anoraks and pumpkins, knee-high socks and jackets, chai lattes and sparklers. She doesn't care where they are going, she is just excited at the prospect of time away with him. They haven't had a single night together in almost four weeks. His wife has been travelling less and less. Linden says it's fine, that she often has long stints at home, but she knows this is a lie. She knows this is the first full month his wife has gone without a work trip since her business took off a few years ago. She worries his wife is growing suspicious, that she can feel Linden slipping from her fingers and into the hands of another woman. So, the two of them must make the most of this night away.

Two more notes have arrived from Millie since that day in the library. *You should be ashamed* and *What would his wife think?* She has decided to ignore her in the hope Millie will grow bored and leave her alone. She is confident Millie won't say a word to Linden's wife because, if she did, she'd have to admit to stalking her lecturer. She decides she will not think about Millie or her notes for the rest of their trip and lets herself wonder where they are going.

Linden is excited. He is bouncy and keeps holding her hand, only

188

letting go to change gear. Eventually, his fingers are squeezing her thigh, five points of heat. He wants her as much as she wants him. She cannot wait to get out of this car, to reach their destination, to feel him inside her.

The tightness of the city loosens around them, houses giving way to greenery, roads giving way to dirt tracks, people giving way to sheep. They drive over a stone bridge and down a lane with a little church until they come to a wooden gate. Linden gets out of the car to open it. She leans forward in her seat and reads the plaque on the stone wall: LOCKWOOD HALL.

He returns and as the car crunches along the gravel driveway, she asks breathlessly, 'Am I meeting your family?'

He laughs. 'No. Of course not.'

She immediately feels stupid for thinking it and turns her face away so he doesn't see her disappointment.

'It was my grandfather's,' he explains. 'Father decided to keep it in the family as a holiday home.'

She can't imagine the kind of wealth that allows a family to have a spare house with the same ease most people have a spare tyre. 'It's beautiful,' she says because it is.

They park outside. While Linden fetches their bags from the boot, she stares up at the handsome double-fronted Cotswold stone home with lead lattice windows and a wisteria-framed front door. Linden told her about this place; the Christmases spent here as a child, the enormous, festooned tree in the foyer, the extravagant lunch at the long table in the dining room, and roasting marshmallows in the evening.

He takes her inside. She is met with a sweeping staircase, a chaise longue and a floor-to-ceiling cupboard with a slatted door painted eggshell white. Past the staircase is a kitchen – she spies the quartz countertops and the large cream Aga. To their left is a lounge with a wood burner and a bay window, and to their right is the dining room. He takes her hand and leads her across the threshold. At its heart is the long mahogany table. There's a second bay window in this room with another, larger chaise longue. In the furthest corner is a drinks trolley.

'Rum? Whisky?' he asks, picking up the bottles and examining the labels.

'No wine?' she teases.

'That's in the cellar.'

'Of course there's a cellar full of wine.'

He grins at her. He likes that she is impressed by this grand house. It's important to him to be admired, and she considers this one of the reasons she appeals to him. As a lecturer, Linden teaches the same thing every year, and maybe what keeps it interesting is the annual intake of new students being introduced to it and them thinking he is marvellous because he learned about it first. And even though whenever they are together she tries not to think about his wife, she finds herself doing just that. They are alike in a lot of ways. They're both from families with less money, both younger than him and with less impressive careers. Or, at least, his wife *did* have a less impressive career when she met him. Linden talked about not being needed by his wife, when really, he meant she had stopped being in awe of him. *That* is what slowly poisoned their marriage. So, she plays up to him now. Eyes wide and voice like full-fat cream, she tells him she couldn't imagine growing up in a house so beautiful. So grand. So expensive. She thanks him again and again for choosing to share it with her.

And her efforts are rewarded when he takes her by the nape of her neck and roughly pulls her to him. They kiss. He lifts her onto the dining table and slips between her legs. His free hand slides up her thigh and then moves her knickers aside. He pushes two fingers into her and she gasps into his mouth. God, she has missed him. She grazes his bottom lip with her teeth and starts unbuttoning his shirt. She wants to feel his skin on hers. She trembles with anticipation.

When they hear tyres on the gravel driveway, they freeze. For one terrifying moment, she is convinced it is his wife. By the look of fear on Linden's face, he thinks so too. He leaps back and races to the window. 'Fuck.'

Her stomach drops. 'What?'

He spins towards her, ashen.

She slips off the table and adjusts her dress. 'What is it?' she asks again.

Then she hears car doors slamming shut. A woman's voice.

Grabbing her wrist, he hauls her into the foyer. He darts to his right and snatches open the door of the floor-to-ceiling cupboard. He tells her to get inside.

'You want me to hide?' she asks, aghast.

'Yes.'

There's the sound of a key in the front door lock.

If she refuses, they will be discovered. Heart in her mouth, she clambers inside just as the front door opens.

Chapter Thirty-Six

The Wife

It's a little before 5 p.m. when the doorbell goes. Heidi stands beneath the porchlight; raindrops glimmer in her mousy-brown hair and on the shoulders of her red coat. Her fringe is clinging to her forehead in wet clumps and she's holding two bulging shopping bags. 'Sorry to drop by unannounced. I tried calling . . .'

I think of the phone I tossed across the room, still lying upstairs where it landed. 'Is everything OK?'

'Colette was going to come over with some documents for you to sign, but I offered instead.' She gives me a private smile. 'Didn't want to add to your migraine.'

And feeling a rush of affection, I grin at her. 'Very wise.' I nod at the bags. 'Surely that isn't all paperwork?'

'Fortunately not.' She tilts her head to one side. 'Fancy some company?'

Heidi has bought ingredients to make us supper. While she cooks, I go through Colette's paperwork. It's comforting, having another person in the house. Heidi serves us lasagne with salad and garlic bread. It's the kind of big, hearty eating I haven't done in months. She tells me she loves to cook. That her mother taught her.

'Are you close to her?'

She passes me a plate of garlic bread and gestures for me to take another slice. No doubt she's noticed how thin I am. 'Very. My parents are great. They even moved from Chester to Bath to help with the children.'

'Your parents are still together?'

She nods.

'How long have they been married?'

'Thirty-eight years. They still go on dates, and Dad buys Mum flowers every week. Darren only gets them for me if they're reduced,' she adds with a playful roll of her eyes.

I can't ever work out whether Heidi is content. She's often arriving at the office frazzled and complaining about her husband. I want to know, and rather than tiptoe around the topic, I channel Addison and ask her outright: 'Are you happy with Darren?'

She pauses, hand halfway to glass. Then she grins. 'Yeah, I am. He can be a bit hapless sometimes but he has a kind heart. I'm a little rounder now than I was before we had children but he tells me every single day I'm beautiful.'

'Isn't that . . . the bare minimum?' I ask gently. I'm a firm believer a woman's weight shouldn't be tied to her worth, especially in the eyes of her husband, and especially not when she's just pushed their child out of her vagina.

'You'd think so, wouldn't you? But one of my friends was gifted scales and a juice diet subscription by her husband just two weeks postpartum.'

I wince.

'Really, though,' says Heidi, 'Darren is so thoughtful. When I was pregnant with our third, I had a craving for this banana bread we got from a café in Reading. He took a day off work and drove all the way there just to surprise me with it.'

I nod, impressed. I'd assumed her husband took a back seat in their marriage. But then, people thought Linden and I were the perfect couple and look how wrong they turned out to be.

'I don't know much about your family,' observes Heidi. 'Are your parents still together?'

I shake my head. 'They divorced a long time ago.'

'That's a shame. Do you see them often?'

I tear a piece of garlic bread apart without meeting her eye. 'It's difficult. My father lives in Belgium and my mother passed away a few years ago.' We lapse into silence. I can't imagine a world in which I pop into my mum's for a cup of tea or enjoy a barbecue surrounded by aunts and uncles and cousins. Heidi is lucky to lead such a wholesome life, enveloped by the love of a bustling family. I tell her so and she reddens.

'It isn't all puppies and rainbows,' she offers. 'My in-laws are pretty terrible.'

'Really?' I ask dubiously, wondering if she's just trying to take the shine off her happiness to make me feel better.

'Really.' She wrinkles her freckled nose. 'Mirriam, my mother-in-law, doesn't understand boundaries. When I was in labour she kept messaging Darren to ask how dilated I was.'

I pull a face. 'I'd have told Mirriam if she didn't stop asking, there'd be a hole in the ground dilated six feet just for her.'

Heidi laughs so hard she almost knocks over her drink. Soon, I'm laughing too. It's the first time in a long while. Heidi is easy company. One of those rare people that feel like a hot drink on a bitter winter's night. 'What about Linden's parents?' she asks. 'Did you get on with them?'

I shrug. 'They were courteous but never welcoming. They wanted him to marry a certain type of woman. Someone from a noteworthy or entrepreneurial family they'd consider equal to their own, that could add value to the Lockwood name without having any ambitions of her own. A pretty accessory to decorate their son's arm. In their eyes, I was all wrong for their firstborn.'

Heidi doesn't know what to say in the face of my belched honesty. I'm about to apologise and change the subject when she shakes her head. 'But you're Verity Rose. A household name. These days, more people have heard about you than about Lockies Shortbread.'

'But that was part of the problem. They wanted a woman equal to, not more than. Like Linden, they didn't approve of how much I worked and how often it took me away from family events. The truth is that I felt more comfortable in business meetings than I did at Lockwood gatherings.'

'But Linden was proud of you and the business,' she says uncertainly. 'Wasn't he?'

I open my mouth to lie then stop myself. What's the point? Though Heidi and I haven't discussed it since the day the police called, she knows about the affair. That my marriage was the last thing from perfect. 'He liked the money and the lifestyle but when we met, *he* was the ambitious one. The best-selling author. The revered lecturer. Neither of us ever expected I'd become the breadwinner and he struggled when I did.'

She's surprised. Of course she is; in public, Linden was forever taking my hand and spinning me proudly into the spotlight. He knew exactly how to put on a show. In private, it was a different story: my achievements were met with silence and the parties to celebrate them were attended with the petulant apathy of a teenager being dragged round a garden centre. Though whenever I picked him up on it, he'd apologise and buy flowers and suggest a minibreak. By the time we arrived home from a few days away of great food and even greater sex, I'd already forgiven him. 'Do you have any contact with his family now?'

The last time I saw them was at Linden's funeral. I stood with the Lockwoods but they made me feel colder than the echoey church had. 'No, but maybe it would've been different if we'd had children.'

She's quiet, mulling this over, and I can tell she has questions. 'You never wanted them?'

I stare into my water glass, not sure how honest I should be. I've spent so many years lying for Linden that it's become more instinctual than telling the truth. 'I did want them,' I say out loud for the first time in years. Heidi's mousy-brown eyebrows shoot up, disappearing beneath her fringe. 'Addison and I aren't sisters, but she always felt like one and whenever I pictured a family, I saw two little girls who loved each other as much as we did.' Regret slides beneath my skin. I pick up the glass and drain it.

'I assumed you never had them because you were so busy with Verity Rose.'

My smile is wry. 'That's what Linden wanted people to think.'

And, remembering my conversation with Amy, I'm sure that's what he told her.

'I don't want to pry. Tell me if I'm crossing a boundary here, but if you wanted children, why didn't you have any?'

'After we were married, I suggested to Linden that we see a doctor. Talk about our fertility. I didn't want any surprises,' I say, thinking of Addison and Harry and the smacking disappointment of years spent fruitlessly trying. 'I wanted to be prepared in case there was an issue. I wanted to know if it would be difficult for us. But Linden kept putting it off. Cancelling the appointment last-minute, never giving me a date to rebook. Until finally, I snapped. We fought. And eventually, he admitted children weren't an option for us because, before we married, he had a vasectomy.'

Heidi's mouth falls open. 'Oh my God. Verity . . .'

'He didn't want to get it reversed.' I push my plate away, feeling sick all over again. Heidi refills my water glass. 'It's the only time I ever thought about leaving him.'

She leans forward. 'Why didn't you?'

'Because I loved him.' The kind of consuming, visceral, aching love I didn't know how to live without. 'He asked me if I was really going to throw away our entire relationship over children that didn't even exist. I thought about it and realised I wanted him more than I wanted them. He told me he couldn't imagine having children. That he didn't want to share me.' My laughter is bitter. 'Little did I know I'd spend the rest of my life sharing him.'

'I'm so sorry.' Heidi reaches for my hand.

'So I threw myself wholeheartedly into Verity Rose. I loved him so much that giving up children to be with him, after everything, seemed worth the sacrifice.' Thinking about it again makes the very bones of me ache. 'I truly never thought he'd stray.'

'We haven't talked about . . .' She clears her throat, searching for the words. 'About Linden's . . .'

'Affair?' I finish for her.

She nods.

'I thought I knew who the other woman was but the more I've unravelled it, the further away the end of the string gets, and now

I have no idea who's at the end of it. I don't even know how many women my husband was bedding behind my back.'

She's aghast. 'You think there's more than one?'

I nod. All the secrets I'm keeping rot on the back of my tongue. I want to rid myself of them. I want to tell her all of it. I trust Heidi. She's just about the only person I do trust. And she isn't judgemental and doesn't push her opinions onto me like Addison sometimes does. Even though I know my cousin would urge me not to, I confide in Heidi about the photograph of Linden and Mimi, the ones I found in Amy's apartment along with the message written inside the book, the pig's head and the attack in the basement. It pours out of me like bile.

Heidi pushes her fingers back through her hair. 'So you think Amy was following him?'

'Definitely.'

'But why would Amy stalk him if they were a couple?'

I shrug. 'Maybe he ended it and she couldn't let it go.'

'Didn't the police say they found a draft message on the burner phone breaking off the affair?'

I nod.

'Do you think Amy killed him after he tried to break up with her?' she asks.

'Maybe. But what about Mimi and the guy with the lip ring?'

Heidi exhales deeply. 'You need to take all of this to the police.'

'I can't. Whoever is behind the pig's head and the attack in the basement doesn't want me talking to the police.'

'And it was definitely a man who assaulted you?'

I nod but don't tell her my theory about Flora and her married lover. Flora and Heidi are friends. I can't accuse Flora of anything without evidence.

'Could it be the guy with the lip ring?' she asks.

'I'd wondered if it was, but why would he want to hurt me? He obviously wasn't sad that Linden's dead, he said as much, but I don't even know how he and Linden knew each other. I'd never seen that man before.'

'If Mimi and Linden were ever . . . *involved* . . . maybe when he ended it she was heartbroken and lip ring man wanted to avenge her?' She blows out a breath. 'It sounds mad, doesn't it? Like something from an Agatha Christie novel.'

'It *is* mad. The entire thing is exhausting. I don't know what to believe.'

Heidi sits up straighter. 'OK. What about Amy and all the photographs? Are you sure you can't go to the police about that? She might be his murderer.'

'And how do I explain that I broke into her apartment? I can't tell the police anything. And if I do, they'll need a warrant, and in the meantime, what about the person who assaulted me? A cut to the head is one thing . . .' My muscles coil tight with fear. I take a sip of my water, trying not to think about what will happen to me if my attacker learns I'm alone and breaks into my house at night.

'And Amy's out of the country?' she asks.

I nod.

'What about Mimi?'

'She hasn't been at her house for days.'

'Then we need to find her so you can get some answers. Maybe the friendship is salvageable. You said she seemed scared. Maybe whoever has been threatening you has been threatening her too.'

I hadn't thought of that. Heidi's right. It could all be connected. 'I don't know where Mimi is. She blocked me on all her socials and she's changed her number.'

Heidi reaches for her phone. 'She hasn't blocked me and her profile is public.' She starts tapping at the screen. A moment later, she says, 'Found her. Let's see . . .' My heart races in anticipation. Heidi grins. 'She's tagged at this "Fitness with Cleo" every Friday.' Heidi slides her phone across to me and taps a bitten fingernail at the address. 'Go and see Mimi tomorrow. It might be the only way you'll ever get your answers.'

Chapter Thirty-Seven

The Other Woman

The cupboard is wide enough that she can stretch her arms out to her sides and just about reach the adjacent walls. There are only a couple of heavy winter coats and some muddy walking boots for company. She dares not move for fear of being found, and holds her breath as someone steps into the house. She is sure it is his wife. Sure they have been followed to Lockwood Hall. She is equal parts terrified and relieved. This moment has played out in her mind a thousand times before. In every version, there are tears and shouting. In her wildest, most private imaginings, she and Linden run off into the sunset together and when they are old and grey, they talk about how incredible their lives are, how he should have left his wife sooner. In this daydream, they sit in wicker chairs on a sunny afternoon, enjoying a coastal view, a glass of wine in hand. They wear matching wedding bands. A spaniel chases a thrown stick. Their children, and their children's children, gather at a long outdoor table for a family barbecue.

The fantasy dissolves as she hears a woman's voice. 'Linden?' Her French accent is unfamiliar. 'What're you doing here?'

Through the slats in the door, she watches as Linden embraces the slim, red-haired woman. 'Céline,' he says silkily. 'It's good to see you.'

Though he pulls back, his hands linger on her upper arms. The smile Céline gives him is intimate. 'And you. It's been a while.'

'Too long.'

There is more noise. More voices. More people entering the house. Céline quickly steps away from him as a man with Linden's golden hair and hooded eyes scowls in his direction. 'I thought that was your car on the drive. Another generous gift from your wife, I assume?'

Linden turns slowly towards him. 'Hello, brother.'

An older man and woman who look so much like Linden they must be his parents, stand to one side. His mother is petite and immaculate. His father is tall and cleft-chinned.

'Linden!' His mother's voice is a clap of delight. She pulls him into a hug. 'What a lovely surprise.'

His father maintains a careful distance and only acknowledges his eldest with a curt nod.

'Did we know you were coming up this weekend?' asks his mother. Then she turns to her youngest son. 'Felix, did you invite your brother?'

'No.'

Silence settles around them like grey clouds before rain.

Linden clears his throat. 'It was a last-minute decision.' They stumble into another silence, waiting for him to continue. 'Our house is being painted,' he lies. 'I had some work to do, so I thought I'd make use of Grandfather's study. I didn't know you'd all be here.'

His mother looks uncomfortable. 'Oh, well . . .' She glances nervously up at her disinterested husband who has the air of someone waiting for a particularly dull business meeting to come to a close.

'We do this every year,' purrs Felix.

Linden raises a brow. 'We?'

'The four of us. Mum, Dad, me, my wife.'

She knows Linden would never have brought her to Lockwood Hall if he'd known about their annual gathering. In this moment, Linden seems to shrink. There is a chasm between him and his family, and Felix has just taken great pleasure in severing the rope bridge.

'Right,' says Linden eventually.

'We would've invited you, darling,' soothes his mother. 'But your wife is always working, and you've said before you don't want to feel like a fifth wheel.'

Linden straightens. 'She isn't *always* working.'

'She did miss our wedding anniversary,' says his mother kindly. 'And she didn't attend your nephew's birthday party.'

There's another uncomfortable silence.

'And where are my nephews?' asks Linden in a bid to change the subject.

'With my parents,' explains Céline. 'They flew in from Bordeaux yesterday.'

In the cupboard, she barely breathes, terrified someone might hear her.

'We've booked a table at The King's Arms,' says his mother. 'We'd love you to join us.'

Though Felix's expression says otherwise. 'Thank you, but I'd better get back,' asserts Linden. 'I've got a lot of work to do.'

'And what work is that?' asks Felix, an edge to his voice. 'I'm surprised lecturing part-time is so demanding.'

There's tension in Linden's jaw. 'I'm working on another novel.'

'That's brave.'

'Felix,' scolds their mother.

'What?' he says, feigning innocence. 'I think it's admirable. I could never fail so publicly at something, dust myself off and try again. Very resilient of you, brother.'

Their father smirks, amused by his youngest son.

'You know, it's very good of Vee to support you, Linden,' says Felix. 'Though the family might see more of her if she didn't have to work quite so much to do so.'

Linden's face is turning crimson.

He looks so desperately alone that she wishes she could step out of the cupboard and join him.

Their mother glances anxiously between her sons before appealing to her husband. 'Jonathan, shall we take our bags upstairs?'

'I'll help,' offers Céline.

Linden's mother turns to him and presses a hand to his cheek. 'Don't leave without saying goodbye.'

Then she picks up her cream leather suitcase and heads up the stairs with her daughter-in-law. His father nods once before collecting the rest of the luggage. Linden waits until they're gone before rounding on his brother. 'What the hell is wrong with you?' Felix stares impassively at him. Then, with a slick dismissal, makes to follow his wife up the stairs. Linden grabs his upper arm. 'Why must you be such a prick?'

Felix lounges arrogantly in his brother's grip before shrugging him off. 'Why must you be the family fuck-up that our mother adores?' His top lip curls. 'Her *golden* boy.'

'Jealous, Felix?'

He shrugs. 'Not particularly. It's only a matter of time before she sees sense. Like our father has.'

'You've been whispering poison in his ear for years.'

'I can't take any credit for his disdain. That, dear brother, is all your doing.' Felix, sure this is game, set and match, moves off, his expensive leather shoes clicking on the stone floor.

'You should thank me,' calls Linden. His words hit the back of his brother's skull like thrown daggers. Felix stops. He turns slowly. 'The only reason you have all that you do is because *I* refused to take over Lockies.'

Felix's laughter is hollow. 'Father only offered it to you because it's a family tradition for the firstborn to take the reins. He wanted to placate our grandfather. He'd *never* actually have let you take over, Linden. You don't have the spine for it. You can't commit to anything. How many times did you change your degree? Two, three? How much money did our parents waste on your whimsy? How many times did you con them into giving you seed money to start a new company, only to abandon it when you had to put in just a little effort? How many different women did you come to our mother about, asking for our grandmother's engagement ring?' Felix closes the gap between him and Linden. 'The truth is you can't commit to anything. Degrees, careers, women.'

'I have a wife,' he says, as though this is his ace.

'She's never around. Have you ever considered she takes all these work trips just to escape you?'

At his sides, Linden's hands clench. She fears he will punch his brother, right there in the foyer. She has pressed herself so far up against the slats, the door creaks.

'You know,' says Felix, 'we all took bets on how long it would be before you tired of her, ruined the marriage, abandoned it, just as you've done with every opportunity ever handed to you. You're reckless and selfish. You blow through life like a tornado, picking up what you want, dropping it when you want, wherever you want, consequences be damned.'

She can see Linden struggling to control himself. After a moment, he takes a deep breath and unfurls his fists. He relaxes, radiating that air of exquisite boredom. 'What's this really about, Felix?' He cocks his head to one side with mock concern. 'You're not still upset about Céline?'

'Don't you dare,' warns Felix.

Linden's smile is lazy. A child about to pull the legs off a spider. 'We were together six months, and if I hadn't broken it off, you wouldn't be married to her now. Let's be honest, Felix, *everything* you have, *everything* you take pleasure in, is only yours because I rejected it first.' He leans into his brother and lowers his voice. 'You're nothing more than a dog feasting on my scraps.'

In the cupboard, she covers her mouth with her hands. She had no idea Linden had been involved with Céline. She wonders whether Linden's wife knows. If she does, maybe that is why she keeps the Lockwoods at bay.

Linden doesn't flinch as his brother squares up to him. What will she do if they start throwing punches? Launching herself from her hiding place will most likely make everything worse.

'We're going to be late if we don't leave now,' calls Céline as she jogs down the steps towards them. Felix takes a step back. Céline looks between the brothers. 'Is everything . . .'

Their parents descend the stairs. Felix moves closer to Céline and takes her hand firmly in his.

Their mother, oblivious to the tension between her sons, says, 'Are you sure you won't join us, Linden?'

Dandy Smith

'He's sure,' Felix answers for him.

Their mother glances questioningly at Linden, who gives her a reassuring nod.

A few moments later, the Lockwoods are gone.

Chapter Thirty-Eight

The Wife

Mimi is carefree, her laughter easy. She's surrounded by a gaggle of women, all of them in Lycra, clutching water bottles and rolled-up yoga mats. Her petite, pear-shaped frame showcased in patterned leggings and a fuchsia-pink sweater. Her mane of dark curls has been teased into a French braid. My pulse kicks at the sight of her. I feel as though I've spotted a rare, exotic bird in the wild.

Yellow queasiness seeps through me as I cross the road and make a beeline for Mimi. She has her back to me. The two women that are with her see me first. One of them, whippet-slim with large eyes and dark skin, touches Mimi's wrist to get her attention and then nods in my direction.

Mimi spins towards me. At first, she is shocked but her shock quickly slides into ire. 'Verity?'

Her friends exchange a look. I get that nauseating feeling of having been thoroughly discussed and pulled apart by a group of women I don't know.

'What're you doing here?' demands Mimi.

She addresses me as though we are enemies. By now, I should be used to her hostility, but it's still jarring and hurtful after so many years of easy, meaningful friendship. The hot wash of anger I felt after uncovering her deceit is doused, leaving me cold and wondering how we got here. 'Can we talk?'

'No.' She turns her back on me. I should probably walk away but I am rooted to the spot, reeling from her icy aggression.

'Mimi . . .' I trail off, not sure what to say. To *Mimi*. My closest friend. The one I ate dinner with every week for almost four years. 'Please . . .'

The other women look uncomfortable, as though I'm a homeless person harassing them for money.

Mimi rounds on me. 'Did you follow me here?'

I want to shake her and will her to remember everything we've been through. How, after her mother died, I stayed with her, cooking and cleaning and watching Mimi's old family videos. I even took care of some of her mother's funeral arrangements because Mimi's grief was so crippling, she struggled to make a single decision. 'I need to talk to you.'

She glowers.

The woman with the short blonde bob is eyeing me as though I'm a mangy stray. 'Mimi, maybe we should—'

'Did you get the photograph I posted through your letterbox?' I ask Mimi, cutting off the other woman.

'No. I've been away.' She belligerently lifts her chin. 'What photograph? Why are you sending me photographs?'

'Why didn't you tell me you and Linden knew each other *years* before we moved next door?'

She blanches. Her friends share another look, this one not of wariness, but of astonishment. Mimi's mouth opens and closes wordlessly. I feel a stab of regret because, despite everything, I shouldn't have aired our dirty laundry in front of other people. She turns to them. 'I'll call you later, OK?'

They leave, heads bent close together, talking in hurried whispers. Mimi doesn't know where to look but apparently the ground is more fascinating than I am. 'Why did you pretend not to know him?' I ask.

She shakes her head and in a small voice, she says, 'How did you find out?'

And my heart sinks. I'd been hoping I was wrong. That the photograph was some elaborate fake. 'Does it matter how I know?

I know, Mimi. I know, but I don't understand. Did you and Linden . . . were you ever . . .'

Her head snaps up. 'No. God, no. Linden and I were only ever friends.'

'*Friends?*' I can't hide my incredulity.

'*Just* friends.'

'If that's true, why hide it from me?'

She presses her lips together, searching for the words, and stares up at the dark, dense clouds above.

'All I want is the truth,' I say.

She rubs her forehead as though trying to ward off a headache. 'I didn't know Linden had bought the house next door until I saw him outside the day you moved in. We were arguing. You appeared on the front steps and Linden acted as though we were two strangers having a neighbourly chat. I was so thrown, I just . . . went along with it. I didn't think you and I would become friends. I wanted to tell you.'

'So why didn't you?'

'Linden warned me not to.'

'Why would he do that?' I ask, struggling to keep up. 'How did the two of you really meet?'

She sighs. 'Before I freelanced for Harrier's as a translator, I worked there doing admin. As an author, Linden was invited to all kinds of events. We met at a party.'

'Right.'

'We became friends.'

'And then . . . ?'

She glances away. 'We fell out.'

'Why?'

She folds her arms and glances down the street. It's getting dark and the sweat from her workout is drying on her skin. She obviously wants to leave but I *need* answers. 'Mimi, *please*, just tell me.'

Her hazel eyes find mine and I worry the thick skin I've convinced myself I have is actually made of paper. 'Harrier's threw a spring party. Linden had too much to drink. So did his editor's assistant, Lyla. He was drunk but she was drunker. I caught them together, found them in a stairwell. He was . . . all over her.'

'All over her.' I swallow thickly. 'What do you mean?'

She closes her eyes, as though willing away the memory. 'Her dress was pushed up around her waist, he had her pinned against the wall, but she wasn't with it. She couldn't stand without him holding her up.'

I turn away from her, a tightness in my chest, and press the palm of my hand against the wall of the fitness studio to steady myself. I am nauseous. That yellow queasiness rushes up my throat. I wish I could deny her story. Tell her that my husband would *never* have done such a thing. But I know better. The times we'd share one too many drinks, the sex I couldn't remember having, the way he'd kiss me in the morning and tell me he loved me and I'd let that simple act dissolve the unease in the pit of my stomach like sugar in water.

Mimi moves closer to me, her expression soft with concern. 'You didn't know?'

I shake my head. 'Was it ever reported?'

'I got her away from him and took her home in a taxi. At work the following Monday, I checked on her. I knew what I saw wasn't right but she *insisted* it was consensual, that she'd always had a thing for him and that she'd initiated it. She was so much younger than him. She refused to talk about it again and asked me not to discuss it with anyone else. I said if she wanted to report what had happened, I'd back her up but she was shocked I'd even suggest it and warned me if *I* went to the police or to HR on her behalf, I'd lose my job.'

I can tell she's upset with herself for not doing more so I say, 'Mimi, if Lyla and Linden weren't going to corroborate your story, telling anyone else about it wouldn't have helped. They'd have denied it all.'

'No, I should've—'

'You made sure she was safe,' I insist. 'You did all that you could and you respected Lyla's wishes.'

She relaxes a little. 'Really?'

I feel a rush of familiarity, as though we are still great friends. 'Yes, definitely.' She gives me a small, grateful smile and it feels so good, I smile back. 'What happened to Lyla?'

Mimi takes a breath. 'She left Harrier's a couple of months after our talk. I stayed away from Linden after I caught him with her and didn't see him again until you moved next door.'

'When did this happen?'

She shrugs. 'Before you were married, I think.'

I wait for the relief but it doesn't come because, no matter what, the man I married was a liar and a predator and a cheat. 'Why didn't you tell me?'

'I didn't know you.'

'But we became friends. *Close* friends.'

The wind picks up, whipping my hair across my face. Mimi shivers. 'I know. I wanted to tell you but the deeper into that lie hole I fell, the harder it was to claw my way out. Linden begged me not to say anything. And the two of you were happy together.'

Happy. Was Linden ever truly happy with me? With anyone? He came from a wealthy, ambitious, high-pressured family. He was born into expectation. Pitted against his younger brother from the start. They were always in competition because, according to their father, competition bred winners. The family legacy, the Lockies brand, always came first. I think Linden spent his whole life wanting to be someone's top priority and the moment he believed he wasn't, he strayed. 'I wish you'd told me.'

Mimi's face colours with shame and regret. 'So do I.'

It starts to rain, coming down on us like icy bullets. We dip beneath the fitness studio awning and stare out across the slick road and the cars that pass by, windscreen wipers swishing. I'm swept up in a memory of driving to a hotel in Wales with Mimi. We got lost. It was dark and it rained so hard, we had to pull over and spend the night in my car. The wind flung fistfuls of rain at the windscreen. We stayed up, sharing a packet of chocolate buttons and talking. It was the first time I told her about my parents' torrid divorce.

'I miss you,' I tell her.

'Verity, don't.'

I swallow around the rising lump in my throat. 'Why?'

She twists towards me. 'You really don't know?'

I stare into her large hazel eyes. 'No.'

Her expression hardens. She is angry. So angry. And I have no idea why. 'I'm trying to protect you,' she tells me.

'From what?'

I think about Heidi's theory that the same person who has been threatening me has been threatening Mimi, too. I want to help her. 'Mimi . . .' But she spins away from me and steps out into the rain. She is soaked instantly. 'Don't just leave.'

She turns and fixes me with a look so fierce, it's as though a hot iron has been pressed against my skin. 'Verity,' she says my name as though she can't bear the sound of it. 'Stop talking to the police. Let it lie. Linden is gone. Move out of Windermere. Away from Bath. Away from me. Go. And don't come back.'

Chapter Thirty-Nine

The Other Woman

They drive back to Somerset in near silence, and she's thankful for the time to think. She replays the conversation Linden had with his brother. Linden was once in a relationship with his brother's wife . . . No wonder they don't get along. Felix was scathing but he wasn't wrong about Linden. He does struggle to commit. That isn't a secret to her. How can it be when he is having sex with another woman behind his wife's back? Maybe deludedly, she'd at least considered Linden was committed to *her*.

He'd told her his wife doesn't believe in divorce and that without her, he has nothing, but she understands now that isn't the real reason Linden hasn't ended their unhappy marriage. It's because doing so would be another failure which his family would beat him with. His marriage is the only outwardly successful thing in his life. It is the garlic, or the cross, he uses to ward off the pointed teeth of those who doubt him.

Maybe she should be angry that he hasn't been completely honest with her, but instead she pities him. It makes her sad to think of anyone wasting years of their life with someone they don't truly love. She imagines Linden and his wife growing old together in their home, souring like spoiled milk. And even though she has been to their beautiful house, it becomes something entirely different in her mind. Draughty and cold, silence spreading throughout it like an icy fog. She doesn't just feel sorry for Linden, but for his wife, too. It is selfish of him to stay married to her only to save face with his family.

She thinks of her own future, the days that will turn into weeks, into months, into years, into decades. Is she willing to only ever be a mistress? The secret kept in the house by the canal?

She stays because she loves him.

The answer is as simple and as complex as that.

She doesn't want to 'fix' him. This is what Anna would have told her she was trying to do. She would remind her that once these men have been fed and nurtured and rehabilitated, they stray. They find themselves a new home with someone who receives them at their best, having never seen them at their worst. No; she doesn't view Linden as a situation to be mended because she accepts him for who he is. Everyone has flaws. Everyone has secrets. She isn't perfect. She thinks of the terrible thing she did to her father at the behest of her mother. An awful, unforgivable act. She likes to think that if she can love Linden despite his flaws, he can love her in return. That is, if she is ever brave enough to tell him what she did. Isn't true love, real, unbreakable, irrevocable love, knowing even the darkest corners of another person and still choosing them? She can't imagine her life without him. Doesn't want to. Though, if he isn't ever willing to give up his wife, maybe she must.

She rests her forehead against the cool pane of glass and watches the world zip past.

'You're quiet,' Linden remarks eventually.

'So are you.'

They are on the motorway now. It has started to rain. 'I'm sorry this trip was ruined.'

'I'm not upset about that.'

'Then what?'

She sighs, long and deep. 'How many women have you proposed to?'

He scowls. 'Eavesdropping isn't polite.'

'There wasn't much else to do, trapped in a coat cupboard,' she snaps. 'How many women?'

'Does it matter?' When she doesn't answer, he says, 'A couple. None that were important. I was just . . . it was like dot-to-dot. Something I thought I ought to be doing, not something I actually wanted to do.'

'Until you met your wife.' He presses his lips together and doesn't so much as glance in her direction. 'You're never going to divorce her, are you?'

Silence. A silence that is as grey and endless as the road ahead of them.

Linden clears his throat and in a voice as silky smooth as dark chocolate, he says, 'Sometimes I think my life would be easier if she were dead.'

Chapter Forty

The Wife

'Protect you from what?' asks Addison.

We're walking around the Frome Christmas market, each clutching an overpriced artisan coffee in our gloved hands. The air is crisp and dry and spiked with cinnamon and orange. It's bitterly cold. The clouds overhead are dense and white. We're forecast snow, but that hasn't deterred the crowds. Everyone is merry and loud, cold and pink-cheeked. People meander beneath twinkling Christmas lights, browsing the stalls of handmade wares and sipping hot mulled wine from cardboard cups.

'What was Mimi talking about?' she asks. Addison's had a fringe cut in since I last saw her. Her hair is still long and thick. That wrench of jealousy remains whenever I think of my cousin's hair. We're looking less alike these days, me with my bob and Addison with her fringe.

I shrug. 'No idea. I thought maybe whoever is responsible for the pig's head and the assault could be threatening Mimi, too.'

'No,' says Addison.

'No?' I raise a questioning brow. 'Why not?'

She stops beside a stall selling stained-glass art and picks up a piece in the shape of holly. 'Why would anyone threaten Mimi?'

'I've been wondering the same thing. Maybe she knows who Linden was having an affair with.'

Addison turns away from me and picks up a bauble. 'If she knew who the other woman was, she'd have told you. Like you said, she was your closest friend.' I stare at the back of her glossy, dark head, not at all surprised by the undercurrent of bitterness to her tone.

'But you're like my sister,' I say, wanting to placate her. Her gaze swings up to mine, searching for sincerity. I give her a small, warm smile and she relaxes a little. 'If either of you knew who Linden was sleeping with behind my back, you'd tell me.'

She sets the artwork down. 'Of course.'

'I wonder if the other woman has threatened Mimi to keep quiet?'

She turns to face me. 'Threatened her with what? How?'

'Well, a pig's head with a knife through its skull was enough to stop me from speaking to the police.'

'Surely Mimi would have told you if she'd received similar threats?'

We move away from the stalls and past a vendor selling fat Brie and cranberry paninis. 'She doesn't know what I've been through. I haven't told her.'

'I don't think Mimi knows who he was having an affair with. She'd have said so when Linden was alive.' Addison veers towards a stand of patterned plant pots. She picks one up. 'This would look lovely in your kitchen.'

The generation of middle-aged men before us bought fast cars or ended marriages to regain a sense of youth; millennials become doting plant parents and get a dog they can dress in Christmas jumpers. Right now though, I'm not interested in any of it. 'Do you still think Mimi killed him?'

The stall owner whitens. Addison sets the pot down with an apologetic smile before taking me by the elbow and leading me away. 'I don't know who killed him, Verity,' she says, voice low. 'But, as I've said before, fleeing Bath the moment she could is suspicious.'

We weave through the throng of people. 'If Mimi didn't know who he was having an affair with, why would she kill him?'

'Maybe she's lying about how she knows Linden. Maybe she was obsessed with him and he rejected her.'

I still haven't told her about Amy. I think the second I do, she'll conjure up some wild theory that Amy and Mimi were conspiring. 'So Mimi murdered him?' I shake my head. 'She didn't kill Linden and she wasn't obsessed with him. She didn't even like him.'

We meander along the high street which has a little stream running through it. Addison ducks into a shop. 'But you believe the tale she spun about Linden assaulting his editor's assistant?'

'Lyla,' I say, following her inside. 'And yes, I do.'

She pulls a face.

'What?'

She gives the slightest hint of a headshake and presses her lips together. 'Nothing.'

We walk down one of the narrow aisles. 'Just say it, Addison. If you don't, you'll give yourself a migraine.'

'It doesn't matter,' she insists, taking a cookbook from the shelf. She thumbs through it, avoiding my eye.

'Well, it clearly does.' I whip the book from her hands and slap it shut.

'Fine.' Her dark eyes narrow. 'You don't think Mimi is capable of murder, but you think Linden was capable of sexual assault?'

Adrenaline pulses through me at the confrontational snap in her voice. I place the book back on the shelf and fight to stay calm.

She folds her arms. 'I would *never* believe anyone who accused Harry of such a thing.'

Indignation flares in my chest. 'Well, lucky for you, Addison, Harry is a good man. A loyal, loving husband who hasn't ever put his dick in someone else. But Linden did, didn't he?' We lock eyes. The air around us spits and crackles. She doesn't back down.

'Cheating and sexual assault aren't the same thing,' she chides.

'No. Not at all. But Linden was *my* husband and *you* didn't know him like *I* did.'

She glances away and takes a moment to gather herself. 'OK,' she says, calmer now. 'Tell me what I don't know.'

All the unsaid things fester on the back of my tongue. Everything I buried so I could believe I was dancing in the centre of a perfect life: the drunken sex I managed to convince myself was consensual; how rough he could be when he'd had a bad day; every time I shrank my achievements to make room for his ego; the nights after our wedding I spent lying awake beside him, feeling as though I was sharing a bed with an apex predator who'd take a chunk out of me if I dared to relax. But I can't share any of it. Not in the middle of all this wholesome Christmas festivity. 'It doesn't matter,' I tell her. 'But I believe Mimi.'

She holds my gaze. I can tell she wants to dismiss my instinct, tell me I'm wrong, push my opinion aside and assert *she* is right. But instead, she turns back to the shelf and reaches blindly for a candle. 'Have you even looked up Lola to see if she's real?'

'*Lyla*,' I correct, trying to douse my rising irritation that Addison has deemed this woman's story so unbelievable, she can't even be bothered to get her name right. 'Yes. I did.' She raises a brow but doesn't comment. 'Lyla left publishing. She works for a rape crisis charity.'

There's a long, stony silence. 'That doesn't prove anything.'

'Doesn't it?' Addison looks up, reluctant to believe it. 'Google her. She's a real person. There isn't a photograph but I found her LinkedIn account. The dates she was at Harrier's, the date she left, everything Mimi said . . . it all fits.'

I can see Addison turning it over in her mind and I watch her reticence dissolve. 'Even if she's real, it doesn't mean Linden assaulted her, but if you believe he did, have you also considered Lyla could be his killer? That's a pretty strong motive *if* she's telling the truth.'

If. I tamp down the urge to yell at Addison for her reluctance to accept Linden was a predator. But then, she isn't the person I should be speaking to about this. 'I need to talk to Mimi again.'

Her head whips up. '*Why?*'

I take a large lily-scented candle from the shelf so I have something to do with my hands and prepare to defend myself because I know Addison doesn't want me anywhere near Mimi. 'I think Linden strayed with more than one woman during our marriage, and I think Mimi might know who they are.'

Addison opens her mouth but I don't get to hear what she has to say because, through the gap in the shelves, a familiar face stares back at me. I jump. Her green eyes widen as they find mine. She stumbles as though she's been caught.

I practically throw the candle back on the shelf and hurry down the aisle. Addison follows close behind, demanding to know what's happening. I round the corner and almost smack into Flora. She's wearing a stone-coloured coat over mom jeans and pristine trainers. Her long red hair is loosely curled and tumbles past her shoulders.

'Hi,' I say.

'Hi.'

Silence. Stretched, strained silence. 'Enjoying the market?'

She nods. 'Yep. It's great. Really great.'

'Great.'

'Great.'

We're wearing matching, clownish grins. I want to know how much she heard. I mean, she'd have heard every word if she was standing there listening the entire time. What, exactly, has she learned? What did we say? 'Flora, look . . .'

Her eyes dart towards the exit. 'Actually, I better go. My friends are waiting for me. I'll see you at work?'

'OK. Sure.'

She nods. Without meeting my eye, she flees.

Chapter Forty-One

The Other Woman

Linden wants her to meet him at his house. He gave her a key months ago but she's had very little cause to use it. This week though, builders have been traipsing in and out of Paddledown, refitting the bathroom after a leak. Linden's wife is visiting her father out of town, so she lets herself inside to wait for him. Their home is set back in relative privacy and their neighbour is rarely home so she isn't worried about being seen. Though not as grand or as sprawling as Lockwood Hall, the house Linden shares with his wife is large and beautiful. Parquet floors and skylights, wall panelling and walk-in wardrobes. She can't imagine ever owning a home like this. She can't even afford to own her own flat, let alone a detached four-bed house.

It's quiet. The October sunset spills across the foyer floor in a wash of gold. She removes her boots and carries them upstairs with her. Despite how lovely the house is, she doesn't like coming here. When she's alone with Linden, in a hotel or at Paddledown, she can pretend his wife doesn't exist, but here, in their house, she is everywhere. In the silk dressing gown draped over the armchair in the bedroom, in the Jo Malone perfume on the nightstand, in the gold earrings left in a trinket dish above the en suite sink.

Linden is late, caught up in a meeting at the university. With nothing else to do, she gives in to curiosity, ignoring what it did to the cat, and opens one of the drawers in the large oak chest. Inside is his wife's underwear. Lace basques and suspender belts, boned corsets and silky matching sets from Gilda & Pearl, all of them in moody hues, emerald greens and damsons. With a wave of humiliation, she thinks of the cheap satin set in cherry red that she's wearing now. She slams the drawer shut and then wanders over to the enormous king-size bed in the centre of the room. It's like something from a fancy hotel or the pages of a home decor magazine with its complex arrangement of pillows and its hand-stitched quilt. Hanging on the walls are framed photographs of the happy couple, all in tasteful black-and-white, documenting their lives together. The image that captures her attention is of them on their wedding day. His wife in three thousand pounds' worth of georgette silk, Linden handsome in a dark green suit, the two of them gazing at one another, beaming with post-wedding euphoria. The way his wife looks at him, as though he is the centre of her universe. She swallows her jealousy like spit before vomit. She wants to be this woman. Wants her life. What she doesn't want is to fuck Linden just metres from this photograph. She doesn't want to be here, in this house that isn't hers, in a bed that isn't hers, with a man that isn't hers, either. She thinks Linden gets a thrill out of having sex with his mistress in his marital bed. He's always a little more excited when they come here. It's as though he isn't just screwing her, but screwing his broken marriage, too. She becomes incidental, a way to secretly punish his wife for being more successful and revered than he is.

Since visiting Lockwood Hall three weeks ago, she has felt cloaked in melancholy. The hot, trembling *need* to be around him, the fever that has burned through her for months, has eased because it has become painfully apparent that he will never leave his wife for her. She is desperately in love with Linden but she isn't at all enamoured with their situation. She knows that by staying with Linden, *she* is part of the problem.

She decides to return to Paddledown. Boots in hand, she turns to leave. Then she hears Linden's key in the front door. She sighs, already drained by the tantrum she knows he'll throw when she explains she doesn't want to stay here. She is about to call out to him that she is in the bedroom when she hears his wife's voice.

'Sorry I couldn't come, Dad. I got half an hour out of Bath and felt so unwell, I had to turn back.'

She freezes. Panic pulls tight, like a cord around her chest. She spins, looking for somewhere to hide. She darts for the en suite then stops, knowing his wife is likely to use the bathroom. She swings towards the his-and-hers walk-in wardrobe. She can hardly believe that, for the second time in a month, she is being forced to hide in a cupboard. She presses herself further into Linden's wardrobe, trying to disappear into his rack of shirts.

'Don't worry, Linden will be here soon.' His wife's voice drifts up the stairs and through the closed door. 'He'll take care of me, he always does.' The bedroom door opens and his wife steps into the room. 'I just feel guilty. Linden is so good to me, Dad, and I've barely seen him these last few months. I'm travelling again, more than I'd like. I miss him. I miss him so much.'

From inside the wardrobe, she can hear Linden's wife moving around the room, ducking into the en suite, running a tap and filling a glass. The rattle of a pill bottle. 'He doesn't know it yet, but I'm planning a huge Christmas gathering this year. His family are coming to stay with us. Linden doesn't realise how much he needs them. I'm so close to our family, and he just . . .' His wife's footsteps draw closer, stopping just outside.

She holds her breath, fearful of being caught.

His wife sighs. 'There's a lot of tension between him and his brother *and* his father. Maybe I can help. I just want him to be happy.' There is the sound of drawers opening and closing. 'I need to slow down and spend more time with Linden. He's right, we can't even *think* about starting our own family until I take a step back from work, but *my* income is what affords us our lifestyle.' His wife falls quiet again, listening to whatever her father is saying on the other end of the phone. 'You're right, people manage, and we will, too. I suppose I just have to wean Linden off the luxuries before we have a baby.'

She feels the wardrobe closing in on her. Baby? Linden's wife wants a baby? She thinks of all the times he has told her *he* wants a family but his wife refuses, always prioritising work over *his* wants and needs, over their future family. Her pulse quickens. Has Linden lied?

'Anyway,' says his wife, 'I've just taken some sleeping pills and I'm going to crawl into bed. Don't worry, I'll be fine . . . Yes, I promise to visit soon. Love you.'

His wife starts getting ready for bed. Linden claimed she is aloof and largely disinterested in their marriage but it's clear she *loves* him. Wants children with him. For the first time in weeks, guilt creeps in.

Heart hammering, she takes her phone from her pocket and turns down the brightness of the screen until it's practically grey. She makes sure it is on silent and then reads the previously unseen message from Linden, warning her to get out of the house. She fires off a reply, explaining her situation. A situation so absurd, if she wasn't terrified of discovery, she might laugh.

A moment later, Linden responds.

Don't move. I'm on my way.

Move? Where does he think she is going to go? Burst from the wardrobe and offer to make his wife chicken soup?

She stands in the dark, contemplating all the choices that led her here. She wonders, if she could go back, would she make the same decisions? Would she kiss a married man? Go to bed with him? Allow herself to fall in love with him? Maybe . . . if she could guarantee he would love her enough in return to leave his marriage.

When she is sure his wife is asleep, she gently pushes open the wardrobe door just enough that she can slip through it. She is light-headed with the fear of being caught. The curtains are drawn. It's so dark, she can barely make out the shape of the furniture around her. She trips over the pillows his wife has stacked alongside the bed.

His wife makes a noise and rolls over.

Heart galloping beneath her breast, she snatches the offending pillow up. She doesn't know what to do next. Light from the landing glows beneath the closed bedroom door. If she opens it, the room will be flooded with light and she can't risk waking the sleeping woman. She checks her phone. A message from Linden tells her he is five minutes away and to stay inside the wardrobe. She turns towards it, not wanting to get back inside but knowing she can't just stand in the middle of the room.

His wife breathes deeply in her drug-induced sleep.

Linden had said his life would be easier if his wife were dead. At the time, she'd been shocked, but hadn't she thought the same of Peter? It doesn't mean she'd ever harm him or want to see him hurt. She understood that when a relationship ends, you don't just mourn losing your partner, but the life you planned together. The grief isn't clean. It is muddied by curiosity and jealousy and the temptation to go back. And isn't it true that *her* life would also be easier if Linden's wife were dead? Then she could stop feeling guilty. Could have everything she wanted: Linden all to herself, their relationship out in the wide world. They could move in together, she could make new friends, host dinner parties, start a family. Could spend the rest of their lives coasting on domestic bliss, their worries no more dire than which of them is going to drive their youngest to hockey and who is going to get up early to walk the dog.

Still clutching the pillow, she moves to stand over his wife's sleeping form. She could smother her. That would allow her to shed the life of The Other Woman and step into the role of wife. She imagines pressing the pillow over his wife's face. Pressing hard enough to cut off her air. Long enough that she never wakes up again.

The bedroom door swings open. She is momentarily blinded by the light. Linden's wide-eyed, fretful gaze locks with hers. He takes it all in: her, the pillow in her hands, his unconscious wife. She waits for him to shout at her, to shove her away from the bed. He doesn't. He watches. He waits to see what she will do next. She feels a rush of something hot and dark shoot through her. Then,

Dandy Smith

horrified with herself and the blackness of her thoughts, her cheeks heat with scarlet shame and she drops the pillow. As she does, she catches the disappointment that flickers across her lover's face.

Chapter Forty-Two

The Wife

I'm certain Flora heard every word. Without a doubt, she knows Linden was having an affair. Is that why she practically ran away from me? I suppose it isn't usual to know the ins and outs of your boss's personal life. I wonder whether she'll speak to Heidi about it. If she does, I trust Heidi not to gossip.

Addison and I don't stay much longer at the market. I'm too distracted. I want to go home and try to talk to Mimi again. Maybe she's back from wherever she's been. When I return to Rook Lane later that afternoon and knock on her door, she doesn't answer. I'm too tired to be frustrated, so I trudge across the driveway to my house.

It's getting dark. I walk around, turning on lamps. I don't understand anyone who uses the big light. It's so cold that I put the heating on before getting undressed and taking a shower. The house feels vast, like I'm a marble rattling around inside a glass bottle. Every now and then, I get the urge to sell Windermere and live in a cosy cottage with a thatched roof and original floors. Maybe, once the mystery of my husband's life is exhumed, I will.

I change into a pair of cotton, robin-print pyjamas and melt half a slab of chocolate into full-fat milk. As I stir the pan, I feel eyes on me. I whip around, but I'm alone. Slowly, I pivot towards the double doors that lead out into the garden. It's pitch-black now and the glare from the ceiling lights makes it impossible to see if anyone is there.

As I stare into the dark, the hairs on the nape of my neck rise, an animal instinct warning me I am not alone.

But then, I haven't felt truly alone in this house since Linden's murder. His ghost lingers. I feel him trailing behind me as I wander the hall and landings. Feel his cold lips against my throat as I lie awake at night. Sometimes, I catch the warm, spicy scent of him and imagine he is nearby, watching me, and when I inhale deeply, beneath his cologne is the metallic tang of blood. I've never admitted this to anyone but occasionally, I talk to him. I say out loud that I hate him, that I miss him, that I'm still desperately in love with him and don't know who I am now he's gone. I wonder, if I move from here, whether he'll follow me or stay to haunt the hallways of the house he loved so much. The first day we viewed it, his face lit up like Christmas lights and he spun me off my feet right there in front of the estate agent. 'This, my darling, is *our* new home,' he said, before dipping me backwards to give me a Hollywood kiss.

I turn away from the doors and continue to stir my hot chocolate. As I pick up my phone from the counter, I remind myself that if someone is watching the house, help is only a call away. Trying to ignore the crawling sense of foreboding, I pour my hot chocolate into a red and white Christmas mug and top it off with whipped cream and marshmallows. It looks like something from an advert. I take a photo and send it to Addison. Her reply is instant: You're making me so jealous.

Then she sends a photograph of her and Harry curled up together on the sofa, both pulling ridiculous, goofy faces. Harry is handsome with his curly dark hair, dark eyes and broad, white smile.

I am jealous of *her*. Jealous that she is part of a team. That there is always someone to come home to. To eat dinner with. To ask after her day. To touch. To curl up with on the sofa and take silly photographs. Addison and her perfect husband. For one moment, I hate her for it, but still I send her a message wishing her and Harry a great night.

In bed, I try to evict the toad of jealousy from my mind, but still it squats, flicking its long, fat tongue out into the blackness of my thoughts. I drink my hot chocolate even though it burns my tongue. Then I pick up my Noah Pine book and read until the words blur on the page and I fall into a deep, dreamless sleep.

I jolt awake in bed, enveloped by blackness. I don't know what woke me. A noise or a feeling. I search for it now and my body coils tightly in alarm. I am not alone. Someone is in this room. I hold my breath and listen. There, in the dark, is the steady, unfamiliar breathing of a stranger. Fear spreads like poison through my body, leaving me paralysed. I feel them move closer.

Get up, I think, *run*. Before I can spring into action, something is slammed into my face. I kick and struggle, my screams are muffled. I can't see. Can't breathe. I claw at the thing covering my face. It's large and soft and smells of lavender detergent. A pillow. With frantic, desperate fingers, I search for the hand crushing it into my face. I rake my nails across slick, cold leather. The pillow is pressed harder. There is a crunch and pain bursts across my nose. I try to flip onto my side but a hand closes around my throat. Blood pounds through my ears. My screams melt into clotted gurgles of terror.

I buck and thrash and hook my fingers into talons, tearing at the clothed arm of my assailant. Still I cannot breathe. My chest tightens painfully and my head spins. I throw a punch. My fist connects with something solid. There's a grunt. The pillow vanishes and I throw myself across the bed. Coughing and spluttering, I tumble to the ground. Then I am up and running. I'm shaking so hard, I fall on the landing. I imagine them behind me, barrelling after me. I push onto my hands and knees and force myself up. I'm stumbling, ping-ponging across the landing and down the stairs. My trembling hands fumble with the lock and then I am spat outside into the freezing night air. I scream and scream and scream, racing blindly around the hedges and trees and the low stone wall that separate my house from the road. Petrified a hand will clamp over my mouth and haul me back, I run faster still. Across the street, a neighbour's hallway light blinks on.

Chapter Forty-Three

The Other Woman

Linden drives her home. He leaves a note for his wife to tell her he is going to the supermarket. She thinks of the disappointment she saw on Linden's face as she dropped the pillow she'd been holding. Had he hoped she'd smother his wife? She'd managed to convince herself he didn't mean it when he said his life would be easier if she were dead, but the look he gave her, that predatory, unwholesome spark in his eyes as she clutched the pillow, and then the disappointment that followed once she dropped it, make her wonder.

'I found out at the last minute Vee wasn't going to visit her father,' explains Linden. 'I am so sorry you had to hide in the bloody wardrobe.' He looks over at her with a grin. 'It's becoming an occupational hazard.'

She stares out of the window at the glittering lights of houses. 'You don't need to apologise. It's my fault.'

'Of course it isn't.'

'It is, actually. You can't enter an affair with a married man and expect never to have a close call, can you?'

They fall quiet and the next few miles are driven in silence. She remembers the first time she set eyes on Linden. He was handsome but that wasn't what drew her in. It was his quick wit and dry sense of humour. His ability to fill a room all by himself. The way others clambered to be near him, to feel the warmth of his attention on their skin. She liked that he was confident, maybe even a little arrogant.

That, where she often felt awkward in social situations, starting a sentence before stumbling into silence, Linden always had an opinion, a point of view, something to offer. She met him at a party. A work party. From across the room, his gaze burned into hers. They were separated by a dozen people, but it felt as though he was standing right in front of her, close enough to touch.

As she moved through the party, everywhere she went she could feel him watching. It was frightening and thrilling. He sought her out. She felt him before she saw him. A heat at her back. When they spoke, her entire body thrummed. The connection, the *pull*, she felt towards him was dangerous. Dangerous for him because he was married. Dangerous for her because he was married to her boss. Dozens of times, she wanted to put an end to their relationship, but she loved Linden and loved the way he made her feel: desired and desirable, powerful and curious, giddy and alive. He gave her back all the things her break-up with Peter had stolen.

'Is everything all right?' asks Linden as they pull up outside Paddledown.

'Your wife really loves you.'

He twists to face her. 'Where is this coming from?'

'I heard her talking about you on the phone to her dad.'

'OK . . .'

She looks down at her hands in her lap. 'I feel guilty.'

'That guilt is mine. As her husband, *I* owed her loyalty. You don't owe her anything.'

Though she reaches out towards his cheap-and-easy get-out-of-jail-free card, she can't take it because she is an adult and she understands the difference between right and wrong. She owes it to herself, and to his wife, to put an end to her affair. In this moment, she is sure that is the right thing to do, even if it terrifies her. 'When I thought she didn't *need* you, didn't *want* you, or *love* you, I could justify what we were doing, but she does love you, Linden. Your wife wants children with you.' He opens his mouth to speak but she holds up a hand to stop him. 'I convinced myself the reason we were together is because *I* am who you're meant to be with, that we are better suited to one another than you are to your wife. That we have a connection so deep it runs beneath the roots of your marriage. I let myself believe you would leave your wife. But you won't. You never intended to. You say I don't owe your wife anything but we both know what we're doing is wrong. And I owe myself the chance to be with somebody who can offer me more. More than just snatched moments. More than the scraps of love I let myself take from you.'

She thinks of Linden's wife and wonders whether he will mention the pillow. She hates that she thought about hurting someone. Worse, ending their life. This isn't who she is. It isn't who she wants to be. She wants to be the person Peter loved, not the jealous, murderous mistress she's turning into.

Linden is incredulous. He stares at her as though she has lost her mind. As though she is rejecting a plate of caviar in favour of a kebab. 'You're ending this? *Us?*'

'Yes.'

'You can't be serious.'

'I have to, Linden. We can't keep doing this. How did you think this would end?' And it is obvious to her that he never thought about it ending. That he believed she would always be there, waiting for him, as the sun waits for the moon.

His eyes search her face and the resolve he is met with makes him pale. 'Don't do this,' he implores. '*Please* don't do this.'

But it is done. It is already done. 'I'm sorry, Linden.'

She gets out of the car. Linden does too. He follows her to the front door and catches her wrist, spinning her to face him. 'Please.'

The grief takes hold and she cannot draw breath. Losing Linden feels like an event she will not survive. But she must. There will be tears and pain and doubts. She will spend weeks analysing every conversation, every action, wondering if she could have done more. She will turn her face into her pillow at three in the morning to muffle bottomless sobs. She will see something – her olive-green armchair, rust-coloured socks, Elephant's Breath – and she will remember him. There will be moments, unexpected, startling moments of missing him.

But not now.

Now there is only her and the man whose heart she is breaking.

It is clear, from the agony on his face, that he loves her. Really loves her. And she wonders if she is making a mistake. She can feel herself softening like candlewax. She reaches deep withing herself to find resolve. She tells herself this pain is temporary. A madness as impermanent as lust. It will pass.

'I'll find somewhere else to live,' she tells him. 'If I can just stay until the end of the month.'

'You don't need to leave.' His fingers move from her wrist to her hand. He squeezes it. 'Don't do this.'

She slides free and turns towards the door. She lets herself inside. Linden follows. She tells him they can't be together. She asks him to leave. But his gaze is fixed on a spot beyond her shoulder. His mouth falls open in a perfect O of horror. She spins on her heel. The lounge door is open. On the wall above the fireplace, scrawled in crimson paint, is a threat: *I'm going to tell his wife.*

Linden pushes past her and stumbles towards the defaced wall. Her heart thunders in her chest. Millie has broken into Paddledown. *How* did she get inside? She feels sick. Feels violated. The irony that she was in another woman's house without her knowledge just half an hour ago is not lost on her. She swallows thickly.

'What the fuck is this?' Linden barks.

With no other choice, she tells him about the notes she's been receiving for months.

He pushes his fingers back through his golden hair. 'All this time and you never breathed a word?'

'You're surprised I know how to keep a secret?' she says archly.

'But this.' He throws a hand out towards the vandalism. 'This is . . . who knows? Who have you told?'

It is on the tip of her tongue to be honest, to admit that Peter is aware of their affair, but Peter isn't responsible for any of it and she doesn't want to put him in Linden's firing line, not when she is sure who is behind it all. 'Millie did it. All of it. The notes, the break-in.'

'Millie?' He frowns. 'Who is . . .' Then his furrowed brow clears. 'No. Not possible.'

'You said she stalked you. Wrote you notes. That she's *obsessed* with you.'

'She didn't do this.'

'Of course she did.'

He shakes his head. 'Millie isn't even in the country.'

She feels a clench of alarm. 'Are you sure?'

'Certain.' He rubs a hand over his face. 'I drove her to the airport myself.'

'Why?'

'To get her as far from me as possible.'

'When?'

'Yesterday. She's visiting family in Germany.'

'Why didn't you tell me you were with Millie yesterday?'

'Probably for the same reason you didn't tell me about the notes,' he says, voice spiked with irritation. 'I didn't want to worry you unnecessarily.'

Her mind whirls. When she was sure Millie was her tormentor, she'd been relieved. Millie was just a girl. A tragic little girl with a crush on her lecturer, posting notes through the letterbox, but the idea of a *stranger* breaking into her home and defacing it is not as easily dismissed. 'If Millie didn't do this,' she says, 'who did?'

Chapter Forty-Four

The Wife

It's been four days since I was attacked in my home and the police are as clueless as ever. To be fair to them, I didn't see my assailant's face and without a description they have very little to go on. But I did report to them the pig's head and the incident in the cellar. They seemed frustrated I hadn't done so sooner but Addison pointed out that Linden's murderer was still at large and our faith in the police isn't stellar.

Harry has called a company to install security cameras. When Linden and I moved in, I did suggest a security camera but he rebuffed the idea. He claimed we didn't need it because Bath is a safe city and he didn't care for the idea of being spied on. Though now I understand he was worried about being caught with another woman. Until the cameras are set up, I'm staying with Harry and Addison.

Where my house has felt cold and grey, theirs is warm and cosy. Harry is always singing or humming. Addison gets irritated that he repeats the same line of a song but I find it endearing and join in. Last night, while we made dinner, Harry and I belted 'No Body, No Crime' by Taylor Swift. Addison shut herself in the snug.

Now, I'm helping Addison unpack the food shop and put it all away, but at the sight of salmon fillets, I feel sick.

'You've gone all pale. Are you OK?'

'Can we store that in the cellar freezer?' I ask. 'Just in case.'

Harry enters the kitchen. He's tall and toned with dark skin and liquid brown eyes. 'In case what?'

'I'm allergic.'

He takes the fillets from Addison. 'You didn't tell me Verity has an allergy.'

She sighs. 'I forgot.'

'Maybe she's had enough of me,' I tease to lighten the mood. 'Maybe she thinks killing me is the only way to get me out of her house.'

Harry grins. 'I wouldn't put it past her.'

'I honestly forgot,' she says, decanting tomatoes and onions into their various plastic storage containers. Addison's fridge is more organised than most people's lives.

'Have you had a reaction before?' Harry asks me, helping himself to a grape and popping it in his mouth.

'Once. At work. An intern gave me lunch contaminated with salmon oil. It was an accident.'

Addison looks up. 'I didn't know about this. When did this happen?'

At the memory, I shudder. 'While you and Harry were in America.'

'Do you have an EpiPen?' asks Harry.

'In my bag,' I say, turning away from them to load tins and spices into the cupboard so they can't see how my hands tremble.

But Harry notices. 'Addison, I think it's best we get rid of the salmon.'

She's affronted. 'Why?'

'Your cousin's allergic . . .'

There's a little friction between them and I feel guilty for being the cause of it.

She pulls a face. 'What am I supposed to do, throw it back into the canal?'

He shrugs. 'Or give it to a neighbour.'

'Who goes house to house offering neighbours salmon fillets?' quips Addison.

'People who buy it even though their house guest has a deadly allergy?' I offer playfully, trying to dispel the tension. Addison isn't amused.

I don't get to hear her reply because my phone vibrates in my jeans pocket. It's a number I don't recognise. I excuse myself and wander down the hall to the lounge in case it's the police. 'Verity, I've just got back from the police station.' It's Mimi. I'm so astonished, I can't speak. I pull the lounge door closed. 'They said you were attacked earlier this week?'

'I was . . .'

'Oh my God, are you OK?'

I frown. 'Do you care?'

'Would I ask if I didn't?'

I take a deep breath, not sure how I feel. 'I'm fine. Mimi, why did the police want to talk to you?'

'In case I saw anything suspicious. Anyone hanging around outside either house. I didn't. I've been away a lot lately. I got back yesterday morning.' She doesn't volunteer where she's been staying or mention the man with the lip ring. 'Where are you?'

'With Harry and Addison.'

'Oh.' She sounds surprised. 'Right. OK.'

'What?'

'Nothing, I'm just . . . I didn't realise the two of you were still so close.'

I stiffen. 'Shouldn't we be?'

Silence.

'Mimi?'

'Who attacked you?' she asks.

'I don't know. The police think it could be the same person who killed Linden.' I hear her breathing. It's getting faster and faster. 'Mimi, are you all right?'

'No. I think . . . I think . . .' She groans. 'I think I've made a huge mistake.'

My pulse kicks. 'What mistake?'

I hear the rushing of traffic and imagine her striding along the pavement. 'Can we meet?'

Meet? After all this time, she wants to meet? Words stick to the roof of my mouth. I open and close it, trying to dislodge them.

'Verity, did you hear?' she says. 'Can we please meet?'

'But why?'

'I think we should talk, in person, in private.'

I hesitate, not sure why the sudden U-turn after more than a year of silence and rejection, but if I don't agree to see her, I might never find out. 'Sure,' I say after a moment. 'Let's meet.'

Tomorrow, I'm going to Cambridge for the night to review a boutique hotel, so we arrange for me to come to her house the day I return. I hang up, excitement to see her mixing with a sense of foreboding. I listen out for Harry and Addison but the house is still and quiet. I turn towards the door and beneath it, I see a shadow. I cross the room and pull it open but the hallway is empty.

Chapter Forty-Five

The Other Woman

It has been two weeks since the break-in and the vandalism. The back door had been left unlocked by the builder dealing with the leak in the bathroom. Linden was livid but she felt better knowing the person who sneaked into the house was an opportunist, rather than a crowbar-wielding nutjob. Still, for the first few nights, she was too afraid to sleep at Paddledown alone so she booked herself into a Travelodge. She decides not to dwell on who is behind the notes. It doesn't matter anymore because she and Linden are over. Done. Which means their anonymous author has nothing to tell.

Rather than giving in to the heartbreak, she has started piecing her life back together. She looks for a house share and attends three meet-ups. She warms instantly to a woman called Cassie who describes herself as a 'plant mum' and has an encyclopedic knowledge of noughties TV shows. She is homely and kind. The perfect antidote to the last wild, intoxicating six months. She agrees to move in with Cassie in just a few weeks.

Now she is no longer spending her time hiding in the staff toilets to message her boss's husband, she has more time to focus on her career. She puts herself forward for content creation and finds she is a talented writer. She tries not to think of the letters she penned to Linden in the early days of their affair, or the notebook he'd given her with pastel-coloured pages. Her appetite has returned, too. Without dining on guilt and anxiety, she has room for spaghetti Bolognese and mushroom risotto. She thinks about her father. She misses him. Longs to see him again. She thinks about her mother, too. The mother who blames her for the choices her father made. The mother who slapped her hard across the face once he was gone, then clung to her when the shock retreated and the grief surged in.

She thinks about Anna and Mel and Lucy. She misses them keenly. She wonders if she can reconnect with them. Explain. They will be shocked but maybe they will be forgiving, too.

She does not respond to Linden's pleading messages, his declarations of love. True to her word, his wife is travelling less and working from home more, which means Linden can't slink off to Paddledown without arousing suspicion. Not certain whether her resolve is made of sand or stone, she is grateful for the separation.

If she isn't working, or cooking, or meeting Cassie for brunch, she is taking up new hobbies: pottery and spin, aerial hoop and a writing workshop. She is determined to fill with love the holes in her life that Linden has left.

At work, it is busy. All the freelancers have come into the office for the day. They are planning content and events and launches for the New Year. Just before lunchtime, the office manager, red-faced and hassled, approaches her. 'Someone called Out to Lunch and cancelled our food order.'

'Who?'

The woman gives her a look that tells her she's exasperated by her existence. 'No idea.' She sighs. 'We've got twelve people to feed and nothing in the office but water and the rejects from a box of Celebrations. So unless you can do whatever the fuck miracle Jesus performed with fishes and bread rolls, can you please run across to Boho Deli?'

Before she can answer, the woman slaps a long list of orders onto her desk with a wedge of cash. Without complaint, she takes them and leaves.

Outside, the sun is golden in the bright blue sky, yet it is unseasonably cold. She slips on her mittens as the icy November breeze whips across her face, turning her nose and cheeks pink. The shopfronts are adorned with Christmas displays, baubles and lights and garlands. She is walking fast, wondering how she will carry twelve lunch orders from the deli back to the office all by herself, when she sees Linden waiting for her just around the corner. Her heartbeat quickens.

His eyes, the colour of caramel, light up as she nears him. He's handsome in his peacoat and boots, his leather gloves and cream turtleneck. He has stubble now, a shade or two darker than his blond hair. It's only as she stops before him that she notices the shadows beneath his eyes. 'What're you doing here?'

'I was on my way to the office.'

'Oh.' She shifts uncomfortably. 'Why?'

'Lunch with my wife.'

She feels a pinch of disappointment that she tries to hide with a smile. She should not be disappointed that Linden is here to see his wife instead of his mistress. *Ex*-mistress. After all, this is what she wanted.

They have tumbled into an awkward silence. And even though he is holding her gaze, outwardly as confident and in control as ever, she notes the quick beat of the pulse fluttering in his neck and a fine sheen of sweat on his forehead. He's agitated and spring-coiled.

'I've actually got to get going,' she says. 'Or you won't have anything to eat at all.'

He frowns. 'What do you mean?'

She pats her cross-body bag where she has tucked the list of lunch orders and money. 'Food run.'

'That's a large party to cater for. How will you carry it all?'

'I haven't figured that out yet . . .'

He brightens. 'I'll come with you.'

'No,' she says quickly. 'No. It's fine. I'll manage.'

'Don't be ridiculous. Let's go.' He turns and strides down the street. She hesitates, instinct telling her this is a terrible idea. That an addict should never be left alone with their favourite cocktail. But wouldn't it be churlish to refuse his help? Linden Lockwood isn't going to vanish from her life. She has to learn to be around him. To be near him without wanting to touch him. Without wanting to be touched by him. Resolute, she takes a deep breath and hurries to catch up.

Chapter Forty-Six

The Wife

I haven't told Addison my intention to meet with Mimi because I know she will warn me against it. Especially since she thinks Mimi killed my husband. So, on my way back from Cambridge, I drive to Rook Lane alone. It's not long until Christmas now and it gets dark early. By the time I've pulled onto my gravel driveway, the sky is a smudge of grey. Soon, the streetlamps will turn on. I get out of the car and make my way over to Mimi's front door. I knock but as soon as my fist meets the wood, the door slowly opens, yawning into the darkness of the hallway.

Apprehension snakes through me as I cross the threshold. She never leaves her door unlocked, let alone open. I call her name and wait for her to appear. She doesn't. I'm greeted only by an eerie, too-still silence.

'Mimi?' I shout into the dark.

When she still doesn't answer, I start walking down the hallway. The tiny hairs on the nape of my neck rise. The air feels charged, the way it does in summer just before a storm.

I turn right into her office. Mimi's house is filled with colour. She once described her interiors style as a child let loose with a tin of paint. The wood-panelled walls are verdant spring green and the soft furnishings in hues of yellow and white. Dandelion colours. On her desk is her laptop. Nothing seems out of place but still unease hisses through me as I wander back into the hallway and down into the kitchen. The walls are ice-cream pink and the cupboards are a pastel rainbow, each one a different shade, reminding me of the fishermen's cottages in Cornish seaside towns. Though the stove is off, resting atop it is a pan of soup. It's cold with a thick skin, as though it's been left overnight. On the counter is a chopping board and loaf of sourdough, the knife suspended in it, mid-slice. I imagine Mimi preparing lunch and being interrupted by a knock at her door. So why didn't she return to eat her food? And where is she now?

Even though I know it's fruitless, I call for her again.

Silence. Thick and bleak.

I pivot towards the closed lounge door. Dread curls tightly inside me as I push it open. A flock of fear swoops down on me as I take in the scene: the overturned coffee table, the mug of spilled coffee, the smashed vase and the wilted flowers that are strewn across the patterned rug. Cautiously, I step inside, half expecting to see Mimi's lifeless corpse in the corner of the room. But there is no body. Relief, as sharp as the crisp, clean air outside, whooshes through me. It doesn't last long though because I see a smear of red across the corner of the overturned coffee table.

'No,' I whisper, feeling sick. 'No . . .'

At the sight of the blood, my hand flies up to cover my mouth. I need to call someone. Tell someone. I fumble for my phone but I haven't managed to dial the police before the front door creaks open. I freeze. I listen. I hear footsteps in the hallway. Terror clenches in my chest. I snatch up a gold candlestick from the sideboard and dart behind the lounge door. My breath is coming hard and fast, like the panicked panting of a dog. I wait, muscles coiled tight in terror.

A figure emerges around the door frame and I swing the candlestick. A woman's terrified shriek rends the air and I pull back at the last second, swinging the candlestick into the wood.

Addison falls backwards against the door frame and stares up at me with wide, horrified eyes. 'What the hell?' she breathes, a hand pressed to her chest as though fending off a heart attack. 'Jesus, Verity. Are you trying to kill me?'

I toss the candlestick onto the sofa as fear slackens into agitation. 'What are you doing here?'

'You were supposed to be back from Cambridge three hours ago.'

'There was traffic,' I tell her.

'I was worried so I drove to your house to look for you. I saw your car in the driveway and then I spotted Mimi's front door was wide open.' She straightens and finally takes in the scene. 'What the . . .' She slowly walks into the lounge.

'We need to call the police,' I tell her. 'We shouldn't be in here.'

She crouches beside the coffee table and rubs a thumb over the red stain. 'Is that blood?'

'I think so.'

She snatches her hand back and stares up at me. The horror on my face mirrored in hers. 'What happened?'

I shake my head, tears stinging my eyes. I picture Mimi being thrown into the coffee table, hitting her head, sending her unfinished cup of coffee and her vase of flowers flying. I can taste the metallic burn of fear as she tried to fight off her attacker. I know all too well what that feels like. Though I won my fight, I'm not sure Mimi was lucky enough to win hers.

Chapter Forty-Seven

The Other Woman

She and Linden weave between early Christmas shoppers and down winding cobbled streets. She swings right, in the direction of Boho Deli, but Linden grabs her arm. 'Green Bird Café will have less of a queue.'

His fingers linger. Even through her coat, she can feel the warmth of his touch. She thinks of that injured house martin. Of Peter insisting that men like Linden don't set women like her free. She looks up at him. His gaze drops to her mouth. She feels her pulse in her lips. If she wanted to, she could reach up and kiss him. Her resolve to stay away from him starts to crumble. Frightened it will disintegrate completely, she jerks back. She stumbles over the lip of the kerb and into the road. Someone screams. She whips her head to the right in time to see the bike careering towards her. Then she is being yanked forward, onto the pavement and out of the cyclist's path. She tumbles into Linden's chest and buries her face in his coat. Her heart hammers.

Linden wraps his arms around her. 'Jesus, you were almost hit.'

Her face burns with humiliation as she makes eye contact with an older man who shakes his head at her as he passes.

She breathes in the familiar spicy scent of Linden's cologne. Then he is touching her face, tilting her head back so he can stare into her eyes. 'Are you OK?'

She nods. 'Fine.'

He smiles. 'Good.' His gaze is penetrative and intense. Desire surfs through her as she remembers what it feels like to have him on top of her. The glide of skin on skin and the breathless thrill of his touch. 'God, I've missed you,' he whispers, not caring they are in public.

She can't return to evenings spent waiting for a call from her married lover. She wants more than that. She *needs* more than that. She thinks of her new housemate, Cassie, of Anna and her other university friends, of proper meals, of her hobbies: of evenings spent working her fingers over cool clay or writing, pen on paper, until her hand aches. *That* is the life she is creating from the ashes of their break-up . . . isn't it? So she swallows her longing. 'We can't do this.'

'I wasn't happy in my marriage. I didn't realise how unhappy I was until I met you. It's true, I get bored quickly. Tire of things, of people, too easily. But I have never been bored or tired of you. The *you*ness of you. I want you. Only you. Only ever you.' He's breathing hard, his eyes searching her face. 'I know I'm not a perfect person. Far from it. But I love you. I will always love you but . . . do you still . . .'

And in this moment, she is in love with his vulnerability. In love with the idea that she is his entire world. That she is chosen. It is now that she discovers her resolve is sand because with his words, he has blown it away. It is granules taken off on a sharp gust of wind. It is nothing. Nothing that matters because all that does is being here, with him. He kisses her and she lets him. He is that first square of dark chocolate after Lent. If she lets herself, she will devour him whole.

He pulls away from her, a satisfied smile stretching his lips. He rests his forehead against hers so all she can see is the tawny amber of his eyes. 'I'm going to take care of you,' he tells her.

'What about your wife?'

'You don't need to worry about her.' And that nervous energy from earlier is gone, replaced by a stillness that makes her heart race.

'But if we're together and you're still married, whoever is writing those notes will tell—'

'I'm going to fix everything.' And before she can ask what he means, he takes her hand and leads her to Green Bird Café.

Chapter Forty-Eight

The Wife

Mimi has been missing for three days and the police aren't telling me anything. Addison and I were questioned thoroughly but we know as much as they do: Mimi's lounge is in a state and she's nowhere to be found. It's obvious to me that the attack in my bedroom is related to Mimi's disappearance but the police seem unconvinced. Even so, I haven't returned to Windermere. Harry was kind enough to insist I spend Christmas with him and Addison.

Usually, they decorate their house on 1 December, but with all that's happened, they haven't done it. Now, with only a week to go, Addison has hauled boxes of labelled decorations from the cellar.

'I could've helped you do that,' I told her.

'No, don't worry. There's all sorts of junk down there.'

Harry is visiting his aunt and uncle in Dorset for a couple of days so it's just the two of us. It feels bizarre to listen to Christmas classics and decorate a tree while Mimi is still missing, but I don't want to let my melancholy impinge on their festivities. I am sick with worry but Addison maintains the police will find Mimi and in giving them our statements, we've done all we can.

'But who would hurt Mimi?' I ask as I carry a clear plastic box into the lounge.

'Didn't you say there was some guy with a lip ring hanging around outside her house? Maybe it was him.'

I didn't catch his name, but I gave the police his description in case they needed to talk to him. Lip Ring, as I'd come to think of him, had been so dismissive of Linden's death that it had made Addison question whether *he* killed Linden. Now though, I wonder whether Mimi told Lip Ring about Linden assaulting Lyla and perhaps that's why he said the things he did. 'But why would that man hurt Mimi?' I ask. 'He seemed to really care about her. If they aren't dating now, they certainly have in the past.'

She shrugs. 'Maybe he's an ex who wanted to rekindle their relationship and she didn't.'

'And so he hit her over the head and carried her off to some cave?'

Another shrug.

We open the boxes and I start pulling out all the carefully organised baubles and fairy lights. Every year, Linden and I would stuff our lights back into a bag and regret it when Christmas rolled around and half our evening was dedicated to disentangling them. I long for another Christmas in my own home. The smell of a real tree. Addison said the needles drive her nuts so she bought a fake one and even though it was extortionate, it still smells of plastic instead of pine. I try to concentrate on hanging baubles but questions fly around my mind like dusty moths. 'What if the person who's been threatening me, who attacked me, is the same one who attacked Mimi?'

'I don't know,' she says, reaching for another decoration. 'Maybe. Maybe not. Why would the two be related?'

'Don't you think it's odd that just as she was ready to meet me, she disappeared?'

She shrugs again. 'Maybe she realised how awful she'd been to you and wanted to apologise.'

'Or maybe she had some more information about Linden and whoever she ran from.'

'Did she specifically say she had a secret?'

I hand her a painted glass bauble. 'Well . . . no . . .'

'Have you ever considered she's faked her own abduction?'

I stare at the back of her glossy, dark head. 'You can't be serious. No one *fakes* their own abduction, Addison.'

'Elodie Fray?'

I roll my eyes at the mention of a local case from three years ago.

'OK. You have *one* example. But faking your own abduction is far less likely than actually being abducted.'

Finally, she looks at me, one eyebrow raised. 'Is it?'

'Well, I don't exactly have the statistics to hand,' I quip.

Dean Martin's 'Baby, It's Cold Outside' fills the silence. And I imagine Linden convincing Lyla to stay for just one more drink even though he knew it would be one too many. 'What if—'

'Stop!' Addison yells. I'm so startled, I drop a bauble and it shatters into a dozen sparkling gold pieces. She sighs, long and loud, before bending to pick them up.

I crouch beside her to help. 'Sorry, I didn't mean to—'

'It's fine,' she says quietly. This close to her, I can see the dark circles beneath her makeup. 'I'm sorry I yelled. I'm tired and it's a week before Christmas. I don't want to talk about murders and affairs and missing neighbours.'

And what can I say to that? She and Harry have opened up their home to me. I can't blame her for not wanting to dwell on the chaotic, morbid mess my life has become. More tangled and complicated than the fairy lights sitting in a bag in my attic.

Christmas is important to Addison; growing up, she didn't get much of one. Her mother rejected it. Rejected the Christian home that raised her and the Christian holiday which meant she'd have to be the kind of parent that decorated and cooked. One year, Addison's mother left her in a Travelodge for three days over Christmas while she partied on a narrow boat in Cambridge. Addison ate vending machine chocolate bars and stale crisps. Now, as an adult in control of her own life, she makes up for every terrible Christmas her mother gave her by doing it bigger and better and more exuberantly than anyone I know.

So I don't talk about Mimi or Linden again and instead, I continue to pick out baubles and hand them to my cousin. After a few minutes of decorating without speaking, Addison says, 'Are you sure you don't want to visit your dad and Agathe for Christmas?'

I feel stung. 'You really don't want me here, do you?'

She stops and turns to me, remorseful. 'I do want you here, Verity. Of course I do. I just don't think it's good for you to be worrying the way that you are. Maybe going away will help take your mind off it all.'

'I can't,' I tell her. 'If I go to Belgium, I'll either have to lie to my father about what's going on or tell him and have him worry himself sick.'

'At least he cares enough about you to worry, Verity.'

'Have you heard from your mum?'

She nods. 'She sent a card. I don't know where in the world she's even living. She talked about moving back to Somerset but I've heard that before.' She falls quiet. She's hurt, of course she is. Addison's mother was more suited to the role of fun aunt than responsible parent. Even though our mothers looked identical, they couldn't have been more different. 'Sorry, that was insensitive. At least my mother's alive.'

'My mum being dead doesn't change the fact that yours isn't around. They're both gone, just in different ways.'

Addison swallows thickly and I think she might cry. 'Anyway, it doesn't matter. She's the *least* of my worries.'

I open my mouth to ask what else she's worrying about when she snatches up the empty box the decorations were in.

'Do you want me to take that down to the cellar?' I offer. 'It seems fair, since you dragged them up here.'

'No,' she says, pushing her fingers through her long hair. 'Like I said, it's dangerous. There's so much junk down there. I'll do it.'

Chapter Forty-Nine

The Other Woman

Green Bird Café is small and crowded. There is a fridge with preprepared sandwiches and a round DIY salad bar.

'Where's your list?' asks Linden.

She retrieves it from her bag along with the money. Linden tells her to take a picture of the list on her phone so they each have a copy. Then he takes half the cash from her. 'Right, let's get this done quickly. I'll grab the salads, you grab the sandwiches and drinks.'

She smiles, grateful for his help.

At the counter, she rattles off the drinks order to a bored-looking barista. While she waits, she wonders what Linden meant when he said he would fix everything. Is he going to find out who wrote the notes and put a stop to it? Pay them off? Or, she speculates with a thrill, is he going to divorce his wife?

Soon, she and Linden are stepping out of the café, laden with bags, and walking back to the office. Despite the cold, she is sweating. On the corner, just down the road from their destination, Linden stops. 'You'd better go in first,' he says.

She nods and takes the bags from him. The handles dig into her fingers. If he hadn't stepped in and helped, she'd have had to do two trips. She wants to talk to him. To clarify what is between them. Even though she loves him, she knows they can't be together until he has left his wife. That is the boundary she is going to set. No secret liaisons, no snatched kissing, no covert phone calls. Nothing until he has a clean break. But this is not a conversation to be had now. 'Can we meet this weekend?' she asks. He grins and her cheeks flush. She shakes her head. 'Not for . . . To talk.'

He frowns in mock solemnity. 'Sure. Absolutely. Just talk.'

'I'm serious,' she says, suppressing a grin. He's being playful. She loves it when Linden is playful.

'Got it.' They smile at one another. He gestures towards the office. 'You'd better . . .'

'Yep.'

As she turns to go, he grabs her wrist. 'Her order is on top.'

'What?'

'My wife. Her salad is in this bag.' He tugs at the handle to indicate which one. 'Right on top.' She frowns in confusion and he says, 'Fish allergy, remember?'

She rolls her eyes. 'Of course. Yes. Thanks.'

Then he pulls her to him. She wants to kiss him. His mouth is so tempting. But she can't. She won't. Instead, she smiles and then moves past him. As she goes, she can feel his eyes on her.

Chapter Fifty

The Wife

I go into Bath for some last-minute shopping. The market is over. Every year, the city is packed full of tourists and now they're gone, the city breathes out and loosens its trousers as though it's polished off Christmas dinner. Above me, tiny lights like champagne bubbles twinkle in high arches. The shop windows are adorned in reds and greens and golds. Crowds of people pass by, clutching glossy bags and steaming takeaway cups of gingerbread latte. The air sings with expectation and cheer. It feels wrong. I feel wrong. Like a lump of coal in a child's stocking on Christmas morning. There is so much joy around me, and I can't touch any of it. Mimi is constantly on my mind. Thoughts of her run in circles around my head like a cat chasing its tail. I'm as far from solving Mimi's disappearance as I am from unravelling my husband's lies.

It's cold. I pull my coat close around me and walk down the high street, glancing in shop windows as I go. Then, in the warm glow of a boutique shop, I see Amy browsing a rail of cashmere jumpers. Her blonde hair is pulled up into a sleek ponytail. She's in profile, her skin like glass as she moves beneath the shop lights. She glows in her white fur coat and ivory silk skirt. She's as tall and as lean and as perfect as ever.

I take a deep, bolstering breath and head inside the shop. I'm so nervous as I approach her that my heart tries to hammer its way through my chest.

'Amy?' I say to the back of her head.

She stiffens.

And, leisurely, she pivots. Her smile is polite and guarded and so cool it makes frost slide through my veins. 'Verity,' she says by way of greeting.

Even though I've practised this confrontation in my mind a thousand times, I can't think of a single thing to say. I just stare up at her.

'Right. Well,' says Amy in the face of my silence. 'I'm actually meeting someone so I'd better head off. Merry Christmas.'

And then she moves carefully past me, as though not wanting to dirty her white coat. 'I know about you and Linden,' I call after her.

She stills. Slowly, she turns, like a ballerina in a jewellery box. 'What about me and Linden?'

'That the two of you were involved.'

She widens her eyes, her long lashes almost touching her pale brows in a show of innocence. 'Involved?'

And like a match being struck along the side of a box, fury flares. She's treating me like an idiot. 'Don't pretend you haven't fucked my husband.'

The women browsing the rails beside us perk up so quickly they remind me of meerkats. Amy gives them a tight smile before taking my elbow and manoeuvring me to one side. She lowers her voice, 'Whatever you *think* you know about me and Linden, you don't.'

I shrug out of her grip. 'Then tell me.'

She glances around the shop. The two women have moved closer. Amy's perfect feathers are ruffled. 'Not here,' she decrees.

We walk outside and stand in the glow of the shop window. It's cold and there's a mist in the air that makes me shiver. 'I know you and Linden were together.'

She flicks her chin up. 'How?'

Before I answer her questions, I have some of my own. 'The night of the Verity Rose Winter Party you had a lilac sheet of paper in your pocket. What was it?'

She frowns. 'What?'

'I saw you waiting for a taxi outside Lullington Manor. You pulled it out of the coat you're wearing now, then scrunched it into a ball.'

She shrugs. 'It was a blank piece of paper. I have no idea where it came from.'

I eye her, trying to work out whether she's being honest, but I'm met only with sincerity. Someone at the party planted it in her pocket. But why? To frame her? Only the author of those lilac love letters would want to pin them on Amy.

'Why would you ask me that? What's a blank sheet of paper got to do with anything?'

I shake my head, refusing to answer her questions until she tells me the truth. 'How did you and Linden really meet?'

She sighs as though bored by the entire conversation but I can see the pin-sharp interest in her eyes. 'University.'

'But that doesn't make any sense. He's older. He—' My mouth snaps closed as I realise. 'He was your lecturer.'

She nods.

I think of all the times he'd come home and tell me about the silly, giggling girls that followed him around campus. He'd feign annoyance, exclaim that he was a writer, not a children's entertainer, but it was obvious he got a kick out of it. That the attention of all those promising young women made him feel relevant and desired and interesting. 'That's why you were so vague about how you met.'

'He asked me to be.'

'Because you were friends?'

'He thought so.'

Nausea washes over me. Lyla came before Linden and I were officially together but what about Amy? She's barely a handful of years my junior. 'Was he married at the time?'

She shrugs again. 'He never wore a ring.'

He very rarely did. His publicist apparently advised he appear 'available' because that made him and his books more accessible. I never questioned it; I was secure in our marriage. Now though, I doubt it was even his publicist's suggestion. 'You didn't think it was odd that you and he had to sneak around?'

She folds her arms across her chest. 'Neither of us wanted our position at the university to be compromised. I could have been expelled and he could have been sacked.'

High risk, high reward. I think of their shared secret, the stolen glances, the hotels he would have taken her to, the breathless, toe-curling sex on the knife edge of being discovered. So much more exciting than the wife he left at home. A fat, hot ball of anger and betrayal lodges in my throat. 'So was Linden the one you told me about? The one who got away?'

Her smile is wry. 'No, I certainly wasn't talking about Linden.'

'Then who?'

She glances away. 'She came long after Linden.'

She? I study Amy, but I can't tell if she's lying. I'm not sure why she would, since she's already admitted she and Linden were in a relationship. Still, there are things I don't understand. 'Why were you following Linden?'

She blinks, surprised by how much I know. 'Are we done?'

'He's dead, Amy. Murdered. Don't you think the police will be interested to know about your relationship with him? That you *stalked* him right up until his death?'

Her cheeks turn the colour of holly berries. 'So, if I don't give you all the gory details, you'll go to the police?'

I lift my chin. 'Yes.'

'I've got nothing to hide. I didn't murder your husband.'

She levels me with a hard stare which I meet with one of my own. 'You've just started your own business. Do you really want to risk bad publicity?'

She studies me, assessing me anew. 'I always thought you were nice.'

'Then you really don't know me, Amy.'

Our gazes lock and I can see her mulling over her options. She shakes her head, as though she can't believe she's telling me anything at all. 'I was barely twenty when Linden summoned me to his office to look over my work. He told me I was gifted and that with his help I could be a great writer. Just as good as him. Soon, he wasn't complimenting me on my writing but on how beautiful I was, how mature. He told me we had a connection. I thought he loved me.' Her laughter is bitter. 'But the only thing Linden loved was power and control and how he could exert it over women.' She leans forward, angry. 'Your husband was a predator.'

The Wedding Vow

I am breathing hard. It's as though she has poured scalding hot water over my head, the truth blistering and burning. 'If you hated him that much, why were you friends with him?'

'I befriended him *years* after our relationship ended and it was only possible because I worked for the accountancy firm the Lockwoods used.'

'But why befriend him at all?'

'To keep tabs on him.'

I shake my head, failing to keep up. 'What?'

'I pretended to be his friend so I could watch him. I needed to know if he was taking advantage of other women. Like he did with me and . . .' She trails off and glances down the street. She wants to leave, but I have so many questions. I need to keep her talking so I ask another.

'You think he took advantage of you?'

'I know he did,' she snaps. 'It took me a very long time to realise exactly how toxic he'd been. How wrong it was of him to get involved with a student. I'm not saying I was entirely innocent. I knew a romantic relationship with my lecturer wasn't right, but he used his position at the university to get close to me. And then, whenever we fought, he'd mark down my work. He claimed it was a coincidence but the threat of him ruining my education, my *life*, always hung over my head.'

'And so you broke it off with him?'

She reddens. 'No. He ended it with me. I got the sense he was seeing someone else. We were together only a few months but it affected me for years. I knew it was legal, consensual even, but it wasn't OK. I was too ashamed to tell friends, especially those who'd been at university with me, so I contacted a charity. Impartial professionals that dealt with women in crisis. And they were great. They put me in touch with a therapist. They validated everything I already knew: that Linden had abused his power. Had coerced and manipulated me. And I wasn't the only one.' She takes a deep breath and I can already feel the weight of what she's about to tell me pressing down on my throat. 'A week later, I received an unofficial email from someone who worked at that charity. A woman who recognised Linden's name.'

I swallow. 'Why?'

'Because he assaulted her.'

My heart canters. 'Assaulted?'

'At a work party.'

'Lyla?' I breathe, remembering Mimi told me Lyla left publishing to work for a rape crisis charity.

Amy's lip curls in disgust. 'You knew what he did and you still married him?'

'No. Of course not. I found out recently.'

The revulsion clear on her face eases, just a little. 'Like me, it took a long while for Lyla to accept what he did. Like me, she was worried their encounter would ruin her career. She was just an assistant when he assaulted her. He warned her that people at the party saw them flirting and knew she had a thing for him. He promised her no one would believe their best-selling author over a junior assistant and even if they did, she was expendable, whereas he was not.'

I don't know what to say. I married a stranger. Built a life with a stranger. Gave up so much to be with someone I clearly didn't even know. 'Why didn't you ever tell me about your relationship with Linden?'

'I didn't know you. Didn't know if you'd believe me and even if you did, Linden and the entire Lockwood family were huge clients of the accounting company I worked for. He warned me our history was private and if I shared it with anyone, especially with you, he'd threaten to leave the agency to ensure I lost my job. He never meant for me and you to meet. He only introduced us because you stumbled across us having lunch in town.'

Which means the reason she's telling me all this now is because she's working for herself and, with Linden dead, she's the only one with the power to disclose their past.

'Amy, why didn't you tell anyone about your relationship with Linden? The university? Your family? You could have had him sacked,' I say gently.

She raises both pale blonde eyebrows. 'Are you really going to be one of those women who asks why it wasn't reported sooner? As if that diminishes or erases what he did?'

'No. No, of course not. I'm just . . . trying to understand.'

Her cold blue eyes rake over me and, seeing my sincerity, they soften. 'Linden once told me women very rarely come out of these situations smelling of roses. I worried for my education, my reputation, how my story would be examined and pulled apart. He knew what he did to me was wrong and so he made it crystal clear that if I ever spoke up about it, he'd crush me. He threatened to tell the university I was *obsessed* with him.' She shakes her head. 'Even after we were over and I graduated, I couldn't be sure if my first-class degree was because I was capable or because I'd slept with my lecturer. Not knowing was infuriating. So much so, I retrained as an accountant.'

I'm so sorry for what Linden did to her, I look for the words to make it right. 'Amy, I—' But she's so caught up in her rage, she speaks over me.

'He ruined everything. Even my relationships. I found it difficult to trust anyone after him. Sex and power and love were so interwoven, I sabotaged every connection. Including what I had with Lyla.'

I'm so surprised, I gasp. 'Lyla? You and Lyla . . .'

She nods. 'She was patient and kind. A *good* person. And I ruined it because being with Linden made me feel as though I was undeserving of being more than someone's dirty little secret.' Linden had been a cancer in Amy's life that she spent years carefully cutting out, but I see the damage he has done, the scars that are left behind. 'Lyla and I started off as two strangers who'd survived Linden Lockwood. Then we became friends . . . Then we became more. And I was the happiest I'd ever been. I tried to convince Lyla to go to the police but she refused. Said it was years ago. That there was no evidence. It was just her word against his. She said she'd dealt with it and now she was helping others to do the same, but I couldn't ignore what he did to her, or to me. I needed to stop him from derailing other women's lives the way he had ours. I became intent on catching him doing to another woman what he did to Lyla and, when she found out, she told me to let it go. I couldn't. So she let me go instead.' Her eyes shine with tears she won't let fall.

I realise now it was never Linden who was the one that got away. It was Lyla. And he was the 'project' that came between them. I think of the framed photographs in Amy's home. The only ones on display were of her mother and the redhead Amy refused to introduce me to at the Rye Bakery. With a swooping feeling in my stomach, I understand why. 'Lyla is the woman that stopped by our table, isn't she?'

Amy appraises me, impressed I pieced it together. 'Yes.'

I remember Lyla had appeared just as confused by Amy's refusal to introduce us as I was. Amy must've taken her to one side that day to explain that I was Linden's widow and once she knew, she left quickly. I don't blame her. She must've felt very awkward knowing I'm the woman who married her attacker. 'You really love her.'

Amy takes a deep breath, that icy facade thawing. 'I do. But it's over now. I let Linden take so much from me. My career, my self-worth, Lyla, even my name.'

I frown. 'Your name?'

'Millie,' she says. 'At university, I was Millie. *His* Millie.'

I'm so shocked, words are lost to me.

'I used to love the way he said my name.' She blushes and I imagine him gasping it into her bare back. 'After university, I couldn't stand to be called Millie. It reminded me too much of him.'

'How did you get Amy from Millie?'

'Amelia,' she tells me.

I nod, reeling from all the information. There are still so many questions. I reach for one but it's like putting my hand into a bag of pick 'n' mix; I have no idea which one I might pull out. 'But why take photographs of him? Was it a case of revenge being a dish best served cold?'

'No. It wasn't. In my experience, revenge is a dish best served hot and bloody.' Her eyes narrow. 'How do you know about the photographs?'

I press my lips together, realising my mistake. I can't lie. There's no other explanation for knowing what I do. Forcing myself to hold her gaze, I admit what I've done. 'I visited your apartment while you were away.'

Her mouth falls open. 'You broke in?'

'No. Not exactly. Your neighbour . . .'

'And you think *I'm* the crazy one?' she snaps. The she turns on her heel and starts walking away. I rush after her and grab her arm.

'Amy, wait. *Please.* Linden didn't only ruin *your* life,' I say honestly. 'I gave him everything and it turns out I didn't even know him. He manipulated me, too. He lied to me, too. He used me, too. Please, Amy,' I add, desperate. 'I *need* answers.'

Silence stretches between us, long enough to make panic rise within me but Amy's anger slackens into pity. I hate that she feels sorry for me but I swallow my pride because I need her to fill in the gaps. 'It wasn't about revenge. It was about justice. What Linden did with me was wrong, but it wasn't illegal. What he did to Lyla was. When she left me, I couldn't let it be for nothing. I doubted Lyla would be the last woman Linden assaulted. So I followed him and took photographs, hoping if he did hurt someone else, I'd at least catch it on camera.'

'Was there ever anyone?' My mouth is dry and I feel sick as I wait for her answer.

She shakes her head. 'Nothing like what happened with Lyla.'

That, at least, is a relief. I'm quiet, trying to organise everything I know. As Amy isn't the author of the lilac love letters, she must know who is. 'At the winter party, I told you Linden was having an affair. That I found love letters. They were typed on lilac sheets.'

She nods in understanding. '*That's* why you asked about that piece of paper.'

I nod.

'It wasn't mine,' she confirms.

'I think my husband's mistress set you up.' I take a deep breath. 'Did you ever photograph them together?'

More silence. A dark tide of trepidation wells up inside me. 'I did.' My heart stops. She knows the identity of the other woman. 'I sent her a note. I didn't see them together again after that. I intended to talk to her face to face to see if she had a similar story to Lyla, but then Linden died. And I finally felt like it was over. A death sentence was better than anything the courts would've dealt him.'

Dandy Smith

I feel my pulse in my lips. 'Do you know who killed him?'

'No. I don't. But I'm not sorry he's dead, Verity.'

'Neither am I,' I say, fixing my gaze on hers. I wait for her surprise or her reproach but I'm met only with solemnity and quiet approval. 'Amy, who's the other woman?'

'Are you sure you want to know?' she asks, stony and intent.

I swallow. 'Yes.'

She holds my gaze a moment longer but I don't waver. I want to know what she knows. She gets her phone out of her Chloé bag and scrolls through it before finding what she's looking for and then handing it to me.

Insides churning, I stare at it. At the photograph of Linden in a restaurant, leaning over the table, kissing another woman. A woman I know all too well.

Chapter Fifty-One

The Other Woman

The office is busy. First, she makes sure Linden's wife has her salad. Then she goes around the room, handing staff their orders. It's only now she realises she forgot to order food for herself. Sighing, she reaches for her coat, preparing to go back out. She's frustrated because it's cold and she'll have to eat at her desk to make up the time. Not that she minds; she struggles with small talk and finds it tedious to feign interest in stories of colleagues' children and what they did at the weekend.

She spins in the direction of the exit but stills when she spots Linden standing beside the rack of bags and coats. He straightens. Their eyes meet and she feels it all the way to her toes. She is thinking of the first time he told her he loved her as they lay naked and entangled on the living-room floor of Paddledown. Her blood starts to sing, desire and love sparkling in her veins. His gaze is still on her when someone screams.

She spins towards the noise. A freelancer with red hair is shouting for someone to call an ambulance. Linden races across the office and drops down beside his wife as she convulses on the floor. Her skin is turning scarlet. Her eyes are wild and terrified and bulging. She cannot breathe. She claws at Linden's shirt with desperate, panicked fingers. The salad box lies beside her, its contents strewn across the hardwood.

'Her EpiPen!' demands Linden. 'Where's her EpiPen?'

The office manager sprints towards the coat rack where Linden had been standing just moments ago, and rummages through the black Gucci bag. 'It isn't here!' she shouts. 'It isn't here! Where is it?'

She looks down at Linden's wife. Her lips are turning blue. Linden fumbles in his pocket for his phone but others are already speaking quickly into their mobiles. A girl with freckles says, 'Ambulance is on its way.'

But it might be too late because Linden's wife has gone slack in his arms.

Chapter Fifty-Two

The Wife

I pound on her door. It's almost 7 p.m. but the lights are on so I know she's at home. I stop banging and listen. I hear footsteps hurrying down the stairs and a moment later, the door is yanked open.

Flora stares at me, wide-eyed and worried. 'Verity, are you OK?'

'Can I come in?'

She hesitates, then steps aside to let me pass. The hallway is small. Flora nods towards the lounge. I don't bother removing my shoes. My mother would throw a fit if she saw me now, standing on a cream rug in my boots. Flora looks small and fretful as she hovers in the doorway. She's wearing sage-green button-front pyjamas. Her long red hair is pulled up into a messy bun, some loose pieces framing her pretty face. I stare at her perfect pink mouth. I can't dispel the image of her kissing my husband. My blood runs hot with fury all over again. She's exactly his type: young and beautiful, promising and naive. Fresh meat. Fresh and tender and easily devoured. How stupid was I that I didn't see it before? It all makes sense. That day I saw her in Novel Wines – Linden's favourite – dishevelled and heartbroken by the mysterious boyfriend no one even knew about. It was Linden. It had to be. And then, at the winter party, Flora had volunteered to run the cloakroom, which would have allowed her to slip the lilac love letter into Amy's pocket. For months, Flora has barely been able to meet my eye. For Christ's sake, she's been dating the Tesco Value version of my husband but I never thought, not for one second, Flora conniving or deceitful.

'Are you OK?' she asks again.

'No,' I snap. 'No. I'm not OK.' I start pacing up and down, trying to rein in my temper.

'C-can I get you a tea?' she stammers. Her large green eyes dart down the hall towards the kitchen, desperate to get away from me.

I must look like a feral animal. I stop pacing but I'm not calm. Rage balloons inside me, expanding until I feel I might pop, leaving chunks of myself all over the stone-coloured walls of her home. 'You kissed my husband.'

Flora blanches. 'Verity . . . I . . .' Immediately, her eyes well up and her bottom lip trembles like a kite on a windy day. 'I . . . I'm . . .' Her breath comes in short, sharp bursts. Then her hands fly to her throat, as though she is choking. She's rasping, struggling for air. A panic attack. She's having a panic attack. She clutches the arm of the sofa and I rush over to her, helping her onto it. I tell her to put her head between her knees even though, just moments ago, I wanted to knock it off her shoulders. She does as I instruct. I sit with her, waiting for her breathing to return to normal. I expected to be met with denial or vitriol, not panic and fear. Soon, Flora is able to right herself. She looks up at me from beneath tear-damp lashes. Her eyes are red and her hands tremble on her lap. 'Verity, I'm so sorry.'

I sink to my knees. 'How long?' I ask.

Her brow creases. 'Sorry?'

'How long were you sleeping with my husband?'

She recoils. 'Sleeping with him? No, no, I didn't . . . we didn't . . . no.'

My brows knit together. 'No?'

'I never had sex with your husband. *Never.*'

I gape at her in disbelief. 'But you kissed him. Don't deny it.'

'*He* kissed *me.*' She rubs her palms against her knees. 'But I didn't want to be kissed.'

I sit back on my haunches. 'You weren't having an affair?'

'No. Not at all.'

'Then what?'

She pulls a plump macramé cushion onto her lap and starts fiddling with one of its ivory tassels. 'It was just supper,' she offers meekly.

'A supper in which you and my husband kissed?' There's a bite to my voice that makes her head snap up.

She looks at me, aching and lost. Her pyjamas pool around her feet and she seems like a little girl. 'I'm not the woman he was having an affair with.'

'You know about the affair?'

She swallows thickly. 'I heard you in your office on the phone to the police.' So it was Flora who had listened in and knocked over the monstera.

'The morning I came to work and talked about going through Linden's things, you were worried. Why?'

'Because I knew someone else had seen Linden and I together. I'd received a note and I was concerned Linden had, too. That if he had, you'd found it.'

She is shaking and despite my suspicions, I feel sorry for her. 'How did you end up at a restaurant with Linden?' I ask gently.

'I met him at that first Verity Rose Winter Party,' she begins. 'I was nervous, it was my first work event. Linden was standing in a corner, drinking alone. He seemed . . .' She trails off, struggling for the word.

'Sullen?' I offer.

'Quiet,' she corrects. I can see it now, Flora on the fringes of the party, hovering awkwardly as strangers dive effortlessly from one conversation to another. She attempts to join in but feels as though she is trying to step onto a twirling carousel. So she hangs back, swinging from wanting to be noticed to wanting to slink home. Linden will have been watching her. Flora, who is young and beautiful and adrift. He smiles to himself, finding her skittishness endearing.

'He started talking to me. I told him I was your assistant. He asked me lots of questions and seemed interested in what I had to say. I admitted I wanted to be a writer, like you, and that's when he offered to take a look at some of my pitches.' He becomes a flickering flame and she a spellbound moth. 'I agreed to meet him for lunch. But, on the day, he called and said he had to move things around.' Lunch becomes supper. He chooses a fancy restaurant; one he knows will impress. The kind where the waiter pours the wine and tablecloths are buttery-soft linen. There is candlelight and possibility. There is dessert and anticipation. There is Linden and my twenty-three-year-old assistant.

'He leant across the table and kissed me,' she says. I can picture them, her reluctant and nervous, him expectant and certain. I see his face, his white smile and caramel eyes, rapt and glimmering, fixed on her mouth as she talks. He isn't listening. He is wondering what she tastes like. He is bold enough to find out. 'I was shocked. Too shocked to pull back right away.' Her gaze finds mine. 'He told me you and he had an understanding.'

And with this, the images dissipate. I laugh, a loud, disbelieving burst of noise. 'Did he?'

She looks unsure. 'Yes. I didn't believe him, though. I read every blogpost and article you ever wrote about your marriage and what he was saying didn't sound right. He made me promise not to mention it to you. He said you'd kill him if you ever found out.'

I surge to my feet. 'Lies on top of lies on top of lies.' I whirl towards her my frustration with him bleeding into this conversation with her. 'And why didn't you come to me?'

She blinks up at me, obviously terrified. 'I was worried about my job. I love working for you. For Verity Rose. I thought you'd sack me just for agreeing to meet him.'

My minds spins. I still have questions. 'Why were you in Novel Wines that evening after Linden died? Did he tell you about it?'

She nods. 'But I already knew about it. My boyfriend's . . .' She winces. '*Ex*-boyfriend's,' she corrects herself, 'brother owns it. When Linden kissed me, I was in a relationship. A really happy one, actually.' She looks down. She is winding the tassel around her finger. 'I made the mistake of telling my boyfriend, Adam, what Linden did and he was enraged. He wanted to confront him but I begged him not to. I didn't want a fuss but I didn't want to lie to my boyfriend either. Adam thought I had feelings for Linden but I didn't, Verity. I swear.' She pleads with me, wanting me to believe her. 'And then a week later, Linden was dead. I panicked. I was terrified that . . . that . . .'

'That what?'

'That maybe he . . . Adam . . .' The words jam in her throat. Her eyes are wild, darting all over the lounge, looking anywhere but at me.

I kneel at her feet and put a reassuring hand over hers. 'What is it?'

She takes a deep, trembling breath. 'I thought Adam had hurt Linden.'

My hand slides from hers. 'You think your ex-boyfriend murdered my husband?'

She worries her bottom lip. 'I thought so. Adam denied it. He was so furious I even asked, he broke up with me. Cut me off completely. Changed his phone number. I was at Novel Wines that night to talk to Adam's brother. I hoped he'd at least tell me where Adam was staying. Then I saw you and I was so mortified I ran.'

Slowly, it's all coming together. Still, I need to find out who sent me that pig's head. Flora's married lover certainly fits the description. 'You're with someone else now, aren't you?'

'No,' she lies.

I get up and sit on the sofa beside her. 'I've seen you with him.'

She closes her eyes. 'Benjamin. I met him at a bar,' she says after a moment. 'But we aren't a couple, not anymore. He ended things a few days ago.'

'He went back to his wife?'

Her brows shoot up in surprise. 'How did you . . .'

'I saw you with him outside a couple of months ago. He was wearing his wedding ring.' I give her a look. 'You really should be more discreet.'

She puts her head in her hands and groans into her palms. 'We are . . . were . . . His wife lives in Northampton. He comes to Bath for work.'

We fall quiet. For the first time, I look around the room. It's painted a terracotta pink and all the furnishings are in pastels and creams. The room is decorated with soft throws and scatter cushions, plants and candles in coloured glass jars. It's so tidy and feminine. The lack of black, flat-pack furniture tells me she doesn't live with a man. I shouldn't be here, in my employee's house. I should leave, but I have a feeling Benjamin is somehow involved and Flora's the only person who can confirm my suspicion. 'At the winter party, I was lured into the cellar and attacked. Just last week, someone broke into my house and assaulted me in my bed.'

The blood drains from Flora's face. '*What?*'

I nod.

'Verity, I'm so sorry.'

'I'm fine, I just . . .' I bite my bottom lip, wondering how best to ask. 'Could Benjamin be responsible?'

She opens and closes her mouth. 'No. No. I mean . . . he doesn't even know you. Why would you think . . .'

'Well, at the party, the person who attacked me was seen. The witness basically described Linden.'

She wrinkles her brow. 'OK . . . I don't understand.'

'The man you were seeing, Benjamin. He looks a lot like Linden.'

She gawps at me. Slowly, I see it all sliding into place. Her face flushes. 'God, Verity, I never even realised.'

'Are you *sure* Benjamin isn't involved?' I press.

'He can't be. He's never even met you. And I haven't ever told Benjamin about Linden. Besides, we aren't together anymore. He broke it off. He just stopped answering my messages and calls.'

If Flora's telling the truth then she's right, Benjamin has no reason to be involved in any of this, but someone matching his description was seen picking the pig's head up from the butcher's and giving a waitress the note that lured me into the basement.

'I'm *still* worried Adam hurt Linden,' she says. 'He was never violent with me but he was protective, and angry that Linden kissed me. What if Adam went to your house to confront him that night? I didn't go to the police in case I was wrong but I should've, shouldn't I?'

I shake my head. 'I don't think so, Flora. If Adam murdered Linden for you, don't you think he'd have stayed with you after? If not, what was the point?'

Some of the tension seeps out of her. 'You're right,' she reassures herself. 'I'm just . . . so sorry, Verity. I should never have met with Linden.' She looks at me, plaintive, wanting to be absolved.

I don't blame her for agreeing to meet with him. He knew exactly what he was doing. Flora didn't. I remember what it was like to be twenty-three, to feel as though you know everything while knowing almost nothing at all. I understand Flora. I feel sorry for her. Heartbreak has torn a chasm in this young woman so wide, she is willing to fill it with married men, but it'll never work. 'Flora,' I say gently. 'You're talented. I always intended to give you a writing position but, with Linden's death and everything else, it slipped off the list. You never needed his help. Women very rarely need to rely on a man to lend them any kind of success. I didn't. And neither do you.' She gives me an appreciative smile. 'As for Adam, and Benjamin, and whoever comes after them, you aren't one half of a person waiting to be completed by another. You're whole, all on your own. Be thankful Benjamin broke things off when he did. He cheated on his wife. He's a liar. He'll always be a liar. Men like that will twist you out of shape. They'll take and take and take until you don't even recognise what's left behind. You weren't his first mistress and you wouldn't have been his last.'

Later, I climb into my car. Flora waves me off and then ducks back inside. She closes the door and, as I stare up at her canal-side home, I wonder if I'm a fool to believe a single word she's said.

Chapter Fifty-Three

The Wife

I barely slept last night. Amy and Flora's stories kept turning over in my mind. Neither of them wrote Linden love letters on lilac paper. Both were impressionable, and he took advantage. I still don't know the identity of the man who collected the pig's head from the butcher or lured me down to the basement. Flora is right; there's no reason her married ex-lover Benjamin would have to hurt or torment me. So, if he isn't behind it all, then who is? And is my attacker the same person who took Mimi?

It's a few days before Christmas. Harry is due back tomorrow and Addison has gone out for dinner with friends. She didn't want to leave me alone in the house and spent the entire day trying to convince me to go with her. Frankly, I'm not in the partying mood. I practically had to force her out the door and I'm glad I did because I'm grateful for the time to think. I haven't told Addison about bumping into Amy or my excursion to Flora's house, but I will when the time is right. I'm in the lounge, trying to unwind with a glass of wine. Addison's house is much cosier than Windermere, where there are so many empty bedrooms. When I bought it, I imagined we'd fill them with children. I don't want to rattle around in a too-big house with only Linden's ghost for company, so when this is all over, I'm going to move somewhere smaller.

It's cold tonight so I've whacked the heating up and pulled a throw across my lap. The wind wails, clawing at the windows with hooked fingers. Hail thunders against the house. I love the feeling of being warm and cosy inside while a storm rages outside.

My phone rings. It's Addison. She's barely been gone an hour. 'I'm on my way back,' she tells me as soon as I answer. 'The weather is atrocious. I'm worried as soon as it stops hailing, the roads will freeze over and it'll be too dangerous to drive home. Is everything all right?'

'Everything's fine.' I pick up the TV remote. 'I'm about to find something festive to watch.'

'OK, good. Great.'

Silence pours down the line along with the feeling that something is wrong. 'Are you OK, Addison?'

'Yep,' she shrills.

I laugh. 'Are you worried I'm going to start rooting through your underwear drawer or something?'

'No,' she says too quickly. 'I just don't like driving in this weather. Anyway, I'll be back as soon as I can but the traffic is a nightmare.'

'OK, well, drive safely.'

I'm about to hang up when she says, 'Oh, I forgot to mention earlier that I saw a rat in the cellar last week. Harry put some poison down before he left.'

'Poison? It's Christmas, that isn't very jolly of you. You could've offered them paper hats and turkey, maybe even a seat at the dining table for Christmas lunch.'

'Just please keep the cellar door closed – I don't want them scurrying through the rest of the house.'

When she's gone, I turn on the TV and start surfing through the channels. Addison is so wound up, I'm surprised she hasn't snapped yet. She takes hosting very seriously and I imagine, in her mind, by leaving me home alone she's broken one of the ten commandments of the etiquette bible to which I'm sure she subscribes. My phone rings again.

'I'm fine, Addison, really, and the rats remain very much in the cellar,' I say by way of greeting.

'And how do the rats feel about that?'

I freeze, fear sliding through my stomach at the sound of an unfamiliar male voice. Is it the man who has been impersonating

Linden? I pull my phone away from my ear and check the caller ID. It's an unknown number. 'Who is this?'

'Max. We met the other day, outside Mimi's house.'

The man with the mop of dark hair and the lip ring. I turn off the TV and sit up.

'I hope you don't mind me phoning,' says Max. 'I have a friend at the police station and he took your number from Mimi's phone.'

I frown, still a little on edge. 'That doesn't sound legal.'

'Maybe it isn't legal but it is important.'

'OK . . .' I can hear that he's upset and even though I don't know what he's going to say, my entire body prickles with intrigue.

'I went to your house a few times but your car was never there.'

'I'm staying with my cousin, Addison. After what happened to Mimi I was afraid to be alone.'

'What *did* happen to Mimi?' Like me, Max is really worried about her. I hear it in the quake of his voice and that makes some of my apprehension dissolve. He may have been rude to me about Linden, but it's obvious he cares a great deal for Mimi. After a fraught back and forth with Addison, who even went as far as to question whether Mimi staged her own abduction, it's a relief to talk to another person who's desperate for answers.

'I don't know what happened to her, but I want to find out. You said you had a contact at the police. Have you asked him?'

'*Her*,' he corrects. 'And I did. The police are clueless.'

I scoff. Aren't they always? This is why people take matters into their own hands. 'I told them everything I know, but I'm sure you have a lot more information than I do. Mimi cut me out of her life right after Linden died. I don't even know where she's been living this past year.'

'She travelled. We ran into each other in Oman, on the steps of the Royal Opera House. I hadn't seen her in years, but when we started talking, it was as though we hadn't ever been apart.'

I still don't know the nature of his relationship with Mimi but, from his wistful tone, I'm convinced they were once a couple. 'How did you both end up in Bath?'

'After a few more weeks of travelling, we came back to England

and stayed with some old friends in Leeds, but I had a job starting in Bristol. Mimi missed her home, so she came back to Somerset with me.'

That's the glory of Mimi's job as a book translator; she can work from anywhere. 'Did she ever tell you why she left Rook Lane?'

'She talked about the day she found Linden's body and how it stopped her from sleeping, but I always had the feeling there was more to it.'

I think of all the cryptic things Mimi has said since she returned and how I had the sense she was running from someone. 'Like she was afraid?'

'Like she felt guilty.'

'Guilty?' I shake my head. 'You don't think she murdered Linden?'

'No. No, I don't,' Max says quickly. 'But I always wondered if she knew who did.'

A rock hits the bottom of my stomach. 'You never asked?'

'She wouldn't talk about it.'

'But she did talk to you about Linden?'

'Yes,' he says, voice clipped.

He knows. Max knows about Linden sexually assaulting an editorial assistant. 'Mimi told you about Lyla?'

'Yeah, she did.'

Which makes sense, given how dismissive he was of Linden's death.

'I'm sorry if I upset you with my comment the day we met,' he says. 'But from what I've heard about your husband, he wasn't a good man.'

I wonder if he thinks I'm not a good person because I married him, but remind myself it doesn't matter. Max is a stranger; I shouldn't care what he thinks of me. What I do care about is if he knows anything that will help us find Mimi. 'Well, for a time, Linden tricked both Mimi and I into thinking he was a good person. You know Mimi and Linden used to be friends?'

'I do.'

'You know she hid that from me. I'd never have found out if wasn't for Addison giving me that photograph of Mimi and Linden together.'

I hear rustling, as though he's switching the phone from one ear to the other. 'Mimi was shocked when you posted it through her letterbox,' he tells me. 'She hadn't seen that photo in years.'

I frown. 'It was hers. Addison stole it from Mimi the month before Linden's death.'

Silence. 'Verity, Mimi never had that photo . . . It was Linden's.'

'Linden's? No. That's not right. Addison told me she took it from Mimi's house.'

'No . . .' he says slowly. 'When Mimi showed me the photo, she said she was surprised Linden had kept it.'

Unease twists my stomach into knots. I get to my feet. The throw pools onto the floor. 'But that would mean Addison lied to me. Why would she lie?'

'Are you sure you didn't find the photo while you were clearing out his things?'

The sound of shattering glass makes me jump.

He's still talking into the phone but I move the receiver away from my ear so I can listen out for another crash. When another doesn't follow, I press the phone to my ear again. 'Verity? Are you still there?'

'Yes,' I say, distracted. 'Sorry, I missed that.'

He exhales sharply. 'I said I'm worried that whoever killed Linden has taken Mimi because she knows who they are. Verity, do you have any idea who—'

Another bang, louder this time. I yelp.

'What is it?'

'I heard a noise.'

'Where are you?'

'At my cousin's house.'

'In Bath? Where?'

I'm so distracted by the noise, I answer on autopilot. 'Camden Road.'

I wander into the hallway and make my way towards the kitchen. I flip on the light but there's no glass and everything is as it should be. Slowly, I turn towards the door at the far end. 'I think it came from the cellar.'

'Rats?'

'Pretty big rat to make that much noise.'

Then I am plunged into darkness. I shriek.

'What?'

'The lights have gone out.' I listen. It's silent. Even the hum of the fridge has vanished. I hurry through the dark and back into the lounge. I bash into the coffee table and swear as pain radiates along my shin. Then I limp towards the window and pull back the curtains. Even the streetlights are out. It's so dark, I can't even see the rows of houses opposite. 'It's a blackout.'

'Do you want me to come over?'

My laugh is shrill and shot through with nerves. 'I don't know you.'

'You don't, but we both want to find Mimi. And soon. What if she's hurt? Trapped somewhere?' he says, the worry in his voice making my heart beat even harder. 'I think we should meet to compare notes. Maybe we can work out what's happened to her.'

Isn't this what I wanted? Someone who would listen instead of dismissing me and casting ludicrous aspersions? Addison isn't going to help me find Mimi, but Max will. 'When?'

'I could come to you now. You probably shouldn't be home alone in a blackout when a killer is still on the loose.'

I feel a shiver of fear. 'Are you trying to comfort me? Because if you are, you're doing a terrible job.'

'Sorry, I just . . .' He takes a breath. 'I just can't stop thinking about her.'

'Me neither,' I say honestly. 'But Addison will be home soon and I'm not sure how she'd feel if I let a stranger into her house.'

Silence.

Surely I haven't upset him? 'Hello?' No answer. I look at my screen and see the call has ended. I try phoning Max back but it goes to voicemail. Assuming he's lost signal and will ring when he can, I turn on my phone's torchlight. Unfortunately, my battery is only just hovering above six per cent. Any less than that and the torch won't work. There are candles in the sideboard but no matches or a lighter.

My phone rings again. Glancing at the screen, I see the unknown number flashing up again. It's probably Max. I decide to call him back once I've found a lighter or match. In a drawer of miscellaneous items, I push aside loose wires and half-used birthday candles, until I come across a blue plastic lighter. I snatch it up and make to close the drawer when I spot a small scrap of paper. I pick it up, turning it this way and that, examining it beneath the bright, white glow of my torchlight. It's such a small piece, I'm not surprised she missed it. One edge is frayed and the other is jagged, as though it's been torn from a book. It's thick and expensive. And lilac. Just like the love letters I found beneath the floorboards of Linden's wardrobe. A perfect match.

My heart spirals down to my stomach and there's a roaring in my ears, growing louder and louder. I grab the work surface because this is proof, it's the ultimate proof. Addison is the author of the letters . . . Addison is the other woman.

Then there's another bang. A definite crash coming from the cellar. I whip in the direction of the noise. The cellar door is at the far end of the kitchen. I turn my torch towards it. Harry had wanted to convert the cellar into a cinema room. I think they even started the project but then the bathroom renovation was more expensive than they thought and so the cellar conversion was put on hold. I haven't been down there in a couple of weeks. I move towards the door but when I try to open it, I realise it's locked. Why is it locked?

I go into the hallway and check the console table drawer where the spare keys are kept. They're missing. Addison's house is so organised, it's odd the key isn't there. Then, remembering that Harry keeps a set of spare keys in his gym bag after he was locked out a few weeks ago, I turn and jog up the stairs into their bedroom. It smells of furniture polish and their combined scents. I open up the second wardrobe and from the bottom of it, I drag out Harry's gym bag. I search the pockets until my fingers clasp around the cool, hard metal of his spare keys. The little brass one looks like the one used to access the cellar. I jump to my feet and run as quickly as I can down the stairs, swinging into the hallway and then sprinting into the kitchen. The key fits. I'm about to open the door when I remember the last time I ventured into a cellar alone. The memory of a stranger grabbing me from behind makes fear tremble through me. I back away from the door. But then, if he is down there, why would he have locked himself in? There's probably nothing down there, but unease needles my skin.

My phone vibrates in my hand, making me jump. It's Max. 'We got cut off,' he says. 'Are you OK?'

'No.' Adrenaline whiplashes through me. 'There are noises coming from the cellar. I don't think I'm alone in this house.'

His voice is tinny, as though he's driving. 'Then you need to get out.'

'But what if . . .' I trail off, the thought so preposterous, I can't even speak it.

'What if what?' he demands.

'Addison was being . . . odd. She told me not to go into the cellar. Said there were rats.'

'OK . . .'

'But I'm not sure I believe her.' I press my lips together to stop myself from saying more, hoping he'll fill in the gaps.

He replies but the signal is cutting in and out, his words broken and impossible to decipher. Then the call dies.

I don't bother trying to phone him back. I need to get into the cellar. I pull open the door and carefully start making my way down the steps and into the dark.

Chapter Fifty-Four

The Other Woman

Dazed, she staggers through Bath. After Linden's wife was whisked away in an ambulance, they were dismissed and the office closed. She can still see the blank expression Linden was wearing the second before the ambulance doors whooshed shut. She doesn't know what to do. She calls him but he doesn't answer. Of course he doesn't answer; he is at his wife's side, waiting in the sterile confines of a hospital.

The streets bustle with tourists and students, early Christmas shoppers and the late lunchtime crowd. Nausea rolls through her, making her mouth water. She concentrates on putting one foot in front of the other as she heads for the bus stop but her heart is pounding so fast, she's worried she will faint. She stops and rummages in her bag for her water bottle. She unscrews the cap and glugs it down. It sloshes into her empty stomach.

What if Linden's wife is dead?

The thought starts small, like a pinprick, but grows quickly until it consumes her. She is crying. Crying so hard that her chest heaves as sobs break from her ribs. She is leaning against a wall but slowly starts sinking to her knees. If his wife dies, it is her fault. She must've given her the wrong order. What will happen if the police get involved? They could find out about the affair and accuse her of murdering her lover's spouse. That is the conclusion others will come to. Will she go to prison? Though she knows she is not a murderer, at the very least she is a killer. It is her fault. All her fault.

People stop to stare, even the sharply dressed businessmen who are in a rush. A man with greying hair and a kind, weathered face crouches in front of her. 'Are you hurt?' he asks.

Something about him, his woody cologne or his grey tweed jacket, reminds her of her father. She cries even harder. She wants to be a little girl again, out on the fishing lake with her dad. She covers her face with her hands and sobs into them. Her incompetence might have just ended another's life. She thinks of Linden, all alone, clutching his wife's hand.

'Can I call someone for you, love?' asks the man.

But there is no one.

When she closes her eyes, she sees Linden's wife, her face contorted in fear, the bulging veins in her neck, the blue-grey of her lips.

'Don't worry,' says another voice. One that is familiar to her. 'I know her. I'll take it from here.'

Then Peter is helping her to her feet and picking up her bag from where she's dropped it. He walks her down the street, past cafés and shops. She is too gripped by panic and anguish to be surprised by his sudden appearance. She leans into the solid safety of his arm around her. He tugs her into an alcove next to a bakery and turns her so she is facing him. She is still crying; her mascara runs black rivers down her cheeks.

'What's happened?' he asks.

She shakes her head, her throat too tight to answer. She tries desperately to gather herself but she can't banish the memory of the paramedics or the stricken look on Linden's face.

'Did Linden hurt you?' demands Peter. 'If he hurt you, I'll kill him. I mean it.'

She doesn't like this darker, angrier side of Peter. She only ever glimpsed it after his neighbour killed his dog all those years ago. Despite spending just minutes in Linden's company, something about him has slid beneath Peter's skin. Is this her fault too? She thinks of herself as poison, winding through the veins of those who dare to love her. She drove her father to do the unthinkable; she transformed Linden, a faithful husband, into a liar and a cheat, and Peter, her first love, is willing to murder.

And now someone is dead. Linden's wife could be dead. Because of her.

Her chest tightens, gripped by horror once more. She cannot breathe. Cannot draw a single breath.

Peter takes her hands in his and squeezes them. His green eyes are focused, fixed unwaveringly on her. 'Take a deep breath,' he tells her. 'In and out, that's it.'

She does as he says, in through her nose and slowly out through her mouth. She can smell the pine and cedarwood scent of him. Can feel the whip and chill of the cold November air and the reassuring warmth of his hands holding hers. Eventually the panic subsides but she can't bring herself to let go of him. To anyone walking by, they would look like a couple. 'Thank you for staying with me,' she says now. Though her heart still flutters in her chest, she feels calm and safe. Peter has always made her feel that way. She takes him in, noticing for the first time how smartly he is dressed: the navy trousers, suede loafers and a tan coat. His lip ring is gone. 'What're you doing here?'

'Interview,' he says. 'I had an interview for a graphic design job.'

And for a moment, sunshine breaks through the clouds of her own miserable situation, and she is happy for him. 'It went well?'

He glances down, biting the inside of his cheek.

'What?' she pushes.

'I, um, I think I've probably missed it. I was on my way when I saw you.'

Her stomach drops. 'Peter . . . No. Oh God, I am so sorry. I—'

'When I realised it was you . . .' He shrugs. 'I didn't have a choice.' His gaze is locked on hers but it is too much, as though she is staring directly into the sun, so she looks away. He sighs.

'I'm so sorry.'

'What happened to you?' he asks. 'Did Linden—'

'No, Linden didn't hurt me.'

He relaxes. 'Good.'

She stares down at their still-joined hands. She should slip hers free but she doesn't. 'Why are you being so nice to me after what I told you?' she whispers. 'I'm not a good person, Peter. I'm the dreadful *other woman*.'

'Because of him.'

Her gaze finds his. 'Because of *me*. I'm not perfect, Peter. Not even close.'

'No, you're just punishing yourself.'

'What?'

'Because of what happened with your dad.' Her stomach drops. She doesn't want to talk about her father. Peter gives her hands a reassuring squeeze. 'Because of what your mum said.'

She feels the sharp sting of her mother's remembered hateful words: *You don't deserve to be loved.*

'She's wrong,' he assures her. 'Penelope was hurt. She lashed out at you and said things she didn't mean.'

'She *did* mean them. She's never apologised or taken it back. She's right, what happened to my father was my fault, and now ... and now ...'

'What?'

She can't tell him about Linden's wife. And she can't let Peter pick up the pieces. He cannot fix her. Cannot fix any of it. She is a poison spell. A hex. Everything around her withers and turns to ash. She whips her hands away from him and steps out of the alcove. He looks at her as though she has slapped him. 'Just stay away from me,' she begs through a veil of tears. '*Please*, Peter.'

'Wait.' He reaches for her but she sidesteps. He freezes, his eyes too wide, his chest rising and falling too fast.

'I'm not who you think I am,' she tells him. He looks wounded and vulnerable, and she knows he wants to save her but she's painfully aware she doesn't deserve to be saved. Or desired. Or loved. Wherever she goes, she wreaks havoc, and she will not let Peter be part of the devastation. 'Next time you see me in the street, don't stop.'

Then she turns and keeps walking until she can no longer hear him calling her name.

On the bus back to Paddledown, she refuses to think of Peter Holland and instead she calls Linden's burner phone five times. He doesn't answer. Out of desperation to know the fate of his wife, she considers calling his personal mobile but instinct tells her it is not a good idea. If his wife is dead, she can't risk the police seeing the call log and unearthing things she'd rather stayed buried.

When she arrives outside Paddledown she is so shocked by the sight that greets her, she almost drops her phone. There is another note from her anonymous sender, pinned to the front door with a knife. She takes a corner of the paper and rips it free.

This is going to end terribly for you.

With trembling hands, she pockets the note. Then she steps up to the knife, grasps the handle and yanks it from the wood. She stares down at it. She feels her face drain of colour because she recognises this knife. The ivory handle and the maple leaf at its base. It is part of a set.

Without a doubt, she knows who has been sending her the notes.

Chapter Fifty-Five

The Wife

The cellar is cold and damp. Without my torch, it would be pitch-black. I swing my phone from left to right as I reach the bottom of the stairs. The space is filled with boxes, plastic and cardboard, with abandoned gym equipment and Harry's fishing rods. Nothing is smashed or broken and I'm struggling to see where the noise might have come from. Still, I have a burgeoning sense of unease. I move through the cellar slowly, listening, but all I can hear is the rush of my panicked breath. It's so dark I feel as though I'm trapped inside a coffin.

Towards the back of the cellar are boxes that have been stacked up, dividing the space into two halves and making it feel much smaller than it is. I stand in front of them and try to peer over the top, but they're piled too high so I start moving them aside.

Then, with the boxes out of the way, I am left staring at a single divan bed. It looks brand new, the cellophane still clinging to the sides. I move to inspect it. It's grey and boxy. On top of it is a stack of gym weights. Two of these plates are lying on the ground. I pick up one of them. Beneath it is a shattered drinking glass. I suppose if it slid off the bed and smashed the glass, it would explain the noise I heard. Crouching down, I start gathering the shards in my cupped hand. Then I carry them over to a stray box beside the bed and set them down next to a screw-top jar of pills. I pick it up and read the label. Harry's prescription sleeping medication. Why're they in the cellar?

I go back to the bed to take a closer look. Running my hands along one side, my fingertips brush over metal. When I shine my torch, I see that they are hinges. The bed is an ottoman, the kind that opens up and is hollow for storage. My heart starts working its way up into my throat. I remove the remaining weights from the bed. My entire body is a live wire, zinging with tension.

I open up the bed. It clicks, locking into place. But before I get a glimpse of what's inside, the light from my torch vanishes and I am plummeted into treacle-thick darkness. My phone has died. Frustrated, I drop it. Then, breathing through my mounting panic, I try to shake the feeling that the walls are moving closer. I gingerly lower myself to my knees and grope along the edge of the frame, willing myself to reach down into the storage space. 'It's probably nothing,' I say out loud into the dark.

When my fingers are met with cold flesh, I squeal. Bombarded with images of pigs' heads and bloodied, dismembered bodies, I scream and scramble backwards on my haunches. Then the light above me blinks to life and I close my mouth so quickly, my teeth crash together. I'm breathing hard, relieved the power has returned. Shaking, I get to my feet and reluctantly step towards the divan.

I gasp, hands flying to my mouth.

Mimi!

She's unconscious, lying on her side in the ottoman, bound and gagged. She's wearing a pair of blood-splattered dungarees. There's a nasty gash on her temple and rivulets of blood have dried across her cheek.

'Oh my God!' I drop down beside her and press my hand to her neck, searching for a pulse. She's clammy and unmoving but I can tell from the shallow rise and fall of her chest that she's breathing. I remove the gag. 'Mimi?' I shake her shoulder, trying to rouse her. 'Mimi, can you hear me?'

Her eyelids flutter but do not open. I scoot forward and start untying her, wincing at the purple bruises encircling her wrists. She's mumbling, too quiet for me to hear. I lean closer. 'Addison,' she whispers.

My stomach clenches like a fist. Addison did this? Mimi's been down here for at least four days. I think of the sleeping pills and know Mimi's been drugged. How many has Addison given her? I have to get help. I scramble for my phone and then, with a thud of dread, remember it's died. Addison doesn't have a landline but the charger for my mobile is upstairs. I don't want to leave Mimi in the cellar but, without knowing the extent of her injuries, I'm not sure it's safe to move her, either.

Then I hear the unmistakable slam of the front door, echoing like thunder. I swing my head up, towards the top of the staircase: Addison is back.

Chapter Fifty-Six

The Wife

Terror thick in my veins, I surge to my feet. Addison is jogging down the stairs towards me, her long dark ponytail swishing behind her. 'I told you not to come down here!' She's furious and I am silent, too terrified to move.

Seeing the open ottoman bed, she stops and her fury quickly bleeds into panic. Her wide, dark eyes find mine. 'Verity . . . I . . . it was an accident.'

'An accident?' I stare at her in disbelief. 'You *accidentally* shut Mimi inside a bed in your cellar?'

She looks at me pleadingly. 'Mimi and I, we got into a fight.'

'When?' I step to the side but Addison mirrors me, blocking my way.

'While you were away in Cambridge. I went to her house. We argued. She fell.'

'Fell?' I scoff. 'You expect me to believe she *fell*? I'm not an idiot, Addison.'

In the silence, her gimlet gaze assesses me. She is deciding how many lies she can force-feed me and when she realises it is none, it all comes spilling out. 'I shoved her. I just lost control and I shoved her. She hit her head on the coffee table and I couldn't wake her. I panicked.'

'You should have called an ambulance!'

'I know. I know. But I was scared, Verity. I put her in my car and I meant to drive her to the hospital but . . . but . . .'

'You didn't.'

'I *couldn't*. I was frightened, I was in shock, so I brought her here. You and Harry were away. I just needed time to think.'

Adrenaline surges through me, whipping my heart into a frenzy. 'We need to call someone. Mimi is barely breathing.' I make to cross the cellar but Addison steps into my path again.

'Verity, *please* don't call anyone. If you do, she'll tell the police.'

'What's the alternative, Addison?' I snap. 'Keep her locked in this cellar forever?'

'No.' She swallows. 'I don't know.'

I try to move past her but she puts her hands out to stop me. I don't know what she's thinking but she's determined not to let me leave.

'Can we just talk?' she desperately pleads.

If Addison could hurt Mimi, attack her in her own home and then drug her and abduct her, what will she do to me? I need to buy myself some time so I say, 'Fine. Let's talk. What were you and Mimi arguing about?'

She blinks. 'What?'

'You said you got into an argument. What was it about? What could she possibly have said that made you mad enough to shove her?'

'I . . . I don't know. I can't . . .' She trails off into deafening silence.

'You were outside listening in the hallway when Mimi called and asked to meet with me, weren't you?' Addison presses her lips together and I know I'm right. 'Mimi was going to tell me what she knew and you went to her to try and stop her. She does know, doesn't she?'

Addison pales. 'Know what?'

I lift my chin. 'That you were having an affair with my husband.'

She freezes. Holds her breath. My entire body tightens as I wait for her reaction. I let the silence hang between us like a noose and watch as she dips her head into it and then leaps into the abyss below. 'Verity, I'm sorry.' And that is it. Finally, the truth. A lifelong relationship dead and swinging. Something ancient and new opens inside me. An endless, black pit of despair. My husband and my cousin. The two people I loved most in the world.

'How could you?' I breathe.

She sobs. Her body shakes with the force of her sorrow but it isn't for us, it's for him. 'I loved Linden.'

The secret she has kept from me leaks out like an oil spill into an ocean, ruining everything. 'You wrote those letters,' I say, thinking of the small, torn scrap of lilac paper I found in the kitchen drawer.

She nods, ashamed.

'How long?' I demand.

She shakes her head.

'HOW LONG?'

She takes a deep breath and exhales slowly. 'Nearly a year.'

My knees feel weak. 'A *year*? You were fucking my husband for a *year*?'

Her brow furrows. 'It wasn't like that . . . it was . . . Neither of us meant it to happen.'

'So how did it?'

She lifts a trembling hand to her forehead, as though she is staving off a headache. 'I'd just found out Harry was sterile.'

'Sterile?' I echo, shocked.

She nods. 'I was devastated. We'd been trying for a baby for years and I thought *I* was the problem but it was him. I came to your house to talk to you but you were gone. Another trip with Mimi.' Even now, I can hear the bitter note of jealousy. 'Linden invited me inside. We talked. He offered me a glass of wine . . .'

'Jesus,' I hiss.

'You were never there, Verity.'

Fury scorches a path from my heart down to my toes. I turn on her. 'So this is *my* fault?'

'He was lonely. I was devastated. It just . . . happened.'

'And kept on happening?'

'I never wanted to hurt you.'

'Then you shouldn't have had an affair. A year. A *fucking* year.' At my sides, my hands curl into fists. 'And what about Harry? He loves you, Addison. But because he couldn't give you a baby, because he isn't perfect, you cheated on him, *lied* to him?'

Instead of being cowed, she is angry. She closes the gap between us, bringing her face just inches from mine. 'You want to talk to me about perfect, Verity? You had it all: the husband, the career, the expensive wardrobe, a mother who loved you, who wanted to be in your life, but you take everything for granted. You always have.'

And this is it, isn't it? This is how she truly feels about me. I see it now, years and years of building resentment, buried beneath affection. But she has no idea how hard I worked for the life I have. No clue of my relationship with my mother. When Addison moved in with me and my family, she was so grateful to be away from her own neglectful, wayward parent, she was happy to do whatever mine asked of her. She craved rules and organisation, everything that my aunt lacked. Addison lived with my family for less than a year before she went away to university. She hadn't endured almost two decades of my mother's constant micromanaging, her criticism, her impossible standards, and the many days of silence that would follow if I dared to disagree with her. My mother loved Addison, but she used her to hurt me, too, lavishing my cousin with affection while acting like I didn't exist because I'd kissed a boy she didn't approve of, or chosen a university she insisted was too far from home.

'Linden told me he wanted children,' she spits, malice rolling from her like smoke from a fire. 'But you were too *selfish* to even consider it.'

My laughter is sharp and contemptuous. 'He told you that, did he? And you believed him?' But of course she did, Addison is a jealous creature and it's so much easier to be cruel if you can convince yourself the person you're being horrid to is actually the villain. 'I wanted a family. I wanted a child. It was Linden who didn't.'

'You're lying.'

'I'm not. The reason we never had children is because Linden had a vasectomy before we married.'

She stares at me, lips parted in horror. She's distraught. I imagine all the false promises he made to her. I see him lying naked with Addison, wrapped around her, whispering how she is his everything, his past and present and future. That he can't wait to start a family with her. That hers are the only children he will ever want. These are the same lies he fed to me. Ones I swallowed happily. Just like her. But they are no more substantial than mouthfuls of air.

'No,' she says. 'You would've told me.'

'Just as *you* told *me* Harry was sterile?' She sucks in a breath, realising I am right. Until Heidi, I hadn't told *anyone* about the vasectomy. I wanted people to love Linden and me together. To think we were the perfect couple. So I kept secrets. 'We were clearly never as close as we pretended to be.'

A tear rolls down her cheek. I'm not sure whether she's crying for the end of us or the lies Linden told. I'm not sure I even care, but I do need to know more. I recall the evening Addison handed me some pills to prevent a headache and how I promptly fell into a fourteen-hour sleep. I assumed she'd given me paracetamol but, having seen Harry's tablets and what they've done to Mimi, I'm convinced Addison drugged me, too. Which can only mean one thing. 'You knocked me out with sleeping pills, didn't you? It was *you* who left the pig's head. You had to be certain I wouldn't wake up and catch you with it.'

She nods and, ashamed, brings her hand to her mouth.

I'm so furious, I have to fight the urge to lunge at her. 'Why the pig's head?'

'I wanted to scare you into keeping quiet. I worried if you continued to talk to the police, they'd find out about me and Linden and they'd tell you and Harry.'

'But the police called and said there was nothing on the laptop or phone to give away the other woman's identity, so why did you lure me into the basement? Why send someone to kill me in my home?'

'I didn't send him to kill you! I told him not to hurt you. It was all to frighten you. I hoped the run-in with him would steer your focus away from the identity of the other woman, but I never meant for him to seriously injure you.' She's earnest, eyes wide, desperate for me to believe her. 'I really didn't.'

She had me assaulted so I'd abandon my pursuit of Linden's mistress and turn my attention to the mystery of my attacker, all the while planting doubts, trying to make me suspicious of Heidi, Amy, Flora, Mimi. Anyone but her. Addison even went as far as to insist Mimi was dangerous so I'd keep my distance because she was worried Mimi would tell me about Addison's affair with my husband. She is more conniving than I ever gave her credit for. 'Who is the man you sent to attack me?'

She closes her eyes. 'Flora's married boyfriend.'

'Benjamin?'

Another nod.

'How are you two involved?' It doesn't make sense. Like Flora said, Benjamin had no reason to hurt me and I can't think why he'd agree to help Addison.

'I saw him again. Found out where he worked.' She shakes her head, as though she is ashamed of herself. 'I threatened to tell his wife about Flora if he didn't help me.'

'You blackmailed him?' It's impressive, really. She hardly had to get her hands dirty at all. I suppose she's the reason Benjamin so abruptly ended things with Flora. I realise, in this moment, that I am a terrible judge of character. Forever putting my trust in the wrong people. I knew Addison could be single-minded and never thought she could be so calculated, so callous. 'You were responsible for it all: the pig's head, the assault in the basement, breaking into my home and attacking me in my bed?'

Her cheeks flame. 'It got out of hand. I never wanted you to be seriously hurt.'

'He tried to smother me!'

She covers her face with her hands. 'I'm sorry. I'm so sorry.'

'Are you? First you fuck my husband, and then you have me attacked and tormented to cover it up? And you have the audacity to call *me* selfish?' I hiss ferociously. 'How dare you? Growing up, I shared my home with you, my parents, everything I had.'

'Your parents chose to open their home to me.'

I shake my head. 'No. I had to convince my mum to let you live with us. I begged her. I even threatened to run away if she didn't help you because just like your own mother, mine never wanted you either.'

'Fuck you!'

'Are you going to shove me and lock me down here like you have Mimi? Or maybe you'll beat me to death like you did Linden?'

She pales. 'I didn't kill him.'

'You really think anyone is going to believe you? You think *I* believe you?'

'We loved each other.'

I give her a spiteful spread of my lips. 'You think you're special? His only mistress?' She's so affronted, the cords in her neck strain. She's battling the urge to attack me but I don't care. I want to hurt her as much as she has hurt me. 'It may have felt shiny and new for you, but for Linden, it was all déjà vu.' Linden chose her because she reminded him of the woman I was when we met: unambitious, lost, yearning for adventure.

'You're wrong.'

'No. You only wish I was. I'm going to make sure you pay for everything, Addison. The lying, the cheating. All of it. You can tell yourself I deserved it. That I was a bad, inattentive, absent wife, but that isn't true. You have no idea how much of myself I gave up for him. Your affair was never about Linden or the deluded fairy tale of love you used to comfort yourself. It was about punishing *me*. Taking something from *me*. Because you're ruthless and tragic, trapped in a life that doesn't serve you. That you've grown bored of. I should thank you, Addison, because you freed me. I'm free of him and soon I'll be free of you, too.' But I'm not done yet. I have kept my parting shot, my poisonous dart, for last. 'Your father didn't want to know you and your own mother ran from you. You're rotten, Addison. You'll never be a mother. You aren't made for it. You don't deserve it.'

She lunges at me. We tumble backwards, knocking over a stack of boxes. Then she's on top of me, fists raining down on my head and shoulders. All the while, she's shrieking like a banshee. I kick and twist, struggling to get away. I lash out. My fist smashes into the side of her head and the force of the blow vibrates up my arm. She falls to one side and I scramble to my feet, clutching my bruised knuckles. I shake out my hand, trying to dislodge the pain.

I lurch towards the staircase, stumbling over the boxes and their spilled contents. I am hit from behind and thrown forward. Flinging my arms out to break my fall, I turn my head to the side to avoid smashing my face into the concrete floor. The air whooshes from my lungs as I land. I flip onto my back but I don't have time to get up before Addison is straddling me. Her hands go around my throat, cutting off my scream. I suck in short, desperate puffs of air. Her bruising grip tightens until I can't breathe at all.

Adrenaline scorches through my veins, forcing me into action. My fingers grope the floor, searching for something, *anything*, I can use as a weapon. I feel cardboard and cloth and then cool, hard metal. Addison brings her face close to mine, so blinded by fury I'm not sure she can even see me. My fingers close around the metal and then I swing my unseen weapon. It cracks against Addison's shoulder hard enough to knock her off me. I roll over, coughing and spluttering into the ground. Then I stagger to my feet and I look down.

I gasp . . .

'Oh my God!' My mouth hangs open as I stare at the brass fire poker in my hand. It's the one missing from my home. The murder weapon. At my feet is the stack of boxes we knocked over during our fight. 'You hid it in the cellar. All this time . . .'

Addison gets up, cradling her injured shoulder. She pales at the sight of it in my hand. 'Verity . . .'

'You killed him,' I scream, throat throbbing and raw. 'You killed Linden!'

His dried blood still stains the brass. I drop it as though it is scalding hot. Then I turn and run for the stairs. Addison follows, charging after me. I make it to the top. I skid into the kitchen and sprint for the hallway. But Addison is faster. She throws herself at me, knocking me into the wall before I can reach the door. We struggle. Addison is yelling but I can't hear her over the blood rushing through my ears. She's trying to pin me to the ground. I fight her. I kick and scream and try to twist beneath her. She slaps me across the face, so hard I taste blood in my mouth. She hits me again and again. And then her hands close around my throat for the second time. I claw uselessly at her arms, protected from my nails by her jumper. This isn't part of the plan. This isn't how I want to die. My vision greys. My throat burns. She's going to kill me.

Just as I am slipping into unconsciousness, I hear the front door being thrown open. Addison's head whips up and her grip slackens. I catch a blur of movement and then she is gone, being lifted up and off me. My arms feel heavy. I'm wheezing, struggling to draw in air. Addison is screaming. I push up onto my elbows and see Max has her pinned up against the wall. She's hopelessly struggling against him. He's bigger than she is, stronger, too. He's yelling for me to call the police, his lip ring catching the light. I drag myself towards the handbag Addison must've dropped when she came home. Once I have her phone, I do as Max tells me, rasping the address into the receiver.

Chapter Fifty-Seven

The Other Woman

Still holding the note and the knife in her trembling hand, she orders a taxi. Within twenty minutes, she is pulling up outside a house. It is end-of-terrace, with a bay window and a duck-egg blue front door. She pays the driver and then strides up the stone path. She uses her fist to pound on the wood. It takes only a few moments before the door is yanked open. A dark-haired woman dressed in navy wide-leg trousers and a cream jumper answers, a look of astonishment on her pretty, lined face. 'This is a surprise.'

She has not seen her mother since she visited Paddledown almost three months ago. 'Can I come in?'

Taken aback by the stony tone, Penelope frowns but steps aside. The house is warm and smells of winter spice candles and laundry detergent. She glances right, into the living room. The wood burner is on, the dancing orange flames casting a cosy glow across the large rug. On the arm of the cream sofa a book rests, pages down.

She continues along the hall to the kitchen. The cupboards have been painted taupe and there are new glossy tiles on the walls in pearly neutrals. It has been almost a year since she stepped foot in her childhood home. After her father, her mother wanted to gut the house, to erase all memories of him. She would start a job, like pulling up a carpet or painting a room, only for the grief to crest on a wave and wash her back to the confines of her bedroom where she would languish for days.

With trembling hands, she takes the note from her bag and slaps it onto the kitchen counter.

Penelope's eyes widen. Then she presses her lips together and tries to arrange her face into a neutral expression. 'What is that?'

'It was *you*,' she spits. 'You've been tormenting me for months.'

Her mother tries to deny it. 'I don't know what you're talking about. I—'

'DON'T LIE TO ME!' she yells.

Penelope's mouth snaps shut.

Silence pours into the space between them. She is the first to break it. 'You've been following me. You broke into my house.'

'I didn't break in,' corrects Penelope. 'The back door was unlocked.'

'You defaced a wall. You anonymously hounded me for months. *Stalked* me. You pretended not to know where I lived even after you'd pushed notes through Paddledown's door. How? *How* did you find out about me and Linden?'

Penelope scowls. 'I saw you. The two of you all over each other, stumbling out of a taxi and into a hotel. I couldn't believe it.'

She glares at her mother and then retrieves the steak knife with the maple leaf from her bag. 'I recognised this,' she says. 'You stabbed it into my front door. Have you completely lost your mind?'

'Have *you*?' retorts Penelope. 'Sneaking around with a married man like that.'

'Why didn't you just talk to me?'

Penelope's laughter is mirthless. 'Are you joking? You don't take my calls. You don't visit. You haven't stepped foot in this house since you abandoned me.'

'I didn't abandon you.'

'Of course you did. You're just like your father.'

An old anger rises within her. 'Don't you dare talk to me about my father.'

'Why not?'

She stares at her affronted mother, baffled by her lack of awareness. 'The father you forced me to disown. The father you made me promise never to discuss with you. The father you claim to others *killed* himself.' Her voice cracks as she struggles to contain the sudden swell of emotion. 'He isn't dead, *Mother*, he just didn't want to stay married to *you*.'

'And whose fault is that?' she snaps back, face contorted in disgust. 'I *heard* what you said to him. Encouraging him to leave me. Whispering to him that being unhappy with me wasn't the happiest he'd ever be. You told him to abandon us. Practically packed his bags for him and pushed him out the door!'

'I told him that if he didn't love you, he should leave you. He never intended to abandon me, too.'

'He left the country!'

'To get away from you,' she spits back.

'Here we go again,' mocks her mother. 'Of course my husband only stayed married to me for *your* sake.'

'After he left, you told me he was dead to us. That you couldn't forgive me for what *I* said to him unless I agreed to cut him out of my life too. So I did.' And she regrets it now, but her father moved to another country, which made her mother's lie plausible, and it was easier to let go of him than it was to let go of her mother and the responsibility she felt for causing her pain. 'When Peter and I broke up, I moved back into this house to take care of you. Yet nothing I did was enough. You berated me every day, chipping away at me until there was nothing left.'

'Yes, because I am such a terrible mother,' she cries. 'Everything is my fault.'

'You aren't a terrible mother, but you have done terrible things,' she reasons. 'You told me that I was the *bitch* who ruined your marriage because I dared to give my father permission to leave a situation that was making him miserable.' She feels the hot prick of tears at the memory of the conversation that finally pushed her to flee her childhood home and move into that little studio. The wretched agony of her mother's hateful aspersions. 'You told me I didn't deserve to be loved. How could you say that to your own daughter? All I did was love my father enough to let him go. Why couldn't you do the same?'

Penelope turns away from her and snatches up the kettle. She fills it with water and then snaps it on.

'That it, then?' she says as her mother fetches a mug from the cupboard and slams it down beside the kettle. 'Conversation over?'

Penelope spins to face her. 'Do you think your father would be proud of you? Do you think he'd approve of you sneaking around with a married man? We didn't raise a *whore*.'

She recoils. 'A whore?'

'You silly girl,' admonishes her mother. 'If Linden were ever going to divorce his wife for you, he'd have done it by now. You know nothing of wedding vows. Of until death do us part. The only way their marriage will end is when one of them is dead!'

She thinks of his wife turning blue on the office floor, and dread slides down her spine. And then, she is hit by a memory of Linden telling her his life would be easier if his wife were dead. She'd brushed it off, sure he'd never harm Vee, but now she is remembering them at Paddledown, sharing a salmon dish and the earnest sobriety on his face when he mused that his wife's allergy would come in handy if he ever needed to kill her off. The room cartwheels around her. She feels sick. Linden had led her to Green Bird Café to help with the lunch order. He'd been the one to put together his wife's salad box. He'd told her he'd placed it on top of the others in the carrier bag. Had Linden used her to kill his wife? The thought slithers beneath her skin.

Her mother is talking but she can't make out the words over the blood rushing around her head. She turns away and stumbles out of the kitchen. She must get to the hospital. She has to know the truth. She fumbles for the front door handle but Penelope grabs her and yanks her back. 'You can't just leave. We're talking. We're—'

'I have to find Linden.'

Her mother's face turns puce. 'You are not leaving this house to run back to that venomous adulterer,' she seethes.

But Penelope doesn't understand. Couldn't possibly know. And she does not have time to explain. She spins towards the door, feeling like a wild animal caught in a trap. Penelope grabs her, squeezing hard enough to bruise. Startled, she whirls towards her mother, arms raised to fend her off. She forgets she is still holding the knife. The blade slices across Penelope's outstretched palm and she staggers back, cradling her bloodied hand to her chest, smearing scarlet across the cream wool of her jumper.

They stare at one another, aghast. 'Mum, I'm ... I'm ...' She drops the knife. It clatters to the floor.

'He's turned you into a monster,' breathes Penelope, tears in her eyes. 'If you go now, you are no daughter of mine. Do you understand?'

Guilt settles in her bones but it is not enough to weigh her down. To stop her from leaving. She must find out whether Linden's wife has survived. She has to know if her lover intended to turn her not into a monster, but into a killer. 'Mum, I'm sorry. I can't stay.'

Queasy with shame and desperate for answers, she turns away from her mother's anguish, and as she flies out of the door and down the garden path, she knows there is no way back. She is lost in the woods now without so much as breadcrumbs to guide her home.

Chapter Fifty-Eight

The Wife

Two days later, I am sitting beside Mimi's hospital bed. She's awake. She has a concussion and bruised ribs but they're letting her come home today. Her freshly washed coffee-coloured curls are piled on top of her head and secured with a green silk scarf I gave her a few years ago. Now, I'm painting her nails lilac. It's a pretty colour against her olive complexion.

'I should be painting your nails,' she says. 'It's the least I could do, since you saved my life.'

I shrug. 'It was a joint effort.'

If Max hadn't arrived when he did, Addison might have killed me. When the phone went dead, he was so worried, he drove to Camden Road. He recognised my car on Addison's driveway and as he approached the house, he could hear screaming. Luckily, Addison hadn't locked the front door when she returned so he was able to rush in and help.

'How're you feeling?' she asks. 'Your neck looks sore.'

It is. It's bruised and it still hurts to talk but the hospital has given me some strong painkillers. I don't like looking in the mirror, though. When Addison choked me, she burst a blood vessel in my eye. I look demonic but the doctors have assured me it will heal. 'I'll be fine.'

Mimi is quiet. I look up. Her face is creased in consternation. 'What is it?'

'We should talk about everything, Verity. I appreciate you not pressing me but we need to clear the air.'

I take a deep breath. We've slipped back into an easy friendship. It's as though we never fought at all. As though she didn't abandon me when I needed her most. I've enjoyed existing in this bubble but it can't last forever. 'OK.' I screw the cap back onto the nail varnish and place it on the table beside her bed. 'How long had you known about Linden and Addison?'

Mimi smooths her hands over the white sheet and rolls her shoulders back. 'A couple of months before he died.'

'And that's why you and Addison fell out?'

'We didn't argue. I never even spoke to her about my suspicions.'

'Why?'

'Linden warned me not to. He said if I breathed a word to Addison, he'd tell you I'd lied about how I knew him. He was sure you could forgive him for lying about how he and I met because he was your husband, but he said you'd never forgive me.' She picks at the sheets. 'I didn't want to lose you and I really wasn't sure I was right about Linden and Addison. It was more of a feeling than anything else.'

'How did you find out?'

'You were away. I'd asked to borrow something from you, I can't even remember what it was now, so I let myself into your house, and Addison and Linden were alone together. Standing too close in the kitchen. It felt wrong. Addison couldn't even look me in the eye. Linden was furious I'd walked in unannounced. She left and I had it out with him. He was so angry, Verity. I thought he was going to hit me.'

It was the second time Mimi had caught him with a woman he should never have touched in the first place. He always considered himself the smartest, most cunning person in any room and it would have infuriated him that Mimi made him reassess that. 'You could have told me. I would've believed you.'

'But would you have forgiven me for lying to you about Linden and how I knew him? Keeping from you what I knew about Lyla? You seemed so happy with him, and he was different with you. Or ... I thought he was.'

I swallow around the rising lump in my throat. 'He wasn't happy with me. Not if he was having an affair with her.'

'It wasn't your fault,' she says, laying her hand over mine. '*He* was the problem. It was never you. You were the perfect wife.'

'I was never there.'

'Yes, you were. You just weren't at his beck and call. You weren't the timid, stay-at-home wife he wanted. The kind that would have a hoover in one hand and his cock in the other.'

And despite the wash of tears, I laugh. She's right. He wanted someone who would shrink themselves to make room for him and his wants and desires. He wanted to be the star of the show and wasn't ever willing to share the stage. 'Why did you move away from Rook Lane?' I ask.

Her hand slips from mine and she doesn't meet my eye. Her reluctance to tell me makes my pulse quicken. 'Because I thought I knew who killed Linden.'

I tense. 'And why didn't you tell the police?'

She looks at me then. 'I thought it was you.'

I feel the blood drain from my body. 'What?'

'The night Linden was killed, I saw Addison leave the house. I watched her from my bedroom window. I knew you were away at Oakleaf. It was so late at night, and that's when I realised I'd been right about them. I tried to go back to sleep but I couldn't stop thinking about you and how I was going to tell you.' She shakes her head. 'Then, in the early hours of the morning, I heard your front door close so I went to the window and thought I saw you leaving the house.'

I am light-headed. I suck in a breath. 'Mimi . . .'

'But now I know it wasn't you. It was Addison. You look so alike and it was dark. She must've returned to the house and fought with Linden.' Mimi sits up. 'It makes sense, doesn't it? I mean, she attacked me, she killed Linden. She's dangerous.'

'But you didn't tell the police?' I clear my throat. 'When you thought I'd killed him, you didn't tell them?'

'No. I thought you'd found out about the affair and then . . .'

I blanch. 'Murdered my own husband?'

She tips her head forward and presses her face into her palms. 'Yes.

I know. I know it's ridiculous. And though I never liked Linden, I don't think anyone deserves to be murdered like that. My God, Verity, I still have nightmares about his body. That attack was frenzied.'

The images of his torn flesh and broken pig nose flash into my mind and I swallow against the nausea. 'Me too.'

She shakes her head. 'I thought that maybe if you had killed him, you'd sent me in there to find his body on purpose.'

'Why would I do that?'

'To punish me for not telling you about the affair? I don't know. I thought if you somehow knew that I had my suspicions and hadn't come to you right away, you'd be angry enough to send me into the house knowing what I'd find.'

I nod. 'And that's why you've been so hostile?'

'Yes. I mean, I was horrified to think you were capable of murder but I know you aren't deranged and, after what he did to Lyla, I knew Linden had a dark side. He broke your heart with someone you loved. With family. Addison was basically a sister to you. And so, although I can't condone murder, I could ignore it if it meant protecting you from the police.'

It all makes sense now. And it means so much to me that even though she believed I was Linden's murderer, she had wanted to keep me safe.

'Obviously, I'm going to tell the police everything I know,' she affirms. 'How I saw Addison at the house.'

I nod, relief rushing through me. 'Thank you.'

'The least I could do.'

She smiles and I long to wrap my arms around her. 'I'm so sorry.'

'For what? You have nothing to apologise for.' She gives me a small smile. 'Will we be OK? You and I, we can move past this, can't we?'

Our eyes meet. Affection for her bubbles up like hiccups. I take her hand this time and squeeze it. 'Of course we can.'

She's relieved. I'm relieved, too. There is so much turmoil ahead. Addison has been arrested and charged with murder. They have the weapons and, with the letter breaking up with her having been found on Linden's burner phone, a motive, too. All that alongside Mimi's eyewitness account, I'm sure they'll be able to convict her. Still, I'm exhausted just thinking about the trial and the news coverage that will follow. I'm glad, at least, I'll have Mimi by my side. 'No more secrets?'

I smile. 'It's over,' I tell her. 'It's finally over.'

Chapter Fifty-Nine

The Wife

Two years later

The café is all wooden floors and hanging plants and black hardware. Colette is already waiting for me when I arrive. I'm not late, but, as ever, she is early. It's a warm spring day and the sun is shining. Colette is wearing a buttercup-yellow wrap dress and her lips are painted petal pink. Out of her power suits, she's softer, less intimidating. I haven't seen her since she left Verity Rose nearly two years ago, only days after Addison's arrest. It's no secret that, for whatever reason, Colette doesn't like me, so I was surprised when she reached out last week and asked me to meet with her.

I join her at the table. We don't hug but she smiles tepidly. We order tea from the waiter and I'm about to ask whether Colette is enjoying her new job when she launches right in. 'I've got something I need to tell you.' She flicks up her pointed chin. 'Something you may not know about Linden.'

I sit up, completely taken aback. Colette didn't even know Linden. I can't recall a single time I ever even saw them in the same room. 'OK...'

She nods once, as curt as ever, but then the waiter returns with our drinks and as Colette reaches for her tea, I see her fingers trembling. I have no idea what she's about to tell me but whatever it is, I'm not sure I want to know. Was she having an affair with him too? The thought is so ludicrous, I almost laugh. I can't imagine Colette having sex. She's so rigid and dispassionate, it would be like rubbing against a plank of wood. She opens her mouth and I brace myself for whatever catastrophic disaster I am about to be met with. 'You aren't his first wife.'

And everything inside me turns to ice. 'What?'

'Before you, he was married,' she says. 'To Vanessa Fernly.'

I sit up. 'Are you sure?'

'Positive. I was the maid of honour at their wedding.'

I stare at her, shocked. She pulls out her phone, scrolls for a moment and then slides it across the table to me. On the screen is a photograph taken on the steps of a stately manor. The sky is bright blue and the sun is shining. Linden is young, in his early twenties, wearing a navy suit and smiling widely at the camera, his fingers laced through those of a willowy woman in a sweeping white gown. She's beautiful, with large doe eyes and long blonde hair. His first wife.

'You really didn't know?' asks Colette, eyeing me shrewdly.

My mouth fills with spit before vomit. I shake my head. 'There are a lot of things I didn't know about the man I'd vowed to spend my life with.'

'He was quite the accomplished liar.' She sips her tea. I haven't touched mine. 'I wondered whether you knew. Bath isn't a large city but I suppose he and Vanessa were very private and she was often abroad, travelling to fairs, fashion shows, the manufacturers. Some people were surprised to learn she was married since she was hardly ever seen with Linden. He didn't support her career, rarely attended functions with her.' Colette raises an eyebrow and I think she gathered Linden had much the same attitude with me and Verity Rose. 'He hardly ever wore his wedding ring, which drove Vee mad.'

I nod. This all fits. Amy told me that when they were involved, he didn't wear his wedding band. And then while Linden and I were married, his ring was often stowed in his pocket because he claimed his publicist said appearing single would sell more books. 'So you knew him before joining Verity Rose?' I ask.

'Yes.'

'But he never once mentioned he knew you . . .'

'I haven't been in the same room with Linden in years.'

I mull this over, trying to think of a time they'd have crossed paths but all the events they were both invited to, like the Verity Rose Winter Party, Colette avoided . . . that is, until after his death. Now I know why. 'But Colette isn't exactly a common name. He knew I worked with a Colette. Surely he'd have put the pieces together . . .'

'I used to be known as Lettie. It was a nickname given to me by Vee when we were at school.'

Vee. Linden would sometimes slip up and call me Vee. I hated it, and although he acted as though he didn't mean to shorten my name, I sometimes wondered whether he did it on purpose just to get under my skin. Or maybe the women in his life were as interchangeable and indistinguishable to him as underwear. 'Is that why you applied for the job? Because you wanted to keep tabs on him?'

'No, I had no idea you were his wife. You went by Verity Rose, not Verity Lockwood. By the time I realised who you were married to, I'd been in the job for months and I loved the work. It paid well. After my divorce, I needed the money.'

I take a moment to process it all. I sit back in my chair. Around us, people are enjoying lattes and fat sandwiches. I feel queasy.

'Besides,' she adds, 'Linden took so much from me, I wasn't going to let him take my career too.'

My head snaps up. 'What do you mean? What did he take from you?'

And though she is usually severe and cold, her brown eyes fill with tears. 'He took her,' she says. 'He took Vee.'

A tight ball of dread rolls around in my stomach, making me feel like I might be sick. 'What happened?'

She blinks up at the ceiling, trying to will away the tears. 'She's dead.'

'*Dead?*'

'The police said it was an accident. She had a food allergy. She'd gone into work. There were more people in the office than usual, freelancers and the like. She'd put on a lunch for everyone and her food was contaminated with salmon oil . . . She was always so careful, so fastidious, she had to be, it was her *life*. We were all shocked when we heard.'

'That's horrifying.' Instinct tells me to reach out and comfort her but I'm afraid she'll slap my hand away. 'Why do you think Linden was responsible?'

'Her EpiPen was missing from her handbag. It was found later at home in her bedside table. She *never* went anywhere without it. I always wondered if he had something to do with it. If he'd taken it out of her bag and hidden it.'

My heart starts thumping hard. 'But how would he know she'd pick up the wrong order?'

'I . . . I know it doesn't make sense but I'm right.' She inhales, trying to compose herself. 'He was there, that day in the office. He met her for lunch. He could've meddled, or . . .'

I'm barely keeping myself together as I ask the question: 'Were *you* there?'

She shakes her head. 'I didn't work with Vee. I wish I'd been with her, though. I think about it all the time, wondering if I could've saved her.'

Colette's anguish is palpable. I dread to think about losing Mimi the way Colette lost Vee. This time, I give in to the instinct to comfort her and I put a hand on her arm. Her smile is weak but grateful. 'Why do you think Linden would hurt his wife?'

'Vee found out he'd had a vasectomy when she came across the medical bill from the private hospital. I told her he was selfish and cruel to do something like that behind her back.'

In part, I think Colette is right, but she didn't know Linden like I did. He had a complicated relationship with his parents. They were wealthy, yes, but there was a great deal of expectation. Of the career he should choose and the things he should want. He always felt as though he was letting his parents down and he was forever in competition with his younger brother. He once told me that siblings were a type of terminal cancer. It shocked me. I'd always imagined myself with at least two children. I should have realised then he wouldn't have any. Linden got bored of people and things so easily; maybe he was self-aware enough to not want to inflict that on his own children. Maybe a vasectomy was Linden's single most selfless act.

'Anyway, Vee had had enough,' says Colette. 'She wanted to leave him. She told me she was going to contact a lawyer and then, a few weeks later, she was dead.' She takes another sip of her tea. 'She was the breadwinner in the relationship. It obviously bothered him. When Linden met her she was just an assistant but she worked her way up. She had a clothing brand. It was successful, though it folded after her death.'

I nod but stay quiet, waiting for her to continue. She's talking more to me now than she did in all the years she worked for me. 'Vee's aunt was very wealthy and had left Vee a large sum of money in her will. I think Linden thought he'd get his hands on it if anything happened to his wife, but he hadn't done his research,' she says, with a surreptitious smile. 'The money came with conditions, a contract Vee had to sign agreeing that in the event of her own death, any money left over from her aunt's estate would be returned to the Fernly family.'

'So, you think he wanted his first wife dead for her money but didn't realise until afterwards that it wouldn't ever be his?'

She nods. 'I do, but I can't prove it, and whenever I told anyone about my suspicions, they didn't believe me.'

'I believe you.'

She looks surprised. I hold her gaze to show her I'm sincere. 'I was wary of you. Of course I accepted there was no way you could know *I* believed Linden had killed his first wife, but I wondered whether you knew he was married before. You have a very similar style to Vee, same ambitious nature, same terrible taste in men.' She sips her tea and then appraises me over the rim of her mug. 'Though I never liked you.'

I raise both eyebrows at her bluntness. 'I gathered.'

She shrugs one shoulder. 'I hated Linden so much, I didn't trust anyone who'd willingly get into bed with him.'

'Vee did,' I say, equally blunt.

Colette nods slowly. 'You're right,' she concedes. 'My animosity was irrational. I was upset to see someone else living the life Vee

Dandy Smith

should have had. All those years were stolen from her. And there you were, running a business like her, married to the man she loved, living in the house they'd planned to buy together.'

I almost choke on my disbelief. 'What?'

'Windermere. They viewed that house a few weeks before Vee's death. And then just a few short years later, you and he were living in it.'

'I had no idea,' I tell her honestly. Within weeks of Addison's arrest, I sold it and relocated to a little cottage in Frome. I was sad to move away from Mimi but we still see each other every week.

'I thought you were blithely living my best friend's life and I resented you for it. I thought you knew about Vee. You know,' she says, leaning forward in her chair, 'you really are a lot like her – driven, hard-working, creative.'

'Maybe that was the problem. When Linden first met me, I was just an assistant too. I didn't have any ambition of my own and Linden liked it that way. It left more room for him.' When I look back now, I realise he was like a virus, slowly taking me over. 'The career and the house and the busy social life came years after we met. He couldn't cope. Maybe you're right, maybe I became too much like his first wife, and that's why he latched on to Addison. Harry was often away. She had a lot of time and no baby or career to fill it. Even her social circle had thinned – all her friends were tied up in careers and husbands and motherhood.'

'I'm sorry he did that to you,' she says. 'I always wondered whether he was unfaithful to Vee,' she says. 'That perhaps one of the reasons he got a vasectomy without telling her is because he was sleeping with other women and wanted to avoid getting them pregnant.'

Colette doesn't know about Amy, who he was sleeping with while he was married to Vee, or Lyla, who fell somewhere between his first and second marriage. I don't tell her. I can see her hatred of Linden and her grief for Vee and I don't want to add to any of it.

'I'm sorry to burden you,' she says. 'I've just been sitting with this for so long and then when I read in the papers about the arrest and the affair, I felt awful. I realised he treated you just as badly as he treated Vee, and my resentment towards you was entirely misplaced.' She fiddles with the saucer, turning it round. 'And I'm sorry.'

I smile. I don't think I've ever heard Colette apologise for anything. 'Thank you.'

'I know you loved him, Verity, but that pig got what he deserved in the end.'

I see Linden lying dead on our living room floor, his nose broken, bent at an unusual angle, and swollen like a pig's snout. I glance down at my tea. It's cold now. I've been here longer than planned. 'Sorry for cutting this short, Colette, but Addison is waiting.'

Chapter Sixty

The Wife

I enter the visitors' room at HMP Eastwood Park. It's arranged in three long rows of metal tables and hard plastic chairs that are secured to the floor. I suppose that's to stop inmates from picking them up and using them as a weapon. Around the periphery of the room are several officers.

It's loud in here. Prisoners and their families sit in small groups around the tables, most deep in conversation, others in stilted silence. At the far end, an older lady weeps across from a woman I can only assume is her daughter. I try not to look and instead pull my long dark hair over my shoulder.

An officer nods towards a table and I take a seat to wait for Addison. I haven't seen her since the trial ended last year. She's serving a life sentence for murdering my husband. Along with the fire poker, the police found Linden's watch hidden in Addison's cellar, stowed in a box. They didn't recover his ring, though and she refuses to tell them where it is. They suspect she took the watch to stage the robbery but believe Linden's wedding band was some kind of trophy.

Addison has sent me dozens of letters requesting I visit but I've ignored them all. Until now. I wanted to organise my life before I saw her again.

I become aware of someone standing by my table. I look up and there she is. Addison is wearing a black T-shirt and leggings. She's gained weight. I suppose it was bound to happen now she can't run around Bath four times a week. Her skin is pale and blotchy, her nails bitten to the quick. The long, glossy hair I'd been so jealous of is dull and full of split ends. She sits down opposite me. She doesn't speak but she takes in my glowy skin and freshly painted nails. My floral dress and long, shiny hair. I've grown it out again, pleased that I no longer feel the ghost of Linden's fingers running through it. Addison and I drink one another in. The gossamer thread that bound us is frayed now, forking in separate directions.

Still, she is silent, but that's fine. I have enough to say for the both of us. 'I moved house,' I tell her. 'I live in a beautiful three-bed cottage in Frome, down a little cobbled street. I've got window boxes with petunias and marigolds. Auntie Claire came over the other day to help plant some wisteria.' At this, Addison's mouth falls open. 'I found her last year. Did you know your mother was living in New Zealand? Well, she was serious when she sent you that card about moving back to England. She has a little cottage right down the road from me and we see each other every week. She even came for Christmas.' I sigh in mock concern. 'I'm sorry she hasn't ever bothered to come and visit you at the prison, Addison. I think she feels guilty that her absence from your life drove you to become a killer.' Addison is gripping the lip of the table so tightly her knuckles are turning white. Initially, my desire to reconnect with Auntie Claire was to spite Addison, but we've become close. She's like the mother I wish I'd had. 'What else? Oh, yes . . .' I lean in as though we are two best friends gossiping over a bottle of wine. 'Harry is *finally* dating again after you broke his heart. His new girlfriend is a gem.'

The veins in Addison's neck bulge. I can see it's taking all her will not to fling herself at me.

'Mimi doesn't know it yet but Max is going to propose this summer. He's nervous but I'm certain she'll say yes. They really are very much in love. And that isn't the only wedding in the calendar.' Then I slide my left hand out from where I'd hidden it beneath the table. Addison's gaze follows the movement and lands on the opal and diamond engagement ring. 'I'm getting married in a couple of months.' Addison's lips part in surprise. 'His name is Sebastian. He's a teacher. We met at a pumpkin farm, can you believe it? And he's taking my surname. In just eight weeks we'll be Mr and Mrs Grey. We would wait a little longer but I want to be able to fit into my wedding dress,' I say, because I've kept the best news until last. This, I know, will cut deeply. I place both my hands on my belly. 'We've just crossed the three-month mark.' Then I take the knife and I twist. 'You know what's wild? We weren't even trying.' I give her a supercilious smile.

Addison's dark eyes fill with tears, and victory sparkles through me. I sit back in my chair and wait for her to speak. I'm being awful to her. Maybe I'll regret it later but, right now, it's empowering. I trusted her completely and she stole everything from me. Then she tried to take my life, too. If Max hadn't come to the house, I'd be dead, and maybe Mimi would be as well. Addison doesn't deserve my kindness. Not anymore. She swallows, choking back a sob. The din of conversation is dying down as tables around us start emptying. And just when I'm thinking it's time I leave too, Addison leans forward. The tears are gone and in their place is an intense steeliness. 'Why did you kill him, Verity?'

I stare at her, cold and imperious. 'You killed him.'

'No, I didn't. You know I didn't. Right from the very start, you were playing with me. You made sure I was with you when you "discovered" my letters, so when you reported it to the police, I was there to back you up. It put you in the clear because if the police could prove you already knew about the letters, about the affair, you'd have a motive to kill him.'

'I don't know what you're talking about.'

'Why drag it out for months?' she hisses, ignoring my denial. 'Why pretend you had no idea who authored those letters? Was it all some elaborate revenge? Were you trying to make me sweat?'

She is desperate for me to confirm what she thinks she already knows. The purple shadows beneath her eyes a result of nights she has spent lying awake in her cell, trying to put it all together. Mine is the final piece of the puzzle she needs to complete the picture. 'You're unhinged,' I tell her blandly.

She inhales sharply, and I imagine injustice burning in her chest. 'You enjoyed it, didn't you?' she counters. 'Like a cat playing with a mouse.'

People often get that wrong. Cats don't play with their prey out of malice but out of self-preservation. To tire the mouse so it can't strike back and injure the cat. I don't bother telling Addison this, though because I don't want to give her theory any credence.

'And Heidi, too. Did you make a show of telling her everything because it lent your story more credit?' she asks. 'More witnesses to your lies? I think the real reason you didn't go to the police about the threats and the pig's head is because you didn't want them involved before you could frame me. I'm right, aren't I?'

I shake my head. 'Really, Addison, you're deranged. You killed Linden because he was ending your affair.'

'No, he wasn't.' She's vehement. 'He didn't write that message. It was staged. It—'

'If he was so madly in love with you, why did he kiss Flora?'

Her lips thin. She really has deluded herself into thinking Linden could love anyone more than he loved himself. I sincerely had no idea about him kissing Flora until Amy showed me that photograph, and thank God she did because it was crucial in winning a conviction. It proved that Linden was tiring of Addison and had his sights set elsewhere.

'Did you wait a year just to plant the watch and fire poker in my house?' asks Addison. 'I suppose Harry inviting you to stay with us for Christmas was perfect, wasn't it?'

'Why are you so certain it was me?' I ask, lowering my voice. 'Did you ever consider *Harry* knew about your sordid affair, and took matters into his own hands? That maybe your betrayal pushed him over the edge? If you didn't kill Linden, if you aren't responsible for the watch and fire poker hidden in the cellar, who else could it have been? I was at a rural yoga retreat seventy miles away, seen by dozens of witnesses. If it wasn't me, or you, it had to be Harry.'

She swallows and sits back in her chair, rolling this scenario around in her mind. After a moment, she says, 'He wouldn't . . .' But she doesn't sound sure.

I raise a brow. 'Wouldn't he? You can't imagine the pain, the *rage*, of finding out the love of your life is cheating? Even if it was Harry who beat Linden to death, I still blame *you*. It's still *your* fault, Addison. The first time you kissed my husband, you signed his death warrant.'

We sit in silence. She starts frantically picking at the skin around her thumbnail until it bleeds. I grow bored and decide it's time to go. I gather my bag. Addison's eyes widen. She doesn't want me to leave. 'Verity, wait,' she pleads. 'I'm sorry. I shouldn't have accused you. I know you didn't kill him. I didn't mean it . . . I . . .' She is shaking her head, her eyes wild and searching. 'I just don't believe Harry hurt Linden and I know I didn't either. I *loved* Linden.' Her voice breaks on the swell of emotion. 'He was going to leave you because he wanted *me*.'

'And now he's ashes,' I tell her. 'He's nothing. Just like you.'

Her face crumples. 'You bitch.'

'*The* bitch,' I correct. I give her a saccharine smile and then push to my feet, glad to be leaving. I'll most likely never see her again. Now I've said my piece, she's as dead to me as Linden is. 'Goodbye, Addison.'

I leave the prison and drive back to Bath. In the car, I cry. I tell myself it's the pregnancy hormones but it isn't. I loved Addison. I loved Linden. Sometimes, the wrench of missing them overcomes me and I turn my face into my pillow in the early hours of the morning and I scream at the unfairness of it all. At the pain and loss and heartbreak. It doesn't mean I'm not happy with Sebastian or excited to be a mother. I've decided, if this baby is a girl, I'll teach her to be more careful with her heart than I was with mine, and to avoid giving it to charming, egotistical men. If I have a boy, I'll instil in him all the values my first husband lacked: loyalty, honesty, altruism.

I do wish my mother was still alive to see me become one myself. Even before Linden, my relationship with her was strained but I'm sure if I hadn't ever become involved with Linden Lockwood, I could have salvaged it. My mother only ever met him once, that day I pretended he was my landlord, but of course, she knew he wasn't.

When one of her friends realised my father hadn't killed himself as she'd claimed but rather migrated to Belgium, she left Bath. She died from an aneurysm just months after that last row we had in her hallway about her taunting notes. She's the only person who knew the truth of how Linden and I really began. The very last loose end. She didn't ever tell anyone what she knew. I think she was afraid that if she exposed the affair, I'd reveal the insanity of her stalking and her threats, on top of the lies she told about my father's 'suicide'.

I pull up outside Paddledown and let myself in. When I moved out of here and into Windermere with Linden, we thought about selling Paddledown but it was *our* special place. One all our own. Now though, in a bid to start over, I've decided to put it on the market. Max works in real estate and thinks we'll sell it quickly. I'm fond of Max, he reminds me so much of Peter, not just his lean build and lip ring, but the way in which he is endlessly kind. Peter is married now with a daughter. I looked him up after Addison's arrest and even though I was happy to learn he'd moved on, I was a little disappointed. Still, I slammed that door shut years ago.

I walk through the house where I started my Verity Rose blog. It was choosing paint colours with Linden and decorating this small canal-side home that sparked the idea for my first post and, as my blog picked up, I started piecing my life back together. I took up hobbies, reconnected with my father, threw myself completely into creating a life I truly wanted. Linden understood why I let him believe my father had taken his own life. He knew all too well what my mother was capable of and what it's like to have a difficult family. Unlike my mother, my father doesn't know the roots of my relationship with Linden and, the few times they met, they got on well. But, thankfully, he gets on even better with Sebastian. This summer, Dad and Agathe came to stay with me and Seb. I made us up a jug of raspberry mojitos – the same recipe I taught to Mimi when I moved to Rook Lane – and we sat on the lawn, a happy family, drinking and talking in the sunshine. I'm lucky my father forgave me for the years I cut him out of my life at my mother's behest. But then, he knew how challenging she was.

I run my hand along the back of my father's olive-green armchair. I'm taking it home with me today to set it up in the baby's nursery. I do not glance down at the floor in front of the fireplace where Linden first told me he was in love with me. I head for the back door, out into the narrow garden and down to the water's edge.

It was a shock to learn Amy and Millie are one and the same. I never did get a good look at her that day by the lake. I always suspected Linden was lying when he said her feelings weren't reciprocated but I was desperate to be wanted so I chose to believe him. Even more of a shock was finding out Colette was friends with Vanessa. Still, I think she believed I had no idea he was married before. I knew from the day I met Linden that I could never be his first wife but I thought, at the very least, I'd be his last mistress. If only he could have loved me as much as he loved himself. Standing on the wooden jetty, I reach into my pocket and take out Linden's wedding ring, still stained with his blood. I'm not sure why I took it. I think I was holding onto the last piece of our marriage but it's over now. All of it. Amy was wrong when she said revenge is a dish best served hot and bloody. In my experience, revenge is a dish best served as cold as the bodies it leaves in the morgue.

Then I take the ring and toss it into the canal.

Chapter Sixty-One

The Wife

Before

'We're nearly there,' says Heidi. She's been chatting endlessly since she picked me up from my house, completely oblivious to my surging anguish. Just an hour before she arrived, I found a stash of lilac love letters hidden beneath the floorboards of Linden's walk-in wardrobe. I'd only gone in there to fetch my holdall bag for the trip to Oakleaf Yoga Retreat.

My husband is having an affair. Who with, I don't know. He was out, due home after I left for the retreat. Not knowing what else to do, I put the letters back where I found them alongside a laptop and a burner phone. After that, I was on autopilot.

My phone pinged with email after email after email. Linden's infidelity didn't change the fact I had a business to run. That I was at the helm of my own brand and that one of my employees was on their way to collect me. So I plaited my long hair, packed a bag and slid into Heidi's car with a smile.

It's only now, less than twenty minutes from the remote retreat, that the fog of shock dissipates and reality smacks into me so hard, I can't catch my breath: Linden has been unfaithful. He has betrayed me and I haven't done a single thing about it. I need to confront him. Now. *Now.* I want to grab the wheel of Heidi's car and turn around. I want to go back to Bath and deal with Linden. To scream at him until my throat splits open. He's ruined me. Ruined us. Ruined *everything*. Heidi's talking but I can't process a single word of what she's saying. My hands are trembling and the car wraps itself around me. I need to get out. To *breathe*. 'Can we stop off?' I ask, speaking over her.

She glances at me. 'Where?'

Up ahead, I see a shop. We're on the outskirts of Oxford and this is the last town before the houses and retail outlets give way to fields and sheep. Inside the shop, as I pretend to browse the shelves, I force myself to breathe steadily. If I ask Heidi to drive us back to Somerset, she'll want to know why and if she asks, I won't be able to lie. It will all come pouring out of me like a bursting dam. I tell myself it's because my business is private but really, there is a small, desperate, deluded voice that whispers it could be a mistake. That there is no *other woman*. That there's an explanation for the lilac love letters hidden beneath the floorboards. And if there is, I don't want to tarnish what Linden and I have in the eyes of those around me.

So, I gather myself. Pretend nothing is wrong. I buy a bottle of vodka and some chocolate. I give the chocolate to Heidi and hide the vodka in a concealed pocket in my holdall because alcohol is prohibited from Oakleaf, but if I want to sleep tonight, I'll need a drink.

'Thanks for the Dairy Milk,' says Heidi as we pull into the retreat's car park. 'I needed one last treat before we're subjected to kale smoothies.'

I'm about to tell her Oakleaf has a Michelin-starred chef and, at over one thousand pounds a night, they'd better provide the best kale smoothie we've ever had, but then we are out of the car and, despite the September chill, a woman dressed in white linen and wicker sandals greets us.

I get through the day. I give everyone my charm and my smile. And no one suspects a thing. I've spent the last few hours coming up with a plan. Heidi and I are staying in a cabin together at the furthest end of the site. After dinner, I ply her with shots of vodka and myself shots of water. Soon, she is passed out and I am stone-cold sober. I stuff my bed with pillows in case she wakes up to look for me. Then I take her car keys. Linden is supposedly home alone tonight. Though that's likely to be a lie. He's with *her*, whoever *she* is. I need to catch them together, to find out who she is so he can't deny it later. If I'm quick, I can get to Windermere and back before anyone even notices I'm gone. Oakleaf is quiet and I slip out easily.

I park Heidi's car a couple of streets away from my house and make the rest of the journey on foot. If I'd pulled up on the gravel driveway, he'd have heard. It's dark and I skirt around streetlights, paranoid I'll be seen by someone I know. Though it's unlikely, given the late hour. My heart is a fierce flutter in my chest as I make my way to Rook Lane. I force myself to keep an even pace. The urge to sprint is almost overwhelming, but I don't want to draw attention to myself which, a woman sprinting through the dark alone, I might very well do.

I creep around the stone wall that separates mine and Mimi's house from the road, staying low. I step into the row of trees, squeezing between two trunks so I won't be seen. I wait. Even dressed in thick joggers and a hoody, I am cold. Seconds pour into minutes. Then, upstairs, framed in our bedroom window, I see two figures.

My stomach plummets.

Linden is in there now, with another woman. The voice that whispered to me earlier, that tried to convince me I'd made a mistake, is replaced by a blood-curdling shriek of despair. I take a step, wanting to run inside and catch them in our bed. But I stop myself. I need to be smarter. Need to take my time.

I don't know who she is, and the idea that it is someone I know makes bile rise in my throat. My patience stretches so tight, it's on the verge of snapping when finally, the front door opens. My breath stays locked in my chest, anticipation thick in my veins. Then she steps out of the house and onto the porch, lit by the golden glow of the hallway light.

No.

No.

I cannot believe. Cannot *believe*.

Addison . . .

She stands on my porch, wearing a little white dress, her dark hair loose and spilling down her back. She is joined by Linden. He's shirtless. He wraps his arms around her waist and she spins to face him. She whispers something into his neck and he laughs with all his toned stomach. They aren't afraid of being caught. Windermere is set back from the road, hidden behind a bank of trees and a low stone wall. Even Mimi can't see our front door from her window. They are bold and arrogant and enjoying the thrill. They kiss. His hands slide up her back. He winds his fingers though her hair and it's as though I am Addison, I feel his fingers in tangling in my hair, feel his lips on mine, taste him on my mouth. Linden kisses his way down her throat. Then lower and lower still. Until he is kneeling before my cousin like a parishioner worshipping at the altar. His hands are on her bare legs. He manoeuvres her until she is pressed against the porch beam. He lifts the hem of her dress. She isn't wearing underwear. He buries his face between her legs. I watch my husband fuck her with his tongue. Bile rushes up my throat and I stuff my fist into my mouth to stop from calling out. He sounds like a pig pushing its snout through a trough of slop. Addison throws her head back, enjoying the feeling of my husband's mouth. Her fingers grip his hair and she cries out into the dark as she is swept up in the rush of her orgasm.

Then she relaxes, bones like silk in the aftermath. Linden gets to his feet. They both laugh, giddy with the thrill of it, the danger, the passion. They kiss again, she tastes herself on his tongue. Then she peels herself away from my husband and saunters past my hiding place, glowing with post-orgasm bliss. She doesn't see me. Her car isn't on the driveway but she's probably parked a street or two away.

Linden goes inside. I fall to my knees in the dirt. She has no idea she isn't special. That I was once her. A married man's mistress. Addison was living in America with Harry when I got involved with Linden. I always thought if she'd been in England, if she'd known about my affair with him, she'd have put a stop to it. Grounded me like she always did but, like the lilac love letters she has written to my husband, she bends and folds to his will. She's more like her licentious mother than she cares to admit.

I catch movement in my peripheral vision. Mimi is standing in her window, watching as Addison leaves Rook Lane. I expect her to look as shocked as I feel. She doesn't. Her expression is blank as she turns away and disappears from view. *What?* Fury unfurls in my stomach and I battle the hot rush of nausea. Does Mimi know about their affair? Is that why she and Addison stopped speaking? My best friend, my cousin, my husband. They've all *lied* to me.

The worst of it though is Linden. How can he do this to us? After everything I sacrificed to be with him. Peter and my mother. After we fought at her house about the notes all those years ago, I cut her off. When I told Linden she had been the author of those threats, he insisted I choose. That with Vanessa's death, we were free to be together, but if I wanted him, I couldn't speak to my mother again because she knew too much. He declared her mentally unwell, stating no parent torments her daughter the way she tormented me unless she's lost the plot. And I believed him. And then she died. I never even got the chance to say goodbye. I even sacrificed becoming a mother myself. I forgave Linden for the vasectomy and prepared for a life without children, all to please him. All because I was desperately in love with him. And he was only ever in love with himself.

I believed so many of his lies. He assured me what happened to Vanessa was an accident and that he had nothing to do with it. I haven't been able to eat seafood since. Even the smell of it makes me think of her. Of her bulging, panicked eyes as her throat closed up. Her blue lips. Her desperate, scrabbling fingers that clawed uselessly at her own neck. So I lie and tell people I have an allergy just to avoid having to be around fish. I've adopted so much of Vanessa that the lines between us blur in my mind: her allergy, her ambition, her close relationship with her father, the man she married, even taking on the story of the day I gave her the lunch contaminated with salmon oil, switching our roles so it's me lying there, gasping for air, and her standing uselessly over me. Now, years on, I wonder what I wanted more: to be with Linden or to *be* Vanessa.

For a while, I managed to convince myself Linden was telling the truth, that he played no part in his first wife's death, but I've always known, deep inside, that he was lying. Linden Lockwood was a fever I could not soothe. I didn't want to believe he could kill anyone or that he could use me to do it. He promised it would be the two of us always. That, as Cinderella went from rags to riches, I would go from mistress to wife. A year or so apart after the funeral and then we could date publicly. Come out as a shiny new couple. All I had to do was say yes. All I had to do was choose him. And I did. I chose him over everything. Even after he turned me into a murderer, I chose him. And now . . . and now . . .

I look up at the house he bought with my money. Up at the bedroom in which I let him have me night after night. The bedroom in which he has just had my cousin. He takes and takes and takes. I won't let him take from me anymore. He has got away with so much, but I can't let him get away with this. Fury mingles with determination in my bloodstream, glittering and dark. I step out of the shadows of the tree line and venture inside the house . . .

Acknowledgements

The most heartfelt thank you to my gorgeous, powerhouse agent Thérèse Coen for making all my dreams come true. None of this would be possible without you. It's been a thrilling year and I'm excited for the future. Thank you to everyone at the brilliant Susanna Lea Associates.

A huge thank you to my new editor Martina Arzu for your wisdom and your insight. You understood this book and expertly whipped it into shape. Working with you has been a true pleasure. And gratitude to everyone at Embla for providing my books with the very best home and being the very best team to carry them forward.

Thank you to my avid readers – Catilin M, Jasmine, Kara, Sarah W – you are exceptionally kind, wonderful people. And to everyone else who has read my books and sends me lovely messages of support. It means the world to me. I can't thank you enough.

Thank you to Andrew Chapman, Duncan Cooper, Hannah Dawes, Louise Friend, Claire F, Rachel Gates, Tiffany Graves, Binny Lascelles, Emily Mitchell, Peter Neville, Jo Nadin, Hannah OF, Dawn Palmer and Jo Wells for your friendship and support. To Clare James for understanding. And to the doctors Rebecca Annis, Matthew Stuttard and Wesley Dean for indulging my many morbid medical queries.

A special thanks to Sarah Goodwin – a witty, interesting and generous friend and fellow thriller author. Without you, I wouldn't be published. If you hadn't encouraged me to apply to the Bath Spa University MA, I'd never have met my marvellous agent or signed with the incredible Embla Books. You deserve every happiness, every success and you are worthy of epic, soulful friendships. I will always cheer you on.

To Rachel Delahaye Lefever for having unwavering faith in me and for avidly devouring *every* book I write before it even hits my editor's inbox. Not only are you wildly talented, but you are also a pillar of wisdom and without you, I'd topple.

I want to thank Mia Kuzniar for tumbling into my life and making an enormous impact. It feels impossible that you haven't always been by my side. Our daily talks bring me joy and your encouragement makes me brave. I'll always help you find your daffodil.

Love and gratitude to Mel Neville for racing through this story and, as always, for offering invaluable pearls of insight. I'm a better writer for your support and input. Almost two decades of friendship behind us and many more to come.

To my sisters. To Charlotte for always telling me you are proud. A piece of you is in every story I write. I love you.

So much love to my mum for instilling in me the belief that my dreams are worthy and achievable. I wouldn't be the woman or the writer I am today without you.

To my husband, Josh Butler-Smith, for never doubting me no matter how determined I am to doubt myself. Thank you for listening to my ramblings about this fourth book. It's the trickiest plot I've ever handled and it was only possible because you offered a patient, if a little confused, ear. Thank you for being the antithesis of Linden Lockwood. I will always love you.

And, finally, to Lucy. Thank you for the last *nineteen* years of friendship. Your compassion, empathy and thoughtfulness are unparalleled. You have achieved so much and I am so proud. Loving you has taught me that sisterhood is so much more than blood. We didn't quite make it to Aruba but I wrote this book for us. For you.

While Bath is a real place and many of the locations in the book are also real, the events that unfold and the characters involved are entirely fictional. I hope you enjoyed this book as much as I enjoyed writing it. Dandy x

About the Author

Dandy Smith lives in the Somerset market town of Frome with her husband and two cocker spaniels. She has an undergraduate and master's degree in creative writing from Bath Spa University, and enjoys all things aerial fitness, true-crime and *Gilmore Girls*.

About Embla Books

Embla Books is a digital-first publisher of standout commercial adult fiction. Passionate about storytelling, the team at Embla publish books that will make you 'laugh, love, look over your shoulder and lose sleep'. Launched by Bonnier Books UK in 2021, the imprint is named after the first woman from the creation myth in Norse mythology, who was carved by the gods from a tree trunk found on the seashore – an image of the kind of creative work and crafting that writers do, and a symbol of how stories shape our lives.

Find out about some of our other books and stay in touch:

X, Facebook, Instagram: @emblabooks
Newsletter: https://bit.ly/emblanewsletter